LEATHER

PART I

Chapter 1

While normally attuned to things which were not as they should be, Jennifer Scott arrived home one October night noticing nothing at all out of the ordinary. Had her attention not been diverted by the latest issue of Cosmo pulled from the mailbox, she would have wondered about the front door, unlocked despite Logan's insistence that it remain thrice-bolted at all times. The lingering odor of scalded soup should have roused her attention upon crossing the threshold, but no smell could compete with the magazine's fragrant advertisements held just beneath her nose. And then there was the silence. Logan played his records so incessantly, the absence of music should have registered as an abnormality; but the remnant of a song from her car stereo bubbled in her memory and on her lips to cloak the unnatural void. It wasn't until she pushed the front door shut behind her that she first sensed something was wrong.

Why is the doorknob sticky?

Bringing her hand up, she was stunned to find blood between her thumb and the underside of two fingers, a discovery followed by her glance down the hall and into the bedroom. Near the foot of the bed was what appeared to be a pile of laundry, or possibly a bundle of sheets and blankets kicked to the floor; but in the span of a single heartbeat she discerned a leg, brown hair, and the form she knew to be Logan.

The magazine slipped from her grasp and crashed to the hardwood floor.

For a moment she considered it all to be some sort of pre-Halloween joke; some bizarre prank from which Logan would leap up, smile, and they would share a laugh. However in the absence of laughter there was only a lingering silence, and the solitary feeling of being the first to witness a scene of violence perpetrated by an unseen enemy.

Around her in the bedroom was the result of both a struggle and a hasty search. The bed had been pulled apart, drawers were open with their contents spilled to the hardwood floor, and the closet door was smashed and attached to the frame by only a resolute bottom hinge. The room was such a wreck she picked out the things left untouched. Pictures still hung perfectly on the walls, items within and upon the bookshelves were in their place, and of the dozens of knights in her chess piece collection, not a single onyx, marble, or glass horse was toppled. Facing different directions from their perch atop the mahogany dresser, the herd silently surveyed the destruction all around them.

She walked closer.

Logan was no longer Logan, but a corpse. Bound to their bedroom chair at the waist and feet, his pallor of death was on his skin. Blood was pooled beneath his head, and had made its way over the floorboards and into the heater vent at the foot of the bed where it still dripped into the ducts beneath the house. His eyes were open but there was no electricity to transfer the image to the circuitry of his brain. All his intelligence and memory were erased, a blank tape in a player without power; and while the sound of Jennifer's sobs and fleeing footsteps quivered his eardrums, their reverberations meant nothing.

Had Logan been alive and able to speak, he could have revealed a description of his assailants or their names. But those words were never spoken, and his murder resulted in neither a conviction nor an arrest. The only clues to the identities of his murderers lay within a journal wedged behind the dresser, encrypted and interpretable only by the knowledge Logan alone had once possessed.

McGarry/Leather

PART II

Chapter 1

Jennifer emerged from her office and surveyed the activity throughout the arena. The Sunday night 7:15 game was moments from beginning, and she noticed the referee perform an awkward balancing act while seated atop the waist-high midfield wall. Extending a meaty leg forward for equilibrium, he reached behind him to flip the switch that began the 25-minute digital clock. High on the wall on the opposite side of East Portland Indoor Soccer, the countdown commenced … 24:59 … 24:58 … 24:57. Jennifer watched as he took a quick gulp of beer, set his cup behind the wall, and licked a layer of foam from his upper lip. Only then did he spring to a standing position on the field. With his massive size, black shirt and shorts, and stern disposition, he basked in the momentary attention.

Nothing says credibility like a ref who drinks.

The whistle blew. This set in motion the only orderly moment in the next twenty-five minutes. With hands upon hips, the captain of the red-shirted team ended his irritated posture in the center of the field and initiated play with the easy kick of the ball to a teammate. The game crept into motion, but the speed soon increased, and a minute later the jumble of red and white jerseys were without any notable order. At each end of the frenzy the teams' goalies stood as sentinels, alternating between boredom with all action on the other end of the field, to crouched anxiety when the other team advanced dangerously with the ball.

Jennifer scanned the entryway corridor where, just behind the midfield benches, exhausted players from the prior game sat against the walls with their knees pulled up so others could pass through the narrow corridor, or make their way past her office to where the restrooms, concession area, and big screen TV were located. Water bottles and phosphorescent Gatorade were raised to mouths, and people rummaged through their bags for sweatshirts and verification that their wallets hadn't been stolen. The jingle of key chains signaled departures, but others changed their shoes, checked the blisters on their feet, and settled in for a longer stay with their friends.

Making her way toward the concession area, Jennifer avoided three players who were carefully kicking a soccer ball between them while, within the triangle, a stiff-legged one-year-old girl cackled gleefully in a staggered pursuit. Unexpectedly, the child's determination paid off when she seized the ball, fell to her knees, and joyfully sank two pearls of bottom teeth into the leather exterior. Her father swooped her up, and finding no punctures, merely wiped off the saliva with his shirt and the game of keep-away began anew.

Reggae music was playing and the song, one she hadn't heard for many years, immediately made her think of Logan. Even ten years after his death, she was surprised what could trigger his memory. A song could do it, but so could the mention of a movie, or a news report of a drug bust somewhere in Oregon. And of course there was Charlie, whose questions about his father, carried with them the remembrance of the time when she was so young and happy.

And naive.

Filling all but one of the eight picnic tables in the concession area were the usual collection of exhausted players in various stages of recovery from their games as rifle-shot reverberations occurred just a few feet from them as shots intended for the southern goal rattled the ten-foot-high Plexiglas that bordered most of the field.

Yelling as they pursued one another, Charlie, and his friend Jonah, raced past the video games, around the picnic tables, and through the door that was the lone portal between the arena and the area in the back where she and Charlie lived. The door banged shut after they'd passed through, a noise she alone discerned above the din of the arena.

She grabbed a rag to wipe off a tabletop, acknowledged a drink order, and eyed the game taking place on the field. It was early in the first half, and as Jennifer plucked a meager fifty-cent piece tip from a tabletop and pocketed it, she paused to watch. Two futile scans of the field led her eyes to the bench where she finally spotted her friend, Helena. Moments later a player sprinted to the bench, and Helena burst upon the field to merge with the flow of the game.

Her aggressiveness shone immediately. She charged at a girl dribbling the ball, blocked her pass, and as the two bogged down in a stalemate with the ball pinned in a corner, players from both teams joined in. The game ground to a halt amid the mire of entangled legs, and at least one prostrate body tripped to the turf within the melee. No infraction was whistled though the referee, who rarely strayed from midfield, had the time to stroll near the action. Just as he raised his whistle to his mouth to call for a free kick to re-initiate play, the ball miraculously squirted free, and a stampede of players sprinted in pursuit.

A player on the opposing team broke free with the ball, but just before he could shoot, Helena clipped his leg, causing his headlong flight through the air and barrel-roll along the ground. Players on the other team howled instantly and the referee blew his whistle to signal the infraction. Play resumed, and the infraction was soon forgotten amid a mix of euphoric goals, blown opportunities, deft passes, clumsy dribbling, diving saves, and monumental defensive lapses.

Afterward Helena made her way off the field and toward the concession area where Jennifer held up a half-full pitcher of beer. "Pabst Blue Ribbon?" Jennifer offered.

Helena laughed, flopped her gym bag to the floor, and said, "Yeah ... Right!" knowing, as Jennifer did, that the consumption of alcohol following the exertion of a game would leave her incapable of driving herself and Jonah home. A tendril of medium-length black hair fell in Helena's face, and while taking a seat she resecured it within her ponytail in an effortless whirl of fingers.

"I'll take some, Mom! Gimme a PBR and make it snappy," Charlie interrupted from behind.

She merely smiled at him.

"C'mon, Mom. I'm thirsty."

"Yeah, right. If you're thirsty then why don't y ... "

"C'mon Mom ... really." In front of him he shook an empty paper cup as would a jittery junkie.

"All right, mister. Tell you what ... why don't we leave it up to fate? Heads you get your cup of PBR, tails you have to go get your pajamas on and get ready for bed." With that, she reached into her pocket and flicked the fifty-cent piece high into the air where it glimmered in the lights of the arena. After snaring it with one hand and slapping it on the back of the other, she lowered both hands for him to see.

JFK.

She poured, and with a wry smile on her face handed him the cup. His bluff called, Charlie stared down at the layer of dingy foam within his cup and anticipated the ill taste of adulthood. After a few seconds he vigorously shook his head back and forth, and upon noticing a few muffled laughs at his reaction, became awash in embarrassment. Tears rose within him, but before they could spill, he sloshed the cup down on a picnic table and bolted across the concession area. She called after him, but could only watch as he headed for the back and what she assumed would be his bedroom.

I should have known better.

Charlie handled many of his emotions with the maturity of a child much younger, and she knew that embarrassment, especially among people he knew well, had more than enough power to trigger an outburst. She made momentary eye contact with Helena, but her friend's attention was diverted by Jonah's shirt-tugging request to go home. She turned to seek out Charlie, but after just a few steps a sweaty hand clasped upon her forearm and drew her closer.

Helena rose, speaking only once they were near enough to whisper. "So how's your love life?"

"In the toilet I'm afraid," Jennifer replied.

"You haven't talked to him?"

"Nope. He hasn't called or stopped by or anything."

"He's a coward."

Jennifer nodded and shifted back to her normal voice. "I gotta go talk to Charlie. If you're up late, call me?"

"I will," Helena said, and shifted her attention back to Jonah.

She disappeared to the back. Once the door slammed shut behind her, she locked it and realized Charlie had placed a gauntlet of books, his backpack, and an assortment of loose papers along the floor. At first she thought he'd knocked them over, either in anger or by accident, but at once she realized why. Atop the low shelf that ran for twenty feet along the entryway to their home, was her knight collection. Each horse was set a few inches apart from the next, and they all faced the door as if guarding the entrance. The collection now numbered nearly one hundred, all gifts from friends, relatives, and acquaintances who had purloined them from little-used but fine sets at home, many she knew had been shoplifted, and one made of deep blue lapis which was apparently subject to repossession at any time and without notice. Lately, she and Charlie had made a game of alternating the collection's location, and the display in front of her was Charlie's latest arrangement. In a week or so she would move the collection elsewhere and cluster the pieces however she fancied. Likely it would be less than a week, as Charlie's arrangement eliminated their most utilized counter space.

Halfway down the hall she heard his sobs coming from a different direction than expected, and upon entering her own room she found him lying face-down and motionless on her large floor mattress. She kicked off her shoes, dropped to her knees, curled up next to him, and ran her fingers through his light brown hair. Its color was exactly Logan's, and as it fell back into place, she found herself transfixed by how it even shared the coarseness of his Logan's hair.

"Charlie, could you please pee in my bed too?"

His sob turned into a sniffle. "Huh?"

"Well all your other bodily fluids seem to be draining onto my sheets."

He pulled himself up and noted on the light blue sheet the amoeba-shaped stain that consisted of a mix of snot, tears, and saliva. Taking a cue from her easy tone, he meekly apologized and grabbed a tissue, with which he tried to dab up the mess.

She stopped him, threw the wadded-up tissue to the floor, and laid him down next to her, hugging him from behind with one arm. "I'm sorry about the beer thing Charlie."

A whole new round of sobbing began.

"C'mon Charlie, please stop crying," she pleaded without success. "Okay, Charlie. Listen … give me the name of a place where you go to have fun."

He didn't respond, and she repeated the question while weaving her fingers along his scalp, slowly lifting her hand away from his head until his hair fell free.

"The moon," he managed between sniffles.

"The moon. Okay, now give me the name of a person you like."

"KC," he replied after some thought, referring to KC Nenn, her lone employee at East Portland Indoor Soccer.

"And give me a reason you like KC."

She immediately got an answer this time. "I like his black skull T-shirt." His sobs had subsided, and he wiped a tear from his cheek.

"Now, give me a place on your body where you're especially ticklish," she said while moving her fingers along his side as would a tarantula.

"My armpits," he said with a squirm.

"Okay, so we have the moon, KC, his black skull T-shirt, and your armpits. Is that right?"

"Right."

"Okay, once upon a time, Charlie woke up one morning and was surprised to find he wasn't in his bed at home. He was on the *moon*. He carefully stepped out on the surface of the moon, took one step, and jumped for joy. But on the moon, you see, they don't have as much gravity as here on Earth, so he jumped really high, like as high as the rooftops back on Earth. He couldn't believe it! He had fun, but so much fun he didn't look where he was jumping, and fell into a crater up to his *armpits*. He couldn't get out and was afraid he'd be stuck there forever, but then saw Spaceman *KC*. Charlie said, 'Spaceman KC, will you please help me?' and Spaceman KC said, 'Okay.' Spaceman KC reached down to help Charlie out and pulled him by the belt loop of his pants, and Charlie also helped by grabbing the back of *KC's black skull T-shirt* to pull himself up. Once Charlie was freed, they wondered, 'Hey, how are we going to get back to Earth?' Charlie said, 'I know!' and stuck out his thumb to hitchhike. Then they caught a ride on a passing spaceship powered by a meteor, flew back to Earth, drank Tang along the way, got dropped off in the ocean, and rode a giant dolphin who brought them home to Portland via the Willamette River. The End."

Charlie didn't move, lost in a few seconds of contemplative

silence. "Mom?"

"Yeah hun?"

"I thought you said it was dangerous to hitchhike."

Chapter 2

Miles away in a rundown apartment building, hitchhiking was also on the mind of Jack Edens. He sat on his couch watching a rerun of *I Love Lucy*, and despite the cool breeze that flowed through the open window, sweat ran down his side, over his ribs, and into the growing stain on his shirt. On a television propped up by cinderblocks Ricky Ricardo attempted to flag down a ride beside his broken-down car while his wife, Lucy, lampooned his mannerisms in the background. An invisible audience laughed and laughed.

Jack tried to laugh with them, but it was no use.

Tiny rainbows suddenly scattered about the room, and Jack smiled as he imagined them as hundreds of angels that danced and pulsed and protected him. The breeze gently rotated the prism that hung in his window, and the rainbows spun in a vortex along each wall. However the spectacle lasted only for a minute, and as the sun disappeared behind clouds to the west the angels abruptly departed, and Jack knew not to expect them again anytime soon.

He lived on the first floor of an apartment building where wide cracks split the sidewalk, wind-blown litter accumulated against chain link fences, and the parking spaces along the street were stained with a continuous stripe of oil. Without shame, his landlord had once declared the apartments 'a place for people down on their luck'. It was a sentiment Jack didn't share.

He considered himself lucky.

He felt lucky despite living beneath a couple who regularly fought, eruptions that served as a prelude to the more piercing cries of their children. He felt lucky despite the landlord's empty promise to fix the gutter outside his bedroom window, leading to sleepless nights as water drummed on a dumpster's metal lid. He felt lucky despite his poverty, his meager job, and the thick scar tissue that covered the pad of the index finger on his right hand. Above all else, he felt lucky for the last six years of his life, six years in which he found himself free.

Six years that were coming to an end.

His thoughts flowed to his mother. Though far away in the rural town of Prineville, Oregon, her presence felt suddenly near, the tone of her voice familiar, and the expression of her face strangely vivid.

As a child he never questioned his status. On occasion he witnessed the unusual warmth other parents showed their children, but such displays were so foreign they generated no envy, and no regret. That his best friends were the animals on their farm seemed to him only natural, for these were the only creatures that didn't tease him or trick him, or regard him with indifference. Even his mother's preference for his brother, Michael, made sense to him, for Michael was made from something different. Something better.

He ran his tongue over his chipped tooth, turned from the laughter of the television, and stared at the door. He imagined himself opening it and walking down the hall toward the lobby where he knew a letter waited in the tomb of his mailbox.

Upon bicycling home after his indoor soccer game earlier in the evening, he'd suddenly remembered that today was the day. His mother had told him to expect her letter, and with it, the news about Michael. However with each bounce of his bicycle tires up the front steps of the apartment his courage ebbed, and he'd hurried past the mailboxes as if the metallic wall would come alive, reach out, and grab him. Alone in the safety of his apartment he'd hoped the letter would wash from his mind just like during soccer, but instead it remained and his room began to feel empty and dreary with the rainbows long departed.

Six years ago, a lifetime of abuse had ended when Jack's brother Michael Edens, and his associate Nick Latourelle, were arrested, convicted, and sent to the Oregon State Penitentiary, not as a result of their violent crimes, but for the activity in which Jack himself had become forcibly embroiled.

Cocaine.

Using a combination of financial and physical control, Michael and Nick had exercised such absolute power over him that Jack began to accept his life would never be his own. Their abrupt arrest and departure six years ago was so unexpected that Jack was convinced angels had intervened on his behalf.

On the morning of their arrest there was no indication the day would prove miraculous. Michael's temper flared as it often did, but on this particular day he worked himself into an agitation that built, and doubled, until it erupted at the news of Jack's failure to make a delivery. In the course of a furious beating, Michael kicked him with such vigor that, when it was over, Jack had barely the strength to crawl from the kitchen to the living room couch. Michael and Nick then left to purchase cocaine from their supplier, a tiny woman who conducted business from various locations around town, leaving Jack behind to struggle to breathe with blood brought up with each painful cough.

But they never did return.

The police arrested them all in the midst of their transaction, and while Michael was being handcuffed, he groused at the irony: it was the first and only time he had failed to take the precaution of forcing Jack to participate in a purchase, and carry the drugs and money on his own body. On the one day it counted his safeguard was for naught, negated by the beating that left Jack home when he should have taken the fall. As they were read their rights, Michael gave Nick a menacing glare to signal that no information be given to the police regarding their activities.

It was the tiny woman, and her drug connections in Mexico the police and FBI were after, but they bagged the bonus of two buyers as well, and with only a little coercion Nick revealed their address. It was the first in a series of helpful pieces of information he would provide, and a short time later multiple police cars converged on their squalid house. After tranquilizing Nick's dog, a creature that gnawed on the yard's chain link fence, they kicked open the front door and found a meager figure lying on the couch with a lung punctured by several broken ribs.

After his hospitalization and recovery Jack was asked to testify, but a base fear made him decline, and the police were reluctant to pressure him. His handicap, the beating, and the lack of any evidence of his direct involvement all combined to deter them from charging him as an accomplice. And his testimony proved unnecessary. Large amounts of drugs were found at the scene of the arrest, as well as in a bag in Michael's room, and in Nick they found a person willing to provide a wealth of information on Michael and the tiny woman in exchange for a reduced charge of conspiracy. With his previous felony convictions counting against him, Michael was sentenced to twenty years, while Nick, with an unblemished record and an attorney provided by his father, received an eighteen-month sentence with the potential of time off for good behavior.

He never even saw the fourth month.

Initially Jack didn't know what to make of the news of Nick LaTourelle's strangulation by his cellmate. Nick hadn't been the plague that Michael had -- patiently teaching him to drive the Oldsmobile, making sure he had a jacket and blanket in the wintertime, and once even treating him to a drink in a tavern. However, these recollections could not erase his more recent memories of Nick acting just like Michael, and he came to regard his death a good thing, a further closure of his involvement in the cocaine trade. As a memento Jack had cut out the newspaper clipping that provided details of Nick's death, and stored it between the pages of one of the three books given to him by the nice people who occasionally knocked on his apartment door, talked about God and religion, and answered his many questions about angels.

Jack reached for the bookshelf where his copy of the Holy Bible lay on its side. Holding it upside down, he thumbed through it, but nothing fell from its pages. His foray into the Book of Mormon however, sent two amber newspaper clippings fluttering to the floor, and he unfolded the one that landed closest to him. It was a single column and only a few inches long, and though he struggled with many of the words, to Jack it read like poetry.

Inmate killed in Prison Fight

Salem An inmate at the Oregon State Penitentiary was pronounced dead after an altercation with another prisoner. Prison guards found Nicolas LaTourelle unconscious in his cell Saturday morning, and transported him to the prison infirmary where he was

> pronounced dead by the physician on duty. "Prison officials are questioning the deceased's cellmate," said prison spokesperson Mitchell Hayden. Hayden added that LaTourelle's death was likely the result of asphyxiation, but said preliminary autopsy reports were not yet available. Latourelle was serving an eighteen-month sentence for drug-related offenses.

He refolded the article and placed it in his wallet between the two one-dollar bills that made up his spending money, and did the same with the second newspaper clipping, the one that detailed Michael and Nick's guilty verdict and sentencing.

Bedsprings creaked as he leaned forward and clicked off the TV, shrinking to a dot a scene in which Lucy was talking to a truck driver while Ricky Ricardo and an older couple snuck into the back of the delivery truck. Settling back upon his bed and glancing over at the wall calendar, he realized the month of April had ended, and flipped the page to May. A yellow field of flowers reminded him of the label on the dishwashing soap at work.

For the past six years he had worked a variety of menial jobs that allowed him to eke out and existence on his own. He did yardwork for a few years after Michael and Nick's arrest, but that ended one day when the company went out of business, and his last paycheck never arrived as promised. He'd resorted to washing dishes at restaurants ever since, a career interrupted only once by the month in which he returned to Prineville to stay with his mother while she recovered from a problem with the veins of her leg. However his constant presence soon inspired in her the same cruel condescension of the past, and the same use of the word 'retard' and 'stupid' he remembered from childhood. Preferring his life in Portland and receiving no objections to his return, he took a bus back at the first opportunity and got his current apartment and dishwashing job.

He worked for Rudy's Diner, one of a vast chain of restaurants that employed young people, many of whom were nice in their interactions with him and invited him to play on the various sports teams the restaurant sponsored. He declined their invitations to play softball and volleyball; but their invitations persisted, and somehow he found more bravery when they asked him to play indoor soccer. While he had no more aptitude for soccer than any other sport, he was assured that neither did many of his co-workers, and was persuaded to give it a try. The league to which their team belonged held for him a new experience, one where mistakes were answered not with physical or verbal abuse, but with understanding and an unending stream of encouragement.

Jack recalled a game two weeks ago in which he had scored for the first time, a goal achieved by nudging the ball across the goal line amid a sprawl of fallen players. He was mobbed by teammates in what he initially thought was a coordinated attack, but when his initial panic subsided he found in that moment a joy that had the power to keep him up at night replaying it over and over and over …

Wind blew the curtains into the room, and the stench of the dumpster's garbage sliced into his happy recollection. With his back aching and his legs stiff, he rose and fingered the mailbox key in his pocket. Leaving his apartment door ajar, he walked from his unit and into the quiet lobby. There were no fighting neighbors, wailing babies, or reverberating stereos as he made his way past a stack of phone books wrapped in taut plastic. He pushed his way outside and took a moment to breathe in the freshness of approaching rain. Golden streaks of sunshine bathed the top half of the apartment building across the street, while directly overhead clouds swelled with ominous grays and blues. The front door of the apartment clicked shut behind him as he thought about the good things in life: soccer, the angels, what it felt like to score a goal.

Carefully he unlocked his mailbox and swung open the miniature door. As if to signify its import, unaccompanied by junk mail or catalogs was a single white envelope that rested diagonally in the box; and without having to even touch it he recognized the black script of his mother's handwriting.

So aware was he that his courage could abandon him, he wasted no time ripping it open, and found within it a smaller blue envelope from the Oregon State Penitentiary that had previously been opened. There was a solitary form letter inside:

Audrey Edens
PO Box 4415
Prineville, OR 96555

Regarding inmate #M3012641 – Michael Bradford Edens

To whom it may concern,

The inmate identified above has been scheduled for early release from the Oregon State Penitentiary on the date indicated below, and has listed you as his/her primary contact. Please make arrangements to meet this inmate between the hours of 11:00 AM and 12:00 PM in Parking Lot F of the Oregon State Penitentiary in Salem, Oregon.

This will be your only notice of release. If you have any questions, please call …

Jack stopped his scan of the letter and let his eyes drift to the date at the bottom of the page, where in bold type **July 1** was engraved. It was only two months away.

Both envelopes fell from his grasp where the wind propelled them along the ground until they found a haven beneath a nearby car. It was then he noticed his mother had circled the date with a red pen, drawn a smiley face, and had written below it: *Just in time for the 4th of July!*

The first raindrops dotted his face, neck, and the letter, one of them smudging the l, y, and exclamation point in her last penned word. The ache in his stomach grew, and his attempt to return to his apartment was thwarted by the discovery he'd locked himself out. With only the thin awning to protect him from the coming storm, he backed against the brick wall and waited for someone to pass through the doors of his apartment building.

That night began the nightmares that would plague him for the next two months.

Chapter 3

An extended electrical *zap!* filled Jennifer's office at 7:30 AM on Monday morning, rousing her from her daydream and alerting her that someone had entered through the main doors of the arena. She grabbed a clean coffee cup from the bottom drawer of her desk, exited her office, and heard the faint cadence of footsteps ascending the entryway stairs across the quiet arena.

It's probably just KC.

She congratulated herself for remembering to unlock the front doors this morning, as KC's recent habit of arriving early for work had not yet become fully ingrained in her mind. Alone for only a few moments more, she stretched and headed for the coffeemaker in the concession area. As she walked, she kept an eye on the corridor that connected the entryway to the arena, and her eyes turned away upon recognizing it was indeed KC. The coffeemaker's digital clock blinked 4:57 PM, a time so preposterously wrong it could only mean KC or Charlie had tampered with it. Upon downing the first blistering sip, she looked up and examined her reflection in the broad mirror on the wall.

I look tired.

Her brown hair, still damp from the shower, dangled about her shoulders, while her eyes looked puffy, red, and in need of the enhancement of mascara. On the positive side though, the scratch on her cheek from a game the prior week was only barely noticeable, her lips were their usual rosy selves, and as she checked her profile, her mother's prominent cheekbones stretched smooth the skin on her face.

Not bad for a thirty-five-year-old who couldn't sleep last night.

KC ambled down the walkway adjacent to the soccer field. With hands in pockets he silently slipped into her office with the ease of walking into his own living room, and she heard the protest of her chair followed by the *Clop!* of his feet upon her desk.

Walking back to join him, she viewed him through the office window. His pale skin contrasted with his jet black hair, and though she'd always thought of him as short, seated in her vast leather chair he looked tiny. As he smiled at her, the dimple on his chin flared, and it spawned a grin that spread across her face. He was in standard KC attire: beltless Levis, crumbling canvas tennis shoes, and a black T-shirt at least a size too small. He was skinny, intractably skinny, and as he reclined with his hands behind his head, his frail arms and the visible band of his abdomen reminded her of malnutrition rather than fitness.

"So … um … boss, did you see how the US women's soccer team beat Costa Rica in the World Cup qualifying? They're basically a shoe-in for advancing out of the North American/Central American Region."

What the hell is he talking about?

"We won 3-1," he added.

"Well … good for us," she said. Shooing him from the seat, she noticed droplets of rain glistening in his hair. Once they'd exchanged positions she could see more water, though this time it was the streaks left upon her desk by his tennis shoes. With the palm of her hand she wiped them away.

"I made a copy of it on videotape if you'd like to see it. It was on ESPN last night."

After drying her hands on her sweats, she settled back into her chair and let her eyes drift to her computer screen. There were no new e-mails in the last few minutes. "Hmmm? Oh … okay, bring it in."

Digging through his backpack, he wordlessly put the videotape on the corner of the desk and turned to greet Charlie who had noisily emerged from the back. A faded label along the side of the videotape read NENN FAMILY VACATION followed by the year of Logan's murder.

KC was an enigma. Even though they'd worked together for over a year, their interactions remained forced. Filling any conversational void with facts about soccer, an improvement for East Portland Indoor Soccer, or some other topic laced with premeditation, KC's awkwardness toward her was so pronounced even Charlie noticed it. It frustrated her some that their relationship had failed to progress to friendship, since she typically found it easy to generate friends. Directly in front of her, KC's fluid interaction with her son made her inability to count KC in the company of her friends almost painful.

After a high-five, KC and Charlie began thumb wrestling. Via the sheer differential in size, KC held the physical advantage; however Charlie was allowed a liberal amount of cheating, either by the occasional use of his offhand or by falling to the floor with a spasm when pinned, thereby making it impossible for KC to hold on for a victorious ten count.

He was her sole full-time employee, and had been with her from the very beginning when she struggled with the enormity of launching East Portland Indoor Soccer. It was his interactions with Charlie, however, like a simple thumb wrestling match that left them both with broad smiles, that elevated his status from employee to family member. From the first moment they met, KC and Charlie had fallen into the instinctual horseplay of boys much closer in age, and she wondered whether gender, a mutual lack of attention span, or Charlie's lack of a father figure forged their unique alliance.

Their thumb-wrestling match finished, Charlie triumphantly retreated to the back to collect his things for school, while KC headed for a closet where he'd stored some supplies from the week before. He carted out tarps, brushes, paint cans, cups, tape, and his portable radio to the far end of the field. His first few loads delivered, he walked back and stuck his head into her open office door. "No games at noon, right?"

Caught in mid-yawn, she covered her mouth and gave an affirmative nod.

He brought the rest of his body into her office and pointed to the palm of his empty left hand. "The key?"

"Okay, okay," she replied. Acquiescing to KC's request to have his own key to the front doors made complete sense. It would make unnecessary her oft-forgotten trips to unlock them for him in the morning, and was also consistent with her feeling of trust for him. And yet, she hesitated. KC had stated his desire to come "hang out" late at night long after the last game of the evening had been played, and promised to do so alone. In addition he cited, as if it were the only conceivable concern, that the big-screen TV couldn't be heard from the back bedrooms where she and Charlie slept. But it wasn't the television that worried her. Even ten years after Logan's murder she was vigilant about security for herself and Charlie. The thought of granting unlimited access to the arena, even to KC, struck her as unadvisable; and she clung to the small comfort of knowing KC could not lose the key, or have it stolen or copied, as long as she retained sole possession.

Whereas she saw security in the key, KC saw freedom. Making his case for the key he proclaimed that late nights at the arena were "by far the best way to avoid my parents," with whom he still resided. Months previously while painting late into the night he'd discovered that staying out late assured his mom would not wait up for him, caution him on his night-life activities, and remind him, with statistical information memorized from *Reader's Digest*, of the need to be conscientious about AIDS.

She knew that had it not been integral to his effort to secure a refuge from his parents, KC would never have shared the story of his domestic plight. Nevertheless she'd made a copy of the key, and for the past few days let it dangle within the metallic cluster on her key chain while waiting for a sign, a feeling, or some undeniable signal of fate to indicate whether or not to hand it over.

With a roar KC started the FlexLift, the motorized hydraulic apparatus that could be driven to any spot within the arena and raised up to twenty-five feet. As he stood atop it and struggled with the controls, it began to move like a decrepit tank. It took him a while to maneuver it from its storage space to the extreme end of the field, but once in place he raised himself to painting height, cut the engine, and continued his meticulous work above the northern goal. A simple ladder might have been sufficient, but to KC the FlexLift was a cherished toy, and he made no effort to conceal his desire to use it. Across the length of the field she could make out his rabid-looking Snoopy taking shape above the goal. Bared fangs, sharply descending dark eyebrows, and demonic glare all contributed to an image Charles Schultz likely would not have sanctioned.

Of all his talents, Jennifer regarded KC's artistic abilities the most impressive, mostly because they were untapped prior to his employment. One day a month ago, she casually asked him "Can you do some painting?" when a beer distributor agreed to supply free kegs every week in exchange for a painted wall advertisement.

"More beams?" he whined, referring to some of the mundane arena prep prior to their grand opening a year earlier.

"More like art. Well … maybe not *art*, but a PBR logo on a beer bottle, and a few words."

Grimacing as if there was a bad taste in his mouth, he leaned forward and said in a serious tone, "Boss, that stuff tastes like cat piss."

"I really don't care what it tastes like. It's an advertiser … we've agreed on the amount of free beer we'll get … and all that's left is for someone to actually paint the logo. Think you can do it?"

He offered to try, and plunged into the task with vigor. Since the location was at midfield near the digital clock, KC had to work when no soccer would be played and his efforts had adequate time to dry. This necessitated some late night and early morning hours, thereby giving birth to the idea that the solitude of East Portland Indoor Soccer late at night could ease his domestic situation. His preparation, including a meticulous sketch on the wall, paid off, resulting in a finished product that was acceptable to the beer distributor, but somehow only shrug-worthy to KC.

Soon after the PBR success and with the desire to paint something less commercial, KC suggested a ferocious Snoopy-as-goalie over the northern goal. Initially she dismissed the idea, but warmed to it after observing Charlie's laughter while watching a *Peanuts* special a few days later. Acknowledging the empty interior walls of the arena weren't going to be snapped up by businesses clamoring to advertise, she relented to KC's vision when he produced the sketch that was to be his model, and the image of a malevolent Snoopy struck her as funny, irreverent, and representative of the mentality of many goalies.

Dipping a brush into a plastic cup, KC worked on Snoopy's head as she and Charlie walked up to him far below on the field.

"You never got to paint your room as a boy, did you?" she called up.

"Huh?" he answered without bothering to turn around.

"Nevermind. Taking Charlie to school. Back in ten."

She got a noncommittal noise in return. Charlie, however, his imagination ensnared by the dual allure of heavy machinery and cartoons, was captivated by the project. Having been previously rebuffed by KC on his offer of assistance with the actual painting, he resorted to constructive criticism and helpful hints as his only means of contribution. "Don't make his ears too light, they're darker than that. Don't make him growl too much, real goalies don't do that. Where's Woodstock gonna go?" were some of his comments this particular morning.

Jennifer knew KC had limits to Charlie's suggestions, and when his responses regressed from "I won't, buddy" to "Okay," to a muffled "Mmm," she ushered Charlie away with the refrain of needing to get to school on time.

As they turned to leave, KC asked nonchalantly, "Made any decision on the Fourth of July party yet?"

She paused. "Umm, we'll talk about that later." She ushered Charlie forward with a hand on his back.

"Oh, and I almost forgot … ", he added from above.

He put his paintbrush down and struggled to fish something out of his front pocket. After making an underhanded throwing gesture to which she responded with cupped hands, he tossed down an object that she identified as a knight while it was still in the air. As she tracked its descent he explained, "My parents have an old set in their garage they never use anymore."

She caught the delicate figurine and admired it. About three inches tall, it was unlike any other in her collection, a sea horse. Carved from a white stone with random gray streaks that seemed an adornment rather than an impurity, it felt strangely nice to touch, and along the serrations of its spine she repeatedly ran her thumb. After handing it to Charlie, she looked up with the intent of saying thank you, but KC had already returned to his painting. Instead she chose a different course.

"Kase?"

He turned, and she gave him the same throwing motion he'd given her. He leaned forward, cupped his hands, and gave her a frown of regret as if he thought the knight was being returned as an unacceptable gift. Instead a she threw a silver key which he caught easily. He stared at it for a moment, only realizing it was the key to the front doors after a few seconds. With a smile he looked down with the intent of saying thank you, but by then she had already turned and was walking Charlie to school.

After Jennifer's inquiry near the stairs, Charlie realized he'd forgotten his lunch, and raced back to retrieve it. All alone for the moment in the dark entryway, the sounds of KC's radio were all that kept her company. As James Taylor sang about daydreaming of Carolina, she fished the sea horse from her pocket for closer scrutiny and considered KC's inquiry about the Fourth of July party.

It seemed like such a great idea a year ago. A few weeks prior to the arena's opening, a dozen friends, as well as the newly-employed KC Nenn, climbed the exterior fire escape to view downtown Portland's fireworks show. However, when it was Charlie's turn to ascend, he was paralyzed with fear. Her hour-long effort of coaxing, encouragement, and even bribery was in vain, and amid the opening pyrotechnics, Charlie and she were forced to abandon their guests to view the show from one of the bridges that spanned the Willamette River between the arena and downtown Portland. Just as they arrived at the river however, so too did a thunderstorm that cancelled the show, and from which they had no protection. While theirs was a miserable trek home in the rain, they were spared the fate of rooftop guests back at the arena who had to choose between scrambling down the iron fire escape amid bolts of lightning, or riding out the storm on the roof.

They chose the roof.

Even a year later, KC's inquiry about giving it another try caused her to shudder, not because of the possibility of another storm, but because Charlie was likely no more capable of conquering the fire escape twelve months later. Twice in the last week she had brought up the idea of another rooftop fete, each time expecting Charlie to say no and kill the whole idea. But to her surprise he was enthusiastic about it, as if amnesia had erased the debacle from his memory.

Without warning KC switched stations, severing James Taylor's words with a jumble of static. Pulsing rap music suddenly burst forth, and after KC turned up the volume, she couldn't resist peeking around the corner where she found him gyrating atop the FlexLift as he mixed a cup of paint. A grin broke across her face. While unable to consider KC a friend, she had to admit that how she now regarded him was far from how she felt at their first encounter over a year ago.

On that day he had wandered into East Portland Indoor Soccer indistinguishable from some of the laborers hired for the renovation. "And just what is it that you're doing here?" he inquired at midfield with his eyes gazing upward. He stood a mere step away from her, oblivious to the fact his feet were pinning down the carpet she was trying to de-wrinkle while on her hands and knees.

His question went unacknowledged. Instead, she stood with frustration and barked, "PLEASE GET OFF THE CARPET!" Her patience vanished when defeated by a task of manual labor, and as he recoiled with a jerky hop, she realized for the first time she was dealing not with one of the laborers, but with an interloper. In no mood to waste time on a stranger, she addressed his question with an acidic one of her own. "What does it look like we're doing?"

He picked up on her frustrated tone and chose not to answer.

Ashamed to have spoken in such a manner, she knelt and returned to her task as her hair tumbled about her face. I'm turning this place into an indoor soccer arena. Either that or an incredible financial disaster."

KC took a second precautionary step back and resumed his panoramic scan. His expression was that of a man who has returned to his childhood home to find details inconsistent with his memory, and after a minute he shifted his focus to her struggle. "You *do* know," he offered, "that they have specific tools for stretching carpet so that it can be laid without … you know … the bumps and wrinkles?"

"You don't say."

"Yeah. Here." He bent down. "Let me show you."

It proved a pivotal moment, and their ensuing exchange revealed his extensive knowledge of carpeting. While sharing in her struggle, he offered up the most useful piece of information of all, the location of a nearby store where carpeting tools could be purchased. After some mutual toil he looked her in the eye. "Say, is it possible you need some help around here?"

His unexpected query, delivered from the intimate distance of twelve inches, rendered her speechless, coming the very day she'd acknowledged the need for more help in bringing the place to completion. She stood, introduced herself as the owner of East Portland Indoor Soccer, and began an impromptu interview. "So how old are you KC?"

But he trumped her. "Did you know that for age discrimination reasons you aren't allowed to ask that question?"

"What are you … a lawyer?"

He laughed his way into a cough, but didn't answer.

She peppered him with other questions, the answers to which revealed he was currently unemployed, had some experience working in his dad's construction company, and most recently worked at a store no more than a mile away that specialized in outdoor sports and camping. This interested her particularly, and she steered the conversation to why he no longer worked there.

"They fired me after finding out I'm gay."

The simple honesty of his reply stunned her, and while her curiosity prodded her to ask further questions about the circumstances of his firing, his previous comment about discriminatory interview questions had her on her guard. Instead, she nodded and grasped for another path on which to proceed. "Sssooo … at this outdoors store … did you have any experience working with people?"

"Is that important?"

"Well yes. Very … actually. When I get this place going I'll need someone to look after the place, collect money, pass out liability forms, run the concessions, do the clean up, odd jobs, et cetera."

"Oh. I was thinking that this was going to be more along the lines of construction."

"Well, there will be some of that. Painting will be critical, all the netting needs to get set up so balls don't go flying off the field and nail people, I want some sort of buzzer to sound in the office whenever someone comes in the main entrance, and most important we need to figure out how to keep balls from smashing the lights." As she said it she gestured with her head toward the lattice of beams suspended over the field, almost all of which contained bare fluorescent lights on their undersurface. At her prompting he wrote down his name and phone number, and once he'd finished she pointed at some construction workers in the distance. "These guys will finish the majority of their work soon, and once the place gets up and running, I'll need someone to work the place in a sort of behind-the-counter way."

He indicated he was more than comfortable dealing with people, and their interview concluded with an awkward handshake. Once his hands were back in the confines of his pant pockets, he gazed around to try to envision himself working in a place that had no more affiliation with his personal interests than the local YarnWorld. "Indoor soccer, huh?" he muttered to himself.

She tossed his name and phone number atop the clutter already maligning her rudimentary office, and weeks later when the scrap of paper resurfaced, she took it as a sign. An hour after she left a message on his parents' answering machine, he showed up and after a brief conversation she offered him the job.

He accepted.

They agreed his wage would be seven and a half dollars an hour, which is to say that she presented the amount, and KC readily accepted it. They specified an 8AM to 5PM workday to start, with an agreement to shift hours to the evening once the place got going. There was an unending list of details to attend to in the six weeks before the hoped-for opening date, and she instilled in him the import of making that deadline, even sharing that she lay awake at night filled with anxiety that East Portland Indoor Soccer would result in nothing more than a spectacular joke.

"Oh, and have you ever played soccer before?" was her query before he left.

He gave a short laugh. "Well not since, like, third grade. My dad always told me soccer was for sissies." He thought about this response for a moment and then added with a grin, "Maybe he was right."

Whether he took her words to heart or it was in his nature to care particularly about the success of his employer, KC threw himself into his job as if he had a financial interest in the place. In no time, he completed the bulk of the painting with an industrial sprayer he rented from a neighborhood store, rigged an electric shock-sounding alarm which was tripped whenever a light beam was broken at the main entrance, helped secure the Plexiglas borders of the field, and advocated a guerilla marketing campaign by which he would personally adorn thousands of vehicles with fliers touting the grand opening. His *coup de grace* however, was the chicken wire.

KC happened upon a solution for the protection of the fluorescent lights by bracing some fluorescent tubes with a bracket crafted out of the scrap iron found in a back storeroom, and wrapping it all with a protective cordon of taut chicken wire. It was cheap, replicable, and was not an impediment to the lighting. The only question was its strength, and once he'd rigged a test section with the help of the FlexLift, he watched as Jennifer and Helena kicked balls upward against it with all their might. As successive direct hits failed to bring with it an explosion of glass, he broke into the broadest smile she'd ever seen from him before or since. It was the first moment she truly believed the arena would be success.

As for KC, at the time of his hiring he considered himself the beneficiary of good fortune for stumbling upon a job that paid him a decent wage, fulfilled the personal requirement of an escape from his parents, utilized some of his previous experience, and had the potential to blossom into a scene that was the social equivalent of a bartender -- a job he always thought would be fun. At the conclusion of his first full week of work he offhandedly announced, "Oh, and boss, you should probably know that you've hired someone who's famous. Well, not really *famous* famous, just sort of locally famous."

She hesitated. "Famous for what?"

"Well, do you remember a few years back or so when there was that giant protest downtown at the Forestry Department building … and there was … "

Her familiarity with that event compelled her to interrupt,

"Oh yeah. You mean that one where that guy … "

KC interrupted back. "Yeah, well … you see … um …

that guy? That guy was me."

Chapter 4

Eighteen months before his employment at East Portland Indoor Soccer, KC strolled through the streets of downtown Portland with Oscar Rittencourt. Independently they meditated on the unraveling of their ten-month relationship. KC reflected how it felt as if his best days with Oscar were a decade ago, and that Oscar now reminded him of a contemptuous older brother rather than the passionate figure to which he was initially attracted. Oscar felt the decline as well, though his immediate focus centered on the carelessness with which KC had treated his leather jacket at a party the night before, the loss of which he was certain despite KC's insistence that it was sure to turn up.

While Oscar was an advocate of environmental and forestry issues in the Northwest, KC was aloof. This attitude was apparent in everything from his politics (he had never once voted) to his clothing (he never considered the weather when choosing his outfit for the day) to his attention span (if he was bored in a one-on-one conversation he would simply walk away, leaving the other person to ponder what affront they had caused). That he could be convinced to care about something so far removed from his immediate personal interests as trees required foolish optimism, a trait Oscar had in abundance, and one he continued to draw upon as his relationship with KC deteriorated.

KC was selfish. Indefatigably selfish. His only outdoor interest ever was rock climbing, where his lean frame and wiry muscularity combined to give him a natural advantage. While KC and Oscar both had an interest in the outdoors, KC felt claustrophobic in the forests, and Oscar got no satisfaction from the causelessness of rock climbing.

On this particular afternoon Oscar led KC to a protest at the Oregon Department of Forestry building where there promised to be the usual mix of local media, assorted diehard activists, and the usual throng of passive participants. For Oscar, though it threatened to be an event that accomplished very little in terms of publicity, forest policy change, or putting forth a sort of coherent message about the evils of clearcutting, he was determined to give it his all. For KC, his attendance was the result of having no more captivating alternatives for the day, and he tagged along in the hope something interesting would come his way.

"You know quite frankly, I couldn't care less if they chop all the forests down," KC blurted.

He said it just as they came to a stop at a crosswalk, and Oscar opened his mouth to respond. If it was a fight KC wanted, he could surely provide it, but he thought it unwise to rile himself up prior to the rally. After holding his breath for two seconds and exhaling, he simply pursed his mouth around his cigarette and noted how chapped his lips were becoming in the autumnal wind.

"I mean, as soon as you get not ten miles out of the city, you're smack dab in the middle of millions of board feet of forest. I need my paper products for God's sake, and at this point, I wouldn't mind a little firewood." As he said it, KC rubbed his hands together and held his palms out, basking in the warmth of an imaginary campfire.

Oscar turned and took measure of the hunched, chilled creature whose hands soon retreated to what little warmth could be found in the front pockets of his pants. Unless it got down into the thirties, KC could be counted on to wear mere jeans and a T-shirt. On this day however, he hadn't counted on the wind, and the morning had turned frigid. Oscar smiled with the knowledge he had risen above the badgering, and for his own jacketed and mittened warmth. He thought a lesson in layering might be learned today, and in an unperturbed fashion eased the cigarette from his mouth and proceeded with his own languid stream of consciousness. "You know, if only people could look beyond paper products and recreation, and think in terms of the extinction of all sorts of species, this entire argument could be framed the way it needs to be. As soon as we get engaged in topics related to housing, government land policy, and all that crap about public right-to-use, we've ceded the most compassionate high ground of the argument ... the part children actually care about."

KC sniffed, "Focus on Bambi, huh?"

"Yes, focus on fucking Bambi! ... and bears and eagles and all the other wildlife that get crowded into smaller and smaller spaces. And I'll thank you not to condense this argument down to something Walt Disney pulled out of his ass fifty years ago!" Oscar simultaneously blew smoke, ground his cigarette into the asphalt, and adjusted his glasses while waiting for the light to change. While KC initially recoiled at the outburst, his mind drifted into a replay of Oscar's choice of words. *Focus ... on ... fucking ... Bambi.* He smiled and stifled a laugh at the mental image of Oscar, caught in the midst of a sex act with a deer.

A moment later the disorganized mob came into view in front of the Department of Forestry building. They split as they approached the crowd with the silent understanding that Oscar would now get embroiled in the proceedings, while KC would endeavor to kill time in whatever way he chose. KC first walked along the periphery of the crowd in a search for familiar faces. Finding none, he began a search for warmth, and found a bit of it in the forestry building's courtyard where a large square was accessible from the street and surrounded on three sides by the four-story glass-and-brick structure. The biting wind eased once KC took a seat on a concrete border that surrounded a leafless tree, and watched from a distance as the mob try to organize itself on the sidewalk. Enviro-types, gawkers, and quite possibly some homeless cluttered the scene. Many of the activists were hardened veterans of years of forestry fights, having blocked logging roads, spiked trees, and suffered the personal bitterness of the cause's newest tactic: climbing the very trees that were threatened to live within their branches until logging plans were cancelled. KC couldn't help but admire the dedication of a person willing to spend a night in a tree amid a 40-mile-per-hour winter wind to prevent, even temporarily, its felling.

The protest finally gathered momentum and advanced from the sidewalk and into the courtyard where KC sat, with Oscar at a megaphone barking various sentiments. The throng's new proximity destroyed KC's panoramic observation, and he rose to his feet just as Oscar bellowed into the megaphone.

"THIS WILL BE THE THIRD MAJOR TIMBER SALE APPROVED BY OUR FORESTRY OFFICIALS WITHOUT DUE PROCESS! THEY'RE CLEARLY ACTING IN AN UNACCOUNTABLE MANNER! WE DEMAND AN EXPLANATION … AND ARE ASKING THAT SOMEONE COME OUT OF THAT BUILDING TO PROVIDE PROOF THAT HABITAT PRESERVATION STUDIES WERE DONE FOR THIS SALE!"

KC sought out a new position. After a quick scan of his options, he headed for an interior corner of courtyard where two walls met at a ninety degree angle. There, standing with arms crossed for warmth, he leaned back to watch, only to find that while his view was improved, his comfort was not. Where the two walls met, individual bricks jutted out in an architectural offset, and after trying more comfortable ways of positioning his shoulder blades against them, KC turned and faced his sharp-edged tormenters. His fingers explored their edges.

Oscar remained in the middle of the throng, inciting the crowd and feeling like things were improving. The only problem was that his words weren't interactive, and each of his barked comments had to be at least one iota more stinging, creative, or forceful than the last in order to elicit cheers from the crowd. Oscar's eyes caught KC standing in a corner of the courtyard twenty-five yards away, his back turned, looking like a schoolboy banished to the corner of a classroom. An amalgam of curiosity and lament washed over him for his inability to understand odd KC, and his sigh, amplified through the megaphone, could only have been interpreted as exasperation by those who knew of their contentious relationship. Before Oscar returned his full attention to the rally, he saw KC raise his hands and move them along the bricks.

Oscar recalled a statistic he knew all too well. "THERE ARE FIFTEEN KNOWN SPECIES IN THE CASCADES TEETERING ON THE BRINK OF BEING PLACED ON THE ENDANGERED SPECIES LIST, AND THEY JUST MIGHT GET THERE IF THE LATEST TIMBER SALES ARE APPROVED! HOW LONG MUST THIS LIST GROW BEFORE

SOMEONE UP THERE … " he said with a finger thrust toward the top floor, " … TAKES NOTE OF THIS?!"

There was a raucous yell from the crowd and Oscar felt people push past him. For a moment he thought everyone had been moved to storm the building, as if he had uttered an incantation that motivated people to violence. Then his attention was drawn to someone pointing behind him. He turned and noted a lone figure ascending the building at the courtyard's interior corner. Bewildered, he put the megaphone down and took in the unreal sight. KC was scaling the forestry building.

The motivation at that moment was not about upstaging Oscar, trying to make a spectacle, or even trying to help the rally's cause by performing a crazy stunt. He was flat-out bored, and when bored, he was prone to respond to any impulse that promised relief. Though the wind gusted as he made his way up, the climb was an easy one with the offset bricks spaced in a manner as conducive to climbing as a ladder.

He reached a small ledge at a series of windows, which, though technically the second floor, was the equivalent height of three stories. The narrow ledge offered a refuge given the uncertainty he felt on the way up, and as he pressed against the window with his stomach, he dimly perceived the crowd surging and shouting far below. Before him was a broad lunchroom with a brightly lit Coca-Cola advertisement above a bank of soda dispensers. A few seated workers ate and read newspapers, and his arrival from such an unexpected direction went largely unnoticed. His lone identifier was an immense cafeteria worker who spotted him from behind the cash register, though from shock she stood motionless with her mouth agape. In the moment before KC turned to climb further, she had recovered enough to raise an arm and point in his direction, an action that made one customer turn, take note of him as well, and suffer the same jaw-dropping paralysis.

Ascending anew, KC encountered the same corner brickwork as before, and found the same eighteen-inch ledge to perch upon at the next floor up. Unfortunately, the wind made his arrival at this new aerie uncomfortably cold, and while he could ascend still one more floor, he decided he'd climbed high enough. Turning carefully and looking down, he studied the crowd for the first time. That individual people on the ground seemed quite small, was not a surprise. That their combined vocal power could produce such a clamor, was. All thought of danger and frigidity faded from his mind as he raised two fists above his head and the crowd responded with an even louder roar.

Robbing him of his euphoria, Oscar's amplified voice rose from the megaphone. "WE'VE TAKEN THE BATTLE TO THE DEPARTMENT OF FORESTRY!"

More cheers erupted, but high above them KC dropped his arms. "Likening me with those tree whores," he muttered before turning to look into the windows of his new surroundings.

A wide wood-paneled office lay before him, taking up the entire space of the cafeteria one floor below. No more than a few feet away, the back of a bald executive huddled over some paperwork at his corner desk. He was obviously someone important, and KC watched with wide eyes as the smooth head rose, a fatty neck and spine stretched, and the man reclined in his chair with his head tantalizingly close to the glass. He wanted to retreat, feeling as if he'd walked into the depths of a room only to unexpectedly find someone asleep. Just as quickly though, he was aware of the width of the ledge, and he became resigned that his detection was assured, if not imminent. Far below in the courtyard someone started beating a drum.

The executive sipped his coffee with one hand and held a memorandum just above his stomach with the other. He kicked his feet up on his desk and assumed a position that would have resembled slumber were it not for what he held. While pondering his next move, KC stared down past the man's bushy eyebrows and tried to read the memo. His stealthy observation was interrupted, however, when in the open doorway a girl suddenly appeared, burdened by a vast stack of papers she carried before her with both hands.

KC's eyes widened.

No sooner had her attention shifted to KC, she exploded with an upright snap of her spine, sending the stack upward in a manner only an adrenaline release could have made possible. Even as the mass was airborne, she belted out a scream that KC could make out through the window, over the wind, and despite the commotion three floors below.

With a spasm the executive reacted. He grasped that something menacing had slipped in behind him, coiled and ready to strike; and as a shower of paper descended swept his feet from the desk. Coffee sloshed, and his feet kicked his in-basket to the floor. When he managed to get his footing, two sensations battled for his attention: the pain of having hot coffee spill upon his abdomen (a condition made worse by standing up) and the incomprehension of what this person was doing on the other side of the window. When it dawned on him that KC was in some way connected to the protest, both sensations gave way to anger at having the distant demonstration suddenly invade the tranquility of his office.

While KC observed the resulting interior drama (confusion, cleanup, people coming in and out of the office to gawk), Oscar's voice boomed from below. "THE FIGHT FOR OUR FORESTS BEGINS RIGHT HERE IN DOWNTOWN PORTLAND!"

The executive fled, no doubt headed to the men's room.

"MAYBE NOW THEY'LL REALIZE TREES CAN HAVE ADVOCATES TOO!"

KC felt the wind brush the hairs on the back of his neck. His entire body convulsed with a chill.

"JUST AS WE HAVE SCALED TREES IN THE PAST, SO TOO SHALL WE SCALE THE EDIFICES OF THE DEPARTMENT OF FORESTRY!"

A security guard appeared in the office doorway, and could only shrug while sorting through the advice of a various office workers.

"IT'S TIME TO TAKE THIS FIGHT TO THE DEPARTMENT OF FORESTRY!"

Numerous coffee-stained papers were scattered about the floor.

"OUR ACTIONS ARE GOING TO GET MORE AND MORE EXTREME AS THE PLIGHT OF THE FORESTS CONTINUES TO BE IGNORED!"

A petite girl within the office waved at KC, and he returned the gesture with a smile. He now knew the feeling of a fish in an aquarium.

"MAYBE NOW THEY KNOW THE FEELING OF A TREE IN AN AREA SCHEDULED FOR CLEARCUTTING!"

KC carefully walked the length of the ledge, avoiding pigeon excrement and other unidentifiable grime.

"FROM NOW ON WE WON'T BE CONTENT TO JUST CLIMB TREES! THE CITY IS OUR FOREST! THE CITY IS OUR FOREST!"

KC tried to communicate with people on the other side of the glass (who were closer, more curious now) using exaggerated mouth gestures and unintelligible nonsense words.

"THE MAN UP THERE IS KC NENN … "

KC experimented with some phony sign language.

"… AND HE VOWS TO STAY UP THERE ON THAT LEDGE UNTIL THE DEPARTMENT OF FORESTRY DECIDES TO CHANGE THEIR POLICY OF SANCTIONED CLEARCUTTING!"

This got KC's attention.

He pivoted slowly to face the courtyard and gazed down. His initial reaction was to try to yell down to Oscar in response, but he realized there was no way to be heard. It wasn't the wind but the howling crowd. KC moved along the ledge to the corner of his ascent, confidently foot-over-foot rather than with his previous sideways shimmy, and began his way back down to the second floor. The crowd in the courtyard had definitely swelled since his crusade to battle boredom, while out on the street an increasing number of police cars with silent flashing lights parked within view. The descent to the second floor was notably more hazardous, and he had to be more deliberate than before with his footing. Once there, he wondered for the first time why he had gotten himself into this situation.

"KC VOWS TO REMAIN DAY AND NIGHT, AS A TESTAMENT TO HIS COMMITMENT TO THE FORESTS!"

The much larger cafeteria crowd congregated at the windows and pointed at him as would children at the zoo, agog at the creature that ventured near the glass. But KC ignored them, so focussed was he on clearing up Oscar's misinterpretation of his actions. Before he could attempt any communication, however, a group of police officers had made their way to Oscar, and, more importantly to them, the megaphone. As they reached him the crowd surrendered its enthusiasm and became almost silent as the police authoritatively negotiated with Oscar for the implement. Only the drummer was unaffected by the drama, pounding away on autopilot from the periphery of the crowd. With arms crossed, KC waited and observed like the rest of the crowd, while below him Oscar put up a spirited argument with the police. For a few minutes Oscar held his own, with one hand holding the megaphone behind his back and the other gesturing wildly at the officers. Then, unexpectedly, he handed it over.

As Oscar separated from the heart of the protest, KC's eyes tracked him through the crowd. Once he'd gotten far enough apart from the others, their eyes met and KC communicated his displeasure through the simple and slow shaking of his head back and forth. At that exact moment, a new voice boomed through the megaphone.

"COME DOWN FROM THE BUILDING IMMEDIATELY!"

KC's gesture, intended for Oscar, had the appearance to all below as direct police defiance, and the mob erupted into rabid cheering. KC's eyes shifted to the crowd, at once aware of the perception he had caused. He tilted his head back and raised his fists, and the crowd gave an approving howl as a reward for his defiance.

"I REPEAT ... COME DOWN FROM THE BUILDING NOW. YOU ARE TRESPASSING ON PRIVATE PROPERTY!"

KC ignored them. Boos erupted from the crowd, directed at the police. He located Oscar again and made the gesture of a telephone with his thumb to his ear and his pinkie at the corner of his mouth, and Oscar immediately plunged into the crowd to find a cellular phone.

A few minutes passed before one was found and volunteered into service. With the donation finally in hand, Oscar picked his way through the crowd to the corner and stared straight up to KC. He practiced an underhanded throwing motion for his own benefit, and unleashed an inept toss that was well short. It struck the wall inches below KC's feet, tumbled to the ground uncaught, and burst into a variety of electronic components and bouncing jagged plastic.

Despite a frantic search, Oscar was unable to find anyone willing to sacrifice a cell phone for another try. Just when his efforts appeared hopeless, an older man stepped forward, produced a cellular phone from within his jacket, and imperiled the device high into the air. This time the phone was on the mark, and it rose until it levitated for a second at the level of KC's chin. All he had to do was produce a palm, and the phone gently settled into his hand, its upward energy spent.

Oscar quickly produced his own cell phone from within his jacket, inquired about the phone number of the one KC now possessed, and disregarded a few comments regarding the selfish protection of his own phone. A hand over his opposite ear, he walked away from the crowd in order to hear better, and within seconds was talking directly to KC. He didn't even bother with "Hello."

"Kase?"

"There's no way, I repeat, no way in hell I'm gonna stay up here until they change their policy! Even … "

"But … "

" … even overnight. I'd either freeze to death or fall asleep on the ledge here and tumble off!"

Oscar walked farther away from the crowd, lest his half of the conversation reveal KC's reluctance. "You don't understand. Right now you *are* the forestry protest. This whole event," he said as he swept his hand across the courtyard, "has been energized by your stunt. We probably have twice … "

KC tried to interrupt.

" … no *ten* times the media coverage thanks to you."

KC stared below and tried to distill the media representatives from the mass of bodies. People were definitely pointing cameras in his direction, and yet another news van was pulling up on the street. Oscar had a point.

"I REPEAT … COME DOWN FROM THE BUILDING NOW!" bellowed the police.

"But this isn't even my issue. I was just bored, Oscar."

"Kase ... you've single-handedly infused this protest with energy. You can't take that away now."

"Watch me."

"COME DOWN FROM THE BUILDING … OR YOU WILL BE ARRESTED!"

"Okay ... look … " Oscar said.

"No, *you* look," KC shot back. "What the hell do I do up here over multiple days? What if I have to go to the bathroom? Am I supposed to poop in my hand and throw it at the cops?"

"COME DOWN RIGHT NOW … OR WE'LL BE FORCED TO COME UP THERE AND GET YOU!"

"Please hold," KC said secretarially. He tucked the phone in his pants and flipped off the police with both hands. The crowd response bordered on deafening, fueled by more and more people now in the courtyard, many just there to see what all the commotion was about, but cheering nonetheless at the anarchy up on the ledge.

Reconnected with KC again, Oscar suggested, "You could use a bucket, and for sleep we could secure you to the ledge with all that mountain climbing equipment you've got."

KC's mind flashed to an image of himself stooping to defecate into a bucket while people stared at him through the cafeteria windows. "I'm coming down right now!"

"Okay. Okay. You win," Oscar pleaded. "I'll tell you what … just stay up there until after the local news tonight. Eleven o'clock. That's all I ask."

The second line on the cell phone rang, and KC again said nasally to Oscar, "Please hold." He deduced to hit the biggest button on the phone right below the digital screen, and a new voice came on the line.

"Hello?"

KC parroted the greeting back, and got an excited earful in response. "Gordon, can you believe it?! The news is showing some character who climbed the outside of the forestry building. He's up on the ledge right now! Whatta nut! But oh whatta stunt! Are you there right now? Gordon? … Gordon? I think it would be a g … "

KC hit the button that he assumed hung up on the inquisitor and got Oscar back on the line. "Oscar?"

"Yes?"

"If you get me a coat … a *really, really* warm coat … and some food, I'll stay 'til eleven o'clock."

"Oh God! Thank you! Thank you for this! Kase?"

"Yes?"

"I forgive you for losing my leather jacket."

KC pondered a response, but instead simply disconnected the phone. After about thirty minutes a coat was produced (bundled into a dense ball, wrapped with duct tape, and heaved up to him), the police retreated from the courtyard (their bluff called), and KC settled in for his stay on the ledge. The excitement of mid-day proved unsustainable however, and much of the rest of the afternoon and evening was spent with KC walking the ledge without a purpose, or in a seated position with his feet dangling as he called various friends on the phone. Oscar and the other members of the protest leadership considered having KC conduct telephone interviews with various media outlets, but then wisely thought better of the idea and conducted such interviews themselves. Forced to deal with the embarrassment of public urination, KC retreated to the extreme corner of the ledge opposite his ascent and bashfully relieved himself into a clear plastic water bottle which, with other food and drink, were hurled up to him by the helpful vegetarians below. Once the peeing was completed, he made a pact with his bladder that if it could hold off until after eleven o'clock, he would never drink cheap beer again.

Oscar organized another crescendo of the rally, complete with drums and other musical instruments, all timed to coincide with the local news. However by then the security guards and police had succeeded in pushing the rally out of the courtyard and onto the street, and the news cameras were left with distant live shots of KC on the ledge and footage from earlier in the day.

Just before midnight KC descended into police custody and spent the night in jail. To his relief and surprise the trespassing charges were dropped (the forestry department didn't want to make even more of a martyr of him), and he gained notoriety as a forest advocate unequalled by those that had dedicated a lifetime to the cause.

Months later in the middle of winter, all that physically remained of the incident was a capped and crystallized bottle of urine which, placed as it was on the corner of the ledge, could only be viewed from across the street. It was removed only after a window cleaner encountered it, puzzled at how a bottle of lemonade could have made it to that unlikely location.

Chapter 5

With Charlie's lunch retrieved, Jennifer left KC and his rap music behind to descend the twenty-seven steps that led to Martin Luther King Jr. Boulevard. On their way down she mused that steps such as these would have been perfect for Charlie's old habit of counting aloud, when his greatest anxiety in life was whether or not he could make it all the way to one hundred. Even though he hadn't counted steps aloud for years, the memory remained with her, and she began to count aloud herself wondering if he would join in. She only got to six.

"Mommmmm! I'm not a baby that counts everything!" Yet when his irritation dissipated he took her hand oblivious that his moratorium on counting aloud was inconsistent with his natural desire to hold his mother's hand.

At the bottom step he broke from her and lunged at the metal bar of the gymnasium-style door, triggering a faint *zap!* that was just audible from her office far away. The door flew open, and they were discharged onto the street with a bang as the door ricocheted off the brick exterior, then slammed shut behind them. Fresh rain coated the sidewalk, while in the sky a pale section within the layer of clouds was the only evidence of the sun.

Hand in hand they headed south along MLK toward the nearest intersection. It was an inconvenience to first walk *away* from Charlie's school to get to the other side of the street, but it was either that or jaywalk -- and the heavy traffic in the morning made them both afraid to go for the shortcut.

"Hey cool, a bug!" exclaimed Charlie, and he broke away to examine a beetle on the ground.

She hit the crosswalk button with her fist and became lost in an accumulation of advertising stapled to a telephone pole. There were fliers touting parties, weight loss, lucrative employment, and a cure for erectile dysfunction. Their one commonality was their inability to withstand the rain, and black drops of ink bled to the bottom of each page where they clung before falling to the sidewalk. She shifted her attention to the impending walk signal, and called for Charlie who reluctantly dragged himself from the beetle.

"Mom, what kind of bug was that?"

The red hand turned into the green profile of a strolling pedestrian.

"Charlie, I didn't even see it … Come on, let's go!" She snared him by the sleeve.

"Do you think it lives in the sewer or something?"

"Charlie. Really. Come on … "

Unaware of the truck bearing down on them, she tugged him off the sidewalk just before the sound of nearly skidding tires caused the muscle in her body to tense. She looked up in time to see the grill of a truck upon them, and it lurched to a stop before she even thought about how to avoid it. Yanking Charlie close to her with a reprimand, only once they were in the crosswalk did she acknowledge her own role in permitting the distraction of the bug just prior to crossing. Just as she felt the first ease of relief, Charlie began sobbing; and once across the street, he froze. Deep wrinkles creased his forehead, cheeks, and chin, and his face contorted in an open-mouthed grimace. His cry was lost in the roar of automobile acceleration, and her plea, "Come on Charlie … don't … " was for naught, and maybe not even heard. Strangers stared at them from a nearby bus stop, but their observations were cut short as she coaxed him toward school with a change of topic. After a few minutes, the distraction was just effective enough to send his tears to remission, and she ushered him red-faced and puffy-eyed through the front doors of his school.

First thing when I get home … ibuprofen.

He gave her a light kiss on the cheek and turned to head for his classroom. She watched him until he rounded a corner, and breathed a back-straightening sigh upon turning to leave. Before she could get to the door though, the authoritative voice of Coach Morris bellowed to prevent her departure.

Gregory Morris, the elementary school's PE teacher, had long since lost his first name to the adults who frequented their children's athletic activities, and was known even more succinctly as "Coach" by the intimidated students. An immense man, he wore gray sweatpants, tennis shoes, and a wide-brimmed Panama hat -- an ensemble that varied only with the different sweatshirt he wore each day.

A tremor shook the floor as he jogged over and introduced himself with an extended hand that swallowed hers. "Ummm, you own that soccer place down by the river, doncha?"

She studied him closely for the first time. Pock-marked cheeks, low-hanging eyelids, and the leathery quality of his skin all galvanized her unease, making her anxious to end the introduction as soon as possible.

Texas. He reminds me of Texas.

"You know ... the indoors place."

At once she was aware of her awkward pause. "Excuse me?"

"That soccer place there? Down by the river?"

"Um …yes, that's my place. East Portland Indoor Soccer."

"Hell of a neighborhood for it, right there off MLK, eh?"

"Well I don't thin … "

"See, I was just wondrin' if I could give you a call sometime." He smiled, revealing crooked bottom teeth. "You gotta business card or something?"

No. Not Texas. Arkansas is more like it.

It sounded like business, but also like he intended to ask her out. Coolly she rattled off the arena phone number. This led to his hurried quest for a pen behind each sunburnt ear, which she ended by mentioning they were in the phone book, and that he could call anytime.

Dammit!

It had come out much more willing than she intended, and she backed toward the door. Retracing her route back home, she found KC's seahorse in the depths of her pocket, and cradled it with her fingers as wisps of steam began to rise from the sun-warmed sidewalk.

She made her way along MLK peering upstream to look for an opportunity to jaywalk. Unexpectedly one, then a second, then a row of cars slowed and stopped for her. It was as if the five drivers were aware of the earlier incident with Charlie, and wished to make amends by stopping where there was no crosswalk or traffic signal. Stepping from the curb, she warily passed in front of them and one-by-one exchanged a wave with each driver.

She stepped over the pitiful dandelions eking out an existence from the cracks in the opposite sidewalk, recalling hers was the exact spot she was in with Charlie when they encountered a family of ducks. Heading toward the Willamette River, the quacking mother and her meandering hatchlings passed close enough to touch -- as if different species shared the use of the sidewalk every day.

Near the arena front door she passed a man she surmised was homeless, but again -- she caught herself with an asymmetric memory. Just a few days prior Helena and she had witnessed a seemingly homeless woman stooping to set out canned cat food for some kittens that lived beneath the a dumpster.

The neighborhood was full of surprises, both good and bad, though her efforts to point out the good to Charlie went nowhere. After visits to Jonah's house in the Lake Oswego his

anxiety was so great, he sometimes refused to even set foot

outside. Charlie saw Jonah's life as idyllic, situated amongst

opulent homes and lush parks. In contrast, Charlie's neighbors

were Mid-City Auto & Glass and Northwest Precision Machinery.

Jonah's bedroom looked out over a valley of tall pine trees too

numerous to count; Charlie's bedroom was windowless, and had it

featured one, would have revealed an alley. The commuter trains

that ran near Jonah's house were painted with the perfect smiles of

the local news personalities; the freight trains that crept between

the arena and the river featured an undecipherable tangle of

graffiti. In autumn, the gutters in front of Jonah's house filled with

multicolored leaves; the gutters in front of East Portland Indoor

Soccer were filled year-round with scraps of metal and fiberglass

from by the nearby autobody shop. While both neighborhoods

featured vacant lots, Jonah's were filled with blackberry bushes

picked clean by children every summer; Charlie's were filled with

litter, discarded furniture, and a sea of yellow weeds whose height

concealed the places where he imagined all the homeless

congregated at night.

Climbing the twenty-seven steps, she longed for a nap before the activity of the lunch hour, and moments later saw her opportunity as KC busied himself behind the concession counter. Just as she was about to call out to him to watch the place for a few hours, the office phone rang, and she hurried to answer it.

"Well now ... *Jennifer,* is it?"

In an instant, she knew the voice of Coach Morris. *How'd he get my name?*

"I was wondrin' about your soccer facility there on MLK ... the Eastern Portland Soccer ... "

"Yes?"

"Well you see, we get enough rainy days to shake a stick at 'round here, and I was just wondrin' if we could march the kids over to your place as a special sort of field trip on one of those downpourin' days this month. You see, when it rains, we have to pack all the kids indoors in the cafeteria to play, and all of them in such tight quarters is a little tough on everyone." He laughed as if he had made a joke. "I'd like to mix it up a little if I could, bring 'em on down to your place, and let 'em ... well ... let 'em have a sort of field trip."

"Oh," she said, relaxing. "And you were thinking they'd play soccer while they were here?"

"Well, ah yes ... let 'em run around awhile, play some soccer, and let 'em see something other than that dirty-ass cafeteria. Pardon my French. Oh, and here's the other thing. We don't have any money in the budget to pay. I was hopin' that wouldn't be a problem."

She felt foolish for her misinterpretation of Coach Morris' amorous motives and they agreed that on the next rainy Wednesday morning -- a time the arena was otherwise unused -- he could call first, then march a class from the school for a soccer field trip. While still on guard regarding his motives (he had announced, "It's a date!" before hanging up), she was pleased at the thought of her arena being a destination worthy of a school field trip.

The rainy Wednesday morning came only two days later, and after Coach Morris' call, Jennifer realized it was Charlie's own class that would be coming to visit. After a polyphony of electric *zaps!* sounded and a chorus of feet clambered up the stairs, dozens of wide-eyed children stood gawking at the cavernous arena many times larger than the biggest structure at their school. A few of the least disciplined ones broke off for a look at the video games, while others marveled at the prominent big screen TV, snack bar, and soccer field -- all of them equivalent jaw-droppers. They imagined Charlie drinking Coke for breakfast while watching wall-sized cartoons, and nights of soccer, video games, and more Coke. Charlie's beaming smile reflected his immediate popularity as his peers said things like "Cool!" and "Wow!" and more eloquently, "Charlie, this is where you *live*?!"

"Mom, can I show them the back?" Charlie asked excitedly amid a group of his classmates.

"No Charlie, you're here for PE."

As if to reinforce her reply, Coach Morris blew his whistle, got two teams organized with amazing brevity, and from a loose sack he carried over his shoulder tossed six balls onto the field. Without instruction, a wild game of multi-ball soccer began. He thanked her for allowing the class to use the facility, and sat down on the elevated single row of bench seats that allowed spectators a view from behind the Plexiglas. Only occasionally did his head lift from his newspaper, and she quelled her last suspicion that there was anything on his mind other than varied athletic experiences for the children.

Minutes later, she looked for Charlie on the field, and saw his earlier elation was gone. His soccer skills were inferior to those of his classmates, and the pressure of playing made him self-conscious of his inabilities. He built to a watery-eyed frustration on the field, but stayed in the game until the moment he had a ball stolen away by a girl who reminded Jennifer of herself at age nine. Bursting into tears, he ran off the field.

He headed for the sanctuary of his bedroom, but was intercepted by her embrace and inquiry. Unaccustomed to the setting, Coach Morris failed to immediately react as he would have on the playground, and in his hesitation she gave him a hand gesture to go back to his paper and that she would attend to Charlie. After failing to console him in her office while the game finished, she left him alone and walked to the field where Coach Morris was rounding up the kids for the walk back to school. "Charlie's not feeling well. He'll be staying home for the rest of the day."

"Okay, and ah Jen, after what I just saw … I was wondrin' er … I was wondrin' if you had, like, sort of a general time where adults can drop in and play soccer. I'd like to get into soccer some. It's a sport I've never … well, gotten into."

She retrieved from her office a schedule of open times in which he might play. He thanked her, and herded the children out of the building with his usual authority. As she walked back to the office, she noticed KC in the concession area, rinsing some paintbrushes in the sink and whistling an unidentifiable tune. His eyes knowingly locked with hers, but then rapidly darted away. Footsteps pounded behind her, but before she had even fully turned to see who it was, Coach Morris blurted out a breathy, "Jen would you like to go out on a date sometime? With me, that is?"

Chapter 6

An hour later, the incident on the field was relegated to its place atop the heap of her memories of Charlie breakdowns, and for the moment he was content to read one of his library books on the field while KC painted high above him atop the FlexLift. She considered taking him back for the last hour of school, but declined in order to cheat any plans fate might have for another encounter with Coach Morris -- to whom she had lied with a generic, "I'm seeing someone." Settling into her office chair, she hit the refresh button of her e-mail, and felt a spike in her stomach upon seeing what awaited her.

A message!

She'd managed to put him out of her mind during the Coach Morris visit and Charlie's breakdown, but now that something from him lay just a keystroke away, she suddenly felt warm nervousness. She drew in a deep breath, held it, and looked around to assure there would be no disturbances for at least a few minutes. The only moving soul around was KC, adjusting the height of the FlexLift on the far side of the field as if its altitude to the exact millimeter was crucial in the depiction of Snoopy's ear. Charlie gazed up at him and appeared to be saying something, though she could hear no words across the considerable distance.

She clicked open the message and exhaled.

FROM: eharrington@hotmail.com
TO: evilsoccermom@epis.org
TIME/DATE: 11:23:02 AM
SUBJECT: APOLOGY

Jennifer, I guess the first thing I want to do is apologize. By now you undoubtedly know I wasn't totally truthful to you about my relationship with Beth. The thing is ... I'm not entirely sure why I didn't come clean with you on the subject. Somehow, I guess I thought this wonderful feeling I have for you ... and felt you were having for me ... would vanish if I brought her into the equation. In retrospect, it was selfish of me. When Helena bumped into Beth and I last week, and I introduced them to each other, I actually felt a sense of relief that I would not have to pretend to you she didn't exist anymore. I have felt bad about misleading you, but I really didn't know what to do. The truth is this ... Beth and I have been living together for a year now. We began dating a year and a half ago, and moved rapidly from seeing each other, to seeing each other exclusively, to living together. We share a lot of common interests. I won't go into them because you probably don't want to hear about them, but I guess I will say our love of a lot of the same things was what initially drew us together. What I am unsure about is whether or not I'm <u>in love</u> with her, and it seems to me I should know that by now. I don't have a view that we are life partners or soulmates, as she does. What I have instead is this feeling that we moved too rapidly in our relationship, and I don't know how to say that to her without hurting her. I don't feel I can talk to her as I can to you, which is why you seem an incredible breath of fresh air to me. What I have with Beth is comfortable and good in a very stable way, but with her I don't get excited about planning an interaction, or feel the regret that comes from playing a conversation back in my mind and thinking of the perfect witty response I could have made. I long to write you and talk to you daily. In you there seems to be a unique quality that attracts me and makes me feel both remarkable and unstable at the same time. I have never felt "remarkableness" in the relationship I have with Beth, only a sense that I am on the same path that my friends and parents have traveled. Lately, this seems to be less and less satisfying, and I find myself wondering … what are the qualities in you, Jennifer, that attract me so? Truly I don't know. It's a little scary really, to feel pulled by something that has more control than I have resistance, and has compelled me to be less than honest. My interactions with you over the past months have been wonderful, and I desire nothing more than to experience those feelings again and again. I hope you know I meant nothing deceitful or harmful ... only that I grew scared that something fantastic would evaporate if you learned the truth. You have put me in a state ... a trance really ... and I find myself thinking about you all the time. I would be lying if I told you anything other than I feel truly happy in your presence. I leave you with this truthful admission ... I won't withhold anything about myself from you ever again.

Ethan

PS ... I have a game Saturday night. Beer afterward?

She wasted no time forwarding the e-mail to Helena with the simple query, "Your thoughts?" and then re-read the message carefully, studying each line for clues or contradictions. Such an outpouring of emotion from the normally evasive Ethan was a salve, but only a partial one, as the recollection of Helena's news that "he definitely has a girlfriend" still had the power to instantly dry her mouth. It was now clear why he hadn't advanced their relationship with the suggestion of some sort of date, and she wondered what evasion he'd have come up with had she taken the initiative to ask him out.

She suppressed the temptation to reply.

Compared to his prior restraint, even a glimpse of his feelings was intoxicating. His wasn't exactly an admission of love, but he clearly felt something for her, though it seemed beyond his ability to define. Above all he sounded scared -- scared that his disingenuousness had threatened something that had resonated so strongly within him, scared at the prospect of continuing a relationship with his girlfriend that was less than satisfying, and yet scared at the prospect of breaking that relationship off. That it took Helena's chance encounter for the truth to be revealed seemed to her both strange and sad.

She felt closer to him than ever before, and though it was tactically to her advantage to have his feelings revealed while hers remained undeclared, the urge to reply rose within her. Instead she forced herself to recall the indignation that had fate not placed Ethan and Helena in the same curio store at the same time, he would be misleading her even now. The memory produced no bile.

A synthesis of thought burst into her mind and she typed out the opening sentence of a reply; but in an attempt to pick out the right words, she paused, and in that hesitation her reply lost its perfection. Returning to her original strategy, she highlighted her half-sentence and pressed the delete button.

Step away from the computer.

As if it would not take hold unless spoken, she whispered aloud, "Do nothing." Besides, whether she responded or not, she'd be plagued by thoughts of Ethan until she next saw him, and didn't wish to additionally obsess over the content of her response. Resolving to wait for Helena's reply, she strove to get him off her mind any way she could. After saving his message, she rose to engage in the only distraction available to her at the moment -- KC and Charlie. They were now together atop the FlexLift, crouched in a pose of concentration while painting yellow tufts of what appeared to be the feathery head of Woodstock. Just above Charlie's shoulder floated Snoopy's ferocious but disembodied head.

"Do nothing," she whispered again while walking onto the field and running her fingers along the Plexiglas. Hers was a position that felt both powerful and pitiable. Taking another deep breath, she neared the FlexLift and called up to them, "Hey you

two! Permission to come aboard?"

Chapter 7

Thursdays at the lunch hour meant attorneys.

Back in the first weeks of the arena's opeing, an employee
from the Portland city attorney's office inquired if a group of
players could reserve weekly time during the lunch hour; and
Jennifer, more than happy to accommodate, gave them their pick of
any day of the week. They chose Thursdays, and it had been theirs
ever since. They consisted of younger athletes fresh from law
school, a few sedentary fortysomethings looking to get back in
shape, and a contingent of females who had grown tired of their
downtown gym. The arrangement was simple. The field was
theirs for the hour for $60 -- with no referee, no working clock, and
no scoreboard.

At 11:45AM the first *zaps!* signaled their arrival, and they
undertook the pre-game ritual of collecting five dollars from each
player, stretching, and signing the liability waiver prominently
installed between the team benches. No sooner had they donned
dark and white colored shirts, each team began arguing about who
would get stuck playing goalie.

Despite the fact that games took place with such frequency
she hardly noticed them anymore, Jennifer could watch the

attorneys anytime. They played not for the glory of winning, satisfying their egos, or as a way to showcase their skill. Joy was their only motivation, and they received doses of it when they saw improvements in their ability, when they cheered a less accomplished player's success against someone more skilled, and when they laughed at their own miscues. She vividly remembered their initial inquiry about reserving weekly time, and how it inspired the exact same feeling as she got from Coach Morris' inquiry -- that, in East Portland Indoor Soccer, she'd created something special. Something worth reserving.

Shattering her nostalgia as she watched from her office, KC emerged from the back and proceeded into her office carrying a just-peeled banana purloined from her kitchen counter.

"Good banana, Kase?"

"Actually no. I prefer them with a slight scattering of brown specks. They tend to be a little sweeter that way. Kinda like me."

She struggled for a reply to that one, and settled for a silent raising of the eyebrows as he smirked and gobbled down a bite despite his critique.

He remained standing and spoke with a mouthful of gooey fruit. "Can I ask you a fabor?"

"Only if you swallow that bite first."

He did so with a gulp that looked painful, and proceeded. "You see, I figure if I'm gonna work here much longer, I've gotta be able to play soccer at least a little bit. Once in a while I get asked to sub for a team that's down a player, and I have to say no because I don't want to embarrass myself. If I'm ever gonna go out there, I need some practice." Another huge bite of white fruit disappeared into his mouth.

"You've got to be kidding. You?"

"Bhy is 'at so incredible?" he smacked and swallowed again while putting his hands on his hips. The last of the banana squished against his left side.

"Well I just never knew you had an interest," she said with an internal smile. The sound of commotion from the field told her the attorneys had begun their game.

He didn't respond, but the severity of his expression told her that, in fact, he was *not* kidding and that he indeed had an interest. She let her smile ebb and cleared her throat, the sound of which was lost as the Plexiglas rattled with a collision.

"Well ... um, I mean ... of course we could ... did you want a lesson or something, Kase?"

"Well yeah ... sort of, I guess. Could you just show me how to kick the thing so that I don't look like a total fool? You know ... just some of the basics? Maybe a few tips? I'll take it from there." He examined the last morsel of his flattened banana, found it not to his liking, and pitched it with the peel into the trashcan near her desk.

She stood to look at the palette of his canvas shoes -- each of them dotted with a colorful array of paint drops. "Okay, but you've gotta wear some appropriate shoes. Those old beaters will never do. You don't need soccer shoes *per se* but at least get some sturdier tennies ... hightops would probably be best so you don't twist an ankle ... and the next time we're in here together when nothing else is going on, we'll kick it around, just you and I. We'll break you in slowly."

"Deal," he said just as a *zap!* sounded in the arena. "I saw the seahorse in the entryway."

She was accustomed to KC's rapid changes in topic, and switched gears with matching fluidity. "Yeah Charlie and I both really like it. It's officially part of the collection now. I counted them last night and I'm up to ninety-five of 'em. Yours is on the fragile side in case you hadn't noticed, and what with Charlie playing with them all the time, I could envision it a casualty at some point."

"Well if you have to send it to the glue factory just let me know. I know where there's another just like it," he said with a wink. He then looked out the office window and changed topics yet again. "I just love that guy."

In mid-yawn Jennifer turned and saw a late-arriving attorney hurrying to the benches. The game had begun with one team short a player, and as those on the field yelled to him of the disparity, he increased his haste, unraveled his tie, and tore into his gym bag.

"I half-expect to see a Superman insignia underneath," she said as his dress shirt was unbuttoned and pulled open, only to reveal a hairy chest.

"What's your opinion of a thick patch of hair on a man's chest?" KC asked.

"Umm ... you mean sexually?"

"Well, I guess I mean just in terms of general appeal."

"I don't know, it's been so long. I guess I don't mind it. As long as everything else is attractive, I suppose I can put up with it. You?"

"I despise it," KC replied with a sour look on his face, as if thinking of someone in particular.

Opting for expediency over the social grace of the men's restroom, the tardy attorney changed into his gym shorts behind the low wall that separated him from the field. He didn't bother with a protective cup or shinguards, and wasn't aware that in his boxer shorts he was clearly visible from the office where Jennifer and KC stood peering at him like voyeurs. Taking a moment to scribble his signature on the waiver, he rushed out on the field without even a moment's stretching, and, in the ultimate shortcut, didn't even bother to tie his shoes, opting instead for an opportunity mid-game to complete that particular task.

When his Achilles tendon ruptured a minute later, it wasn't a total surprise.

Occurring on the office side of the field as it did, Jennifer actually heard the *pop!* as she and KC chatted, but at the time registered it as nothing more than a shoe scuff on the artificial turf. Moments later, an odd silence from the field alerted her something was amiss, and emerging from the office to see what had happened, she saw someone on the ground surrounded by a congregation of players.

"Looks like our Astroturf is made of kryptonite," uttered KC from behind, clarifying for her who was hurt.

She felt relief in the recollection of his signing the waiver prior to playing, however seeing the anguish on his face between the picket fence of legs turned made her feel guilty that liability had come foremost to her mind. She walked onto the field with the intent of helping, but by the time she got there he was upright, though in need of a person supporting his weight beneath each arm. A glance down revealed why -- his right calf was completely devoid of muscle tone, and while there was no bruising or swelling, past experience told her it was a torn Achilles tendon, an injury whose full recovery can take nearly a year.

She felt useless as he hopped feebly off the field toward a waiting car, a trip to the ER, and a tortuous regimen of physical rehabilitation. A female teammate grabbed his clothes and stuffed them into his bag, and the game ended prematurely. Jennifer watched the mass departure before sensing someone standing close behind her. As she turned, KC leaned forward and uttered a succinct word in her ear.

"Lawsuit."

"Shut up … I doubt it." She elbowed him away.

"Whattaya mean? ... they're *attorneys* after all!" A series of *zaps!* indicated their final departure.

"Attorneys *that signed a waiver*, you mean."

He turned to her in an erudite manner. "Did you know that when people get hit by foul balls at baseball games, they can sue the ballpark even though there's a waiver on the back of the ticket that says they can't?"

She was quick with her reply. "Yeah but this guy *signed* the waiver. Those tickets at the ballpark just have some words printed on the back."

"What difference does that make?"

She opened her mouth to reply but truly she didn't know, and while willing to continue arguing with KC on the topic she was silenced at the sight of a cameraman and a reporter whose entry had been cloaked by the *zaps!* of the attorneys' exit.

(*Oh shit!*)

Her first conclusion -- albeit an irrational one -- was that they were doing a story on the propensity of people to get hurt at East Portland Indoor Soccer, and she hadn't enough time to come up with any more plausible reasons by the time they walked up to where she and KC stood on the field.

"Hi. We're looking for a KC Nenn?" the reporter said hopefully.

"You found him!" chimed KC.

A series of handshakes and introductions took place amongst all of them as the reporter identified he worked for one of the local television stations. He addressed KC directly and with a big smile.

"We were hoping we could do an interview with you on the forestry protest from a few years ago. It's part of our series of retrospectives on people who've made an impact on life in Portland. Maybe you've seen one of them?"

"I don't watch a lot of television," KC lied.

"Oh. Well no matter. We want to interview you about, you know, the ledge thing and all that."

"Let me get this straight. You want to interview me about the forestry protest right now?" asked KC with budding enthusiasm.

"Well yes, if that'd be good for you."

"Oh sure. I'm willing to do it right now … " he paused for a moment and thoughtfully added, " … but only on one condition." There was an unnatural break in the camaraderie as Jennifer, the reporter, and the cameraman waited for KC to utter his solitary requirement.

"The condition is this … I get to wear an East Portland Indoor Soccer hat during the interview."

The reporter shifted uncomfortably and responded, "Umm, well, we sort of have a station policy against product endorsements during interviews."

"Well I get that. But this isn't a *product*, it's a *place*. Hell, it probably actually adds to the story. Think about it. It's my only condition, you can get your interview today … now, in fact … be done with it, and move on to your next assignment. I'm sure you guys are plenty busy."

This seemed to strike a chord.

"I'll answer any question you have for as long as it takes. I just want *the hat*. That's all. Do we have a deal?"

The cameraman thought for a second, and maneuvered for a compromise. "Could we at least *see* the hat?"

"Sure," said KC, and he ran off the field to the apparel display while Jennifer, feeling the guilt of an accomplice, struggled with the dilemma of how to make small talk.

"You know, this guy really made a name for himself at that protest," the reporter said to no one in particular. "He's apparently real hero amongst the forest preservation groups."

She kept to herself the truth about KC's ranking of the trees somewhere between Judaism and trigonometry on his list of interests. The reporter shifted his attention to KC who had returned wearing a black hat with bold white stenciling that said EAST PORTLAND INDOOR SOCCER. The cameraman and the reporter made a few hushed comments between themselves, happily indicated agreement, and the three of them headed to the picnic tables.

An hour later it was over and KC transitioned to prepping the concession area for the evening ahead. Jennifer busied herself by calling team captains to remind them to send in their money for the upcoming season, but the combination of the mundane task, the stench of KC's banana peel from the trash can, and her nagging curiosity drove her from her office. She walked up to him as he was crouched down at keg level behind the concession counter.

"Kase, why did you do it?"

Quickly he looked up, stood, and flung his cleaning rag over his shoulder. "Because I want this place to succeed as much as you do." He removed the black hat and admired it.

"I'm not talking about *the hat*. I'm talking about the interview. Why do you still pretend you care about the forests? You and I both know you don't give a rip about the trees."

He thought for a moment and put the hat back on. "Well that's true." Evasively he offered no other information, picked up an empty keg, held it against his waist, and began to make his way past her.

She blocked his path. "So why do you do it?"

He sighed and set the keg down between them with a soft thud.

"The truth …?"

She nodded her head expectantly.

"Well I kind of hate to admit this, but the truth is …" He stopped, but her gaze would not release him from answering. "The truth is, boss … I do it because it reminds me of Oscar."

The following day, KC tossed a pair of shoes onto Jennifer's office desk, toppling a pile of checks she'd arranged in a two-inch high stack. "My new shoes," he announced.

Technically they qualified as shoes, or at least did at one time. Tattered like a dog's chew toy, they weren't high tops as she'd advised, and offered absolutely no ankle support. After reforming her financial pile, she picked one up and turned it over, revealing a tread that was worn smooth. The other shoe was in similarly poor shape, but for the fact it was missing its shoelace altogether.

"They were in the lost and found."

"Are they even your size, Kase?"

"Well I admit that they're a little big, but I'll get by with multiple pairs of socks. Umm … speaking of that, can I raid your sock drawer?"

"Oh sure. 'Door's open. Bottom left dresser drawer."

He headed for her bedroom, emerging a minute later with four pairs of white socks. On his way back he picked up a new pair of shoelaces from the display case, and had them unwrapped and dragging along the floor. Discarding his flimsy canvas shoes, he began to augment his foot size with the socks, and as Jennifer spoke he pulled on one with enough vigor to rip a considerable hole in it with his heel.

"Tell you what we'll do … " she said while managing to ignore her sock's demise, " … we'll kick it around at four or so after I pick Charlie up from school. Oh, and unless you want the notoriety of being the second cripple in two days, I suggest you stretch beforehand."

"Four o'clock? Excellent. It'll give me a chance to break these beauties in." Minutes later he stood and registered the sensations on his feet. If he was wriggling his toes, it could not be detected through the mass of cotton.

"So what did you end up doing last night after you left?"

"Oh nothing. I ended up coming back late and just hanging out 'til like two o'clock or so. Say, it's been three months since I asked, so here goes … you sure you won't reconsider letting me go back to putting fliers on windshields all over town?"

"You know Kase, it was one thing to do it when we were just starting out, but now I think it's just not right. Especially targeting the cars parked at the other soccer facilities. They almost caught you that first time you tried it. I just don't think it's ethical advertising."

"First off … there are no ethics in advertising. Second … I wouldn't just target the other soccer facilities. I'd hit other venues and neighborhoods as well. Did you forget how many people came in here … and still come in here … talking about how it was that first flier that told them about East Portland Indoor Soccer? Besides, I guarantee if we had a parking lot, SoccerCity would do it to you. Thirdly, even if I *did* get caught, I'd just tell them that some stranger paid me to put them on the windshields, and I didn't know who it was."

"And what if they don't believe you and call the cops. The police are familiar with you, you know."

He considered this for a moment, but then struck upon an answer. "Well of course if that happened … I'd tell them Jennifer Scott, the owner of East Portland Indoor Soccer, forced me to do it."

KC's flier ambitions quelled for the moment, she retrieved Charlie from school and had him start his homework at the picnic tables. A team from a local community college had just finished their bi-weekly practice, and a little after four o'clock she inquired if KC was ready to take the field. "Game on?"

"Game on!"

Before they could start however, Charlie yelled from the concession area. "Mommm!"

"Wha-ut," she sang back over her shoulder.

"My homework's sticky." From the picnic table he held up a piece of paper that had evidently gotten stuck to the surface of the table.

She turned to KC. "Did you remember to wipe the beer from the tables last night?"

"Maybe I forgot," he said lamely.

She yelled for Charlie to do his best, glanced at her watch, and spaced herself twenty yards away. "We've got about an hour before the 5:15 game. Oh, and of course, you'll need some shin guards if you're ever gonna actually play, and you might want to make them extra large with that sock-layering technique of yours."

KC looked down self-consciously and said, "Shin guards … come … in different sizes?"

At that moment she kicked the ball in his direction. He was startled to see it rolling toward him, but had time to adjust, shuffled his feet in order to get the timing right, and then met the ball firmly with the toe of his right foot. It sailed far to her left.

"Sorry!"

She chased it down and deftly move the ball back to her previous spot without a wasted motion.

"I've never seen shin guards in the lost and found," he called out. "Maybe you can give me a discount on some of the stuff we sell?"

"Ohhhh, why not," she replied. Her next kick came at him with such precision, he didn't have to move a stride in either direction. Stepping into his next kick with the intent of a powerful return, he instead sent the ball up to the rafters where it ricocheted twice and bounced back approximately to the spot where he was standing. As he grabbed it with his hands, a veil of dust drifted down to the field between them.

"Okay, a couple of quick tips to start," she announced. Closing the distance between them with a brisk walk, she dispensed some pointers on the accuracy and aesthetic of kicking the ball with the side of the foot rather than the toe. "Give me your shoe."

"Huh?"

"Give … me … your … shoe."

He sat on the ball, unlaced his shoe, and handed it to her.

"You see where it's worn on the side but not the toe? … that's because the ball made repeated contact at the ball of the foot, and not at the tip. *That's* where you want to kick it. If you feel that's awkward right now, then kick it off the side of your foot … like at the arch … which'll give you a hell of a lot more control than the toe. And don't worry about kicking it so hard, Kase." She tossed his shoe back to him. "That'll come later. Just work on the fundamentals for now."

He retied his shoe, and was again ready. They settled into a more successful exchange of kicks from a lesser distance, a repetition punctuated only by the sounds of Jennifer's occasional advice and their easy repartee.

After a while KC became adept at a controlled kick using the side of his foot. When he tried to get fancy however, he was prone to errors, and on one occasion his foot missed the ball completely when he tried to return a kick to her. While he chased down the ball, a *zap!* filled the empty arena, and with a glance at her watch Jennifer estimated the first players of the 5:15 game were likely arriving. Seconds later out of the corner of her eye, she noted a man at the benches rifling through a backpack. Soon he came onto the field in their direction.

" ... kick it?" Jack Edens inquired.

Jennifer thought she simply didn't hear part of his request to join in, but his stance created a perfect triangle between the three of them. KC had understood him though, replying with an energetic "Sure!" and sending him the ball.

He looked awkward, with pale skin, wild red hair, and think eyebrows. His upper body was muscular, but his legs were thin, even scrawny, and this incongruity made him appear disproportionately top-heavy. Like KC, his shirt was a size or two too small, but was bright yellow and bore the name and logo of *RUDY'S DINER*, a restaurant chain she recognized as a new team in the Adult Co-ed Beginners' League.

All banter between herself and KC ceased, and the three of them spread themselves out in order to kick the ball to each other with more force. The greater distance posed no problem for Jennifer or Jack, but KC's form deteriorated, and Jack was soon initiated with the thankless task of chasing down KC's errant volleys.

She watched Jack intently, though she didn't know why.

His running gait was loping and not especially fast even though he exerted himself fully, and after only a few minutes, various sections of his shirt were stained with perspiration. On one

occasion KC kicked the ball into the gap between herself and Jack,

and as they drew close to each other, she noticed the numerous

freckles that dotted his face, neck, and arms.

I've met him before.

She joked about KC's errant kicks, but Jack said nothing,

sent the ball back to KC, and returned to his prior position.

Preceded by more *zaps!* other players began drifting into the arena,

including the recognizable presence of Ian, her boozing referee,

whom she watched head straight to the concession area for beer

before beginning his nightly duties. As KC chased down a ball,

she used the opportunity to walk over to Jack and introduce

herself.

"Hi. My name's Jennifer. Do I know you from

somewhere? You look really familiar to me."

He'd had his back turned to watch for his arriving

teammates, and actually jumped when she said "Hi" -- so startled

was he to be addressed from behind at that moment. His eyes first

flashed, but then calmed as he fixated on her hand as it hung in the

air between them waiting for his handshake. Clamping mostly

onto her fingers, he looked her in the eye and responded, "From where? … "

It sounded more like 'fum air' but she understood him nonetheless. "Well I don't know." She slowed the pace of her dialogue as he continued shaking her hand mechanically. "What's your name?"

"Jack," he replied clearly, only then letting her hand free from his grip. He didn't give a last name.

He's handicapped.

"What's your last name, Jack?"

He didn't immediately answer, and she sensed he was uncomfortable with the series of questions. His silence continued, and as he glanced back for his teammates again, she hastened to make herself less threatening by creating a friendly tone in her voice.

"Jack, you look familiar to me. Do I look familiar to you?"

He re-established eye contact, but his left eye trailed off in a way that made it seem he wasn't able to fully focus, and after a few seconds in which she felt thoroughly scanned, he shook his head back and forth.

"D … Do … w … work ah … here?" he asked.

More *zaps!* sounded. "Well yes, and live here too, actually. I'm the owner."

She made some small talk to which he was unresponsive, and felt certain that unless she asked another question, he wouldn't bother to say another word. With relief she found a vehicle of conversation in his T-shirt. "Oh, you work for Rudy's Diner? Your team's new, isn't it?"

He looked down at the front of his shirt. In his clearest sentence yet he said, "Rudy's. Yeah. In the kitch … kitchen." He seemed to relax now that a few of his teammates making their way onto the field. Charlie ran up with a loud "Mom!" but she scolded him for interrupting and told him to wait. Jack received a yelled greeting from the bench, and with a slap on the back a female teammate made a motherly inquiry whether or not he had remembered his shin guards. It was easy to see he was drawn to the camaraderie of his team, and she made a final attempt to re-acquire the meager momentum of their conversation.

She asked him how his team had been faring, and he replied with some partially- understandable details of how they'd won their last game. He spoke excitedly, got bogged down in a stutter at one point, and used the first names of teammates with whom she had no familiarity. His diction was that of a child, but it

mattered not, for while he spoke she only half-listened and

observed his face trying to place him from anywhere in her past --

previous soccer games, her childhood in Arizona, the country club

or the bank where she worked years before ...

Nothing.

The field was now a confluence of bodies, some stretching,

some jogging, and some just talking. One of Jack's teammates led

him to the bench, and as KC approached from behind and kicked a

ball softly against her heels, she watched as Jack's shoes were re-

tied for him. Players from both teams began to fan out onto the

field, and Jack received some instructions from a teammate before

being led to his position.

She was about to question KC about what he knew of Jack

when Charlie tugged on her shirt, this time near tears. In each

hand he carried half a piece of homework that had been ripped

from the sticky surface of the picnic table.

Uh-oh.

But before Charlie could utter a single lament, KC

intervened. Calling him "buddy" in a tone that completely

disarmed him, he suggested the use of the office copy machine to make a replica of the homework, and ushered him in that direction. She followed well behind, awed that KC had in the span of a few seconds negated one of Charlie's breakdowns. As she followed them toward the office, she turned her head back to observe Jack one final time, and in doing so collided with Ian, who was hurrying toward the field with his pint.

"Bloody hell!" he exclaimed. Most of his beer was splashed upon the front of his black shirt.

She apologized and inquired if he had ever before seen Jack, who she pointed out on the field.

He wiped his hand on his shorts and followed the direction of her finger. With his reply came the vapor of beer. "Mmm. New player. New team from the looks of it. Ahh, who can keep track of 'em all?" he said as if burdened. He studied Jack further, standing still on the field with a broad smile on his face. In as hushed a tone he added, "Fellow looks a bit daffy if you ask me," -- an observation punctuated by a back-straightening hiccup. Then he sipped at the remains of his pint and without waiting for any other conversation, walked away, and blew his whistle to get the players' attention.

She retreated back to the office where she saw Charlie's face aglow as he leaned over the copy machine to make a picture of his face. KC stood smiling to the side with his finger on the green button.

"All right you guys, cut it out. Kase, have you ever seen that guy before … the guy we kicked it around with?"

With a laugh Charlie retrieved his image from the machine.

"The retard who got hit by the a freckle grenade? Nope."

Charlie showed her copies of both his and KC's facial profile. Due to the pale stripe down the center of the page, it looked like the toner was running out again, even though she'd replenished it just last month. Fawning over the images for a requisite amount of time, she tasked Charlie with putting his homework in his backpack, and the facial images on their refrigerator in the back. He ran off.

"Don't you have a game tonight?" KC asked.

"Yeah, right after this one. Hey, could you do me a favor, Kase? Could you look up a 'Jack' on the roster of the team from Rudy's Diner? I'd like to get his last name."

"Sure. And by the way, we're running out of paper for the copier again." He headed for the bookshelf that held the rosters for all the league teams, and mumbled "Rudy's" to himself as he thumbed through the pages.

How could we be out of copier paper already?

"Aha! Rudys!"

"And what do you think his problem is?" she asked. "Personally, I don't believe it's mental retardation. He plays soccer after all."

KC answered without lifting his eyes. "Mmm. Maybe he's dyslexic or something."

"Uh, no Kase … that's the disease when you read numbers in the wrong order. I think you're thinking *autistic*."

"Edens."

"What?"

"Edens. Jack Edens. You know, like the garden? Adam and Eve?"

She said it aloud three times in an attempt to jar her memory. "It's not familiar. Is it familiar to you?"

"No, but remember, I've got horrible people memory. Maybe his mom hit the sauce during her pregnancy, or he's got one of those genetical abnormalities."

"*Genetic* abnormalities. Maybe." She changed the topic, hoping it would remind KC of the need to clean the picnic tables before things got busy tonight. "Thanks for helping Charlie with the ripped homework by the way."

"No problemo," he replied. As his memory kicked in he added, "Oh yeah!" and sprung toward the concession area to clean the tabletops.

More *zaps!* spoke of heavy foot traffic at the main entrance. She looked at the binder left open on her desk and found the name on the roster for Rudy's Diner. "Jack Edens," she said aloud, but its utterance did no more to jog her memory than her finger's tracing beneath the nine letters.

Chapter 8

Helena and Jonah arrived shortly after halftime of the Rudy's Diner game, and once the boys ran off to the video games with a roll of quarters, Jennifer wasted no time asking her if she recognized Jack.

"Gosh I don't know," Helena replied while staring at the players on the field. "Let's take a closer look."

They approached the Plexiglas at one end of the field, and in the time it took for play to advance toward them, Jennifer spoke of her intuition of knowing Jack from somewhere, and went through the places from her past she suspected as their common ground.

"That's him with the ball, right?" Helena asked.

"Yep."

"Odd, isn't he?" she observed as Jack had the ball stolen from him and frantically pursued an opponent. Play took place near them now and Jack, red-faced with effort, faced them only a slight distance away. Helena was silent in her study, and once the play had moved away with Jack in their midst, she turned away from the game. "Sorry, but he's not familiar. Jack … what's his last name again?"

"Edens. Like the garden."

It triggered nothing, and Helena summed-up her observation with, "I don't think I've ever seen as many freckles on one face before."

"I actually talked to him earlier, and I'm pretty sure he's … well I guess he's handicapped in some way. Are you *sure* he doesn't seem even a little familiar to you? You're memory is so much better than mine."

"Yeah. He's pretty … " she struggled for an apt yet kind word, " … distinctive. I'd remember him if I met him before."

After some silence Helena moved to the topic that most interested her. "So you still haven't responded to Ethan's e-mail?"

"Oh no. If I had, I'd have forwarded you a copy."

It suddenly occurred to Jennifer that the diversion of Jack Edens had displaced Ethan from her mind. It had been at least an hour since she'd thought of him -- possibly the longest span in the past few days -- and it gave her hope that there were other distractions that could break his stranglehold over her thoughts.

"So, are you regretting you didn't respond?"

"No. It's not likely he'd reply to it."

"Really? How can you be so sure?"

"Well he invited me to have a beer after his game tomorrow night, and trust me, he's the type who only opens up when *he's* ready to. I really don't think he intended to initiate a long back-and-forth series of e-mailed feelings. I mean let's face it, his message came about only because *you* happened to encounter him with his girlfriend. It was just his way of getting a word out to me to say he was sorry and say he got caught. Had you not bumped into him, he never would have *had* to send it. I imagine if he wants to talk to me about it, it'll happen tomorrow night."

"Mmm," was Helena's reply, and within it, Jennifer sensed disapproval.

"What would you have done if you were me?"

"Oh Jen, it's impossible to say. For one, it really all depends on your feelings for him. Also, I've been married for so long, I don't think I'm even in touch with the nuances of a new relationship anymore. I just know that I'd be profoundly disappointed in his deception, and I'd be wary of his inability to tell you the truth. Still, he's very good at the whole 'written word' thing. That's maybe why he sent you an e-mail instead of talking to you directly. Or maybe he just took the coward's way out.

Either way it's probably going to be a bit wrenching for him to face you the first time." She paused and spoke while absently watching the game. "I guess I shouldn't be so hard on him because I truly believe what you feel for a person can sometimes be so powerful, it can override everything else. I guess I don't doubt that he feels *something* for you. What I don't know is how truthful he's being even now. Most of all I don't want you to end up getting hurt."

"I know," Jennifer replied, "and trust me, it's going to be a little wrenching for me too. I'm thinking about him all the time. Even *more* than before you saw him and he sent that damn e-mail." Jennifer turned to stare at the game on the field as well. "Well one thing's for sure, playing in a game is sure to get him off my mind for a while. You got the boys okay?"

"Oh yeah. They're fine. Game on. I'll just pour Charlie a cup of PBR if he gets out of line."

She gave Helena a light laugh and disappeared to the back to change into her game clothes. By the time she returned the Rudy's Diner game was in its final minutes, and the rest of the members of her team -- The Snipes -- had arrived. She joined them in their normal pre-game routine of sparse conversation and stretching, and at the benches she came close to Jack Edens again. He was drenched with perspiration that flattened the curl of his bangs against his forehead. Only the section of his shirt nearest his shorts remained dry, and he drank water with such urgency, it spilled down his chin as he gulped. Looking to see if he would make eye contact with her, she was disappointed to find she didn't even merit a glance.

I'm getting obsessive.

The Snipes took the field. They were made up of a reserved circle of friends in which she was the lone interloper. Far from feeling like an outsider however, she felt a special distinction in her ability to parlay her role as a one-time emergency substitute into a full-time spot on their team. In addition to the fact that they let her play her favorite position -- the left forward spot -- being on the Snipes and *not* on Helena's team enabled one of them to play while the other kept an eye on the boys.

The Snipes' primary strength was its women. Blessed with a combination of fearlessness, and a skill-level forged from decades of competition, they never panicked, and were accustomed to physical play against opponents of either gender. While they never initiated rough tactics themselves, if an opponent resorted to them, the female Snipes instinctually followed suit to make it known they were versed in a variety of styles of play, and would not tolerate an advantage based on aggressiveness. The other main strength of the Snipes was a quiet fellow named Quinn who played goalie. He was experienced, had no fear of the inherent dangers (being hit in the face by the ball, collisions, getting kicked in the hand, etc …), and asked to play no other position. Even without Quinn's skills, just having a designated goalie would have been an advantage for the Snipes, as other teams simply rotated their reluctant or tired players into the position, and their inexperience led to goals Quinn would have thwarted with ease.

The Snipes' weakness was its men. They lacked talent, weren't particularly tough, and had no instinct for how to develop an opportunity for their team. They were practitioners of the 'kick and chase,' and instead of maneuvering around an opponent using feints, guile, or passing laterally and moving upfield -- they sent the ball forward however they could and hoped to be able to run to it faster than the opponent. It was a tactic that rarely worked, not because they weren't fast, but because its success required considerable space, and an indoor field filled with three men, three women, and a goalie per team, simply lacked the real estate to pull it off.

They were, however, devastating defenders.

They found an unnatural joy at foiling the other team, and they readily responded to whatever instructions Quinn urgently barked at them from behind. They played hard, but not dirty, and there was rarely an opponent who was angered by their play during, or after, a game. On rare occasion one of the Snipes men scored a goal, it was regarded as a small miracle of being in the right place at the right time. On some teams such a talent and scoring differential would have led to intra-team strife, but on the Snipes everyone knew their role, and there was only contentment as their team chemistry led to more wins than losses, and their opponents respect.

Conversely, the Snipes' opponent this evening -- Portland Software Products -- was regarded with universal loathing.

Cocky, arriving all at one time as if they just got off a team bus, and radiating arrogance even in warm-ups where they went through choreographed drills and chanted "PSP!" in unison -- Portland Software Products had a knack for making even the most gentlemanly opponent entertain felonious ambition. They were at the extreme end of the competitive scale, verbally sparred with players on other teams, and wore black shirts which matched their in-game demeanor. They pushed, grabbed shirts for an advantage, and it could be counted on that one of their number would get into an altercation with anyone who stood up to their tactics.

And that was just their women.

The men on PSP embodied all the dark traits of the women, and even worse they discarded the notion of easing their aggressive play against women on other co-ed teams, a sacrosanct but unwritten rule whose repeated violation put them in the lowest quadrant of sportsmanship in nearly everyone's eyes.

Including Ian's.

Unlike any other team, PSP unabashedly argued with the referee, and regarded Ian as the buffoon of the stable of referees that officiated games at the arena. This tested his impartiality, for he could be counted on to bark back, mock their conduct, and generally call all marginal infractions in favor of their opponent. A game pitting PSP against the Snipes, and officiated by an intoxicated Ian, was a game brimming with combustible forces.

Even KC's passion was roused. "God how I hate *those bastards*," he blurted from his seat atop a picnic table.

Charlie, having tired of the video games Jonah continued to play, joined him. "Who?"

"Oh, those smug bastards from Portland Software Products … with their fancy chants and all that," he said with derision.

Charlie watched the warm-ups on the field, searching for his mom amid the bodies. He then asked, "KC, what's a bastard?"

"A bastard is a kid that doesn't have a … " He stopped and contemplated an evasion, but thought better of it and continued with shame in his voice. "A bastard is a kid that doesn't have a dad."

"Oh," Charlie said. He hung his head in contemplation.

"You know … I'm sorry Charlie. I didn't really mean to say that. It's just kind of a word that came out of my mouth. I just meant that that the team playing your mom's is full of jerks."

"So being a bastard is kinda like being a jerk?"

"No! It's not like that at all, buddy. It's really just a figure of speech."

"But a bastard is someone without a dad, right?"

"Technically yes, but you're no bastard Charlie."

"How come?"

"Well, in order for someone to be a bastard, the father has to leave the kid. I mean … like never want to be part of his life. Even though you don't have a dad, he didn't choose to leave you. He never even knew about you … and, well … and he died before you were born. If he were alive and knew you were here, he'd be with you right now."

Charlie thought about this while KC closed his eyes and pondered his fumbling response. With the scream of Ian's whistle the Snipes/PSP game began.

"In reality Charlie, I'm more of a bastard than you," he added.

"How come?"

"Well, it's a little hard to explain, but basically I get along better with my mom than my dad, because in some ways … many ways actually … my dad doesn't know me, and he doesn't *choose* to get to know me. That's the difference between you and me, Charlie. My dad is here on Earth and has a choice to love me or not. Yours never got that chance."

KC turned away from Charlie and stared at the game that suddenly had little interest to him, all the while perplexed how Charlie had managed to draw out of him a topic that he kept guarded from everyone else. He made sure Charlie couldn't see the watery-eyed prelude to a tear that he quickly wiped away with his knuckle. The picnic table creaked as he dismounted, and before he moved even a step away he turned back to face Charlie.

"Don't ever let anyone call you a bastard, Charlie. You dad loves you, and is looking down on you right now from heaven. Don't doubt for a second that if he were here, he'd be lovin' you every day." He paused and saw Jonah and Helena at a video game. "Now why don't you go back to playing video games with Jonah. Did you run out of quarters?" Charlie nodded and KC quietly gathered a two-quarter tip from a tabletop, handed it to him, and walked behind the concession counter with an ache in the back of his throat. Before he could busy himself, Charlie walked up to the opposite side of the counter.

"KC, do you know how my dad died?"

"Oh jeez Charlie … " His incredulous smile faded when he noticed a puddle of beer spilt on the countertop. He couldn't find his rag to clean it up, and checked to see if it had fallen to the floor. "You know I'm really not the right … ", distractedly he scanned the countertop for it. "I mean, I just don't think … ", he craned his neck and stood on his toes to see if he left it at the picnic tables. "I mean, you know if you really want to … "

"It's on your shoulder KC," Charlie interrupted.

KC dipped his chin and pulled his rag down to the countertop. While his hands swirled in slow circles he looked directly at Charlie. "You know … if you really want the answer about how your dad died, it's gotta come from your mom."

Chapter 9

Jennifer had long known the reputation of Portland Software Products, and as expected the first half felt like an ugly hybrid of soccer and rugby. On three occasions she was tripped to the turf, the last of which resulted in a scrape on her knee that sent blood trailing toward her sock. With measured synchrony both she and the rest of the Snipes adjusted the ferocity of their play, and pushing, elbowing, and collisions became the standard of play. Even the men on the Snipes fought back, and the result was a vocal, penalty-filled game. The score was tied 1-1 near the end of the first half when Quinn suffered a kick to the forearm just as he grabbed a ball, drawing a two-minute penalty on PSP, and requiring a time-out for bandaging at the team bench. While play was stopped, one of Jennifer's teammates -- a girl known as 'Red' despite her blonde hair -- couldn't contain her agitation any longer.

"Those motherfuckers! If I see them try one even more maneuver like that last one, I'll …", she blurted out to no one in particular.

Ian over heard the comment while downing his beer and broke in. "Now now, let's just play the bloody game. You've got to calm down, darlin'. *It's … just … a … bloody … game.* I won't take kindly to any retaliatin'. You'll find yourself sittin' on the bench permanently, ya got that?"

Red started to protest, but Ian would have none of it, and held up his pint-free hand as if to block her words from reaching his ears. "I don't mind saying, I'll call this game off if ya folks don't start calmin' down." He said it loud enough for both benches to hear, then warming to the idea of a general announcement, backed a few steps onto the field and addressed both teams. "HEAR THAT? LISTEN UP FOLKS! I'D RATHER WE CALL 'ER OFF THAN HAVE A SERIOUS INJURY OUT HERE! LET'S KEEP IN MIND NOW ... *IT'S ... JUST ... A ... BLOODY ... GAME!*"

Despite the ironic use of his favorite adjective, his words had a palliative effect. A few heads nodded with understanding, and Quinn's unperturbed nature led everyone on The Snipes -- even Red, who sported a fresh scratch on her cheek -- to harness their vengeful impulses. The game restarted, but before any incidents could escalate, the buzzer sounded, Ian's whistle blew, and the eerie calm of halftime arrived as unnaturally as the eye of a hurricane.

The second half resumed without incident, but as it wore on and the score remained tied, Ian's warning receded from the players' memory. Tripping, pushing, shirt-pulling, name-calling, and penalties became regular features of the game.

One of the men on the Snipes was assessed a two-minute penalty for rough play when he retaliated and flattened a member of PSP into the Plexiglas with a rumble that could be heard throughout the arena. Red further rubbed salt in the wound by giving him a high-five as he headed for the penalty box -- a gesture that infuriated the PSP collective. Tempers eventually cooled and the game restarted, but contrary to Red's accolade, the penalty was a costly one for the Snipes. With only a few minutes left in the game, they would have one less player for all but the last ten seconds.

The assault began immediately.

PSP channeled their anger into a quest for the winning goal, and brought their entire team forward to maximize their numeric advantage. Quinn, however, was of an equal determination, and made several saves, the first of which was a shot that careened off his chest to the height of the rafters above --

followed by a diving stop that kept the score tied. He popped up and whipped the ball out to Red.

And a frenetic pattern developed.

The Snipes attempted to counterattack immediately after Quinn made a save, but the numeric advantage was too much to overcome, and the ball was stolen away. PSP would then re-form an attack -- resulting in another shot, another save by Quinn, another counterattack by the Snipes, another failure, and a repeat of the cycle. Before long, players on both teams were gasping for air with hands resting on their knees or hips, and few were left with the stamina to do more than jog.

Quinn stopped another shot and flung the ball out to Red. Summoning the energy to get upfield, Jennifer joined her, received her lateral pass, and pressed the counterattack. After a feint to the left she cut to her right, but as if her intent was known the defender poked the ball away, the momentum was reversed, and PSP advanced to take another shot at the imperturbable Quinn.

He stopped it, bounced up, and again flung the ball out to Red. As before, Red lateralled it across to Jennifer, and she sent the ball deep for Red to run to. Again it seemed as if her intent was known, this time by the PSP goalie. Charging forth from beneath the ill-tempered Snoopy, he intercepted the ball, sidestepped a malicious kick by Red, and initiated his team's counterattack himself for a while before passing to a teammate for a shot.

Quinn stopped it, bounced up, and again flung the ball out to Red. Red lateralled it across to Jennifer. And this time she pre-planned nothing. Maneuvering to an open area to her left, she advanced downfield with a stampede of players expending their last energy in pursuit. Suddenly, within the pack, a flash of a white surged ahead of the black shirts, and instinctively she nudged the ball to the center of the field.

Fresh from his two-minute rest in the penalty box and running faster than anyone else, Jennifer's teammate saw a tantalizing sight -- a barely-rolling ball fifteen feet in front of the opponent's goal, with only the goalie to beat. With time for only one attempt, he kicked the ball as hard as he could and without aiming, and it flew into the low corner of the goal as the game's final buzzer sounded.

A whirlwind ensued.

En masse the Snipes from the bench ran onto the field to join their teammates already engaged in a spasm of celebration. It was a display like none other, and as their jubilation peaked, Jennifer felt a high from soccer that she hadn't felt in years. After a two-minute group hug the Snipes finally came off the field with Jennifer and Red draping arms over each other's shoulders. They headed for the concession area where the first-aid kit was located, and after applying disinfectant to their abrasions, they parted and Jennifer approached Helena with a beaming smile upon her face.

"Wow! I mean Wow!" exclaimed Helena.

"Ha! Oh man! That may have been the most satisfying game I've ever played in! I mean … I'm talkin' ever!" She caught her breath. "Did you see the last goal?"

Helena nodded that she had while Charlie, sensing excitement, interrupted them. "Mom, did you win!?"

A *zap!* sounded. "Yes hun, we won … at the very last second," she said while running her fingers through his hair.

While she described her the winning goal, KC was busy doling out pitchers of beer in the concession area, and was soon struggling to meet the needs of the standing-room-only crowd made up of players from Snipes, PSP, Rudy's Diner, and the usual assortment of friends and spouses connected with them. She noticed KC's glance in her direction at one point, and moments later he extracted himself and approached while wiping his hands on his pants -- even though his rag rested in its usual place over his shoulder.

"Hey, there's a guy here who wants to t ... "

But before he could finish -- a shout, a burst of commotion, and the sluice of beer from a thrown cup erupted from the picnic tables.

Oh my God ... a fight!

She pulled her hand from Charlie's hair where it snagged, leading to his brief yelp, and brushed past a startled and immobile KC to make her way toward the brawl. She couldn't make out the combatants at first, but once past a few people on the periphery of the fray, she recognized Red and one of the girls from PSP wrestling with all their might. No sooner had she identified them, both players tumbled to the ground between two picnic tables with Red on the bottom. The phrases "You bitch!" and "Get the fuck off me!" filled the air interspersed with the grunts and screams of their struggle. Jennifer pushed her way near them, but hesitated once she was a stride away.

I've never broken up a fight before.

Fortunately, she didn't have to. Ian had been helping himself to a Guinness behind the counter when the altercation first erupted. Not wanting to spill a single drop, he finished filling his cup to capacity, set it down carefully on the countertop, and only then moved from behind the concession counter to intervene. Arriving at the same time as Jennifer, he showed none of her hesitation, and extracted the top combatant from the pile as efficiently as possible.

Having never seen anyone picked up by the ponytail before, Jennifer was awestruck as Ian lifted the girl from PSP into the air. His forearm muscles bulged with the effort as he peeled first her head, then her torso from atop Red. Her body took on the paralysis of a cat carried by the scruff, though the look on her face was that of a viper, and she eventually fought through the pain to utter a few words between her gritted teeth.

"LET ……… GO!" she spat while twisting and lashing out at him with an arm.

But Ian lifted her imperceptibly higher, and the increase in pain left her grasping at his hand to lessen the pressure. With experience at breaking up his share of fights, Ian inserted his mass between the combatants and addressed the girl whose hair he held,

"Now take it easy darlin'. Be takin' a breather now. There'll be no more o' this brawlin' 'round here!" Continuing with a handful of hair, he ushered her away and through a parting sea of observers. Profanities polluted the air, and from their different locations Jennifer and Helena cringed with the knowledge that obscenities were finding their way to Charlie and Jonah's attentive ears.

The girl from PSP cobbled together a full sentence. "LET ... GO OF ME ... YOU DRUNKEN ... PIECE ... OF ... SHIT!"

"Now that's not very ladylike," Ian said while loosening his grip. He then unleashed a savage hiccup, and suggested, "I think you'd do best ta settle down 'n leave ... or do we have to call the police to sort this all out?"

The mention of the police tempered her fury somewhat and after a few odious glances in Red's direction and a yelled threat, she left with a coterie of her teammates -- a departure that magically restored the arena to order. As if the role of peacekeeper was merely one of his many job responsibilities, Ian blew his whistle and got the next game going to make up for the lost time the brawl had consumed. It was only after the game had begun that he realized his pint remained behind on the concession counter instead of within the protected enclosure between the benches.

"Bloody hell," was his private lament.

Jennifer returned to Helena, Jonah, and Charlie. "Well *that* was exciting."

"Mom, why were those girls fighting?" asked Charlie.

I'm sure Red's nasty slide tackle had something to do with it.

"Whoa … that one girl said some bad words!" added Jonah.

"Well guys … that's the ugly side of sports sometimes. That's what happens when people forget about having fun and take it all too seriously."

Jonah broke in excitedly with both hands over his mouth, and said to no one in particular, "Did you see how he picked that girl up *by her hair*?! That was soooo cool!" While Charlie and Jennifer giggled their way to laughter, KC approached them from behind with a rag dripping from the beer spilt during the fight. "Um … boss?"

"Yeah Kase?"

He pulled her aside and whispered, "Like I was saying before, there's a guy here who wants to talk to Jennifer Scott -- *the owner.*"

Her smile melted to a look of blank inquisition, and as KC pointed, she located at one of the picnic tables an older man dressed professionally in slacks, a white dress shirt and a tie. He would have looked refined were it not for the fact that the upper half of his torso and an entire arm were soaked with the beer that had been used as a weapon at the outset of the fight.

"Uh … thanks Kase." She left him behind with the others and approached the man. He stood to introduce himself, tossing aside the rag KC had given him to dry off. "Hi. I'm Jennifer Scott."

"Pleased to meet you Jennifer. I'm Preston Richardson."

He was an older man, with receding gray hair and a goatee. He was small but distinguished, and wore delicate wire-framed glasses that reminded her of a university professor. She doubted he played soccer.

"I'm really sorry about that," she said while pointing at the stains on his shirt. "Sometimes the players … they … get a little carried away."

"Oh, not to worry. I've seen fights that needed a little more than dry cleaning to make right." He removed his glasses, rubbed them on a dry portion of his shirt, and meticulously set them back on his face. "Jennifer, I'm with SoccerCity. Perhaps you've heard of us? We're an indoor soccer facility on the West side."

"Of course. I used to play there all the time."

He stepped closer. "Jennifer, is it possible we could talk in private?"

"Oh well sure … we can … " she looked around and found the picnic tables full. "Why don't we use my office?"

"Wonderful," he said, and followed her past KC, Helena, and the boys. As soon as she pushed open the office door, she found dozens of knights placed on chairs, her desk, the copy machine, the file cabinet, the computer monitor, the paper shredder …

"Ohmygosh. I'm sorry," she said as she stooped to clean a dozen horses off the chair opposite her desk. "My son likes to … well … these chesspieces are a little game we have." She set them atop the paperwork that cluttered her desk.

"Oh … and do you play chess?"

"No, I actually I just collect the horses. I mean the knights." A *zap!* sounded.

"What was that?" he asked.

"Oh, I had that rigged up so I could tell when anyone entered the front doors. Kind of an early warning system, in case I'm in here alone."

"Mmm," was his reply. He saw his opportunity to steer the conversation toward the purpose of his visit, and stepped toward her desk. "The knight is my favorite piece actually. It's unique. Did you know that no other player on the board can move in their direction? You know … the L shape?" Picking one up, he scrutinized it and took a seat. He happened to choose the sea horse given to her by KC.

"Oh yeah, well … like I said, I only collect them," she said while closing the office door and watching Preston from behind.

"It's kind of like yourself I imagine. The knight, that is."

"How do you figure?" she responded while walking around her desk, clearing a row of knights balanced upon the armrest of her chair, and taking a seat.

"Why, for the very uniqueness I mentioned. It's not just anybody who can transform a warehouse into a soccer arena. I mean, the cost alone must have been prohibitive. It's no wonder there's not a lot left in the budget for marketing techniques more refined than fliers." She was puzzled by his flier reference and wondered if he spoke of KC's marketing effort back when the arena had just opened. He continued, "At SoccerCity, we have a variety of investors ... shareholders actually ... who have a financial stake in its success. Yet you own East Portland Indoor Soccer outright?"

She nodded her head and smiled, but a feeling came over her that seated across from her was an adversary.

"Quite commendable," he remarked, holding the sea horse up to the light. He added as an aside, "Actually this one's quite beautiful," before setting it on her desk as if reluctant to part with it.

He smells like beer.

There was an awkward silence. "So what is it can I do for you Preston?"

"Yes. Jennifer ... as I said before I represent SoccerCity ... "

She knew all about SoccerCity. It was the suburban soccer facility near Helena's house where the two of them had played for many years. It was impeccable, and featured none of the adornments, advertising, or painted cartoons that filled East Portland Indoor Soccer. Its high ceilings that gave it a spaciousness compared to her rafter-filled tangle, featured an actual locker room with showers, had an apparel shop that put her meager display case to shame, and was built, lit, and operated with the sole objective of being an indoor soccer facility -- not adapted to fit that purpose. SoccerCity also charged exorbitant prices for everything from food, to lessons, to team fees; and she knew that she'd had stolen away many of the teams that had once played there, lured by reasonable rates, and a friendly atmosphere tonight's fracas completely contradicted.

"I'd like to inquire about ways that we might work together more closely in the future," he suggested.

She nodded her head, not knowing how to interpret his general offer. He went on to describe in eloquent business terms the "market penetration" of soccer facilities, the demographics of the growing popularity of soccer among females, the "collateral revenue potential" and "marginal growth" attributes of athletic facilities, and the generalities of capital financing -- all to which Jennifer nodded her head in polite assent. It wasn't until his use of the word "synergy" that it first occurred to her what he was getting at.

She waited for a pause in his stream of business consciousness and asked a direct question. "Preston, are you by any chance here to inquire about purchasing East Portland Indoor Soccer?"

He was evasive. "Well that's certainly within the realm of possible scenarios that could be explored, although there are many … "

"Because if you were," she interrupted, "I would have to tell you that I'd be very interested in hearing what you have to say."

Chapter 10

On the seventeenth ring, the phone on the break room wall was finally answered.

"Yes, um … Rudy's Diner."

"Hello young man. Could I please speak to a Jack Edens?" After some silence the voice added in a lower octave, "He washes dishes there," in a lower octave.

This information was of assistance to the cook. He was new, and didn't know people by name yet, but he thought 'Jack' might be the name of the red-haired dishwasher working tonight.

"Hold on a sec … I'll check."

He dropped the phone to spin on its cord and ventured into the depths of the restaurant, behind the stoves and ovens, and around the bank of massive refrigerators. There, at the back of the kitchen, he found the red haired dishwasher bent over a mass of dishes and glassware. The stainless steel surfaces all around him were cluttered with an array of dirty pots and trays, and the high faucet of the sink was running with such force, it created a noise that left no other sound audible.

"Are you Jack?!" he yelled from a distance.

He thought he was heard when Jack turned off the water, but no sooner was there silence, Jack flipped the switch of the garbage disposal causing a roar twice as loud as before. He stood staring downward at whatever was in the sink.

The cook approached him until he was just a stride away. "Hey!" he yelled at the same time he put a hand upon Jack's shoulder.

As if a current of electricity was shot through his back, Jack jerked his arm up to ward off a blow.

"Whoa … dude! Sorry …"

Jack fumbled for the switch that killed the disposal. His wide eyes recovered to a more normal state by the time the blades fell silent, and he managed a breathless, "Wha?" as his fingers twitched at his side.

"Sorry dude. I didn't mean to scare you. Are you Jack?"

He nodded.

"The phone's for you. In the break room. Some lady. Just don't make it long … remember what Allen said."

Allen, the mercurial restaurant manager, had recently identified the break room phone as a source of inefficiency, and had announced he would no longer tolerate its abuse. Despite the fact Jack rarely used the break room, it was a busy night, the dishes were backing up, and anyone caught on the phone at that moment risked Allen's wrath.

Jack walked to the break room, picked up the slowly spinning phone, and said "Hello?" -- already knowing who was on the other end.

"Jack it's your Ma. How are ya?"

"F … Fine," was his simple response.

"Good. How's things at the restaurant?"

Jack looked around the break room. It was the usual sight: a few beat-up sofas, some tattered magazines, his bicycle parked in a nearby corner, and a bulletin board that spoke of minimum wage laws. Below the forms someone had pinned a schedule for the soccer team, and Jack grinned upon seeing someone had scrawled a W next to last night's game.

"You there Jack? Listen … I don't got all day. Did ya get my letter about Mikey?"

Jack's memory flashed to the day he was locked out of his apartment during a rainstorm. "Yeah, J … July first."

"Good. Now look. I'm throwing a party when he gets out of the penitentiary, and I need you to pick him up. You know … on July first?"

"Uhh."

"You still got that car o' yours, right?"

Jack thought of the Oldsmobile currently parked behind his apartment. The last time he had driven it was prior to the ice storm last winter, before it inexplicably wouldn't start and he had been forced to use his bike to travel between his home, Rudy's, the soccer arena, and his other neighborhood destinations.

"It 'ont … w … work so good."

"Whattaya mean *It 'ont w … work so good*?!" she parroted.

"Itn't start … t …t. Since … l … l … long time."

"Well what's the matter with it?"

Jack stammered an unintelligible response until his mother tired of his effort and broke in, enunciating words as if he were a child. "Look here. You … have … to … get … that … car … fixed, pick up Mikey, and bring him home to Prineville on July first. You got that? Just seven weeks from now. Damned phlebitis o' mine! 'Do it myself if it weren't for these infernal legs."

He didn't respond, thrown off by the reference to her legs. He waited.

"I says ya got that? Fix the car, pick up Mikey, and bring him here."

"Ain't g … got … don't have m … money to get … t … t … fix." Repetitively he stabbed a lone thumbtack into the bulletin board. The clatter of dishes from the next room meant the bus boys had piled up more plates and silverware in the kitchen.

"Well how you gettin' 'round then?"

"I … my b … b … bike," he said. Gouged pieces fell from the bulletin board to the floor.

"Well, whattaya think you're gonna do, jest bike around for the rest o' your life? You gots ta get it fixed."

Jack started to speak, but opted for silence and waited to be told what to do.

His mother sighed and said, "Well then here's what we'll do. I'll send you a bit o' money to get your car fixed, and you get it ready so's to pick up Mikey. And I don't wanna hear no more excuses! You're to fix up the car, get yer brother, and drive here to Prineville on July first. Easy peasy Japaneasy. I'm planning a big party … ", her tone suddenly grew more animated, " … a big party for Mikey. Cake and everything. Ought be fun! We'll welcome

him back proper. Family and friends and all. I've invited your

cousin Keith … "

His memory honed in on his older cousin's laughter when

told of how Michael had tricked Jack into touching the glow of

orange from the car cigarette lighter. With his thumb he rubbed at

the scar that remained on the pad of his index finger from that day

year ago.

" … yer half sister Jessica … "

Jack's mind flashed to his last visit to Prineville, when he

overheard Jessica's young daughter ask what was wrong with Jack,

and the response was that she had better stay away from Jack

because "retards are stupid and they hurt people."

" … and Byron Chambers and the rest of the boys."

Jack's mind raced to the image Michael's friends -- all who

still lived in Prineville and regarded Jack as less than human, and

worthy of only ridicule.

"Yessirree, we're gonna have a party and do the fourth of

July here at my place. Gonna be a true In-dee-pendence day!

Fireworks and everything. So you hear? I'll be sending you some money to get that car o' yours fixed … and pick your brother up like the letter done said. On July first. Ya got that?"

Jack heard Allen yell from the kitchen, "WHERE THE HELL'S JACK?!"

"I says ya got that!?"

"Yeah. I … on the … on … f … first."

"Good. Get him here as quick as you can. Seems like forever since the family was back together. Been a long time. Don't be messin' it up now, ya hear?"

"I get … p … p … pick up h … him," Jack stammered, at once aware of the approaching sound of Allen's footsteps.

"Good boy. Look for some money comin' in the mail. Oh I can't wait!" she exclaimed. Her voice trailed off, and a moment later he heard the line disconnect. Upon hanging the phone upon the wall, Jack turned to find Allen staring at him from the break room door with his hands upon his hips.

Chapter 11

After brushing his teeth, Charlie bounded from the bathroom and dove headfirst into a tangle of covers atop his bed. As Jennifer followed, she scanned the room Charlie had said he'd cleaned. Though some of his toys and a book still adorned the floor, there were no significant obstructions between the doorway and his bed, and she decided his effort was good enough for now.

"Okay, what do you want, hun? *Squirrels on the Loose?*"

"No, I'm tired of that one."

"McGrowl III, the Great Cat Caper?"

"Oh mom, you *just* read that one!"

"Really? Oh … well, I don't know Charlie. What do *you* want to read?"

"Why don't you tell me a story instead."

It was a change from their routine, but she went with it, and began to troll for story material in her usual manner.

"Letsee … give me a name of a person who you think is really cool."

He didn't hesitate. "My dad."

Uh oh.

She gazed at him, but he did not return her look. "Okay … " she continued warily, "Why don't you give me the name of … your favorite cartoon."

"Mom, I don't want a silly story. Can you tell me a story about my dad? Like … something that really happened to him."

"Well … okay hun … let me think of something." She discarded the first tales that came to mind -- memories containing material she knew was inappropriate for Charlie to hear. Finally, after a pause in which she twice said "I'm thinking," she recalled a long-lost story. She told of Logan's witnessing an accident in which a dog was struck by a pickup truck, and how he had jumped out of his car, tended to the injured animal in the middle of the street, carried it back to the car, and comforted it while a friend drove them to a veterinarian's office.

The tale stirred Charlie's imagination, because he didn't interrupt or ask a single question while it was told. She concluded with a decisive "The End" and asked why he was suddenly curious about his father.

"I was talking to KC about him."

"Really?" She'd assumed the two of them didn't have serious discussions. "And just what did KC say?"

Charlie gazed upward toward the ceiling. "He said that my dad watches me from up in heaven all the time. Maybe even right now." Then he waved upward as if Logan could see him at that very moment.

The image of Charlie trying to make a connection with the father he never knew was both touching and sad at the same time. Softly she said, "Well I think that's probably true, hun."

They were silent for a while, lost in the ease of their meandering thoughts of Logan in heaven, until Charlie asked, "Mom, how did he die?"

"Well that's a long story hun, and maybe it's best for some other time."

"C'mon mom," he pleaded. "You never tell me stuff about my dad."

It was true. She avoided the topic whenever she could, and when she couldn't, relied upon distractions, delays, and evasions in order to forestall the truth.

Reluctance tinged her voice. "You know, Charlie ... I ... "

"Please mom?" He looked her in the eye. In addition to having Logan's light brown hair, Charlie's eyes were purely his father's in their color as well as their sad shape. Staring into them now she saw the piercing similarity, and felt that while the voice of a child had asked the question, the eyes of Logan were pleading that the answer be truthful. A chill ran through her.

"Okay Charlie, but I have to warn you, this is kind of a hard topic. It's hard even for me, and besides it's late … but I'll give you a few answers to any questions you have about your dad. Are you sure you're okay to hear how your dad died?"

He nodded.

With a sigh of uncertainty, she chose her words carefully. "Okay. Well hun, your dad had some people he did business with that had bad tempers and never learned how to treat people right … like the kind that had been in jail before. The business was good though, and he made lots of money, so he kept doing it, even though he knew these people were dangerous to be around. Now I don't really know for sure because I wasn't there when it happened, but it's likely he got in some sort of argument with some of them. There was some sort of fight, and your dad got hurt. He got hit in the head … ", she touched the back of her own head with her hand, " … and he ended up dying."

There was silence for a moment, which Charlie broke with a question. "Are the people in jail that did it?"

"Hun, they never did figure out who did it." There was more silence until she asked, "How does that make you feel, hun?"

"I dunno," he mumbled as he tried to integrate the smiling photos he had seen of his father, with the image of a fight resulting in his death.

"One last question."

He thought for a while. "Ummm ... oh yeah ... did the dog live or die?"

"The dog? ... oh right, the dog. Well, the veterinarian had to put a cast on his broken leg, but then it got better, and he was okay. And best of all ... the kids in the dog's neighborhood all got to sign the cast."

This appealed to Charlie, and he asked further questions about the dog -- its name, what kind of dog was it, what color it was ...

"Oh hun, I don't know. 'Truth is, it happened before I even met your dad. Now please try to get some sleep. Night night."

"Night night," he replied.

She turned off his bedroom light, worried the revelation about Logan would lead to insomnia. Happily though, she found him asleep just ten minutes later, a slumber that would end up lasting through the night. She congratulated herself for

withholding from Charlie the truth about Logan's death until he

could handle it, and rationalized that the one lie she *had* told him

was worth it. In truth, the dog died in the backseat with its head in

Logan's lap before they even got to the vet's office.

With Charlie asleep, she grabbed the baby monitor she used

to listen for him, clicked it on, and slipped it into the front pocket

of her sweatshirt. It chattered with intermittent static as she

weighed how best to spend the next few hours. Bittersweet

recollections of Logan filled her head --- and she wondered how

many hundreds of memories of Logan had drifted away never to be

recalled again. Opting for work over leisure, she passed through

the doorway and into the arena, and headed to her office just as the

last game of the night had begun.

Before she could get there, KC placed his hand on her

shoulder from behind. "You won't believe it! Tonight's the

night!" He took no note of her sullen mood.

"The night for what, Kase?"

"The night for the interview! My mom just called. She

just got off the phone with them, and said they'll be running the piece tonight! I've got the news on now. C'mon!" He took her by the hand and pulled her toward the big screen TV.

"Okay, okay … I'll be right there. Let me get a beer first."

She felt her malaise magically lift. Just as she viewed KC as nothing less than a saint for his energy and dedication in readying the arena for opening, so too was she thankful for his ability to lift her spirits with his contagious excitement. She headed to the concession area, plucked a paper cup from the top of a tall stack, and leaned over the countertop to push the beer tap forward. It sputtered with foam before her cup was even halfway full, and assuming KC would replace the keg, she pulled back the tap and walked over to the benches where a dozen others had been coerced by KC to watch the news. Sitting down at the closest open spot at a table, she knew none of her fellow viewers, but they all knew KC, who in the span of a year had gained first-name familiarity with nearly everyone. It wasn't until she heard his familiar voice that she realized Coach Morris was sitting at the same table, his identity obscured by the fact he had been leaning far to his right to talk to someone from a neighboring table.

"Well hello there little lady!"

"Oh … Coach Morris … " she stammered. "I'm sorry … I wasn't … It's just that I wasn't expecting to see you here. Are you playing in a league now? I thought you were just doing lunchtime pick-up games?"

"You know my schedule pretty well, doncha?" he said with a wink. "I got asked to fill-in for a team here tonight. And by the way, it'd be fine with me if you just call me Coach."

"Mmm … okay."

The silence between them grew, but was broken when Coach motioned toward KC. "He's certainly excited about this TV … whatever-it-is."

"An interview. I guess it's not everyday you get to see yourself on the big screen," she said.

KC was standing in front of the TV, yelling at the newscaster to "get on with it". "The thing is," she offered to Coach, "KC insisted upon wearing an East Portland Indoor Soccer hat during the interview, so I think he's excited about generating some free publicity for us."

"That right?" Coach said easily. "Well you'd think he owned the place, not you, the way he's carrying on."

He certainly does seem to be carrying on.

She watched him ensnare a bystander with the story of his hat negotiation prior to the interview, and finished off a sip of beer that was mostly foam. "Well, Coach ... all I can say is ... KC is definitely not like most people."

"All right! Finally!" yelled KC. "Here it comes! Turn it up!"

While the newscaster spoke, the words 'Where Are They Now?" appeared on the screen, and the crowd -- animated and talking of other subjects just a moment before -- fell into silence. The newscaster spoke of the forestry protest from over two years ago, and the screen cut to footage of KC pacing along s high ledge of a building, above a sea of bodies.

Everyone at the picnic tables cheered at the sight of KC on TV.

Two years ago, KC Nenn stunned forestry officials, local police, and onlookers by staging his own 'sit-in' atop the Department of Forestry building in downtown Portland, drawing massive media attention to the department's plans to harvest timber on land in the Cascade Creek Wilderness Area. It was a watershed moment in the battle between the interests of the logging industry and those of environmentalists, a battle that continues to this day. We tracked KC down to his current place of work on the eastside of Portland to see what he's been up to since then, and to see how he's carried on the fight since that landmark moment. Glenn Hubert has the story. Glenn?

The screen was filled with a far-away shot of KC talking to the reporter, followed thereafter by a tight close-up of his face and just the brim of his hat, coming just short of revealing the stenciled writing of East Portland Indoor Soccer. It was hard to hear anything amid the exclamations and laughter at the picnic tables, but Jennifer managed to hear KC saying "caring for the forests" and "in bed with the timber industry." KC got hold of the remote control to turn up the volume as the camera switched to another interview shot just distant enough and of such an angle, the words on the hat remained unreadable. The story was winding up, and it became clear that 'East Portland Indoor Soccer' was not going to be seen or heard in association with the story. Soon there was only a still photo of KC on the ledge in arm-raised exaltation, and the newscaster moved onto a story about a shooting at a barber shop in North Portland.

KC wailed, "Ahhhhhhhhhh! They screwed us! They screwed us! They didn't show the hat! … or mention East

Portland Indoor Soccer at all! That's the last time I give an interview about that damn protest!" He then yelled in Jennifer's direction, "Did you see the way they panned in real tight so they didn't have to show the writing on the hat?!? Those media SOB's are the most deceitful, unethical, self-serving, conniving ... " He ran out of adjectives without finishing his sentence, but he was talking more to himself anyway. The crowd lost interest and dispersed into their own conversations, many having nothing to do with KC.

"I don't know why he's so upset about that silly hat," said Coach Morris. "I mean, he got to say all that stuff about the forests. That seems like pretty good publicity to me."

She finished off her last sip, swallowed, and held up the empty cup. "See this cup, Coach?"

He nodded.

"This cup holds the amount of interest KC has for the forests." She then slowly tipped the cup upside-down, spilling nothing. Then she crumpled it in her hand. "He only did the interview to get publicity for the arena."

Coach looked disturbed. "But then why? ... how come he? ..." he paused and thought for a moment. "Out there on the ledge

… why in blazes would he go to all that trouble? … I mean if he didn't … "

She rose. "Coach take it from me. If we were meant to know what made KC tick, he'd be a clock."

After tossing her crumpled cup into a trashcan, she walked up to KC who stood facing the TV with his hands on his hips. The news was well into the weather forecast, but KC stared at it nonetheless, as if they'd soon run a retraction to apologize for their camera trickery. Eventually he noticed her. "Oh I'm sorry, boss. Those … I … "

"Kase, really … it's no big deal. Come on! I'm touched you wanted to get the place free publicity, but its not like we'll fold up tomorrow just because we didn't get mentioned on the Channel Two news."

He breathed heavily, ridding himself of his pent up anger. His hands left his hips and plunged into the familiar front pockets of his pants. "Oh I know. I guess it's really all pretty silly isn't it? It's just that I hate being used like that. Plus I feel like an idiot." He glanced at the TV again, as if a ray of hope lay within a satellite picture of a swirl of clouds sailing across the Pacific Ocean for a collision with Oregon. "I just wanted to help is all."

"Kase, you help this place every day. I mean look all around. I don't know about you but I see signs of KC everywhere. From the paintings to the advertisements to the chicken wire … to the camaraderie you infect this place with by your very presence. I swear, you know twice as many people by name than I do. I mean it Kase, this place wouldn't exist if it weren't for you."

"Oh come on, it'd exist … "

"No, no, really Kase … I mean it … I don't think we'd be where we are right now if it weren't for you. I thank my lucky stars for you every time I think about what a unique thing we've built here, and I'm eternally grateful you happened to drop in here that day way back when I was working on the carpeting. I really regard it as fate. If I've never said it before let me say it now … I don't think I could have done it without you."

A startled look came across his face. "You really mean that?"

"Yes I do," she said with a beaming smile. She felt an impulse to hug him, but hesitated in the certainty he would be the one to initiate their first embrace.

She was wrong.

Looking her straight in the eye for a few seconds, he gave a response that came across as a heartfelt, but made her feel her sense of a connection between them was illusory.

"Thanks" was all he said. With his hands firmly anchored in the confines of his front pockets, he turned and walked slowly away.

Chapter 12

For reasons beyond her understanding, she was automatically angry upon seeing Ethan Saturday evening.

It might have been the amicable way he spoke with a female teammate, triggering a virulent mix of jealousy and the suspicion that she was not the only one who had received heartfelt e-mails from him in the past week. It might have been the fact that despite the declaration of his feelings, she felt a malignant insecurity that *he* was the one unfettered by thoughts and fantasies of *her*. It might even have been her recognition of his ability to come and go from the arena at his whim, while conversely she had little control over their encounters.

Over the past four months their relationship had gathered steady momentum, first with an introduction by a mutual friend, progressing to the intermittent conversation of acquaintances, and then to some subtle flirting she thought little of at the time. By the second month they were seeking each other out for interactions, and they plunged into the ocean of friendship. If she made herself available in her office, he would join her before or after his games simply to talk, and before long they were trading e-mails -- at first light and frivolous -- but then of feelings and confidences. It was the first time she had ever felt such a strong connection with someone so quickly, and often she thought it impossible he was developing the same feelings she had for him. Yet each time she doubted him, her uncertainty was allayed by a gesture, token, or expression of his similar amazement that he felt such a connection with her. By the third month, he began stopping by to see her unannounced even when his team did not have a game -- either after his work or on other random occasions while games took place, and they spent whatever time they had contented in each other's presence, talking of whatever came to mind.

As their intimacy blossomed, so too did his inquisitiveness. Even the most random tidbit of information about her interested him intensely, and before long she felt he knew her on terms that were equal to that of her closest friends. He even made a recurring game out of it, stating "Tell me something about you I don't know" with such frequency, her pat response came to be that he already knew everything there was to know.

But that answer would never satisfy.

He would persist, saying, "It could be anything. It could be your favorite ice cream flavor, or something that happened at a childhood birthday party, or why you voted the way you did in the last presidential election … ", and on and on and on until her memory was jarred, the curtain drawn back, and some new aspect of her was revealed.

She told him about the origin of her team's name (The Snipes were a band admired by a teammate), how she had broken her leg at age one (her mom set her upon a horse for a photograph, and she'd tumbled off the other side), her hip problems at age three (which compelled her father to lie her on her back and peddle her legs in the air for thirty minutes every night), and the story of how, in junior high, she'd found in soccer a way to escape after her mom's death. She even told him about Logan, though she lied about the details of how he died and his profession as a drug dealer.

Watching him now as he repetitively bounced a ball on his knee, she became aware that for all the knowledge he'd acquired of her, she knew comparatively little of him. He was animated and equally conversant with her in any frivolous topic, but when she probed to know why he felt a particular way about something, he only went so far -- stating his answer with simplicity and revealing nothing of its cause. If she continued prodding, he grew evasive, even shrugging his shoulders as if it were a mystery even to him why he felt the way he did. Even before Helena stumbled upon him with his girlfriend, she was perplexed why he kept details of himself private. As she watched him now on the field, it dawned on her how little she really knew him.

Suddenly, she was filled with the impulse to decline any outing with him this evening out of spite. However, just as the feeling arose, it was doused when he noticed her, jogged over, and began talking. Mutually and conspicuously they avoided the topic of his e-mail, and in fact their exchange contained nothing consequential at all until he re-inquired about his post-game invitation.

"So are you able to go for a beer afterward?"

"Yeah, I've got Helena coming to watch Charlie."

"Great. Then I'll see you after?"

She nodded her reply and they parted, he to his game and she to the back where Charlie's favorite dinner -- macaroni and cheese -- bubbled in an orange goo in the oven. Toward the end of their meal Helena and Jonah arrived. Once the boys ran off to play, Helena mentioned she had seen Ethan on the field.

"I know. We talked real briefly … " she replied, but before she could say any more, the boys ran back, preventing further conversation on the topic.

"Are you boys up for going out and getting some ice cream?" Helena announced in an offer she and Jennifer had planned.

"Yeah!" the boys replied in stereo, and they tore off to Charlie's bedroom to retrieve his shoes while Jennifer began cleaning up.

"So how are you feeling?" Helena asked.

"Like an absolute fucking nervous wreck."

"Mmm. But in a good way?" Helena asked with a smirk.

She leaned back upon the sink. "You know how I feel? I feel like he'll try to pretend the e-mail never happened, or maybe he'll tell me he never wants to see me again, or he'll tell me he's breaking up with his girlfriend. Or maybe he'll tell me that he's an alien come down on a mission to torment single moms." She tossed Charlie's plastic cup into the sink behind her. "God I really don't know, all I *do* know is that I'm a bit of a basket case to be honest. One moment I hate him, the next moment I … ". She stopped herself from finishing the sentence.

"Don't tell me you think you love him."

"Honestly, I don't know. I'm all mixed up right now."

"Well that's probably natural. If I have any advice that's worth listening to, it's this: just be yourself … and do whatever it is that makes *you* happy. That's really all there is to it."

"Thanks. You make it sound so simple. Wish me luck." They hugged just as the boys burst in from the bedroom.

"Wish you luck for what?" Charlie asked.

"Luck for … cleaning all the macaroni and cheese that splattered all over the inside of the oven. Okay remember hun, I won't be here when you get back. Aunt Helena's gonna stay with you and tuck you in. I'll check on you after you get to bed. Understand?"

"Can Jonah spend the night?"

"Not tonight hun, his dad's gonna pick him up a little later after you guys get back. Next time, okay?"

Charlie groaned and gave her a woeful "uh-huh" followed by a peck on the cheek. His disappointment was short-lived, and he soon headed out astride Jonah engaged in a spirited debate about which was the best ice cream flavor.

"Good luck," Helena mouthed over her shoulder as she headed out with the boys.

"Thank you," she mouthed back.

The din of the night's activity drifted to her ears between the opening and closing of the door to the arena. Somewhere amid that tangle of noise was Ethan. Waiting a few minutes to assure that Helena and the boys had departed, she emerged into the noisy world she'd created -- one where girls fight, teams celebrate, referees drink, keys are thrown in the air, spectators get doused with beer, school children come to play, artwork gets painted, Achilles tendons rip, and television interviews are given and criticized.

She headed to the office where some paperwork awaited, but it was no use. As much as she tried to focus, the combination of dozens of *zaps!* and Ethan's presence on the field distracted her from her work. It felt good to watch him, and even moreso once she'd gravitated from her office to the empty spectator's row. All her conflicting sentiments calmed as she replayed his simple inquiry in her mind, '*So are you able to go for a beer afterward?*' For the moment, all that mattered was that he wanted to spend time with her, and a languid happiness washed over her as she watched his game.

With his considerable height, he was easy to pick out on the field. His wavy black hair bounced when he ran, and with his agility and the distance he covered with only a few strides, he had a physical advantage most of the opposing players. Yet it wasn't his soccer skills that drew her attention. With a manner befitting a politician, he continually talked with players on both teams, gaining nods and smiles with his quips. One moment she saw him exhort a struggling teammate with the warmth and encouragement of an older brother. Minutes later, his mock-tantrum brought laughter from players on both teams after he fumbled away an easy opportunity to score. Toward the end of the game he instinctively -- but illegally -- extended an arm to knock the ball to the ground near the other team's goal. While opponents yelled for Ian to call a hand ball, Ethan's wide smile revealed his duplicity even as he tried to score, and when the whistle was belatedly blown … smiles, laughs, and the collegial banter of "Nice try!" and "Almost got a way with one!" accompanied hearty slaps on his back from players on the other team.

Why these incidents made him so endearing, she didn't know. It could have been that he simply seemed so boyishly human on the field, or maybe it was because his expressions and actions were so heartfelt, it was as if he withheld nothing of himself while playing. Or, maybe it was that within league play, it was a rarity to see someone not take himself too seriously, and even call attention to his foibles. It occurred to her that if his actions on the field were of the power to make opponents feel a connection with him after only a few minutes -- it was no wonder months of one-on-one interactions with him had resulted in his constant place in her thoughts.

His game ended, and while walking to the benches he spotted her and ran over. Being a foot shorter than him, it felt unusual to have him look up to address her through the Plexiglas. "How long have you been watching?" he shouted with a wide grin.

"Long enough to see your epic blunder," she called back.

At this reply he smiled and shrugged. "Let me towel off, get some water, and I'll be ready to go."

An odd rain fell as they walked side-by-side up MLK in the dark. They each were hit by a single drop every dozen or so steps, and in the glare of cars' headlights the intermittent drops fell like

embers lit only in the moments before they struck the ground.

Ethan's presence made her feel safe as they walked past the vacant

lots of MLK, the depths of which existed in blackness beyond the

lighting of the street lamps. She felt happy and slowed her pace,

not wanting to propel the evening any faster than necessary. By

the time they got close to the Eastbank Tavern the wind had picked

up and the raindrops were falling more frequently. Yet their

leisurely pace never quickened, so lost were they in each other's

presence. As he spoke of his day, she thought to reveal her

encounter with Jack Edens earlier in the week, but changed her

mind and elected to keep it to herself. Ethan's inquisitiveness on

such a topic could consume much of their evening, and she wanted

to ensure there was time for him to broach the topic of his e-mail.

As they approached the door, she wondered if she should

have suggested a more private destination for their evening than a

raucous tavern, and feared that in such an atmosphere he would be

reluctant to talk openly. She longed for the power to set in his

mind the desire to go somewhere -- anywhere else. While he

moved ahead of her to get the door, she closed her eyes and

thought she would be willing to walk miles in the rain to a more secluded destination if he would just say the word.

"Vomit."

Her eyes popped open. "What?"

"Vomit. There's vomit on the sidewalk next to your foot. You might want to watch your step."

Disgustingly, it was true, and as she sidestepped the objectionable orange substance, all concerns about the tavern evaporated from her mind.

Compared to the freshness of newly fallen rain, the pungent smell of yeast, hops, and smoke within the tavern was unpleasant at first. However the warmth, noisy camaraderie, and the instant cessation of the wind drew them in -- and within minutes she no longer distinguished aromas. A mass of patrons stood in a pack near the door, all but blocking the entrance while engrossed in a Chelsea vs. Manchester City replay from earlier in the day on two ceiling-high TVs.

They found a seat at a booth and ordered their drinks -- Irish coffee for her and a pint of beer for him -- and after their waitress left she felt the unease how the conversation would next progress. They had found a booth of relative privacy toward the back, but despite her longing to speak of his e-mail, she wanted

him to be the one to broach it. No sooner had their drinks arrived

than cheering erupted from the crowd, not for events related to the

game which was still minutes away from starting, but for the

familiar sight of Ian McMannus who had just arrived still dressed

in his black referee garb. It took no more than five seconds for a

beer to materialize in his hands.

"Say, isn't that …?" Ethan remarked.

"Yep, none other than East Portland Indoor Soccer's best

referee."

"He certainly seems to be in his environment."

"*His* environment is any place that combines soccer and

beer. I imagine this place and the arena are interchangeably dear

to his heart. He must have gotten someone to ref the last game for

him."

They drank. She found herself detailing the saga of last

night's fight, a story that concluded just as the crowd reacted en

masse to the start of the game. Eventually, they took their eyes

from the commotion, and he smiled and leaned forward. "Sssooo

…"

She awaited what he had to say, a little puzzled at why he was smiling just before bringing up the serious topic of the e-mail.

" … tell me something about you I don't know."

She hid the disappointment in her voice. "You know, you always manage to ask that question at a time when I don't have anything ready. I swear, there have been five times in the last week where I thought of things that would have been perfect responses, but now I've forgotten them."

"C'mon, it could be anything. Your first beer bong. Something about your senior prom. Your favorite Halloween costume as a kid. Anything."

She sat in silence and tried to come up with something while warming her hands around her cup. "Have I told you what's my favorite movie of all time?"

"Breakfast at Tiffany's. You told me that, like, way back in April."

"Okay … did I tell you about the time I almost drowned as a kid?"

"I think so. Was that when you were a little kid and a wave almost swept you out to sea before your dad jumped in to save you?"

"Rats!" she said, and while scratching the back of her head. Suddenly she thought of something. "Okay," she said, and rose from her seat. As she did so a loud lament erupted from the crowd at an early penalty called against Manchester City. Someone hurled an expletive at the television. She sat down on Ethan's side of the booth, turned away from him, and parted the hair on the back of her head. "When I was about ten or so, my family took a trip to one of the rivers north of Phoenix. You know, the kind of event where people just go to hang out and drink beer? I got this scar when I was horsing around with a cousin of mine. We were tossing a Coke can back and forth to each other, and when it got a little hole in it and started spraying everywhere, I bent down to grab it and show it to my mom. When I stood up, I cut my head on a tree limb."

He moved aside some strands near her fingertips, and located a fishhook-shaped scar. "How many stitches?" he asked while gently angling her head downward in order to get a better look.

"I don't remember exactly. Probably like six."

He pulled more hair away, isolated as much of the scar as he could, and bent forward to give it a long kiss as if it had the power to heal. While symbolically the kiss was that which a parent would give a child, the lingering touch of his lips to her head was distinctively sensual, and she closed her eyes until well after he drew back and closed the curtain of hair over the white line on the back of her scalp.

Without turning or looking back at him, she slowly made her way out of the seat and back to her side of the table, fortifying herself by pretending the kiss was platonic. Now it was her turn to avoid how she felt. "I pretty much ruined the outing because they had to rush me to the ER. I remember the look on my mom's face when she saw the blood pouring all down my head. Not a pretty sight. I felt guilty about ruining the outing and I remember in the car on the way to the hospital … I thought if I could just hold my dad's shirt to my head tight enough, the bleeding would stop and we could all go back to the river." She smiled at the recollection which she hadn't thought of in many years, and lifted her coffee to her lips with both hands. It radiated wondrous warmth, and by the time she sipped and set her cup back down, there was a new expression on his face.

"I'm serious about what I wrote in the e-mail. I'm so sorry. Really sorry. I handled this … this … " he fumbled, straightened himself, and exhaled deeply, " ... this entire situation all wrong."

He then paused as if assessing whether the apology had been

accepted, and getting no indication either way, continued. "Have

you ever found yourself in a situation where you knew what the

right thing was to do, and it gnawed at you constantly because you

were torn between going ahead and doing it and ... well ...

basically chickening out and *not* doing it? And the longer you

procrastinated, the more it tormented you?"

"Who hasn't?" she said softly.

"The thing is, I didn't expect to feel the way I do about

you. I didn't plan it, and it's totally snuck up upon me.

'Blindsided' is probably the better word. I'm a believer that you

can't *tell* yourself to feel something or not. You either do or you

don't. And with you I feel ... ", he edged forward and snaked his

hands through the glassware cluttering the table between them.

Their hands joined, and from his fingers she felt the coolness from

his pint contrast against the warmth from her cup.

" ... with you I feel as if I've been blind all my life, but I

just had this operation that restored my sight, and I'm seeing things

for the first time."

The crowd at the bar muttered a universal "awwwwwwww" in disbelief at another penalty, the timing of which made it seem as if the patrons were eavesdropping and adored Ethan's surgical analogy.

She smiled at the coincidental timing, but he seemed not to notice as his hands held hers and his thumbs lightly stroked her knuckles and the back of her hands. It felt delightful, but when they intertwined their fingers, it was ecstasy. For a few minutes he spoke of his state of confusion, and as he struggled for the right words, she seized the initiative, took one of his hands in hers, and kneaded his individual fingers. It instantly relaxed him, and after taking a few deep breaths, he spoke at length of the sentiments and regrets trapped within him.

Another round of drinks came and she continued with the hand massage, fearful that if she stopped, so to would his words. After the waitress was gone he stated simply, "I just don't want you to be angry with me, Jennifer. I'm really sorry."

The crowd at the bar breathed a loud sigh of relief as a shot from Chelsea bounced off the crossbar.

"Well I'd be lying if I said I didn't feel deceived. But I'm not angry, at least not anymore." The truth was, some pain still lingered, however the more time she spent with him, and the more she fell under the intoxicating influence of her drink and his sincerity, the less it hurt. "Instead of being mad, I've just come to accept that our timing right now is really rotten. In fact it stinks."

He nodded in agreement.

"I can't tell you how often the mis-timing of relationships has been an obstacle for me." She felt slightly teary, but fought it off with a sputtering laugh, fearing she'd appear pathetic. "I don't suppose you've been plagued by the unavailability of love-interests in your life?"

"Is that what we are? Love interests?" he said, and for a horrible moment, she thought she'd grossly overstated their relationship. She contemplated a retraction, but slowly he nodded his head in agreement, "I guess we are, aren't we?"

The crowd at the bar suddenly cheered at the prospect of a corner kick for Manchester City.

"That feels really good," he said as she massaged his fingertips one at a time. Then, he looked her in the eye. "So what do we do now?"

The crowd moaned as the corner kick failed.

"Well, as I see it we just back off from where this thing otherwise would be headed." She was glad to have managed a businesslike evenness in her voice.

"Agreed," he said as he lifted his pint and finished off the final portion of his beer. After a pause that concluded with a significant swallow, he stared at her and added, "The trouble is … that goes against everything I'm feeling right now."

The uttering of this single sentence filled her with instantaneous glee, at once eroding her resistance. A chill ran down her back. It was as if his heart had burst forth and seized control of his voice, so contradictory was it to the accord they had just made. To hear his words spoken from such proximity, all while their hands stroked one another, compelled her reciprocal honesty.

"Me too Ethan."

Lost in the solitude of their own thoughts, they said nothing for an entire minute. Only their hands continued as if nothing had happened, indicating their preference for ardor over the spoken pact to resist.

He worked his hands free and ran his fingertips past her wrists. An icy prickle developed on her skin as he moved them slowly to her elbows and then back, touching only the light hairs of her forearms. Closing her eyes, she gave him a smile that she used to still the tiniest of trembles. It occurred to her to give him a simultaneous caress, but so complete was her immobility at that moment, she knew she'd not do it justice. Instead she succumbed to the languid feeling she wished could last forever.

There was a wild cheer as an infraction was called against Chelsea, and then another when a red card was dished out, indicating the disqualification of one of their players.

"I have had *such* dreams about you," he said suddenly. At the uttering of this confession which completely matched her own experience, she opened her eyes and was moved to action from which she had no resistance, and from which she knew there would be no regret. Pulling her arms free, she rose and seated herself on his side of the table as before, only this time facing him.

The crowd hushed with anticipation as a forward push developed.

The last filament of her resistance collapsed as slowly, and with both his hands, he reached up and cradled her jaw. With his fingers barely touching the lobes of her ears, he gently angled her head upward, and amid wild cheering for a goal scored twelve hours ago by a team halfway around the world, their lips touched.

She felt everything -- his slightly chapped lips, the softness of his tongue, and the slight roughness of his whiskers -- but the sensation she would revisit over and over in her mind was not the contact of their mouths, but that of his fingers as he dropped one hand from her face and ran it softly down her spine, gently feeling the contours of her vertebrae through her shirt. By the time his hand got to her lower back, she reached the point of being insensate to the raucous cheering, the discomfort of the bench seat, the painful scab on her knee, and the smoke that swirled in the air of the tavern.

It took the massive belligerence of Ian McMannus to fracture the moment as he plopped down across from them. "Hey, sorry to break up the swabbin' but 'Man City' just scored! Thanks be to god for that red card on Bastiste, eh? 'Don't think we'd have a pot to piss in if he hadn't been sent away at the thirty-eight mark, eh?!"

They looked at him as if he were from another planet, but he noticed nothing out of the ordinary and took a considerable pull from the pint that seemed as natural a part of his hand as his thumb. He wiped his mouth on the back of his arm, and proceeded to yell a friendly obscenity to an acquaintance in the crowd.

They still held each other, and his hand remained conspicuously close to the gap between her T-shirt and her shorts, but when it became clear Ian was not getting up to leave any time soon their embrace eased. For the moment they settled for the contact of a hand on each other's thigh. Amid some small talk between Ethan and Ian, she pondered what tactful comment she could give to cause him to vacate their table.

Then her cell phone rang.

She fully detached herself from Ethan, fumbled through her bag, and answered on the fifth ring.

"Hello?"

"Hey, it's Helena."

She knew it could only mean trouble with Charlie.

"What's up?"

"Hey look. Um ... well it's Charlie."

A sick feeling came to her stomach. "What's wrong?"

"Well I'm not sure, but he seems to have woken up from a nightmare screaming something about his dad's murder."

Chapter 13

Hours later, Jennifer lay awake listening to sounds audible only in the middle of the night. From the kitchen the refrigerator hummed to life and then abruptly stopped -- placing in her mind the worry of a malfunction. The soft buzz of a fly wound an invisible path to the high windows above her bed, where it raged against the glass before falling silent. From MLK, the lonely rumble of a truck grew, reached a crescendo, and then dissipated as it bounced along the rutted lane that led to the freeway onramp.

And incessant thoughts of Ethan prevented her sleep.

The last game of the night was near halftime by the time they returned to the arena, and the concession area was full of its usual Saturday night boisterousness. Ethan had volunteered to "wait out here" while she headed for Charlie, but his patience lasted only ten minutes, and she returned to find only his meager message taped to her closed office door:

11:45PM. I'll call you tomorrow. – Ethan

Rolling to a new position and checking her bedside clock for the fifth time since laying down, she saw it was now past 2AM.

As if her mind could only tune into a single frequency, she plunged into thoughts of Ethan -- their conversation, his light touch on her hands and forearms, and the electrification deep in her body when his hand moved slowly down her spine as they kissed.

Like earlier in the evening, Charlie interrupted her moment with Ethan. Drifting from his bedroom, through the baby monitor, and to her ears, his garbled phrases, "The water's cold … " and "Cut it out!" were decipherable within a mix of mirthful laughter. With a smile she lay comforted in the thought that his subconscious had switched gears and cast aside the earlier nightmare involving Logan's murder.

She yawned as words from Charlie trickled away to a soft mumble, and all was silent again. Achieving a yawn and desperate to thwart her mind's gravitation toward Ethan, she began a mental exercise she used to lull herself to sleep. Picking the name of someone in her life, she used the letters in that person's name to form a list of things she'd physically like changed about herself. Having used Ethan's name so many times before, she instead chose a name that until a few days ago was unknown to her.

Jaw	No TMJ pain ever again.
Achilles Tendon	Never torn or injured.
Cerebrum	I immediately have an IQ of 150
Knee	All soccer scrapes magically heal -- no scabs.
Eyes	Blue instead of brown. 20/10 vision.
Deltoids	Muscular and toned
Epidermis	Flawless tanned skin. Perfect complexion.
Nose	Supermodel perfect. Never another cold or sneeze.
Spine	…….

At the selection of 'Spine' she found herself replaying the feel of Ethan's hand along her back, not even realizing she was trapped in the memory until the rumble of distant thunder shook her mind free. In frustration she rolled over and tried a different sleep-inducer. She imagined herself a floating apparition in the night sky, looking down through an illuminated and roofless arena, and studying every inch of the structure -- the office, the field, the concession area, and the back where Charlie and she lay in their separate rooms, quiet and alone.

Then it occurred to her that maybe they weren't alone.

For all she knew, KC was on the internet in her office, drinking beer in the concession area, refining his few soccer skills, or attempting to do all of these things for a few minutes at a time. Or maybe he wasn't in the building at all, and the arena was dark and motionless but for the video games that endlessly blinked 'Insert Coin' and the coffee maker whose digital clock ticked off the minutes of mid-afternoon. She eased toward sleep, but was startled awake by the clear pitch of Charlie's voice. She rose to check on him in his room. Though the path consisted of two turns in total darkness, she wound her way there having walked it hundreds of times before in the night.

The faint orange illumination of his nightlight allowed her to gaze at him from the doorway where she leaned against the frame. He lay on his stomach with his elbows tucked in, his fists beneath his chin, and his eyes closed to everything but the images of his dreams. Asleep and still, he was such an embodiment of comfort and peace, she wondered if she'd dreamt his words. Few things gave her as much contentment as her peacefully sleeping boy, and she smiled anew when his mouth wiggled and opened with words that, for the moment, remained unspoken.

She moved toward his bed.

His pajama top showed an insipidly happy dolphin leaping from the water and saying *Visit Ocean Park!* in a cartoon bubble -- a souvenir from a trip they made to California with her father years ago. It barely fit him now, but remained his unwavering choice of nightwear no matter what the temperature, and despite the fact that it was threadbare and the collar was separating from the rest of the shirt. Standing in silence, she drowsily stared at the fading dolphin, wishing some portion of its happy spirit could magically weave its way into his psyche, replacing the fear, insecurity, and self-doubt she was powerless to fray.

I gotta get some sleep.

Like thoughts of Ethan, worrying about Charlie was a proven hindrance to her sleep, and she vowed to think of something else. Navigating back to her room and climbing within the envelope of her sheets, only a faint trace of her body heat remained. Pleasant coolness sandwiched her legs, arms, and shoulders as she slipped beneath layers of blankets. As she lay still, an icy tapping drew her attention to the windows high above her bed.

Rain.

The storm's intensity grew, and drops began to beat against the glass not with the high-pitched tics of sleet, but with the anger of a downpour. A high street lamp on MLK cast three parallelograms of blue light on the opposite wall of her bedroom, and she stared at shadows of water spilling down the panes. She fell under the spell of sleep.

" … splashing me!" came Charlie's voice through the baby monitor.

Her eyes fluttered open, but then powerless to resist any further they relaxed and fell again, She was swimming. Just beneath the surface. Her body rhythmically churned forward, her speed increased, and in a sudden spasm that flexed her body to its fullest, she broke into the air, and beneath her in the water shone her reflection.

She was a dolphin.

She jumped again and again until the water faded away and her attention was drawn instead to a distant city whose buildings were ablaze with light. Above the biggest buildings exploded a succession of fireworks, and she closed the distance, in no time arriving at the city center where motionless yachts took on the hues of the colors filling the sky, and the surface of the Willamette sparkled with flecks of light.

Passing beneath a bridge, she emerged on the other side as an apparition that scythed over the surface of the water and headed for the riverbank. An eddy churning froth and trash near her as she sped toward a large pipe split by the waterline, and entered it. The pelting rain ceased, and the light from the fireworks receded into a distant semicircle.

Then the darkness became complete.

An echoing rush of water filled the tunnel until flashes lit the interior of the pipe, and she emerged onto an empty city street. An explosion shook the buildings around her, and an umbrella of sparks filled in every quadrant of the sky. Looking up, she saw movement atop the building facing her where a lone figure pulled back behind the edge of the roof. It was only then that she saw the familiar painted soccer ball on the wall, and beneath it, the words EAST PORTLAND INDOOR SOCCER.

She levitated upward where a soft pop lit the world from above, revealing pipes, vents, an antenna, and just as the light faded -- a distant human form on the far side of the roof. Cloaked in darkness, she began moving forward. Raindrops thrummed in a constant percussion as she closed the distance between them, halving it, then halving it again. She longed for light, and as if responding to her wish a burst of yellow radiated from above revealing the profile of a man just a few strides away.

It was Jack Edens.

Saturated by the rain, his Rudy's Diner T-shirt clung to his slumped shoulders, and water streamed down the contours of his freckled face. A series of explosions burst overhead, illuminating the area in extended light and causing her to flinch at its power. All the while Jack's eyes held a downward gaze. Following them, she was galvanized by a sight that had lain undisturbed in her memory for years.

Logan.

He lay as she had found him in their bedroom almost a decade before, curled in the same position, and bound to the same fractured chair. As before blood flowed from his head, but instead of pooling in a thick circle, it now ran in a red stripe toward the gulping maw of the downspout. When she looked up again, Jack was gone.

A booming thunderbolt shook Jennifer's eyes open, and sitting up in bed, she felt alive with the knowledge that she remembered Jack Edens from her past, and with the certainty that he was involved in Logan's drug dealing and murder. Her breathing grew more regular by the time a brilliant flash of lightning struck nearby and burnt the image of the parallelograms into her eyes.

"Mom!" called Charlie, who by now was also awakened by the storm. There was fear in his voice. Another thunderbolt struck nearby.

"MOM!"

"COMING!" she yelled back in a wavering tone as she threw her covers from her lap. Her legs ached as she felt her way to Charlie's room with red squares dancing in her vision. As the storm peaked, she reached him with a tight embrace that gave them a mutual feeling of security and comfort.

After a few minutes the storm's fury abated, and Charlie relaxed with his head upon her thigh. While lightly scratching his back, she hummed a song from her childhood -- one that her mother used to sing while tucking her in. By the time the song was finished he wasn't stirring, and was breathing with deep regularity. For a minute more she scratched his back, then rubbed with only her fingertips, then stopped. After shifting his head to his pillow, she pulled his shirt down to find the smiling dolphin staring back at her.

And the vivid details of her dream returned.

While tempted to climb into his bed in a reversal of the way in which he, without invitation, often climbed into hers -- she instead rose and made her way out of his room. As the storm spent its fury on neighborhoods to the east, she returned to her room to fetch the baby monitor and key chain. Opening the door that connected to the arena, she was greeted not by dark silence, but by light and the sounds of MTV.

KC's here somewhere.

She squinted beneath the visor of her hand, but saw no one on the field, and headed for her office. After only a few steps she stopped and looked back. Hunched down at the far picnic table in the concession area, was KC. Using his forearms as a pillow, he was clearly asleep, and as she walked near him his snoring could just be heard.

Sorting through her keys, she made for the storage closets that held, amongst other things, the few items of Logan's she still possessed. The box with the prominent L on its side was where she expected to find it, and she rummaged through some LPs, photographs, his high school yearbook, his buffalo nickel collection, and the specific object she sought -- the journal with the black fleur-de-lis on the cover.

Behind her KC snorted, shifted, and resumed his slumber, resting the side of his head directly on the surface of the picnic table.

It haunted her to think that she held one of the last things Logan touched before he was killed, as she recalled there were entries from the very afternoon of his murder. Flipping through the pages until they went blank, she thumbed her way back to the last entry. A variety of numbers adorned the left-hand border of the page, each of them next to what the police had surmised were codenames used to indicate drug buyers. BUSTED NOSE, MR. LIPSMACKER, SHAR-PEI, and the more cryptic THE PREACHER were traits Logan alone had observed and ones that Jennifer, having distanced herself from the unsavory people with whom he dealt, failed to connect to anyone. All about the page other random information was scrawled. Among them were the listing of records he had listened to that day …

Frank Sinatra   *Greatest Hits 1962-1966*

John Coltrain	*A Night in Harlem*
Stevie Wonder	*Songs in the Key of Life*
The Beatles	*Abbey Road*

… mundane descriptions of the weather …

Dark clouds drifted in by mid-morning. Leaves blowing everywhere.

The rain didn't stop until 3PM. The fence may be rotting from the wet.

The usual wind from the west brought the smell of fireplaces.

… all mixed with random lists and information such as the top five movies he wanted to rent, a compilation of the states he had visited in his life, a listing of his teachers from kindergarten through high school, and other miscellany he thought particularly poignant or noteworthy that day. Going back a few pages from the date of his murder, she noted more of the same content that filled his three years' and eleven books' worth of journaling. In midst of her scan, her eyes were suddenly drawn to a word that stood out as if it were the only English word on a page full of Braille.

The day before his death, next to the number 6000, was the codename FRECKLES.

The word seared into her, and stirred all of her past frustration of being unable to give the police any useful leads on who may have murdered Logan. It also instantly transformed the fiction of her dream into something very real, and thumbing back further she found FRECKLES to be one of the most frequent codenames, and associated with some of the biggest numbers on the left side of the page. After a few minutes she inserted into the journal's pages the photo of Logan, tucked it under her arm, replaced the box on the shelf, and shut the storage room doors. While jangling her keys, she walked up to KC as a bouncy acne medication commercial blared from the TV. Clicking off the remote control brought forth a piercing silence she thought sure to rouse him.

But he slept on.

Seating herself across from him, she stared at the long curls of his eyelashes unfairly wasted on a man. As was particularly true of KC, the beauty of one feature was offset by the repulsiveness of another, and in this instance the drool seeping from his open mouth onto the picnic table provided the requisite balance.

"Kase," she whispered.

He didn't move.

"Kase!" she blurted while slamming the journal down on the table.

His eyes popped open, but he otherwise didn't move while familiarizing himself with his surroundings. As his pupils adjusted to the light, his brow furrowed, his eyes blinked a few times, and he used the back of his forearm to wipe the stale wetness from his mouth. His right cheek bore crazy striations from its contact with the wooden table, and only after a minute did he manage steady eye contact with her.

"Oh good. You're awake," she said with a huge grin.

He didn't answer, and instead took the time to stretch his back. He noted from her anxious tone she wanted to talk to him about something important, and he braced himself for some sort of I-met-the-man-of-my-dreams recitation of her evening with Ethan. To his surprise he found himself listening to a lengthy story about Jennifer's past with Logan, his unsolved murder, a found fortune, an unexpected pregnancy, a nine-year period of "moving on", a chance encounter at the arena with Jack Edens, and newly-discovered details in an old journal that revealed a link between Jack and the murder. It was far more engaging than the dream he had been having in which his father had banished him from his house, and he was cast out into a thunderstorm homeless and alone. By the time Jennifer finished her tale he was wide-awake, only managing a soft "Wow!" when she'd finished.

Not satisfied with his response, she asked, "Well, what do you think?"

"What do I think? Hmm. Well … I guess I'm wondering why it is that you're telling me all this."

"Because I want you to help me find out about Jack Edens."

PART III

Chapter 1

From the passenger seat of Logan's Honda, Jennifer reached over to twist on the radio, bringing forth a peppy commercial to rouse her from her catatonia. Only rarely had she and Logan carpooled since they'd begun seeing each other, but since she'd moved into his house riding to their common place of work together had become an automatic part of their morning routine. Sinking back into her seat, she felt the contentment of being an increasingly important part of his life -- a fixture rather than an accessory.

And it felt good.

Disregarding the speed bumps along the winding entrance of Eastmoreland Country Club, Logan drove. He flipped the heater off, and tried to find a station -- any station -- playing music rather than advertisements. He settled for Elton John just as the Honda entered the wide, bowl-shaped parking lot.

Stopping in the middle of the lot, he shifted the car into reverse and put his hand on her headrest. Then he maneuvered the car uphill to his favorite spot far from the clubhouse. Just as the back bumper snapped a branch from a manicured shrub growing beyond the asphalt, dozens of golf balls rushed forth from beneath her seat like a wave upon the shore, surrounding her shoes and backpack, and compelling her to tease him about the messy state of his car.

He smiled and killed the engine, leaving the radio on. "Well, you know it's just so easy to throw stuff in the back when you're in a hurry."

She shifted in her seat to be closer to him and put a hand on his thigh. He looked good in the clothes required of him by the country club, and his dark blue polo shirt brought out the matching color of his sad eyes. His brown hair, trimmed short, was immune to dishevelment as she ran her fingers along his scalp. "What's funny is you don't even play golf."

He paused. "Oh I know, but … you know … I plan on learning sometime."

"Hmm," she said while edging closer and inviting a kiss.

"They say its good for business contacts and all that. I don't plan on being a minion in the bag shack all my life." Displeased by a weather forecast that followed the music, he changed the radio station.

"I suppose," she murmured.

"So, you gotta game tonight?" he asked.

He's too distracted.

Hiding her disappointment, she initiated only a simple peck and disengaged with "Yeah. Eight o'clock at SoccerCity. I'll probably go over to Helena's beforehand." As she pulled her backpack from the floor, golf balls rushed into the vacuum. "Why is it that you park way up here anyway?" Her eyes surveyed the sea of closer spots between them and the clubhouse.

"Oh, I just like to be up high so I can look around. Besides, I don't think Hodge would find *elegance* in someone smoking a cigarette in a car right outside the main entrance."

His reference to the pet word of the micromanaging club president made perfect sense, and put her on her guard. Over the past few weeks Lionel Hodge had routinely invaded her place of work -- the dining room -- dispensing recommendations of how things should be run, checking for cleanliness like a public health official, and even showing disdain for particular items on the menu. Despite all his criticism, the replacement of BLTs with crab cakes was Hodge's lone contribution to date -- the first ripple in the wave of "elegance" he vowed would return to Eastmoreland Country Club during his term as club president.

"Yeah," she said, "I suppose cancer smoke near the entrance would give him an *elegant* coronary."

He gave a cursory laugh. "Yeah, and ... Oh shit! I totally forgot. Close your eyes."

She took her hand from the door handle and complied, a thin smile curving across her face. Reaching across her lap, he opened the glove compartment only to have it bang against her knees. "Sorry," he said, followed by an enthusiastic, "Aha!" The deejay was rattling off numerous traffic alerts, and Logan flipped it off after slamming the glove compartment shut. "So ... I sorta got something for you on the six month anniversary of us going out."

Her smile instantly vanished. "Hun that's not fair! You didn't say anything, and I didn't even get you anything ... "

"You can open your eyes."

Silenced, she saw that he held his hand in a fist. "Jen, just take it. It's not like it's jewelry or anything." Uncurling his fingers, he revealed a small crystalline horse rearing up on its hind legs.

"It's a unicorn," she said with uncertainty.

"A knight actually. As in chess. You can see the felt on the bottom."

But I don't even play chess.

She turned it over to reveal its smooth green fabric on the underside. "So it is. But I'm not sure I … well I'm not sure I get it, hun."

"Well, I know you like horses, and I remembered how you once said your mom got you collecting those plastic horse replicas back when you were a little girl. I saw this unicorn and thought I'd see if you wanted to start a new kind of horse collection."

She stared at his gift, dumbfounded that it was tied to the offhand comment about her childhood made months ago, and never repeated since. At that moment, the last remaining doubt about what she felt for Logan dissolved. She loved him, and all the angst of not having a reciprocal gift melted away.

"Where'd you get it?" she said softly.

"Oh come on now! You know better than to ask that. You think singular chess pieces are just for sale here and there? Let's just say it galloped up to me, poked me repeatedly with its horn, and wouldn't stop 'til I took it home." He placed his fingertip on the unicorn's horn, and in doing so noticed his watch. "Hey, you

gonna be late punching in? Ol' Hodge e checks for tardiness."

"Oh yeah," she said dejectedly. In a more upbeat tone

suggested, "Meet at our spot at nine?"

"You can count on it."

They shared a kiss and she hurried out across the parking

lot while he stayed behind, the beginning of his shift still thirty

minutes away. He studied her as she went, pressing in the car's

cigarette lighter as she fumbled to secure the unicorn within a

small pocket of her backpack. Just as she disappeared into the

employee entrance, he lit up. The cold tobacco crackled as it

burned. Not wanting to let the car's warmth escape, he rolled

down his window only a few inches and smoked leisurely, holding

the cigarette so the ash tumbled down the outside of the glass. The

first cigarette of the morning was always a shock to his lungs, and

when it was done with he rolled the window down further and cast

it into the pristine landscaping behind the car.

In the time since he parked only a few other employees had

arrived, each of them selecting spots on the opposite side of the lot.

Satisfied with his solitude, he reached between his legs to extract a

journal from beneath the seat, opened it to the page that contained notes from the prior night, and set it on the passenger seat where he could consult it easily. He then spun around and pulled down the back seat, and from the darkness of the trunk brought forth his backpack.

Unzipping it, a variety of items spilled forth: an unopened box of sandwich-sized Ziploc bags, six three-ball sleeves of golf balls, a scale, a windbreaker, several golf tees, and a full-sized plastic bag containing dozens of marijuana buds. While taking note of what was written in his journal, he lifted the scale by the handle and made sure the platform below registered no weight. Then he began the meticulous process of creating eighths and sixteenths of an ounce of marijuana buds. As each of the six Ziploc bags were filled and sealed, he paused to scan the parking lot for any movement toward his car.

All was still.

Working as quickly as possible, he poured golf balls into a pile between his legs, and within each empty sleeve he stuffed one of the Ziploc bags. Then he topped each off with one or two balls depending on how much space was left. Feeling vulnerable in this moment and relieved to be done, he closed each sleeve and impaled them with a different colored tee. After tossing everything else into the depths of the backseat, he resolved to dispose of the rolling mass of golf balls as soon as he got home so Jennifer would never again wonder about their presence.

Moments later he stiffly exited the vehicle, his senses alert.

He could see his breath, and his short-sleeved shirt failed to protect him from the morning chill. After locking the car, he heard a soft rush of air behind him. Quickly he turned, only to see a flock of starlings pass just overhead and land on a nearby lawn where they began plucking worms and insects from the sodden ground. His heartbeat returned to normal as he shouldered his backpack, within which lay his balled-up Eastmoreland Country Club windbreaker, six golf ball sleeves each impaled with a different colored tee, and one 35mm film canister that had been carefully prepared the night before.

Throughout the entirety of Portland's eastside, only the Eastmoreland neighborhood could come close to the wealth and opulence so common on the opposite side of the river. For a generations it was the preferred neighborhood of Portland's elite, but as time passed newer developments in the hills west of downtown attracted the city's rich, and Eastmoreland's status was relegated to that of a bastion of old money. Its antiquity and

spaciousness were found nowhere else. Two-story colonials,

mature oaks and maples, and expansive lawns were common in

Eastmoreland; and while no season failed to suit it, the region

possessed awe-inspiring beauty in autumn when the wind filled the

air with a cascading flight of leaves, the smell of burning wood

drifted down the wide streets, and amateur photographers tried to

capture the grandeur of burnt colors against blue sky.

The Eden within the region was Eastmoreland Country

Club, with its circuitous golf course, tennis courts, and massive

white clubhouse. ECC's fairways wound their way through the

neighborhood and back again like an atoll, a crude circle touching

only the grandest of homes. It was the oldest and most expensive

country club in the city, and as if drawn by those twin distinctions,

the profile of the average member was one of extreme age and

wealth. The only consistent youthfulness at ECC -- other than the

children and grandchildren of members – lay within the

employees, all of whom joylessly toiled through servile

responsibilities having long surrendered any aspirations of

affording the luxuries all around.

All, that is, except Logan.

He worked in the bag shack -- the corrugated structure that encompassed the members' golf bags and a stable of ninety electric golf carts. Working in shifts of three, the crew at the bag shack maintained and cleaned the electric carts, loaded and unloaded members' bags, cleaned clubs, and performed any task collateral to a member's day on the course. It was busy, social, and -- as Logan discovered -- lucrative work, having struck upon the perfect mix of service and amicability to garner considerable tips.

And it was chronically unsupervised.

Graham Finnery, a crimson-faced octogenarian tasked with the supervision of the bag shack, favored a hands-off management style that enabled him to spend the bulk of his day drinking in the 'club' room. Through the gin-fueled haze of his daily visit, he never found anything materially amiss at the bag shack, and Logan and the rest of the crew -- intolerant of the inanities delivered within the noxious fumes of his breath -- had long ago taken to lampooning him behind his back. When they tired of even this activity they intentionally dropped a scorecard or a piece of trash to the ground, thereby creating something for Finnery to point out and fulfill his sense of contribution. Only then could he be counted on to retreat to the clubhouse where gin, the stock market ticker, and

his even more sedentary peers awaited his company.

As Logan approached the bag shack to begin his shift, he became

immediately aware of the opportunity that presented itself.

Usually at this time of morning there was a flurry of people, carts,

golf bags, socializing, loitering …

But on this morning -- nothing.

"Dobbs? … Rick? … "

His voice trailed off and there was no reply. As odd as it was,

there did occur moments throughout the day when the bag shack

was unmanned, usually when members sent them on personal

errands or when a cart broke down on the course. Wasting no

further time, he took a final look around and plunged into the area

where the members' bags were stored.

He started with the closest aisle -- the one visible from outside the

bag shack. Identifying a bag from which he recovered money the

day before, he inserted inside its main compartment a sleeve of

balls stabbed with a blue tee. He zipped it up and turned around.

Aside from a few golfers far away on the putting green, all was quiet, and nowhere could be heard the whirr of a golf cart or the crunch of golf shoe spikes on cement.

Hastily filling more bags, he only relaxed upon arriving at the second and more hidden aisle. The last sleeve delivered, he felt around in his backpack for the film canister, locating it only once he removed the windbreaker. The cocaine within had been surprisingly easy to obtain -- and while staring at it in his hand, he calculated that the profit made from this one little canister was more than all six marijuana deliveries today.

"Logan? ... "

He jumped.

" ... Rick? Hey, is anybody here?"

It was Finnery, and from his voice Logan could tell the man was near and coming closer -- into the bag shack itself. Judging there was no time to complete his final delivery, he mentally sorted through his options, but instead did something to which he thought he was immune.

He panicked.

With time to slip it into his pocket or even keep it within the closed confines of his fist, he did neither, and instead tossed it toward the mouth of the closest golf bag. His heart raced as he sent it airborne

-- almost too late -- as Finnery was just rounding the corner of the second aisle. Turning to face him, he heard the awful sound of plastic carom off a golf club and bounce to the pavement behind him where he could only hope it would tumble from sight.

"Where the hell … Oh! … Logan! You startled me!" Finnery said. He clutched his chest as if suffering a heart attack. "Don't frighten me like that, boy! Didn't you hear me calling?"

Logan felt like having a heart attack as well. "I … well I don't know, Mr. Finnery. I just … um … sorry about that."

Finnery, turning pink, stammered before speaking again. "Logan, do you have any idea what would happen if Hodge came down and found the bag shack unmanned? He'd have my head, that's what he'd do! And yours too!" He took a deep breath, spent from the energy exerted in his brief scolding.

He doesn't see the canister, thought Logan. Even at this early hour, he could smell alcohol on Finnery's breath.

"Look, you get together with Rick and that other fellow, and you boys figure out a plan so that at all times there's someone visible here out in front. I don't care what crisis occurs. I want at least one person here, visible, and ready to serve. No matter what. You got that?"

It must have rolled behind my foot, or beneath a bag, thought Logan. His unzipped backpack dangled in front of him. Finnery glanced within the open backpack, a spark of curiosity finding its way through the inebriation. He spied only an ECC windbreaker however, and the spark was extinguished. "And to think! Hodge'll likely be down here any minute. He's playing this very morning you know. I may have to check in on you guys more often," he threatened before turning to walk away. Without warning, he pivoted back toward Logan and pointed beyond him with a finger whose curvature indicated not all was right rheumatologically. "And while you're at it, pick up that trash on the ground behind you." Ashen, Logan turned and gazed at the film canister lying in the middle of the aisle behind him.

With Finnery's departure, the unnatural calm at the bag shack came to an end. Rick and Dobbs returned from their tasks, a few members arrived -- one of them tossing keys to him and asking if he'd retrieve a pair of sunglasses left in a Mercedes -- and he ran off with the canister tucked away in the depths of his pants pocket. He soon became embroiled in his duties and instinctively engaged in some banter with a member, hopeful it would lead to a tip. The adrenaline rush of his encounter with Finnery lessened, and was

forgotten, and soon he noted it was nearing nine o'clock. Without

a word to anyone else, he hurried off to join Jennifer for their pre-

arranged break.

No sooner had he arrived at the side door of the dining room, she

burst from it. "I only have sixty seconds," she announced

breathlessly. Without waiting for any reply whatsoever, she

backed him up against the wall and initiated a kiss that was broken

only when she said, "Turn around and close your eyes. I've got

something for you."

He did as he was told, and crossed his arms and soon felt her hand

as it made its way into the front pocket of his slacks. While

sneaking a kiss was dangerous enough, to be caught fondling one

another on club property was probably grounds for termination.

With alarm he realized her hand was dangerously close to the film

canister lying in the depths of his pocket, but just as quickly as it

had plunged in, her hand left. By the time he spun around she had

disappeared, and the only thing that moved was the closing side

door of the dining room just before it clicked shut.

He reached into his pocket and pulled out a single piece of ECC stationery upon which she had traced the unicorn he gave her earlier in the car. Beneath it she had written:

I Love You, Logan Salinas

-- Jennifer

He pulled out a pen and wrote a return message beneath hers. After folding the paper along its previous creases, he placed it into their secret spot -- the crevasse in the brick wall behind a removable fragment of cement. As he made his way back to the bag shack, his mind focussed on seizing the first possible opportunity to deliver the canister that remained in the depths of his pocket.

"Alice, get the hell in here!" Hodge yelled from his office. His secretary rushed to join him, but warily remained on the opposite side of his desk. Blue cigar smoke hung in the air as he slammed the phone down. "I'll have you know I just called down to the clubhouse, and they informed me my clubs haven't been re-gripped yet. Didn't I tell you to have that done two days ago?

There's supposed to be twenty-four-hour turnaround on these things."

"Yes sir ... Mr. Hodge ... but you see ..." she said as she wrung her hands, "I didn't get to it until that afternoon, and by the time they were sent for, the fellow that works on the clubs had gone home early."

"He had all day yesterday, didn't he?" Hodge angrily reasoned.

"Well sir, I don't know. Something must have happened."

"I'll tell you what's happened! I've got a tee time in exactly five goddamn minutes ... with a prospective member in fact ... and I don't have my clubs ready like I thought!"

"I'm sorry sir. I can't imagine what ... "

Red with anger, he sprang from his leather chair to a standing position. "THIS IS JUST ...!" he hollered, but before saying another angry word, he regained his composure and spoke in a normal tone that seemed almost a whisper in comparison. "This is *just* the kind of screw-up that has allowed this place to slip over the past ten years." He spoke not to his secretary but to himself, and a nod was all she could muster to placate him.

"Never mind!" he snapped. "I'll use my son's. Are Jones and Langston, ready?"

"They just called from the dining room, sir. They said to have you call them when you were ready."

"Judas Priest! They took a prospective member to the *dining* room?!" he bemoaned with a hand held against his forehead. " ... goddamn place is like an old age home with all those gray hairs sitting around in a stupor watching their investments. We'll be lucky if he ... what's his name again?"

"Dr. Anzalone. Dr. Wade Anzalone. He's a cardiologist."

"We'll be lucky if the good doctor hasn't run screaming from the place. Well? Don't just stand there! Call down and tell them I'm on my way!"

A minute later Hodge headed down, with a detour through the dining room to make sure Langston and Jones weren't still loafing inside. By the time he got to the bag shack he noted with displeasure that only two of the three boys were available to assist. Walking up to one of them, he ordered that his son's bag be brought out to their waiting cart. Only then did he join the three men he would be playing with today, and with great effort tried to bury the morning's frustrations behind a veneer of pleasantry.

Chapter 2

Nick Latourelle, sitting in the passenger seat of his Oldsmobile, broke the silence with a few calming statements. "It's okay, Jack. Just calm down and get used to what it's like to sit behind the wheel. We won't start 'er up until you're comfortable and ready." The white car sat quiet and still in the middle of an empty school parking lot. Despite the fact it hadn't been started, Jack's anxiety was so heightened, Nick considered a driving lesson was way beyond Jack's abilities.

"S ... scr ... scared," Jack stammered.

"I know Jack. It's a little scary. Just like a lot of other things in life you do for the first time. Like riding a bike or jumping off a high place into water."

The bike comparison hit home and as Jack recalled his fear of bicycles before he learned to ride one.

"But Mike and I got big plans for you here in Portland, and part of them is for you to learn to drive a car. Understand, buddy?"

Jack nodded.

"We wouldnta brought you all the way out from Prineville if we didn't think you could do it, now would we? Why don't you just turn the key and start 'er up? The car isn't gonna go anywhere. Trust me. Just … turn … the … key."

With his confidence somewhat buoyed, Jack twisted the key and stared at the RPMs which leapt from 0 to the space between the 1 and the 2. His eyes widened as he imagined if the needle ever got to the red area beyond the 6, the car would explode.

"What part's scaring you right now amigo? The engine noise?"

Jack gave a quick nod.

"Look. See how the car is in P right now?" He pointed to the gear display behind the steering wheel. "That stands for Park. P-A-R-K. Get it? P for Park. It means the car ain't gonna go nowhere right now. Even if you hit the gas. Besides, I set the emergency brake before we switched seats. Why don't you press down on the accelerator like I showed you earlier."

Jack declined with a shake of his head.

"C'mon. Just tap the thing with your foot."

Again Jack declined.

A burst of anger pierced the façade of gentleness. "PRESS THE GODDAMN ACCELERATOR, JACK!"

Jack tapped the gas pedal and listened to the bridled power of the engine as it roared from somewhere beyond the steering wheel. While initially terrified to see the needle move toward the red area and the 6, he calmed upon seeing the needle return to the safe place between the 1 and the 2 once he took his foot off the pedal.

"Now do it again," Nick ordered. After a few minutes of alternating revs and idles, he coaxed Jack forward in a more friendly tone. "Whattaya think compadre? Time to go for a spin?"

Jack's meager confidence vanished, and he shook his head from side to side. Driving meant turning over control to the engine, and the danger of the needle going beyond the 6.

"C'mon Jack. This is the next step. You don't want me to tell Michael that you refused, do ya? I think that might make him angry. Don't you?"

Going forward with the lesson seemed like the safest alternative, and Jack indicated he would give it a try. Trickles of sweat ran down his neck.

"Good boy. Now I want you to release the emergency brake there by your knee." Without waiting for Jack to find it on his own, Nick leaned across and touched it with his hand. "Don't worry though, the car's not gonna move an inch." True to his word, once it was pulled and the lever near the floor slammed back into place, the car remained still. "Now, the first thing you gotta do is put your foot on the brake … "

Jack didn't move and looked confused.

"The pedal on the left, Jack. Press it with your foot." Only Nick's helpful fingerpointing directed Jack's attention to the right place, and he placed his foot on it as told.

"Okay, you're pressing down on it?"

At that moment the sun pushed out from the clouds, and Jack was transfixed by a miraculous sight.

"Jack?"

Hanging from the rear view mirror of Nick's car was a prism, and as hundreds of miniature rainbows dotted the interior of the car, all concerns about the engine, Michael's anger, the emergency brake, and his new life in Portland, evaporated. Immersed in the wonders of the rainbows, Jack's trance was broken only when Nick placed a hand on his shoulder.

"What is it?"

"The clol … col … colors … s," he managed, looking down with a grin to find the rainbows adorned even his gray T-shirt.

"Yeah, they're nice, huh? I've had that prism since I was a little boy. My old man gave it to me." He grabbed it with his hand and peered deep within it as if looking for a flaw.

Jack took his right hand off the steering wheel and pointed a bent finger toward the prism. "C … Can I … "

"Hmm? Oh yeah. Sure." Nick pulled his hand away and Jack's took its place with equal reverence. "You know back when I was a kid, my mom told me that when you saw a rainbow, it was a sign an angel was nearby protecting you. That always made sense to me … rainbows being up in the sky and all … pushing the storm clouds away. Then my old man gives me that prism," he motioned at it, "and all of a sudden I had angels all around me whenever I wanted. Er … at least whenever the sun hit it."

With his thumb irresistibly stroking each facet, Jack marveled at the story of the power of the prism.

For five seconds they lost themselves in their separate thoughts, a hiatus Nick broke once he got the impression Jack would stare at the prism all day if allowed. "But enough about that. Why don't we see you actually drive this jalopy. 'Still got your foot on the brake, hombre?"

Jack reluctantly pulled his hand away from the prism, tore his eyes from it as well, and only then set his foot back on the brake pedal.

"Okay now press down on it."

"Pss down," Jack said while stomping on the pedal.

"That's it," Nick exhorted. "Okay now let's ease 'er into drive." He reached over and helped Jack shift the handle behind the steering wheel past R and N where it finally locked in position at the D.

"Now take your foot off the brake *real* slow-like."

The engine sounded different to Jack. He knew that control lay in the brake and in the safety of the P -- and by relinquishing both he was at the engine's mercy. He hesitated, and turned to Nick for guidance with beads of perspiration forming on his forehead.

"Go on now, don't be afraid. You can do it," Nick said with an encouraging smile and a forward motion of his hand. His words rang hollow, but as Jack looked at Nick, he noticed the angels on his face, on the ceiling of the car, on the seat between them, and on his own outstretched arms. In that moment they infused him with a feeling of calm. With angels in the car, he felt he could overcome things. Anything actually.. Once he wiped perspiration from his brow, he gripped the wheel with both hands and eased his foot off the brake. Gradually the Oldsmobile began to creep forward.

"Well, how'd the retard do?" asked Michael upon emerging from the kitchen. He spoke only to Nick although Jack was standing nearby.

Nick hadn't yet grown accustomed to the commonplace cruelty Michael showed toward Jack, and was taken aback at the question. "Uh, Jack, why don't you wait out on the front porch for a minute?" asked Nick, adding, "Thanks" as Jack silently headed for the door.

"I don't know why you gotta treat 'im so nice," said Michael upon flopping onto a tattered chair and taking a long pull from his can of beer. He wiped his mouth with the back of his hand. "We both know why we brought him out here."

Advocacy for the better treatment of Jack rose within Nick, but two days of snorting cocaine and no sleep left him suddenly exhausted, and he knew it would only lead to a futile discussion and what he most sought to avoid -- an argument. He reasoned that Michael had been treating Jack this way all his life, and he knew Michael's capacity to change was even smaller than his capacity for compassion.

Besides he was right.

They had sent for Jack to come live with them only as a means of protection, and how he was treated while he served that role was really not important. What mattered most was that Jack be trained to drive, established as their courier for the delivery of drugs, and positioned to take the fall should the police ever make an arrest. For now there were dozens of details more important. The car had to be registered in Jack's name, they'd have to somehow get him a driver's license, they had to secure a supplier to buy from, and Jack had to be minimally fed, clothed, and healthy if he was to be of any use to them. But first there was the little matter of Jack learning to drive a car, something Michael had never mentioned was so far beyond Jack's capabilities. Until it was mastered, Jack's usefulness was on hold, and he was no more than a cost to them – a mouth to feed. Nick mentally congratulated himself for his one noteworthy discovery of the morning. Jack was responsive to the simplest of courtesies, and he concluded that in comparison to Michael's ruthlessness, a dose of kindness could be an effective tool to get him to do as told.

But no amount of kindness could turn the driving lesson into a success.

Nick relayed to Michael how Jack had to be coerced even to get behind the wheel, how only a few of his starts and stops could be considered smooth, and that many more lessons would be needed.

Michael listened but did not speak or break his vacant stare. Taking a final pull of his beer, he belched, and tossed the crumpled aluminum can onto the sofa where Jack had slept for the last three nights.

"Where's the blow?" Nick asked.

"In the back bedroom. Usual place," Michael responded with disinterest. Then, as if regretting his answer and reading Nick's mind he added, "Don't be taking too much of it now. It's gotta last us."

"Hey, c'mon. It was me who just spent two hours with your dumbass brother teaching him to drive. My nerves is shot."

To Michael, if any argument made sense, it was that getting high was necessary after prolonged time with Jack. He felt relief at not having to undergo the torture of a driving lesson himself. "Go have a party," was his resigned reply. Nick wandered down the hall.

Two hours later he was passed out on the bed in the back room, Michael was asleep on the living room chair, and Jack sat on the porch in search of angels amid the clouds that had blown in and taken the color from the sky.

Michael awoke in the quiet house with unpleasant sobriety. He took the car keys from Nick's jacket pocket and headed out the front door, where he stumbled upon Jack.

"Oh. It's you. Say, why don't you come along with me to the store to get more beer?" It was a command and not a request, to which Jack responded by following in silence. Rain dotted their shirts as they walked the short distance from the porch to the car, where they found the Oldsmobile's windows open and the seats wet.

"GOD DAMMIT YOU GUYS!" Michael snapped. He said nothing more as he wiped his seat with his hand, started up the car, and backed out of the driveway.

Jack broke the silence when he asked, "Where … g … go?"

"I said to the store," Michael snapped, and returned to his gloomy state. He thought about many things, all of them bad. The maddening delay in establishing a contact who could provide them with a reliable supply of cocaine. The impatient customers he had worked so hard to line up, only to have them begin to look elsewhere. The hunger in his belly. The ache of sobriety. And next to him, his brother, whose meekness was as irritating as ever.

Cowed into silence, Jack turned his attention to the prism. Though it swayed as it had throughout the driving lesson with Nick, its magic was switched off, and no matter how long or how hard he stared, not a single rainbow burst forth. Michael parked in the supermarket parking lot and instructed Jack to stay put in the car. Following with his eyes, Jack watched as his brother headed not to the store, but to a pay phone between some vending machines. Turning his attention to the prism, Jack reached out to caress it in the hope the angels could somehow be called upon.

Nothing.

He sighed and looked up from the failed effort, only to see something that made his heart race. Michael's casual posture at the phone was gone, and in its place was the embodiment of fury as he yelled into the receiver and stabbed at the air with his hand. Jack winced when Michael slammed the receiver down. For a while Michael stood facing the phone, his shoulders bobbing with each heavy breath. Eventually he grabbed the receiver again and had an uneventful conversation before disappearing into the store. Five minutes later he emerged carrying a single grocery bag which he took directly to the trunk of the Oldsmobile. After slamming it shut, he came not to the driver's door but to Jack's.

"Shove over. You're driving us home," he announced.

Keys were thrown into his lap, and a panic gripped him as he was forced from his seat into a position behind the wheel. He fumbled with the key ring, not remembering which one went into the ignition. Choosing the copper one, he tried it, but it didn't fit. Before he could gain hold of another, Michael grabbed the keys from his hand.

"It's the silver one dipshit," he spat, handing it back to him with a single key pinched between his fingers. "I'm not happy about your driving lesson, Jack. The way Nick tells it, you had a lot of trouble today."

In Jack's mind, the lesson had gone beyond his wildest dreams of success, but he dared not contradict his brother. "Um, I … "

"You didn't even get out of the parking lot, did you?

Jack shook his head.

"I've got big plans for us Jack. Big plans. In a year or so, I see us driving back to Prineville like kings. Get me? I gotta dream that we go back there and show everybody we made something of ourselves here in the city … not scratching out a living in some shithole like we're stuck in now."

He leaned toward Jack and spoke in a controlled manner. "Part of that dream is for you to be a driver for us. You readin' me?"

Jack said nothing. Sweat ran down his side.

"Drive."

Jack inserted the key and turned it, his bottom lip quivering when the RPM needle jumped. He muttered, "I c … c … can't."

"Oh you c … c … can't huh?" Michael mocked. "Listen. Jack, look me in the eye and listen to me good. You lookin' me in the eye?"

Jack raised his head and looked at his brother for just a moment, but then let his eyes drop. He began to sob.

"It's not … you're not lookin' me in the eye!"

Jack felt Michael's hand grip his jaw and manually turn his head until their eyes met. He didn't resist.

"It's not like you got mom around to protect you and make life easy and simple like before. Life is hard. This is the real world now. And it's my world. And in my world, you can either do things my way … or I fuck you up. Understand?"

Michael nodded Jack's head for him with his hand as he said, "Say yes Jack."

"Yes."

Only then did he release his grip. "Good. Because in my world, things are going to work my way. Now look, I gotta proposition for you." He depressed the knob of the cigarette lighter. "It's real simple. You see the cigarette lighter?"

Jack looked at it.

"You know what it does?"

Jack didn't answer.

"It lights cigarettes. Like a match. You still got that scar on your finger from when we made you touch the cigarette lighter back when we was kids?" As if on cue, the knob jumped with a hollow click, and Michael reached for it, holding the glowing orange coil so Jack could clearly see it. Jack felt the scar tissue on his finger as his face broke into a grimace of tears and grief.

"It's as hot as fire. Probably hotter. Just like when we was kids? You got two choices facing you. You can either drive us home, or you can feel this burn your skin, just like before. Here, let me show you what it can do." He picked up a scrap of trash from the seat and held its corner against the coil. Immediately it burst into a soft flame that Michael let burn almost to his fingers before blowing it out. A wisp of smoke flattened against the roof of the car.

"So those are the simple choices Jack." He moved the coil gradually closer to Jack's face. "Burn or drive? What'll it be?"

With tears running down his cheeks Jack looked one final time at the prism, hoping for the angels. In vain, all he saw was still glass, and with it, the pain that would come from the searing orange touching his skin.

"Drive," commanded Michael.

Jack wiped the mixture of tears and sweat on his sleeve and placed his trembling hands on the steering wheel.

"That's the spirit," Michael said as he fished for a cigarette in the glove compartment. "Whoever said you was stupid has another thing coming. Just don't get us killed on the way home."

He shifted the car into D just as Nick had showed him, lifted his foot from the brake, and the car began to creep forward.

Chapter 3

Dr. Anzalone, sitting in the passenger seat of the golf cart, broke the silence with flattering words about the golf course.

As he spoke Hodge drove, mentally calculating how to respond given that he had already forgotten the man's name. "Yes, we're extremely proud of our club, doctor. It was originally founded in 1911 -- one of the oldest country clubs on the West Coast."

"That right?" was the response. "Oh and please, call me Wade. *Doctor* sounds so officious."

"Very well," Hodge replied. Crisp morning air blew in his face. "I have to say, it looks like it's going to be a beautiful day." Mentally he frowned at the informality of a first name basis, as he considered it one of the thousands of ways the club's prestige had spiraled downward.

"A beautiful day indeed!" the doctor replied while gazing at the blue sky. "I've heard a lot about the opening hole. Water on the right, big trees on the left. It's supposed to be the toughest opening hole in the city."

Hodge at least gave the cardiologist credit for appreciating the course and knowing its distinctions. Much less could be said of the retirees who loafed around the clubhouse and hadn't been out on the course in years. They reached the first tee, and brought their cart to a halt directly behind that of Jones and Langston -- who were always available to court a prospective member if it involved a round of golf. After introductions, Hodge invited Dr. Anzalone to tee off first. "Thank you," was the confident reply, and after pulling a driver from his bag, he ascended the stone steps carved into the side of the elevated tee box.

Hodge took in the moment. Morning fog had lifted, there was a redolence of pine in the air, and dew sparkled as it clung to every perfectly-cut blade of grass. He frowned at Jones and Langston who were sharing a too-loud private joke, and turned his attention toward the tee box.

After a few practice swings accented by the plaintive quacking of a distant duck, Dr. Anzalone said, "Well, here goes nothing … " and unleashed a mighty swing. The ball flew straight and long, much farther than Hodge, Jones, or Langston could equal. As if blessed, it landed in one of the few stripes of sunshine running across the dark green fairway.

"Hell of a drive!" congratulated Jones.

"Farther than any of us old-timers hit it, eh Hodgy?" teased Langston.

"Yes, mighty fine. Mighty fine," Hodge said with a sniff. A stab of trepidation fired within him. He was up next, and as he climbed the steps of the tee box he cursed the fact that he had his son's clubs and not his own. Amid the silence of the morning, he took his practice swings, placed the club behind the ball, and began his backswing.

Bursts of quacking and honking interrupted the quiet morning as Hodge's ball landed with an explosion of water in the midst of dozens of unsuspecting ducks. "I thought you never sliced the ball?!" exclaimed Langston, mocking Hodge's insistence he never mis-hit the ball to the right. Hodge simmered but maintained composure, even as Langston tossed another ball up to him. "Take a mulligan, Hodgy! We all know you had the first hole jitters."

Offended at the suggestion of nervousness, yet unwilling to use his son's clubs as an excuse, Hodge managed a thin smile and teed up another ball and hit an unremarkable shot into the fairway. He stewed while descending to his cart.

Certain that he would be losing more than just this one ball today, he placed the driver back into his son's bag and unzipped the compartment where the golf balls were kept. Fishing around with his hand, he felt around until he found what he sought -- a sleeve of three new balls. He noted the sleeve was oddly stabbed-through by a blue tee, which he removed before tossing both tee and punctured sleeve into the cart.

By the fourth hole, Dr. Anzalone was playing well, Langston and Jones were well into their carefree rounds, and Hodge -- strapped with the handicap of unfamiliar clubs -- was playing far worse than his abilities. He found it increasingly difficult to engage in friendly banter, and by the time he sliced another drive -- this time into a lush hillside bordering the fourth fairway – he'd turned sullen and uncommunicative. He retreated to the driver's side of the cart while Langston hit, grabbed the sleeve taken from his son's bag, and poured two new golf balls into his hand.

Two.

Normally there were three, and peering into the box, he saw something stuffed in its depths.

"You know, this course has a real nice feel to it," the cardiologist commented. "I really like the big trees and the way the … Ho! You know, its been a while since I was in college but I'd say that was a bag of marijuana you're holding."

Hodge stared at the contrast of dark green and brown against the white cabretta leather of his glove, which he then held up for closer examination. "You know … I got this from … the bag … it … it belongs to … "

As if in a trance, he then rose from his seat, plunged the bad into his trousers, and proceeded to the tee where Langston had just hit his shot. He put the pieces together in his mind. The blue tee, the marijuana, where it was found -- as if the bag itself was a vessel of delivery. He hit his best drive of the day, then approached Langston and Jones -- his lucidity rapidly returning. After a brief discussion, he walked back to his cart and explained to Dr. Anzalone that he had forgotten some urgent business, and would need to get back to the clubhouse. He forced a smile, wished him a good round, and shook hands abruptly. With an anger that increased with each step, he marched off vowing to extract the truth from his son within the hour.

Chapter 4

That night after her soccer game Jennifer arrived home, parked in the driveway next to Logan's Honda, and walked back to the curb toward the mailbox. It was one of the simple pleasures of living in a house rather than an apartment -- having your own mailbox -- and she hummed while ducking under the branches of the pine tree whose canopy protected it from the rain as effectively as an umbrella.

Empty.

After flipping the tin door closed she noticed a sizeable pinecone had fallen from higher up and had become wedged between two limbs at human level. Yet another advantage to living in Logan's rented house -- having a fireplace -- and the pinecones that filled their yard and driveway were perfect kindling for the blazes that would warm the house in the coming winter. Reaching up she pried it free, feeling sticky sap on her fingertips.

Making her way to the front door, she alternatively tossed the cone into the air with each hand, feeling the barbs against her fingers with each delicate catch. She reached the door and turned the handle.

Locked.

One of these days she'd get used to the fact that Logan kept the front door locked at all times, even when he was home during the day. For now however, the quirk remained unfamiliar, and upon keying her way in she immediately heard music from behind the closed bedroom door.

He's journaling again.

A more fastidious chronicler she had never known, and though her curiosity was roused now that she saw firsthand how much time he put into his journals, she'd resisted the temptation to read them the first few times she had the chance. With similar respect, she was reluctant to touch any of his LPs, a collection that numbered in the thousands and he said was worth "a fortune".

She headed to the kitchen, stopping to toss the pinecone onto the andiron of the fireplace while walking by. The lights were on above the table where the day's newspaper and mail lay scattered, and absently she picked through the desultory collection of catalogs. Satisfied there was nothing important, she turned her attention to the answering machine where two messages awaited. After a press of the button, she walked to the recycling can where she flung the mass of paper. The first message was from a man who identified himself only as "It's me" and asked Logan to call

him back. By the time the second message was played, she had
her head deep within the refrigerator and was deliberating between
strawberry and boysenberry yogurt. She would end up choosing
neither.

> *This is Lionel Hodge, president of Eastmoreland*
>
> *Country Club. I'm calling for Logan Salinas. Mr.*
>
> *Salinas, I deeply regret that we can't have a face-*
>
> *to-face conversation on the discovery made today at*
>
> *the club. Specifically, I speak of your little ... shall*
>
> *we say ... side enterprise run out of the bag shack.*
>
> *You've betrayed the trust of the club, the members,*
>
> *as well as your coworkers, and while we consider*
>
> *whether or not to pursue this matter with the*
>
> *Portland Police Department, please take the*
>
> *following threat very seriously: If you EVER show*
>
> *your face at Eastmoreland Country Club again,*
>
> *you'll be arrested immediately, and with God as my*
>
> *witness I'll see to it you are prosecuted to the fullest*
>
> *extent of the law. I hope I've made myself indelibly*
>
> *clear.*

By the time the message ended, she'd shut the refrigerator door and was standing next to the machine. To hear Hodge's voice in their home was shock enough, but the civility of his tone mixed with the threat of calling the police baffled her, and led her to conclude some awful mistake had been made. She played it again and when it was finished, headed for the bedroom where Billy Joel was singing about growing up in Brooklyn. She called out Logan's name before pushing open the door.

He sat on the bed in only his shorts, scrutinizing one of his journals. His hair was messed up on one side -- something only a nap could do -- and across the bed were strewn at least a dozen LPs and their jackets. Calmly, he lifted his head, smiled, and yelled above the music, "Hey, I didn't hear you come in."

"Hun, have you listened to the answering machine?"

He walked across the room and turned down the volume of the stereo. "Yeah. I was actually standing next to it when Hodge left his pompous message. That prick. Could you believe his tone?" He took a seat back on the bed, marked the page in his journal, and closed it.

Momentarily off-balance by his blasé reaction, she waited

for him to continue. "You know, I've got a good mind to show up

at the club tomorrow just to call his bluff." As he spoke he stared

off into space, relishing the imaginary clash.

She walked toward him and said, "Logan, would you

please explain to me what the hell's going on?"

He broke from his daydream, cleared a spot for her to have

a seat, and looked her in the eye. He told her almost everything.

How he had begun selling marijuana via the bag shack, how he

developed a system of placing bags of marijuana buds in the golf

bags and receiving payment via the same, how Hodge himself had

stumbled upon a delivery when he borrowed his son's clubs, how

the son had squealed once Hodge confronted him, and how he

talked with the son just before Hodge left his voicemail that

afternoon. The only information he withheld was his recent

progression from marijuana to cocaine.

"In a way I got lucky," he reasoned.

"How's that?" she asked, stunned.

"Well, Hodge has aspirations for his son. He wants him to

go to Ivy League schools and all, and I know for a fact he doesn't

want to make a big scene out of this. He'd go to the police only if he was sure he could keep his son's name out of it … which he can't."

She was dumbfounded. What he told her was startling enough, but his casualness floored her most of all. Fragments of it made sense. Logan had access to marijuana, though he smoked it infrequently. He did have some friends that bought from him on occasion, but this was different. Bigger. More of a business. And it left her with the feeling that he had crossed over from being a casual and somewhat reluctant supplier to friends -- to the entrepreneurial persona of a drug dealer.

"So how long have you been selling pot through the bag shack?"

He mentally calculated and bobbed his head back and forth as he neared an answer. "Approximately?"

He nodded her head.

"I'd say about four and a half years."

"Wow, four years?" Helena asked.

"Four and a half. Basically ever since he started working there. Apparently he's got a nice little nest egg from it. He sold a little bit back in high school too, but nothing compared to what he's sold at the country club."

Helena swirled the ice in her glass as she listened.

"I guess a few of his high school 'friends' had fathers who were members at the country club. Before long word spread and he started supplying dozens of people, mostly members' sons and grandsons. The thing is … I always knew he sold some pot now and then. Hell, every once in a while I'll smoke some myself. I just didn't know he'd made such a business out of it. I get the impression he was making more money from the drugs than he was from his job."

Helena rose from her couch to get herself another Long Island iced tea. "Refill?"

Jennifer agreeably held out her empty glass while crunching on an ice cube. She stretched out on the leather couch, but reclining felt so contrary to her mood, she pulled her knees up and wrapped her arms around her legs in a tight ball.

"So what's he gonna do now?" came Helena's voice from the kitchen.

"He hasn't said. He always thought it was pretty menial to just be at the beck and call of the rich members all day long, so I doubt he'll go back and do anything similar ever again."

"Well I don't blame him. In fact, I can't believe both of you have put up with all that snobbery for so long."

"Aww, it's not that bad," Jennifer responded. She thought it ironic Helena would decry the country club elite even though she and Roy had just moved into a three thousand square foot home and recently hired a maid.

"Well, I just know that I couldn't do it," Helena said. She returned from the kitchen, handed Jennifer a replenished glass, and sat cross-legged on the couch. "So, what's he got, like, a massive pot stash at home? I mean, have you ever seen any sign that he's got a major operation going on?"

Jennifer took a swig. "Well, it's not like he's got piles of pot on every surface, or little plants everywhere. He keeps to himself in the bedroom a lot. You know … listening to his records and whatnot … so I bet he's got whatever supply he has in there. Probably in one of his boxes in the closet, or under his side of the bed. Or maybe in the attic. I don't know … it's not like I've been living there a long time. In some ways, the place feels as unfamiliar to me as your new house here."

"Well maybe … "

"I do have to say though," Jennifer interrupted, "he's always been such a fanatical journaler. I just bet he keeps some drug information in there."

"Have you ever thought to take a peek?"

"Ohh. Lots of times. Especially now that I see him working on it all the time. I used to only be curious about what he's written about me, but now … ", she trailed off. The combination of alcohol, the exertion of their soccer game, and the comfort of the leather couch suddenly made her feel exhausted.

"How's your knee?" Helena asked, referring to the scrape she'd suffered in her game. It was already a grotesque combination of pink and yellow.

"Oh fine." She lifted it up for closer examination. "I think the booze is helping. I'm sure it'll hurt like hell when I take a shower tonight."

"Foot massages?" Helena suddenly suggested.

"You're on."

They set their drinks to the floor, separated from each other on the couch, and put a foot in each other's lap.

"My bunion's absolutely killing me," Jennifer remarked as they started in on each other's feet.

"It cracks me up that you have a bunion" said Helena while examining the foot as would a podiatrist. "It's such an old-lady's ailment. Does Logan ever rub it for you?"

"Oh no. I save it just for you. Does Roy ever rub your feet?"

"Only if I ask him to … which I rarely do anymore. He's so busy with work. Even when he's here at home it seems like he's so preoccupied he's never really got the time for something like that."

"Mmm," was Jennifer's only reply.

"I gotta tell you, I'd be a little cautious …" Helena said as she gulped her drink and set her glass back down on the floor.

Jennifer raised her eyebrows in response, inviting her to continue.

"If drug dealing is that lucrative for him, why would he ever go back to a straight job?"

"Well, its not like he has Eastmoreland Country Club and its client-base anymore."

"Yeah, but … look … I certainly don't know him as well as you do, and I really don't care if he continues or not. It's not like it affects me one way or the other. My only concern is that I don't want anything bad to happen to you. You still love him, right? I mean … this marijuana thing at the country club doesn't change that, right?"

Jennifer paused, nodded that it didn't, and took a sip from her glass.

"Then just be careful," Helena said, stopping the massage and looking her in the eye for emphasis. "If you ever get in a spot, or need anything. I'm always here for you."

"Thanks. But really … you don't have to worry about me. I know what I'm doing. After all, I'm following my heart."

"I know you are. That's what I'm afraid of."

Chapter 5

For Jennifer Scott, the ensuing four years were some of the happiest in her life. Though her normal inclination would have been to worry about the ECC drug scandal for months, the instinct was trumped by Logan's carefree attitude. She loved him, saw her life conjoined with his, and if he found his firing to be of little concern, so too did she.

But hers was an ignorant bliss.

Weeks after Hodge's voicemail, Logan announced he was going into the music business. For years he'd bought LPs for his own collection, and professed it would be an easy transition to become an independent proprietor seeking, buying, and selling music for individuals, store owners, and collectors. He'd travel anywhere in search of a rarity, and his business forays took him throughout the Northwest. In cities big and small he tracked down leads on hard-to-find albums, checked out the inventory of new music stores, purchased entire collections at estate sales, and gained notoriety for his expansive knowledge of rare music. The LPs multiplied, filling the space in the garage that used to house their Honda. Combined with his personal collection kept within the bookshelves that lined most of an entire wall in their bedroom, the total volume of LPs in their house numbered in the thousands.

Because his enterprise was legitimate, Jennifer disregarded signs, even evidence, that Logan continued dealing drugs to more than just his friends. Whenever a sentinel thought leapt from her subconscious, he looked her deep in the eye and explained away her concerns with such sincerity, she was rendered incapable of doubt. Though he was careful to shield his activities from her -- acquiring the privacy of a cell phone and conducting the majority of his transactions while she was away at her new job as a bank teller -- she couldn't help but notice how a single phone call could wrest him from whatever else he was doing, and how much time he spent in the privacy of their bedroom journaling and playing his music. And then there was the time she came home early for lunch and witnessed Logan hastily concluding a transaction on the street in front of their house -- a transaction that appeared to have little to do with music.

On occasion she encountered the people with whom he associated, and found they spanned the gamut. Most were only eccentric or even meek, such as the jittery man with the comb-over – or the silent, freckled man who knocked on her door one

Saturday morning, and silently returned to the white Oldsmobile parked on the street when she said Logan wasn't home.

Others, however, inspired fear.

It could be their size, such as the massive, bloated man with droopy eyes who asked for a private moment with Logan when they ran into him at a neighborhood bar – or the gaunt Hispanic man who argued with Logan at a party and had to be restrained at one point while she and Logan left.

But none of it trumped her love. While under the impression he still made some money on the side selling small amounts of marijuana here and there, she believed it made up just a fraction of his income, a misperception furthered by his tales about the huge profits he made in particular music transactions, and his success at 'putting his money to work' -- as if he had interest and dividends continually compounding. In truth, diversification was an investment strategy for which he saw no need.

For Logan Salinas, the ensuing four years were ones of uncomfortable success. While a judge would not have seen a distinction, dealing drugs away from ECC suddenly felt like a felonious activity, and it initially it nearly made him give it up..

What before was conducted amongst the latest golf technology from Maxfli and Ping now took place in cars, rundown homes, parking lots, and only when absolutely necessary -- his own house. While he occasionally feared for his safety, most of his clients were meager users, and profits made the distasteful interactions tolerable.

And cocaine quickly replaced marijuana. The promotion was made possible when a friend told him about the opportunity; and while the friend ultimately declined due to the increased risks inherent in cocaine dealing, he passed along to Logan information about the tiny woman.

And Logan seized the opportunity.

Traveling the college towns between Santa Clara and Seattle, the tiny woman sold large quantities of cocaine to local dealers, never staying in any city longer than a day. Logan made quarter-pound purchases at first, and moved to full-pound quantities after only a few months. Within six months, his was a significant operation, selling to both addicts and small-time dealers alike.

And Logan found ways to make it even more profitable.

He would have made nearly a thousand each week selling eighth and sixteenth ounce increments alone, but by making his own cuts, adding Vitamin B^{12} and a powdered baby laxative to the drug, he further drove up his profits. He worked his cuts in gradually, arriving at a standard of never selling cocaine that contained more than thirty percent of his own additives -- an amount he gauged was the limit his customers would tolerate without recognition.

And the profits rolled in.

Over time, he expanded his customer base as well, eschewing the security of a static clientele for increased growth and profits. It didn't hurt that the tiny lady made sure to contact him whenever she was in the vicinity, leading to his sudden trips to Corvallis, Salem, Seattle, Tacoma, and Olympia. Lastly, it didn't hurt that he crafted an image consistent with negligible success -- driving a fuel-efficient Honda, wearing simple clothes, and insisting that any cuts to the cocaine came before he took possession.

Continuing to deceiving Jennifer however, proved to be more difficult.

Lying became automatic. He knew there were moments she suspected his drug dealing was greater than the occasional marijuana transaction he conceded, and he became adept at explaining away the phone calls, hushed interactions, and sudden trips that sparked her suspicion. She would have been shocked to know that ten feet from where she slept each night, in the crawl space beneath the house, lay his supplies of cut, his scales, and his most recent purchase from the little woman.

He gave himself two years -- two years to make as much as he could, and then get out; but having accumulated a sum beyond even his most optimistic projections, he kept promising himself he'd quit once he'd acquired just a little more. After the third year, he developed a network of middlemen whose presence eliminated his contact with the drug addicts, and instantly the business became far less distasteful -- more of a business than an illegal activity. After the fourth year he stopped making promises to himself to stop, and devoted all his time to the enterprise. Then one week, unbeknownst to him, the tiny woman began some significant cuts of her own, and he sold a batch comprised of more additives than drug. The addicts noticed and a pair of Logan's middlemen suspected they'd been cheated.

For Michael Edens and Nick Latourelle, the ensuing four years did not lead to the fortune they forecasted. The reasons varied, but none was simpler than their inability to create a significant differential between the amount they paid Logan -- and the amount they collected from their erratic clientele. Within Nick lay only the inclination to satisfy his own drug habit, but within Michael lay a simmering discontent that they'd not emerged beyond the fringe of success in a business where success seemed to come easy to others.

For Jack Edens, the ensuing four years began with the realization that he was indentured servant in a drug operation. His coerced participation initially brought on guilt, but years of exposure to Michael and Nick's customers dulled that emotion. From location to location he drove, gaining comfort with the Oldsmobile, familiarity with the city, and a complacence that there was little he could do but what Michael and Nick ordered. He was no longer repulsed when the packages he delivered were sometimes opened onto countertops, drugs were consumed in his presence, and human detritus lay sprawled on the floors and sofas of the filthy domiciles he entered. He merely drove about the city,

trapped within the simple understanding that his own survival

depended on the apt performance of his duties, and sustained by

the hope that one day angels would descend to rescue him from the

life in which he himself was powerless to escape.

Chapter 6

Jennifer trailed Helena down the stone steps that led into the backyard of the Hamlet -- the Victorian coffee and dessert house they frequented with regularity. While the interior of the house held the allure of bizarre paintings, multicolored lighting, antique couches, and billowing fabrics that crisscrossed the ceiling -- they preferred the backyard when the weather was fair, as it represented to both of them an enchantment. They followed the waitress around the corner near the waist-high statue of St. Francis of Assisi, and found the yard unusually deserted, which was to their liking. Only two tables were occupied. At one, a party of four surrounded an ornate hookah from which they took turns smoking apple tobacco -- the sole flavor featured by the establishment. In a far corner a couple was locked in a kiss of such ardor, the waitress had dared not approach their table to clear the dirty dishes piled before them. Tiny white lights shone everywhere -- woven through the delicate branches of the trees, strung atop the bordering fence, and even randomly through the grass as if spilt from the abundance of stars in the obsidian sky. As they crossed a vast carpet that covered part of the lawn, a formation of geese called out in the air high above, reminding

Jennifer there was indeed a separation between Earth and the heavens.

"I just *love* this place," she said devoutly as they were led to their table.

Helena replied with a different sense of appreciation. "I know. I can't wait to get some of that cheesecake."

They stated their preference for a table with a couch, and before taking a seat Helena pulled from her bag the two birthday presents she carried. She set them between two candles in the middle of the coffee table. One present was a large and shoebox-sized, while the other had the dimensions of a bar of soap. Jennifer studied them and tried to guess their contents from their size and shape.

"You want to open them before or after we eat?" Helena asked.

"After. They're almost like a centerpiece they're so pretty," she replied upon twirling their matching scarlet ribbons.

"It's *your* birthday … "

"First we eat, then presents," she said resolutely.

A light breeze brought the smell of the hookah their way, and sent the lights in the branches to sway above their seat. For the next hour they spoke of trivialities and consumed their cake and lattes. Only a few new customers joined them in the backyard the entire time they were there, replacing the hookah quartet and corner amours with a boisterous pack of middle-aged women and a second pair of young lovers who immediately began making out.

"Someday we're gonna have to try the hookah," Helena said with a kindled sense of adventure.

"Oh I don't know. I suppose. It can't be any different than a bong though. When was the last time you tried one?"

"A bong? High school. But a hookah is totally different. It's so … so … "

" … *sixties?*"

"I was going to say … *Turkish.*"

Jennifer motioned with a nod of her head. "I'm more drawn to the make-out corner myself. Maybe Logan and I need to try out that seat sometime. See what I mean?"

Careful not to be conspicuous, Helena turned slowly to look over her shoulder at the couple. While she did, Jennifer covertly slipped her crumpled napkin in the mug Helena held in front of her, ruining her last sip.

Sucker.

"But enough of that. On to the main event," Jennifer blurted out as the last scintilla of her resistance collapsed. Rubbing her hands together, she leaned forward and extracted the bigger package. At the same time, Helena sat back and intended to finish the last of her latte until with pursed lips she realized she was the victim of her friend's prank. In no time the gift was unwrapped and opened, and Jennifer rose from her seat to hold against her body a full-length black skirt.

"I hope you like it. It's got one of those high slits on the side to show off your soccer legs."

"Oh I love it! You knew I would. It's elegant and sexy at the same time. Thank you so much." With a grin, she meticulously folded it and replaced it in the box. Then she reached for the smaller package.

"This one comes with a story," Helena began. The wrapping was shredded, the box opened, and Jennifer pulled forth a knight. "You know, I've never really approved of your collection … you know, since so many of them are stolen … so I thought I'd contribute a shred of legitimacy to it."

Jennifer studied what she held. It was woven with intricate bamboo reeds with darker thatches for the horse's bridle and mane.

It was worn, but in a way that only added to its look of antiquity, and scrawled on its base were a few letters of faded script she thought could be Thai.

"I'm at a garage sale in the neighborhood … you know, just browsing … and all set up on this ping pong table is this chess set. It looks very old, and the board is made of a dark polished teak. Very pretty. Anyway … it's got a bunch of pieces where the bamboo has rotted or frayed, but this knight was in good shape. I saw it and I just had to have it. I asked him if I could buy the knight off him solo, but he said no. He figured he could never sell the whole set with a piece missing. So I left him my number and made him an offer that if he hadn't sold the set by the end of the garage sale, I'd pay him top dollar for the knight. Well, he called me back that Sunday night … and the rest is history."

"Is it from Thailand?" she asked, pointing to the letters on the base.

"You know, I totally forgot to ask the guy. He was definitely Asian though." Referrign to the lettering she added, " Why don't we just pretend it says TO MY BEST FRIEND IN ALL THE WORLD."

It was a status that exactly matched her own sentiment of Helena. "That sounds about right." They embraced.

"Happy twenty-seven, Jen," Helena said softly in her ear amid the hug they both held for nearly half a minute. Whereas Helena's eyes were closed, Jennifer's drifted toward the kissing couple. Once they separated Helena asked, "So how many in your collection now?"

"I think this makes eleven. Maybe a dozen. I gotta hand it to Logan. He somehow started something with this knight collection idea. Just about all of our mutual friends know about it, and I get the feeling they think of me if ever they see an opportunity to, you know, acquire one."

"Acquire. Yeah. That's *one* way of putting it," Helena scoffed.

They left the Hamlet, and once on the street were surprised to encounter the corner couple that had been making out in the backyard when they first arrived. The duo were seated on the hood of a car -- presumably their own -- parked directly behind Helena's Saab. As they approached, the pair broke their embrace and strolled away hand-in-hand, murmuring to each other a private mixture of words and laughter. The encounter had little effect on

Helena, but left Jennifer with pangs of jealousy, wishing the

spontaneous passions in her relationship with Logan hadn't

disappeared. After another hug Helena departed and Jennifer

watched her drive off. Carrying her gifts to her car parked a block

away, she broke into tears and swore she'd tell Helena about her

and Logan's the next time they spoke.

After unlocking all three locks of the front door and

pushing it open, reggae music spilled down the hallway to greet

her. It was the first time she could recall hearing Logan play

reggae music -- and upon pushing open the bedroom door she

found him sound asleep in bed with the record player on. Cloaked

by the music, she crossed the room to where her knight collection

adorned the top of the mahogany dresser. In the midst of the herd

she placed Helena's gift.

At Logan's side lay his latest journal -- the one with the

black fleur-de-lis on the cover -- and the temptation to read its

contents rose within her. She took a step toward it, but seeing him

asleep and incapable of greeting her on her birthday left her with

an empty feeling, and in her sadness rose an apathy for his music,

his journal, and her desire to spend the remainder of her birthday with him. Leaving the room with the light on and music still playing, she walked to the kitchen with tears welling up from within. She fought them off upon reading the note on the kitchen table.

Your dad called to wish you a Happy Birthday. --

8:10 PM

She picked up the phone and dialed her dad, reclining on the couch while waiting for him to pick up. On the fourth ring, he answered. "Hello?"

"Hi Daddy."

"Hey, baby. Happy Birthday. Did you get everything you wanted this year?" His voice was playful.

"Almost."

There was a silence that amplified the distance she felt from him.

"Daddy?" she asked with a wavering voice.

"Yeah hun?"

Her voice steadied. "Tell me again the story about how you and Mom met."

Chapter 7

The kitchen phone rang, waking Jack from his slumber atop the tattered cushions of the couch. Picking an accumulation of crust from his eyes, he rose to grab it from the wall, answering with the same, "Yeah?" as Michael and Nick always did.

"Michael there?"

The voice wasn't familiar and he didn't respond, torn between the twin dangers of waking Michael and *not* waking him, should he be expecting the call. The ringing had brought forth no stir from the back of the house, and Jack was forced to make a decision.

"Jus minit."

He walked down the hall to Michael's room with the phone in hand, and after a prolonged hesitation, knocked softly on the door.

There was no answer.

He considered retreating or knocking on Nick's door instead, but still fresh in his mind was the beating he had taken months earlier when he failed to pass on a message Michael was expecting, and in Nick lay someone whose kindness had ebbed away, leaving in its place an indifference that now seemed permanent.

He knocked louder and stammered Michael's name, but what came from his mouth was a ragged gasp, and again there was no answer. Left with no alternative but boldness, he knocked a third time, this time kicking the door at the same time.

Through the door Jack could hear the protest of bedsprings, the clatter of a bottle, and a dazed voice coming closer. The door opened, and in Michael's squinting eyes Jack could see simmering anger. Before it could grow he held up the phone, and Michael wordlessly snatched it from his hand. Jack retreated a step, but Michael snapped his fingers in such a way that Jack knew to stay where he stood. He remained within the confines of the dimly-lit hallway, unable to do more than listen to Michael's half of the conversation.

"Yeah? Uh-huh. I know."

"Well it's early … what'd you find out?"

"You're shittin' me! Uh-huh."

"So what you're saying is it's being cut?"

"Yeah."

"Uh-huh. What .. more than half!?"

He held the phone down at his side and looked at Jack wide-eyed, as if viewing an apparition that had materialized behind Jack in the hall. "That mother … fucker," he whispered, and brought the phone back up to his face.

"Yeah, yeah. Shut up for a second. No."

"Now you're sure about this. He didn't fuck up the test, did he?"

"Uh-huh. Yeah. Uh-huh. Okay."

"No, don't worry. Look, I said don't fuckin' worry … you'll get your stuff. Yeah, alright. Bye."

He pressed the button to disconnect the phone and held it at his side, stewing with thought. Jack had seen that look before, and he knew it could recede just as easily as it could build to a rage. Suddenly Michael tossed him the phone -- a projectile Jack miraculously caught -- and ordered him to hang it back up in the kitchen. Then he headed into Nick's room without knocking, and shut the door behind him.

That night, Jack drove the Oldsmobile down the moonlit streets, turning as instructed and parking the car in front of an unlit schoolyard. On many occasions he had been to the nice house a street away -- sometimes alone and sometimes with both Michael or Nick -- but never at night, and never parked a street away like they were tonight.

As soon as he stomped the emergency brake down with his foot, whispers drifted to his ears from the backseat. He checked the rearview mirror.

"Turn the fucking radio on and don't look at us again."

He immediately did as he was told and the whispers disappeared beneath a song. Not long afterward Michael and Nick got out of the backseat, walked behind the car, and disappeared behind the Oldsmobile's open trunk. Not a single person or car moved down the quiet street, and only the soft sounds of the radio kept him company in the darkness behind the wheel. With unnatural gentleness the trunk closed, and after a brief word with Michael, Nick approached his window and indicated for Jack to roll it down.

"Remember, we'll be back in a little while. Listen to me, Jack. It's important that you stay ... right ... here. No matter what you do. Don't follow us, don't leave, and for Christ's sake don't do anything to draw attention to yourself. In fact, don't be gettin' out of the car for any reason. Understand? Not even to take a leak, you got that? Stay in the fuckin' car."

Jack nodded and said, "R … radi … o … okay?"

"Sure, if it makes you happy. Just keep it down. But Jack, what is it you're gonna do?"

Jack took his time, concentrating to get the answer right. "Gon … s … stay."

"And where is it that you're gonna stay?"

"Gon stay r … right here … "

" … in the car. I left them in the car. Of course!" Helena ran from the kitchen and soon returned from the garage with container of infertility pills in hand. Her agitation at being unable to find them was gone, and without delay she headed to the sink to fill a glass of water. By the time Jennifer made her way there, Helena was sobbing. Wordlessly she stroked her friend's back.

Helena gradually calmed and rubbed away the tears on her cheeks. "Oh jeez Jen. I'm sorry. It's just that it's getting to me is all. Two fucking years I've been taking these pills and so far … nothing. I'm beginning to think that maybe Roy and I aren't destined to have a kid."

"Is two years more than it usually takes?"

Helena wiped the moisture from her eyes and dried her hands on her shirt. "Oh, they say it can take more. It's not just that though. I'm lonely here at home all day. I really want this. Roy really wants this. The only thing that's stopping us is that my body won't ... " She trailed off, unwilling to utter words that had brought her to the precipice of another round of tears.

A variety of suggestions came to Jennifer's mind. Adoption. That she and Roy should be patient. How taking fertility drugs could lead to quintuplets. Instead, she only uttered, "I'm sorry."

Helena blew her nose and rallied. "Tell you what? Why don't you make us a couple of drinks. I'm gonna go jump in the shower. Maybe if I wash all this dried sweat off me from the game I'll feel better." She grabbed a handful of tissues and left Jennifer behind in the kitchen.

"What should I make?" she called out.

Helena yelled back, "Surprise me. Just create something from the liquor cabinet. I'll be out in ... "

" … three minutes or so. No more than five. When you hear the commotion, you come on in with the rope and the bat. You just make sure you do whatever it takes to put him down if I'm still fighting him. Got it? I'll make sure the door is unlocked behind me. Got it?"

"Got it," Nick said. He could sense Michael's agitation. "What about Jack?"

"What about him?!"

"You think he knows? He saw the rope and the bat and all."

"That retard doesn't know a bat from a fuckin' golf club. For Christ sake, he even thinks there's angels flyin' around all over the place. Don't worry about Jack. Just worry about gettin' in the door quick when you hear the commotion, got it?"

"Got it."

They walked together in silence before Michael signaled for Nick to hide in the darkness around the side of the house. He made his way up the walkway and pressed the doorbell. Upon getting no answer, he pressed it again. Footsteps sounded from within, followed by the illumination of the porch light. Michael heard a voice call from behind the door, "Who is it?"

"It's just me. I'm putting your drink on the countertop," Jennifer said. She reached into the bathroom and placed the glass next to Helena's contact lens case.

"What'd you make?" Helena shouted above the noise of the shower.

"Greyhounds," she yelled through the opening. She retreated to the bed to lay down and thumbed through one of Helena's scrapbooks -- the one she knew contained pictures of the two of them. Soon she heard the water shut off. Helena emerged, wearing only a towel and holding the glass which was now only half-full.

"You make 'em strong," was her only comment before disappearing into the walk-in closet. Moments later she joined Jennifer on the bed. They began reminiscing about the pictures on each page, but before they were fully engulfed in nostalgia, Helena looked up and said, "You're my best friend, Jen. Thank you. I'm sorry I'm such a mess. I really think it's messing with my hormones, these infertility ... "

" … drugs is a little light. And I been telling 'em I don't know what they're talking about."

"Well I don't know what they're talking about either," Logan responded. After years of dealing with these people he knew not to show weakness, and let his irritation transition freely toward anger. "I just sell what I get, dammit! Nothing more, nothing less! Just like I always told you! What are you saying? 'You saying I've been cheating you? You listen and you listen good … if your people don't like it, then you and them can just get their stuff from someone else! And you don't ever come here again unless I tell you to meet me here, got it?!" He moved closer to Michael, not realizing the danger. "You tell your people they don't like the stuff they're getting, then they can go find some junkie in North Portland to buy from. Got it?!" He placed a finger in the middle of Michael's chest. "Now get the fuck outta my … "

" … house is over three thousand square feet, and I find myself alone in it most of the day. It just gets to me sometimes. I really want a baby."

"I know," Jennifer said sympathetically. She closed the scrapbook.

They said nothing more while they drank, and Helena shifted to a topic she thought would be cheerier. "So tell me what Logan got you for your birthday."

A peck on the cheek.

"Anything good?" Helena added.

She breathed deeply. "Not much. You know your complaints about Roy being busy, never home with you, and distracted by work? Well … Logan's been acting real distant lately as well. For a while actually. We're … to tell the truth we're not doing so good."

"I can't believe you never said anything." After a long pause she added. " How long has this been going on?"

"A few months. Maybe more. It's been building … or I guess 'slipping' would be a better word."

"Oh Jen. Why didn't you say something?"

"Well I sort of thought it would get better on its own. But it hasn't. You know how you always talk about how Roy is busy with his job? All those dinners, golf, and working on the weekend? Well Logan's acting the same way, only he doesn't even have a real job. All he seems to do all day is monitor his investments, travel around to buy and sell his LPs, and write in his goddamn journals. I swear, he's writing in them when I leave, and when I come home it's the same thing. I got home after we went to the Hamlet and you know what? He was sound asleep in the bedroom. No gift or anything. He's been exhausted lately, and later apologized, but it still hurt. This is the same guy who started my knight collection with a gift on our six-month *dating* anniversary."

Helena nodded but said nothing.

"It used to be so different. He used to always give me little gifts, and take me places. He really made efforts, you know? Those days seem long gone. And now ... now I'm not sure if he'll ever ... "

"Come around, Logan. That's it. Come around."

Michael slapped Logan's cheek, helping to rouse him from unconsciousness. The last thing he remembered was the knock on the door, and his surprise that one of the people he sold to -- the fellow with the wild look in his eye whose name he couldn't recall -- was on his front step. Now he saw there was another man ransacking the room. It was then he realized that he couldn't move his arms or legs, and that his head hurt.

"I'm glad you're back with us. Now … don't fade out on me now … " Michael said as he shook Logan's face lightly.

Logan blinked repeatedly, recalling his surprise when the man -- Michael, one of his middlemen -- lunged at him.

"Maybe you can explain to us why you have all these powdered vitamins and shit here in the room," Michael said. "You on a health kick or something?" Nick laughed from across the room while lifting the mattress from the bed. "It seems to me you been cheatin' us. Mixin' in all sorts of things."

Logan stared at the containers he had just pulled from beneath the house when the doorbell rang. Only now they were spilt on the bedroom floor instead of in the closet where he had stashed them before hurrying to answer the door. He remembered getting the upper hand in the chaotic fight, getting atop the man who was strong but slow, and hearing the noise of someone approaching from behind.

"Where's the money, Logan? The way we see it, you been cheatin' us for years. So here's what we're gonna do … "

He could taste blood in his mouth, and felt it ooze down the back of his throat.

"I'm gonna give you a chance to tell us where the money is. The money you been cheatin' us out of. Our money. You tell us where it is, and you get to live. It's simple. Tell us, and you get to live. I really don't think you want this to cost you your … "

" … life was carefree. We used to sneak breaks at ECC in a little alcove and just make out. It sounds so juvenile and yet it was so great. Get this, we even found a hunk of cement between the bricks that could be removed and we would hide love notes for each other. Love notes! I can't remember when we last wrote a love note, or even the last time he told me he loved me. I don't know where we're headed, but it isn't good."

"Do you still love him?"

She nodded her head, and they sat in silent contemplation for a moment, this time with Jennifer wiping the tears from her eyes. "Why can't we just capture in a bottle how we are early in our relationships and save it for later on?" she asked, not expecting an answer.

Helena shook her head. "Oh Jen. That's the million dollar question. There's probably no one alive who knows … "

"Why don't you go fuck yourself," Logan said. He spat blood at Michael. His vision blurred, then sharpened, and with satisfaction he noticed scratches on the man's face, and that his projectile of blood and saliva had hit home. Michael wiped his arm with the ripped portion of the sleeve of his shirt.

"You don't think we'd do it, do you?" Michael asked as Nick continued to ransack the closet. Using the bat as a crutch, he rose and circled behind Logan. "I'm gonna give you to the count of three to tell us where the money is. If you don't, I swing the bat at your head. It's that simple. You don't take me seriously, do …
"

"You okay?" Helena inquired.

"Yeah, I'm fine. So when did you know Roy was the one you wanted to marry?"

"To tell you the truth, I didn't. He really surprised me when he proposed at his parent's place way back when. It was so early in our dating, or at least it was to me, that I hadn't really thought about it by the time he popped the question."

"Well you said yes. Something must have told you he was the … "

"One," said Michael calmly.

"You're wasting your time," Logan responded.

Nick took a break from his search and peered into the room from the closet. "Michael, what the fuck do you think … "

"You're doing the right thing though … asking these kinds of questions and all. I mean, you've been going out for five years now, right?" asked Helena.

"About."

"Is this about a desire to get married or something?"

"Really it's not. I've never set a time table for that. I just want to be moving forward in a relationship … not backward. If Logan and I were at our best at some point in the past … then I want to know that. And if he's done making efforts in our relationship, then I want to know that … "

"Two."

Logan said nothing while Michael placed both hands on the handle of the bat that rested on his shoulder. Nick stopped his search and watched the drama in silence from the closet doorway, certain Michael was bluffing.

"I'm telling you," Logan finally said, "you're completely wasting your time. There's nothing here. Do you think I'd be stupid enough to keep all my money in cash here in the house? Just take whatever drugs you find and get the fuck … "

" … out if you guys are in a spiral you can reverse or not. I mean, I go through funks. I know Roy does. Don't tell me you don't."

"That's true, but do yours or Roy's last months at a time?" Jennifer asked.

"No," Helena admitted. For a while they were silent, before Helena spoke again. "Have you talked to Logan about any of this? I mean, don't you think a five-year relationship deserves that conversation?"

It did, and Jennifer was filled with the desire to speak honestly to Logan about their relationship and what they felt about one another.

"Follow your heart, Jen. That's what you always say, isn't it? That's what I'd do. That's what I did when Roy asked me to marry him out of the blue that one day way back when. So talk to Logan and follow yours. Maybe it'll show you what to do."

"For you it was easier. Either an 'I do,' or 'I don't,' or a 'Let me think about it.'"

"Yeah, but the point is, once I stopped, took my time, and looked at where my heart truly was, it was really easy to pick amongst the … "

"Three," Michael announced with regret in his voice.

"How many times do I have to tell you? I don't have any … "

They were Logan's last words, cut short by the sound of wood cracking against human skull.

Chapter 8

Soon after arriving home and in the midst of contemplating his evening drink, Roy heard a car pull up in the driveway and a door slam. "I think someone's just pulled up," he called to Helena, followed by the suggestion, "Scotch?" Before she could respond to either his observation or his offer, there came a frantic knocking at the door and Helena went to answer it while Roy trailed behind holding two empty glasses in his one hand.

Jennifer burst in.

Roy initially thought she'd been in a car accident, for while Helena held her he noticed blood on her hands and her face. But upon interpreting from her hysterics that something horrible had happened to Logan, he called 9-1-1 on his cell phone and drove to their house on the other side of town. Though he had only been there twice, as he turned onto the street thirty minutes later, a jumble of police cars in a vortex of red and blue light instantly marked its location. He parked eight houses down and approached on foot, making his way past a few robed neighbors blocking the sidewalk. A hatless officer who stood in the middle of the front yard was as much an authority figure as anyone, and Roy approached and identified himself as the one who had called the police. He received a nod of acknowledgement from the officer, and asked about Logan.

The man opened his mouth to reply, but then ushered him farther away from the listening crowd. "He's dead," was the hushed answer, and any further elaboration was cut short by another officer who approached and whispered something in his ear. "Excuse us," the policemen said as they retreated to a position near the front door.

Roy stood alone in the yard while an ambulance pulled up to the house, causing a stir among the onlookers even though its siren and lights were not activated. Two men walked toward the house while pulling on latex gloves, and a series of camera flashes pulsed from the bedroom window. A television news van added to the vehicular chaos on the street, and finally the two policemen finished speaking. Roy approached the hatless officer again, and stole a furtive glance inside the front door.

"Um ... excuse me, officer? His girlfriend? The one who discovered him first? She's at my house."

"Oh good. Right. We're going to need to talk to her. Let me get your address." He flipped open a notepad and led Roy by

the arm back to their prior position in the middle of the lawn.
"What's her name?"

Roy answered and warned that Jennifer was in a state of shock. He asked for permission to get some of her things.

"I'm afraid that's impossible. We're collecting evidence inside. There's nothing more you can do here … *Roy* is it? We've got your info and we'll send an officer over to your house tonight, Roy. Let us take it from here. We've got a lot of work to do tonight if we're gonna catch whoever did this."

Whatever *this* was, it was being fully documented by the continuing camera flashes in the bedroom window, leaving him to imagine the horrors being photographed behind the curtains. He disengaged with a "Thank you officer," put the madness behind him with each step, and called Helena from his cell phone as he walked back to his car.

"Hey, it's me. How is she?"

"Well not very good. She's lying down in the bedroom and I gave her a tranquilizer. Are you at the house right now?"

"Yeah. Me and about thirty cops."

" … and Logan? Is he …?" she asked in a quieter voice that lacked the strength to speak the next word.

He paused at his car and looked back at the patriotic jumble of lights down the street. "I'm afraid he is."

By the time an officer arrived at the Powell's house, Helena had passed along the news to Jennifer. Though she already knew it to be true, it triggered a fit against which the tranquilizer and Helena's embrace were powerless. She cried to such an extent, she became insensate to anything else -- the time (it was almost three o'clock in the morning), the pain in her stomach (which had been getting worse), and her answers to the officer's questions (which were barely comprehensible). She wrapped her arms around her abdomen as she sat on the bed, awash in a permanent tremble.

"I'm not feeling too well."

"Please ma'am, just a few more questions," the officer implored from a chair across from her. "It's of the utmost importance that we get as much information as we can right now. We don't want the trail to go cold."

"Okay," she murmured while rocking back and forth slightly. Beside her Helena rubbed a hand lightly across her back and shoulders.

"Now you say you know for a fact that Logan was involved in dealing drugs?"

She answered hesitantly. "He … yeah, he sold some."

"We found what appears to be a portion of cocaine in a container in the closet, along with some drug paraphernalia. Also a gun. Unloaded."

The news of the gun's discovery failed to register. "He only … Officer … Martinez is it? He only sold some now and then. I'm sure of it."

"Uh-huh. And was there anyone he argued with recently that you saw? Or anyone you think would be capable of doing something like this?"

She tried to stand, but while Helena's hand released her, the officer's fell upon her shoulder, gently keeping her in front of him. "Please ma'am, I know this is hard. But think back … is there anyone that stands out to you at all? Anyone who made any threats? Strange messages on the phone?"

"Really officer, I don't think I can … "

"Anyone at all?"

She exhaled heavily and mumbled through her fingers, "Officer Martinez, I'm afraid you … going to have to … "

"Jennifer, we're on your side. We're just trying to catch whoever did this, but we need you to cooperate."

At the word "cooperate", she lifted her head and covered his shoes with the contents of her stomach.

The police gathered evidence all night and into the morning, concluding the murder was the result of a drug deal gone awry. Helena was allowed to return to the house two days later, and was intent on cleaning it for Jennifer's eventual return. While a sense of dread filled her as she struggled with the front door locks, she found nothing that immediately shocked her beyond some dried blood on the interior doorknob. The house did not smell of death as she had anticipated, and aside from fingerprint dust and some scattered furniture, the kitchen and living room looked completely normal.

But what awaited her in the bedroom was a shock.

It was in a state of wreckage beyond her imagination, and most ghastly of all, in the middle of the room was a hardened stain of what could only be Logan's blood, part of which looked as if it had drained into the heater vent. For a long time she stood staring at the maroon circle, knowing she lacked the fortitude to clean it up with the knowledge he'd died in that exact spot. Commencing

with the room's easier tasks, she couldn't chase the stain from her

mind, and eventually covered it with a rug from the kitchen. Not

once in three hours did she feel in danger as she went about her

tasks, but as she finished two police officers yelled "Anybody

home?" from the open front door, and entered with their hands

tense upon the handles of their guns. Their explanation of

"checking up on the place" struck her as unnecessary, but their

departure left her feeling vulnerable, and soon after their car pulled

away from the curb, she locked up and left.

The days following the murder were a blur for Jennifer.

Logan's parents flew into town to claim his body for a ceremony in

Seattle to which she was not invited, the repetitive questions of the

police officers lessened, and feeling confinement within Helena

and Roy's house, she indicated a readiness to return to the

bungalow to get some of her things. Insistent that both Roy and

Helena accompany her, she trailed behind them as they made their

way from Roy's Mercedes to the house. As if consistent with

Logan's wishes the front door was thrice locked, and as Roy

meticulously undid the bolts and latches, it dawned on her why

Logan had been so manic about front door security, and what a false sense of protection those three locks had provided.

"Where's his Honda?" she managed.

Roy turned his attention from his struggles with the third lock. "Oh. The police took that a few days ago. You know … evidence."

The answer sufficed, and was immediately forgotten while a cold dreamlike state filled her -- a catatonia that worsened as she entered and walked down the unlit hallway. Aware of Helena's cleaning effort, it didn't surprise her that the bedroom was in its original state. Fighting her lightheadedness she gathered some clothes, but unease and then nausea overcame her, and she dropped her things to the floor and rushed to the bathroom. She hovered over the sink not caring what Helena or Roy might see or hear through the open door, and five minutes later the wave mercifully passed. Without saying a word she emerged with a washcloth curled around the back of her neck, and silently picked up her clothes -- only then realizing what the displaced kitchen rug eclipsed.

She had to get out of the house.

Her flight was interrupted at the front door, where, with a hand extended in front of her, she froze, not knowing if any of Logan's blood remained on the handle. She asked Roy if he would get the door for her.

Once outside, she calmly set her things in a pile atop the hood of Roy's Mercedes. From there, it was only a five steps to the nearest section of lawn, where, with her hands on her knees, she completed the act which compelled her earlier rush to the bathroom sink.

It wasn't until the next afternoon that her stoicism returned, and she decided to give it another try. Helena accompanied her while Roy left town on a business trip, and once they'd keyed their way in and made their way to the bedroom, Jennifer mumbled "Oh God … " and took a seat at the foot of the bed. Uncertain if her emotion or her propensity to get sick had sent her there, Helena headed for the bathroom and emerged with the wastebasket.

"Thanks," Jennifer said as it was handed to her, but she sat it on the ground as if unnecessary. Instead she scooted further onto the bed until her back rested against the wall. She held her head sideways, cradled by one of her hands. "You know, this was the last position I saw him in. Sitting up and journaling before I left for work that morning."

Helena knew not what to say, and from the foot of the bed watched her friend's troubled profile. She expected tears, but instead Jennifer broke the pose, leaned far to her side, and struggled to extract something wedged behind the dresser.

"Oh my gosh, it's his journal!"

Helena asked, "What?"

"His journal!" Jennifer added with reverence.

"I don't understand. I thought the investigators took away all his journals as evidence?"

"They did. But I guess they only found the older ones he kept on the floor of the closet. This … This is the last one he was working on though. I'm sure of it. I remember the big fleur-de-lis on the cover." She held it up, but Helena was already coming around the bed and could see the cover for herself. Drawn by the same curiosity Helena plopped down on the bed, and Jennifer opened it to a random page so that half of the book rested atop each of their thighs.

September 4

John Coltraine	*Blue Train*
Carole King	*Tapestry*
The Big Chill	*Soundtrack*
Led Zeppelin	*The Song Remains the Same*

SOMBRERO	*2500*
THE ACCUPUNCTURIST	*700*
FRECKLES	*3500*
OLD SPICE	*130*

The neighbor's goddamn dog is barking again.

It's foggy like yesterday. Probably will burn off later.

Squirrels going crazy in the back yard -- taunting

neighbor's dog?

E-mail mom back about Uncle Frank.

See about calling plan options. Using too many minutes.

Eugene	*Lacomb*
Terrebonne	*Clatskanie*

Bend   *Cannon Beach*

White Salmon   *Corvallis*

In silent synchrony they tried to make sense of the entries, but with each turn of the page gained no clarity and became further lost in the bewildering listings of music, code words, numbers, mundane daily observations and random lists. Page after page it went on in the same manner, some entries consuming multiple pages, some days containing multiple entries, but with no day skipped entirely.

"It's so … " Helena began, but in her befuddlement an apt description remained elusive. "Is this what you expected?"

"Well, no … I mean … I remember him telling me that he always kept a record of the music he listened to each day. Beyond that … I think he once mentioned listing out the details of the records he bought and sold. But those numbers … they can't be right … that is if they mean money. And those … " Jennifer's finger underlined the code words and numbers while slowly shaking her head, " … I just don't get it."

"He's no accountant that's for sure," Helena said, carefully injecting a sliver of humor into the conversation.

"I guess I don't know what I thought he wrote about … just that it would be more, you know, meaningful. Like his thoughts and stuff, maybe poetry or something. Something about me. Or maybe the other extreme, like a detailed ledger or spreadsheet. This is neither." She flipped ahead absently, glancing but not reading, and feeling more numb with the turn of each page. "I just don't get it," she said again as a tear built and hung on an eyelash. She began to shut the journal, but Helena intervened, reaching across to insert her hand into the closing pages.

"Hey, September 29th. Your birthday. Wasn't that the night you said he was playing reggae music and basically slept through most of the evening?"

"Yeah," she said, as Helena flipped it back open. Her tear broke free, catching Helena on the forearm.

"Well don't you see? He didn't list the reggae music he was listening to that day." Helena's finger ran down the page.

Otis Redding	*By the Bayou*
The Guess Who	*Wheatfield Soul*
The Kinks	*Something Else by the Kinks*
Charlie Parker	*Ornithology*

| *A Clockwork Orange* | *Soundtrack* |
| *Fleetwood Mac* | *Mystery to Me* |

Reggae music was nowhere to be found.

Helena moved first, scooting off the end of the bed and accidentally kicking over the empty trashcan in the process. "Oops. Any idea which album it was?"

"What?"

"The reggae music silly," she said while righting the receptacle. "Do you know which album it was?"

"Oh, it was Bob Marley for sure. You know … *I Shot the Sheriff* and all that."

"Well thankfully he alphabetized everything," Helena said after a moment's study. "And it looks like he's only got one here." She used a single finger to pluck from the middle shelf an album between Manhattan Transfer and Dean Martin.

Watching from the bed with the journal still in her lap, Jennifer sat up with the expectation something remarkable was about to happen. But when Helena opened the album and extracted only an ordinary black disk, her attention returned to the journal, and she flipped forward to the day of the murder hoping for something -- anything -- that resembled an answer rather than a question.

"What was it he listed? The soundtrack to A Clockwork Orange?"

"Um yeah. I think," Jennifer answered absently, and didn't bother to look up.

"That's like, the strangest soundtrack to own. Who would even think there was music worth listening to from that bizarre movie." Helena found it on the top shelf under 'A', and pulled it free.

"Mmm yeah. I know," Jennifer mumbled.

"I mean … it was all so violent … and that creepy scene where they held that one guy's eyes open and forced him to watch …" Helena went silent, and after a lengthy delay said, "Um … Jen?"

"Yeah?" Jennifer replied without looking up.

"I think we're in trouble."

Jennifer lifted her head to the sight of her friend, rigidly holding A Clockwork Orange album cover. All about the hardwood floor in front of her lay bills of multiple denominations.

"A lot of trouble," Helena added gravely. She reached down to pick one up for Jennifer to see.

That's a one hundred-dollar bill.

It dawned on her what Helena had meant by *trouble*. Logan had likely been killed for the money Helena had stumbled upon, money likely not limited to what lay on the floor, money that could be in any number of record jackets.

Money they could come back for.

She felt the fear of a horror movie heroine who realizes a serial killer has been lurking in her attic all night, and from Helena's wavering voice she knew the feeling was mutual. Tossing the journal aside, she swung her legs from the bed and got to her feet. Her instinct was to flee the house, but before she could act, Helena began counting the money aloud.

"One hundred, two hundred … "

Jennifer approached the bookshelf, careful not to step on any of the bills Helena was gathering up.

" … six hundred, seven hundred … "

She looked for Fleetwood Mac amid the collection, but couldn't find any of their albums.

" … eleven fifty, twelve hundred, twelve fifty … "

Grabbing a random LP from the top shelf, she could tell it was of unnatural weight and thickness even before opening it.

" ... thirteen ten, thirteen thirty, thirty fifty, thirteen seventy! There's almost fourteen hundred bucks here!"

She cracked open the compartment that normally contained the record, reached in and pulled out several loose one hundred dollar bills. Pinning the jacket between her elbow and ribs, she counted out nine hundred dollars -- aloud, just as Helena had -- only then peering down at her friend to say, "And there's a bunch more in this one alone." Together, their eyes strayed to the bookshelf, crammed to the last millimeter with over a thousand LPs.

"What should we do?" Helena croaked, her voice breaking with resurgent fear.

She had no answer. While the money represented danger, the fact that it was midday represented safety, and they agreed the first thing to do was make sure the front door was locked. Once all three locks were fastened, Jennifer felt the return of her nausea and headed for the bathroom -- this time closing the door behind her. Alone for the moment, she waited for her stomach to settle and weighed her options. Calling the police was the right thing to do.

The law-abiding thing. The safe thing. They would want to know about the money, and about the contents of Logan's last journal. Yes, it was definitely the proper thing to do. But then again, hadn't the police already concluded that the killers took whatever they were looking for? Hadn't that even made it into the newspaper article Helena had read to her? Hadn't she overheard a detective at the police station refer to it as an 'open and shut' case? And hadn't she seen consistent apathy from the police, leaving her to doubt their investigation would be thorough, or even undertaken? Ultimately, only one person in all the world was worthy of her total trust and faith, and she waited for her on the other side of the closed door.

She opened it, and found Helena sitting on the bed, looking as if her stomach churned as well.

Helena stood. "Jen, I'm really fuckin' scared. Let's get the hell out of here."

Grasping her by her shoulders, Jennifer felt a foreign strength course through her. "Listen to me Helena. I'm scared too. God knows I am. This is gonna be really hard, but I need you to be strong and do something for me. I want you to back the Saab up as close to the front door as you can. I want us to load the LPs up and get them out of here ASAP. It's daylight, and I can't imagine anything happening to us. But we've got to get it all out of here now, before … " she stopped herself, certain it would not help to forecast the return of the murderers, " … well, as soon as possible. Will you help me?"

Helena said nothing. She shook her and broke the question into pieces in order to get an answer. "Will … you … help … me?"

"Okay, but you're gonna have to do it Jen. I don't think I can drive right now." With that, she held open her trembling hand, within which lay her key chain.

After scanning the street and gaining a fragile confidence that no one was observing them, Jennifer backed the Saab as close to the front door as possible and popped open the trunk.

Nothing to it.

Upon re-entering the house she headed to the bedroom and grabbed her gym bag.

"Wh … what's that for?" asked Helena.

"In case anyone should see us, you know, the police or whoever. I want it to just look like we're packing up or something."

She felt galvanized by a strange strength, and took it as a sign that hers was the right course. Without saying another word she headed out to the Saab where she placed the gym bag on the hood while Helena began the task of pulling LPs from the long bookshelf.

Together they made several trips with as much as they could carry. On several occasions records tumbled to the floor and bills fluttered from individual LPs, but eventually the sight of cash at their feet became commonplace, and like pieces of trash they crumpled them up in their fists and deposited them into the trunk and backseat. The only moment of alarm came when Helena crossed the threshold of the front door with her last armload, only to hear the sudden squeal of brakes in front of the house. She let out a scream as the records slipped from her grasp, bounced off the car's rear bumper, and disgorged twenty-dollar bills to the cement of the driveway. Having heard the scream, Jennifer ran out the door thinking she would find Helena in the grip of multiple thugs, but instead saw Helena had reacted to the sound of the mailman who had pulled his boxy vehicle up to the curb. Listening to his headphones, the mailman stuffed his deliveries into the mailbox oblivious of clean-up. After the final armful was cast into the trunk, they slammed it shut and Jennifer went back to lock the front door while Helena waited by the car.

A new stab of panic coursed through Helena as she heard a motor from the street, and stood paralyzed as a sedan drove toward them at a menacingly slow pace. However Jennifer read her thoughts, and gently reached for her arm and whispered that it was just her elderly neighbor, Mrs.Klarc. Sure enough, within the car's interior could be seen a tuft of white hair barely the height of the steering wheel.

Helena laughed, fracturing the synthesis of fear and tension that had rendered her motionless. Feeling capable of driving, she took her keys from Jennifer's hand and got behind the wheel.

It was only then, when they were on the road, that Jennifer succumbed to panic.

Thinking there could be drugs within the LPs, and fearful of both the police and the killers at this point, Jennifer kept an eye on the traffic behind them -- muttering to herself when particular vehicles changed lanes suspiciously or followed in their lane for more than a minute. Though Helena was spared Jennifer's concern that they could be transporting drugs, her anxiety grew once she saw the worry on her friend's face -- a stress that abated only once there could be no doubt theirs was the only vehicle on the sapling-lined street of Helena's home. By the time the garage door closed behind them, Jennifer alternatively wept and laughed from the strain, while Helena stroked her hair until the sobbing stopped.

"I need a drink. How 'bout you?" Helena offered.

Jennifer nodded, and broke away from the soft caress to wipe her eyes. "You have a tissue?" she sniffed.

"Inside."

After a silent whiskey sour in which Jennifer twice rose to scan the street from the living room windows, they relaxed and made light of their unraveling composure from the moment the first bills fell from *A Clockwork Orange*. After Helena had made them each a second drink, they agreed on what to do next. Carrying their glasses with them, they made their way back to the garage where Jennifer inquired, "Ready?"

"Ready," answered Helena.

Over an hour later Logan's LP collection had been unceremoniously dumped upon the guestroom floor. Helena had polished off her second drink, though Jennifer had taken just one sip of hers. Helena offered, "Freshen yours?" as they walked back to the kitchen.

"Actually I've hardly touched this one. Could you dump it out and replace it with some water?" As Helena reached for the full glass, Jennifer plucked an ice cube with her fingers and tucked it in her mouth. "Tummy trouble you know."

Helena emptied the whiskey sour into the sink. "Well my *tummy's* fine, but my arms and back sure as hell are gonna be sore after today. How about yours?" She nearly tripped when she opened the refrigerator door into her leg.

"Mmm," Jennifer said with a shrug.

"Ouch!" Helena said while rubbing her shin. She then picked through the contents of the freezer. "Well then … what's next?"

"I haven't a clue." Jennifer thought while chewing the ice cube into oblivion. "Wait. Yes I do. I know what I want to do." She moved the shards to the space between her teeth and the inside of her cheek. "How much time do you have?"

"All day," Helena replied with a glazed grin as she mixed another drink for herself. "As usual. Why?"

"Because I want to count it."

To Jennifer, counting represented therapy -- but not just as a monotonous activity to distract her from the events of the past four days. The money represented the truth. She could get her hands around it, touch it, value it -- and as she dove into the task she pondered what else Logan kept hidden from her. Whether or not he even bought and sold rare LPs. At what ratio he sold marijuana vs. cocaine. Whether he even had friends that were not in some way connected to drug dealing. Whether he considered her safety as he plumbed the depths of his new found profession. Whether he loved her.

Helena intended to help, but three drinks had left her impaired, and she instead reclined on the guestroom bed to sip and observe. Jennifer first emptied the LPs of all contents, finding that the majority of them contained money, and less than half contained records. A few were empty, some contained both money and records, and to her relief none contained drugs as she had feared during their cross-town drive. Eventually there were three segregated piles in the room -- a mountain of LP jackets near the door, a pile of black discs thrown in a far corner, and a cartoonish stack of money on the bed at which Helena gaped.

As if sorting laundry, Jennifer next pulled handfuls of cash to the floor and began parsing them into mounds. While some bills looked as if they had just been printed, others were so deteriorated she was almost reluctant to touch them. Most were in hundreds, fifties, and twenties, but there was a smattering of fives and ones as well, some change, a buffalo nickel collection, a gold chain, and some Canadian currency. Once the sorting was done, Helena retrieved a pad of paper and a pen from the kitchen, handed them to Jennifer, and the count began.

Gradually, each pile was reduced and reconfigured into stacks on the floor, and by late afternoon the task was finished. With her hands on her hips and a pencil behind her ear, Jennifer stretched her lower back mightily. "Okay, the grand total is … " she said while walking on her knees to the bed upon which Helena lay. She took a sip from her friend's glass and grimaced. "Ugh. Care to take a guess?"

Helena stared drunkenly at the rows of money and tried to fathom the value. "Really, I couldn't even … "

"Okay, I'll just tell you." She kneed her way back to her notepad. "According to my calculations, what we are looking at here is eight hundred and sixty-four thousand, two hundred and twelve dollars and eleven cents. That's counting the Canadian

dollars."

Helena stared at her with incomprehension. "Could you …

say that again?"

"I said that's counting the Canadian dollars."

Helena gave her a vapid look, and Jennifer laughed at her

friend. Then she repeated the figure.

"As in … almost a *million* dollars?"

"Well not quite … but … yeah. Nearly, I guess."

"I'm gonna need another drink. Sure I can't get you

another?"

"I'm sure."

Helena was certain she'd have had an accident on the

freeway had she known there was nearly a million dollars of drug

money in her car. Even now, drunk and safe in her home, it was

unreal to contemplate such an amount, and she burst into soft

laughter while pouring another drink. The porcelain clank of an

uplifted toilet seat resounded from two rooms away, and her mind

flashed to the image of Jennifer saying "tummy trouble" while

holding her stomach. Reaching for her daily dose of infertility pills, she stood staring at the bottle while the sound of Jennifer's

retching filled the house.

Minutes later Jennifer emerged from the bathroom to find

Helena walking toward her and carrying something behind her

back.

"God I swear, my stomach's a … What?"

"Well, I've got a little something for you. Care to guess

what it is?"

"A trash can."

"No."

"A breath mint?"

"No."

"A piggy bank that can hold eight hundred thousand

dollars?"

"No."

"Then I give up."

Helena brought her hand out from behind her back, and

gave Jennifer one of her dozens of pregnancy tests.

The next day Jennifer gave the journal with the fleur-de-

lis to the police, hopeful it would lead them to the killers. She sensed disinterest, however, when she handed it over, as if it was a hindrance to the case rather than a help. Particularly troublesome was how the detective on duty didn't even bother to crack it open upon delivery, and instead led her into a room adjoining his office where he merely set it atop a box filled with dozens of Logan's older journals.

"We still have to go through them all," he explained, "but once we do we'll let you know what we find. If nothing comes of them, we'll call so you can come down to the station to retrieve them. That is if you like. Oh, and I'm glad you came by … " He reached for an evidence bag and unsealed it. "Here are some of the things on his … well that he had with him when we found him." He handed her Logan's wallet, silver ring, necklace, watch, and comb. "I don't suppose there's any chance you want his clothes?" he asked hesitantly.

She shook her head and buried the items deep within her purse without examination, knowing they had the power to shatter her temporary stoicism. Quickly she changed the subject. "So you'll call me once you've study it?"

The detective looked confused.

"The journal? You'll let me know what you find?"

"Oh yeah. Absolutely. We'll get right on it. Thanks for bringing it in," he said while ushering her out of the room.

Certain Logan's last journal held information helpful to the case, she persisted with two weeks worth of daily calls to whichever detective she could get on the line, with each conversation finding out more about Logan than the identity of the killers. Logan's gun, the existence of which she had never even been aware, had been at one time registered to a man with a long list of drug and weapon charges. Of the fingerprints taken in the house, three matched people who were on file with the police department and whose alibis were being checked. Programmed into Logan's cell phone were literally dozens of people who were considered worth questioning, though none of them was considered a primary suspect.

As the days wore on, her concerns about the lack of progress in the case gave way to thoughts about the baby, and she called to tell her father the news.

She feared the pregnancy, coupled with her announcement of Logan's violent death, would result in the backlash of being disowned. But if he harbored any negativity, it went unspoken, and instead he offered only his concern and support. He even encouraged her to come back to Phoenix to get away from it all, rest, and have the baby in the environment of her extended family and childhood home. Compared to the turmoil into which her life had veered in Portland, his offer shone with the promise of tranquility and security, and she needed little coaxing to accept it.

"Oh, and dad?" she asked somberly before hanging up.

"Yeah hun?"

"I uh … I just wanted to say thank you."

He paused for such a long time before replying, she wondered if the line had gone dead. At last his voice leapt forth with understanding of her unspoken meaning. "I love you too baby."

A month later she was gone, torn from the city she called home and the once-happy life into which a pathogen had crept, metastasized, and killed. Apart from the memories held by her friends, the only evidence of her time in Portland lay gathering dust on the shelves of the closet in Helena and Roy's guestroom. Amid Roy's old suits, cases of wine, board games, and Helena's wedding dress, lay fifteen boxes. Seven contained her things, seven contained Logan's illicit fortune, and one -- a box marked with an L -- contained the items on Logan's body when he took his

dying breath.

Chapter 9

She named him Charlie, and for more than a year following his birth, they lived in Phoenix in a world free from the nightmare of the past. It was a dreamlike existence, where joy came from the actions of a creature as helpless as a kitten, where the support of her extended family knew no end, and where the details of Logan's murder blurred with each passing day. But for all the escapism of her time at her father's house -- the spacious security, the stable of willing babysitters, and her father's offer to facilitate employment at one of the companies with which his accounting firm had connections -- she knew her fate and her future did not lay in the city of her childhood. A few months after Charlie's first birthday, she returned to Portland to live with Helena and Roy and their new baby boy, Jonah.

It was an uncanny symbiosis -- providing Jennifer with free rent, Helena with assistance in the art of child rearing, and the boys with constant playmates. Even Roy benefited, finding the house filled with a boisterous energy to which he was attracted; and as much as his personality would allow, he shifted some of his career energy toward home. In their communal arrangement the two infants were doted over, Helena established a workout regimen for their return to soccer, and Jennifer -- with Logan's drug money idling in the closet -- began to wonder how the next chapter in her life would unfold.

Within the first two weeks of moving in, they sat Roy down and informed him of the boxed-up fortune. At first he was shocked, but then to their mutual relief he responded with an interest in what Jennifer was going to do with the money. The thought of nearly a million dollars devaluing on a shelf struck him as an atrocity, and he advocated the financial advantages of investment. While his advice made sense, the most persuasive part of his hour-long tutorial were the three sentences he devoted to the impossibility of buying anything significant with boxes of cash whose origin was beyond explanation.

It was an aspect of the fortune she hadn't even fathomed.

Armed with the amalgamation of her own banking knowledge and Roy's investment advice, she spent the next year legitimizing the fortune. Depositing it at levels low enough to draw no suspicion, she put some of the money into an assortment of interest-bearing savings accounts, and plowed the rest into dozens of annuities, CDs, stocks, and other tax-free investments hand-picked by Roy. With no immediate need to spend the money, she contented herself with letting it grow, knowing it could be liquidated once it occurred to her how best to use it.

But for years, no such epiphany occurred.

"Why don't you buy a house with it?" suggested Helena one day as they sat on lawn chairs and watched their sons play in the shade of the backyard.

"You know, I could. It'd be sort of like a home and an investment all in one. Part of me says that's a good idea, but another part of me … a much bigger part … says this is an opportunity of a lifetime. An opportunity to *define* my life. Somehow buying a house just seems so … ordinary."

"So what is this great destiny? Do you even have any clue what it could be?"

"I only wish," she said while freeing a bug Charlie had managed to capture in his hand.

"Maybe it's a restaurant? You know, a cool place catering to the hip crowds and the nightlife? Maybe some place with a bar? Or maybe a place like the Hamlet? That'd be so cool!"

"Yeah right. Like I know the first thing about running a restaurant. I don't exactly think my country club waitressing days qualify me. Besides, don't half of all restaurants fail in the first year?"

"Yeah. Something like that," Helena conceded while handing Jonah his juice cup. "Well you know all about banking and investments. Can't you do something with that?"

"It's really Roy that knows about all that stuff. Don't get me wrong … I'm learning. But really I just follow his advice. I was only a peon teller when Logan died. Besides, it's not like it really interests me. And really, what would I do? Open the Bank of Jennifer Scott?"

Helena's face went blank.

"Sorry. I don't mean to put down all your ideas. They're all good. Really good. It's just that I'd rather wait and not take a chance on something that *could* be my destiny. It's gotta jump out at me, say 'Take me!' and strike me as so convincing, it's not possible to deny it. I'm sure I'll know what it is when I see it. I just have to keep my eyes open."

"So it'll just come to you … this idea? You don't have to go out there looking for it at all?

"No. If there's one thing I'm supremely confidant of … it's that my life is leading up to something. I just know it. It's something that I can't even see right now. Something I have no concept of. I just have to wait and be ready to pounce on it when it comes around the corner. I'll wait for years if I have to."

And for years she did.

Even after moving into her own apartment, Jennifer and Charlie's integration with the Powells deepened. With few job skills beyond that of bank teller and waitress, she left Charlie with Helena during the day and accepted an offer from Roy to work at his commercial real estate firm. She started as a secretary while learning the business, and after a few years became an assistant to one of the firm's top agents. It was boring work, filled with forms, faxes, and only the occasional interesting client; but it expanded her breadth of job experience while Logan's fortune churned through the cogs of capitalism, swelling to over a million dollars.

Seven year's time began to erode her romanticism about fate and destiny however, and the idea of spending at least part of the money on a house for her and Charlie gained a persuasive place in her mind. On a random Monday morning after dreaming of the small but cozy houses in the neighborhood where she and Logan used to live, she secured the phone numbers of a few real estate agents recommended by her connections at work, unaware that fate

stirred with a different plan that morning.

No sooner had she picked up the phone to call one of them,

Roy approached at her desk looking more harried than usual. "Get

your coat."

"Hmm?" she replied while hanging up the receiver.

"I said get your coat. Barbara just called in sick.

Something about a migraine. I checked with Georgeann, and she

said I could borrow you for the morning. I'm meeting a guy at the

place on MLK in ten minutes, and I need someone there with me to

show him around. You know, make him feel like a bigshot."

The place on MLK was a term synonymous with defeat at

their firm, as it had been listed for ten months with no takers.

While it was in the warehouse district, had good freeway access,

and boasted considerable square footage for storage space, its

detractions held more weight. It leaked, had poor lighting, was

dusty with disuse, and generally didn't "show" well. In addition to

its liabilities, it had a key structural handicap in a steep entryway

with multiple stairs -- an impediment to the transportation of

anything sizeable to or from the structure.

"I swear, the day we took on this turkey was a mistake. I can hardly get anyone to look at the place, let alone buy or lease it." As he drove he dialed his cell phone to see if the client was at the location already. Worried about his distracted driving, Jennifer wordlessly took the phone from his hand while he steered his Mercedes through traffic.

I'll dial. You just drive, Mario.

"Thanks, it's the number on the bottom," he said as he handed her a business card with multiple phone numbers scribbled on the back. "The place used to be a roller skating rink, beginning back in the fifties. Then ... get this ... after it shut down, it was reopened as the same thing, but only a gay version. Sort of a part nightclub, part roller disco thing. The place had a cult following for years. A fruity Xanadu, I guess. Anyway, you can still see where the rink was, oval and all."

She finished dialing the number, handed him the phone, and listened to his half of the conversation while staring out the window at the vacant lots and warehouses. Once he finished the call he resumed his lamentations. "Anyway, it's a real low-end place. Probably on its last legs, and really only good for storage ... or those late night rave parties where all the kids get high on ecstasy. It'll be nothing short of a frickin' miracle if we can move it. Personally, I don't think the gay history helps its cause one bit, but I'm sure Mr. Marofski here … ", he motioned to the man standing outside the building as they pulled up, " … knows nothing of its past. So let's just keep that little tidbit from him and his two thousand vending machines, shall we?"

"What tidbit?" she replied coyly.

"Exactly"

After a brusque greeting from Mr. Marofski, they entered the structure only after Roy defeated an inauspiciously stuck front door.

"You know," Roy offered, "Frank Lloyd Wright used to intentionally design his homes with nondescript entrances so that as a person made their way inside, the house would appear to open up for them."

Sensing Roy's tension, she kept quiet and tried to relax by counting every step of their twenty-seven stair ascent, passing wallpaper turned jaundice with time and a boarded-up ticket window whose glass was cracked from top to bottom like a lightning bolt. They passed through a series of double doors and made their way into the vast structure.

"Hmpf. Too bad I seek no such fancy house," was Mr. Marofski's lone retort. After only three steps, he flinched, snared by a tendril of cobweb that tangled about his scalp and shoulders. Polish obscenities filled the air, and Jennifer had to look the other way in order to prevent her laughter.

As conversation resumed between the men, she took note of what surrounded her. The place was in need of a Herculean cleaning, and even though it was listed as empty and unused, crates and other debris were strewn across the floor. There was a long countertop on the far side near what appeared to be a dance floor, and behind it, even more space. In the dim light she could discern the oval of the former roller rink, and its shape uncannily reminded her of the dimensions of an indoor soccer field.

And in a flash she saw it. All of it.

She gauged the beams that striated the air twenty feet above the ground would be an impediment to high, booming kicks. But the bar area was perfect. It could be converted into a concession area, the dance floor could be removed, and the space in the back was even big enough for an athletic store or a full restaurant.

Hell, you could even live in the back space if you ...

" ... Isn't that right Jennifer?" Roy asked.

"Oh without a doubt," she added automatically, hoping to sound neither preposterous nor servile.

"Bah! I just do not think so," said Mr. Marofski. "How must I get my machines in and out?" He flailed both his arms toward the entryway while a flagellum of cobweb trailed from each sleeve.

"Well, I can see how that might cause a problem, but with a little ingenuity and maybe a ramp in the front, there's no reason to think … "

"For the time, I thank you," he said with straightforward rudeness, and didn't bother to wait for an escort back out to the street.

His capacity for pleasantries exhausted, Roy said nothing, simply watched the man storm out and whispered, "Have a nice day!" once he was out of earshot.

Good. He's gone.

Roy produced his cell phone and began dialing a number.

"Roy, about this place … "

"I know. A nightmare isn't it? The only way this place gets sold is if I had a time machine and could instantly make it

nineteen frickin' fifty-two all over again. I mean, I'm ready to …
"

"Roy."

" … throw up my hands and say 'I surrender' on this one. Even on my best day I don't think I could … "

"Roy!" she snapped, cutting short his rant.

"What?" he said with surprise.

"Would you put the phone down and just shut up for just one second!"

He stood in stunned silence, unsure of what was coming next.

"How much did you say this place was going for?"

He pocketed his phone, gave her the figure, and followed it up by smiling and asking playfully, "Why? You wanna buy it or something?"

A chill ran down her back as she gazed around. She knew. It was no accident that she was standing in the middle of a warehouse and was able to see possibilities to which all others were blind. It was no accident that she had been called to fill in for a coworker who had called in sick. And she knew she had been right all along to hold onto the money until the right opportunity came around the corner, jumped out at her, and screamed, "Take me!"

She said nothing, and instead focused her look upon him, letting the irrepressible smile on her face answer his question.

PART IV

Chapter 1

Fighting off the frustration that built with every word, Jennifer listened to KC while picking at a knot in her shoelace. He listed off the things he'd learnt about Jack Edens, but the longer KC talked the more she realized he'd discovered very little. From the information he *had* found out -- which restaurant he worked at, that he washed dishes and had done so for years, that he was somewhat of a loner, and that he used a bicycle to get around -- it was clear that his stint as a private detective resulted in of little use. When he baselessly concluded that Jack was Logan's killer, she stopped him.

"And that's all the information you found out?"

"Well yeah. That and he's got a game tomorrow night."

"The schedule told you that," she said, having checked it herself just the other day.

"Well … yeah. I guess that's true."

"And when you went to Rudy's Diner, what did you find out?"

"Hmmm … I have to say, they make really lousy fries. You know, the big wedge kind? I prefer the fast food ones that are thin, skinless, and … "

"Come on Kase! I'm serious."

"Nothing! I didn't find out anything. It's not like I could just march back to the kitchen to hang out. I'm not even sure he was working the time I went. Now that you mention it, I'm not even sure why you wanted me to go there in the first place."

"I guess … well … I guess I don't know what I thought." In truth, she had such reverence for KC's capabilities, she imagined he'd have wrangled a murder confession from Jack by now. It dawned on her that her expectations had been unrealistic. "Kase?" She paused long enough to make sure he looked up and their eyes met. "Thanks anyway for trying. I owe you one."

"I'll remember that."

She finished tying her shoe, stood, and began stretching while preschoolers and their parents concluded the 'Little Kickers' class on the field.

"So tell me the truth. Am I getting any better?" he asked.

"Compared to your first lesson? Without a doubt. The more you practice, the more you'll be ready to join in a game.

That's the real test … when you're in a game. It's there you'll have to deal with the pressure of people charging at you, bumping you, and that sort of thing. But you've come a long way, that's for sure."

He grinned throughout the compliment.

" … despite your shoes."

"Hey!" he said, taking mock offense. "I won't have you talk to Hansel and Gretel that way."

She looked down at each of them as he stepped onto the field. "Cute. I hesitate to ask, but which one's Hansel?"

"The ugly one. So what's next?"

A whistle blew, and parents and children gathered in a huddle where they yelled "Soccer!" to conclude their class.

"Well, I say we kick it around for a half an hour like always, and then I'll play goalie for a while so you can … "

"No. I mean about Jack Edens. What's the next move?"

"Oh." She thought for a moment. "Well, I guess I'm really left with no alternative but to confront him here … I guess tomorrow night. Maybe in private and after his game so he doesn't have the distraction of all his teammates like last time."

"Do you want me to be there too?"

She visualized KC sitting beside her and glaring while she asked Jack about Logan. "The thing is … I don't want to scare him. I want this to come off casual. Tell you what ... what time is his game?"

"I forget. Let me go check." He ran off to consult the printed schedules posted near her office, and ran back just as urgently, darting between the children and parents who were streaming off the field.

"Eight-fifteen."

"Okay, so they'll be done a little after nine. You'll be here?"

"Of course."

"Okay, here's what we'll do … I'll get him alone with me in my office. I guess I'll just ask him if I can talk to him privately or something, take him back, and I'll lay it all out for him. How I remember him … who Logan was … the whole thing. I want you to watch from outside the office the entire time. You know … inconspicuously. And whatever you do, make sure Charlie doesn't know what's up. We both know he's got enough bothering him about his dad right now. I'll get him in bed by eight-thirty and I'll give you the baby monitor and the keys to the back. It'd be just my luck that he'd have another nightmare while I'm talking to Jack."

KC listened and nodded with attention.

"Now let's synchronize our watches," she added.

He actually lifted his forearm up, but alas -- it was not adorned by a wristwatch, and his intensity was broken by a pursed-lip smile that said *you got me*. "You should show Jack that photo of Logan you showed me. You know, that big eight by ten?"

"Maybe I will … and now that I think of it, maybe I should see if Helena can make it too … just to be safe. If he jumps me or something, I'm gonna want you in there as soon as possible, so just sort of hang out near the video games so you can see us through the window. Got it?"

"Got it."

"Got what?" inquired Charlie from behind.

"Got it … that KC's gonna have to get some shinguards so he can play in a soccer game some day."

"Mom, that's not what you were talking about."

"Hey bud, any more bad dreams last night?" KC asked.

Charlie calmly shook his head. "No, not since that one about my dad a few nights ago."

She didn't even know what dream Charlie and KC spoke of, and marveled at the secret relationship the two of them had built.

It takes a village to raise a child.

"Well *I* had one last night, and it was a doozy. It started out with me … "

As KC elaborated about a dream in which he jumped from an airplane only to find he wore no parachute, she admired the deftness of his change of topics, and wondered if his skill was natural or was learned from watching her own interactions with Charlie. The story soon ended with KC's miraculous escape from certain death, and she backed further out onto the field while coaxing KC to follow.

"Game on, Kase?"

"Game on," he confirmed.

She addressed Charlie. "You want to join us hun? We're just gonna kick it around a little."

"No. You know I'm no good at soccer."

"Well, neither is KC … but you don't see that stopping him, do you?"

"Mom, I don't want to."

"Okay hun, but just know you're always welcome. Did you finish your fractions homework?"

"No."

"Well why don't you go do that."

She thought having to choose between homework and soccer might propel him to opt for athletics, but instead he marched off and disappeared through the doors that led to the back. "I woulda never thought any kid of mine would choose fractions over soccer," she said as a series of *zaps!* signaled the departure of the last participants of the preschool clinic.

"And I woulda never thought the SoccerCity folks would want to buy us out."

How'd he know that?

She'd said nothing of her conversation with Preston Richardson, and had deflected Helena and KC's questions after Preston left. While Helena had probed no further, KC sensed deception, and had taken several stabs at what it all meant -- coming closest to the truth with this latest comment about SoccerCity buying her arena.

"Yeah right," she deadpanned. Part of her felt comfortable sharing with him her strategy in dealing with SoccerCity, but another part of her knew she would never hear the end of it if he knew the extent of their conversation. She offered nothing more while increasing the distance between them and kicking him the ball, and sure enough he transitioned to a new topic moments later.

"So … do we have a green light on the fourth of July party?"

"Yeah I suppose. Weather permitting," she added in reference to both the rain last year -- and the current day's downpour that showed no sign of stopping. "Charlie won't be talked out of it, even though I think the fire escape could flip him out just like it did last year. I'm trying not to pressure him though."

"Can I bring a date?"

"Sure, but try to limit it to just one. I'm thinking I want to keep it the size of last year's disaster. Oh, and I guess … you know I'm not really sure how to say this Kase, so I'll just come right out and say it." She looked around to make sure no one could overhear and closed the gap between them until she could speak without raising her voice. "I haven't told Charlie about you being gay, so just make sure that … well you know that he doesn't see any sort of … well anything that would … "

"No blow jobs on the roof. Got it."

Her embarrassed smile said *you got me*. "Yeah, something like that."

"Speaking of sex, you gonna invite your new man Ethan?"

"Yeah. I'm thinking him *and* his girlfriend."

"Oh! I didn't know. Sorry."

"Me too. It's all very … let's just say … it's complex."

KC let the topic die and they spaced themselves farther apart again and resumed kicking the ball back and forth. Sparked by KC's comment about her "new man", thoughts of Ethan took flight in her mind. While he had resumed his attentive ways, fobbed off his abrupt departure after their return from the Eastbank Tavern as a case of being "late for curfew", and had dropped by on a few occasions other than his scheduled games -- something was missing. There was no mention of the confluence of their sentiments, and worst of all, no attempt to steer their interaction in the direction of their prior intimacy. It was as if time had moved backward, and only in a dream had his heart surged forth to overcome his resistance.

Maybe I'm giving off the wrong signals.

Could he have changed his mind?

Maybe he's not even thinking about me.

I wonder if he's dreamt of me since?

She meditated on these and other uncertainties while wordlessly kicking the ball back and forth with KC, an exchange as natural to her as a game of catch to a baseball player. The grip of her thoughts wasn't loosened until KC was sent chasing down the ball near the Snoopy goal, where he stopped in his tracks, turned, and called out to her.

"I think we're in trouble!"

They were the exact words Helena had uttered so many years ago when she first discovered Logan's drug money in the LPs, but there was no scattered fortune on the Astroturf. KC was merely standing still with his hands on his hips and his attention drawn to something near his feet. By the time she approached him however, it was clear what he meant. Darkened green near Hansel and Gretel was a patch of water the size of a manhole cover, and every few seconds a new drop of water completed its free fall from the interior of the roof.

Fuck. A leak.

"What should we do?"

"Well … I don't know. Why uh … why don't you go get something to catch the drips."

KC ran off to the concession area while she stripped off her T-shirt, balled it up, and placed it on the ground to absorb as much of the water as possible. By the time he returned with an empty pitcher, the T-shirt was sopping wet.

"Nice bra. Victoria's Secret?"

"Lady Foot Locker."

He placed the pitcher in the middle of the stain and tossed her the shirt, which she put back on despite the unpleasant feeling against her skin. Together they stared at the ceiling as the drops began to form a layer of murky water in the bottom of the pitcher.

"I don't think this is a good long-term solution," KC said.

"I have to say, I agree. What do we have … forty-five minutes until the next game?"

"About that."

"You wait here. I'll be back with something bigger. And if you're able to think of a solution so that we can play our games tonight … any shinguards you want are on the house."

With her incentive left to turn the gears in his mind, she ran off to the back while weighing whether to bring out her kitchen trash can or her largest stewing pot. She opted for the pot. While wrestling with lids, pans, and other kitchenware beneath one of their countertops, Charlie dutifully worked on his fractions homework at the kitchen table amid the clatter. Just as she managed to pull her stewing pot free Charlie asked, "Mom? If my dad were still alive, would we be living here?"

She rose from her crouch and kicked shut the cabinet door. "Oh … probably not, hun."

"How come?"

She contemplated not answering, mindful that with every two-second delay another drop of rain had penetrated the roof and was in a freefall toward the pitcher. "Well, I just think things would have worked out differently. Chances are I wouldn't have been working at the company that was trying to rent this place, and your dad and I might not have agreed on this as our home."

"Oh," he said, giving her answer a thoughtful pause. "I wish he was still alive."

"Me too hun," she said while taking a step toward the arena.

"Because if he was we'd be living somewhere else."

She stopped and turned. "Charlie, I'm getting sick and tired of your attitude about our home. I saw the way your classmates reacted when they saw where you live. Heck, even *you* got excited showing them around. I don't understand how it can be that you truly dislike this place so much."

"It's just that I get scared mom," he said with a troubled expression. He turned his attention toward his homework and began vigorously erasing.

"Scared of what?"

"Just everything." He swept bits of eraser from his paper. On the verge of tears he added, "It's just ... everything."

She moved closer to him. "Charlie, if this is about being afraid to go up on the roof for the Fourth of July party ... "

"No mom, no! That's not it! I'll make it up there this year, I'm sure of it."

"Is it those homeless people we sometimes see on the sidewalk?"

"Sometimes."

"Do you feel like we're in danger living here in this neighborhood?"

"Sort of."

"Look Charlie. I've got a leak in the roof that's dripping onto the field right this instant, and the night's games start in less than an hour. When you figure out what you think it is, you let me know and we'll talk about how we can work on it together." She edged toward the arena again.

"Mom? Jonah asked me if I could spend the night at his house this Saturday."

The grip of her impatience eased. Setting the pot on the kitchen table, she pulled out a chair and took a seat next to him. "Charlie … look at me for a second … "

He did.

"Hun, the worst part about your dad dying isn't that we could be living in the suburbs like Jonah. It's that you don't have here on earth another person that loves you as much as I do." She ran her fingers through his hair. "You're just like me hun … having only one parent. Except you lost your daddy before you ever got to know what it was like to have him love you. I remember what it was like before my mom died, and let me tell you, it was wonderful. She'd hold me in her arms, scratch my back with her long fingernails, and tell me fantastic stories I never knew were real or made-believe. When I think back on it now, it was like a dream and a fairy tale all in one. After she died, it was all gone, and my dad couldn't fill her shoes. No one could've really. I'd have given anything to go back to having two parents to love me."

He was listening, but his eyes had drifted back to his fractions.

"But at least I had one, and so do you. Some kids don't even have that."

There was a silence between them as they fell into the labyrinth of their own thoughts. It was only broken when Charlie blew bits of eraser from his paper.

"And yes Charlie, you can spend the night at Jonah's on Saturday night." She slid the pot from the table and started for the arena, but his voice beckoned her from behind yet again.

"Mom?"

She stopped but did not turn around. "Yeah hun?"

"You're not just one parent, you're more like one and five eighths."

She ran back to the field, relieved to find the pitcher only partially full of dirty water. Nonetheless, KC scolded her, "Jeez, what in hell took you so long?"

"Sorry. A little unexpected conversation with Charlie."

"Mmm," he said with a nod, having experienced Charlie's capacity for asking questions with the power to ensnare.

"Come up with a solution yet?"

"Let's put it this way … I'm partial to those blue Adidas shinguards with the silver stripes on the front."

An hour later, the first game of the night was being played thanks to KC's improvisation. Using the Flexlift and a staple gun, he attached two of their four plastic tarps to the ceiling in such a way that it channeled the drips from the field to a spot near the entryway stairs. There, they fell into the plastic trashcan normally used for recyclables. While it made for an inauspicious sight for all those who entered the arena, it left the field playable, and KC took the remaining tarps outside and up the fire escape to try to thwart the water from the other side of the roof. She offered to help but was turned down, and instead remained behind to watch the start of the night's first game with relief and a renewed appreciation for KC's industriousness. Far across the arena, she could make out people's bemused reaction upon entering the arena and avoiding the recycling can. Into the snack bar sink she poured the cloudy water from the stewing pot, and headed to her office resigned that there was little more to be done about the roof for now. Gathering up the scattered knights from her desk and gingerly placing them into the empty pot, she calculated there was time to arrange them in Charlie's room while he finished his fractions at the kitchen table. As she plucked them from the varied locations, her eyes drifted toward her computer screen, where in the upper corner she saw a flashing envelope that indicated new e-mail.

As always, she tried not to get her hopes up, and was vindicated when she found it only to be an inquiry from a parent about her son's lost jacket. There was nothing from Ethan, and weary of waiting for him to make the next move, she took the initiative to extend to him an invitation.

FROM: *evilsoccermom@epis.org*
TO   *eharrington@hotmail.com*
TIME: *05:23:17 PM*
SUBJECT: *DOING ANYTHING?*

Ethan. Haven't heard from you in a while. I wanted to let you know that I've got a free night coming up this Saturday (Charlie doing an overnight at a friend's house), and I wanted to see if you were up for doing anything. Let me know. Am pretty sure I can get KC to watch the place.

Jennifer

PS ... You're frustrating me.

She pondered a few changes, but then decided that her words were the right mix of desire and honesty -- and hit the SEND button with a burst of bravado. Giving her one last chance to reconsider, the spellchecker flagged the word 'Ethan' and suggested it be replaced with 'Euthanasia'.

Chapter 2

The next afternoon Jack Edens stood in front of his inoperable Oldsmobile and stared at the mass of dark clouds boiling in the eastern sky. Though brilliant blue loomed overhead, it was obscured by the intersecting tangle of branches from two nearby oak trees; and every few minutes when the wind picked up, spoonfuls of rain were loosened and fell to the ground below.

"Hey Jack, pass me the Phillips screwdriver, would ya?"

Jack heard nothing but the wind. From the parking lot behind his apartment building, he had a clear view of the retreating storm, and could just make out a faint rainbow against the gray. Somewhere, not too far away, the angels had descended to Earth.

"Hey Jack … when you get a second," called the voice again from beneath the hood, "I really need that Phillips. I've got this screw in place and I don't want it to slip."

Jack's attention was roused not by the man's voice but by the open hand suddenly thrust in his direction, and he tore his eyes from the sky. An assortment of tools lay between the man's feet, and recalling the word 'screwdriver', Jack reached for one and placed it in the open palm.

"Thanks. I think we're just about … No! I said a Phillips! The one with the black handle."

Jack scrambled to find the right tool while the wind dislodged more gobs of water from above. By the time he handed over the one with the black handle his eyes were back searching the sky, but by then the rainbow had disappeared.

"Well that ought to about do 'er," called the voice, and from beneath the hood emerged the part-time cook with smears of grease marring his yellow Rudy's Diner T-shirt. From where he had been working an impeccable battery shone next to a tangle of grimy pipes, tubes, and belts. "Why don't you try to start 'er up?"

"K … Kay," Jack said softly as he felt the pockets of his shorts for his keys.

"They're in the ignition Jack."

With a nod he headed to the driver's side door that only a two-handed pull forced open. The hinge squawked with protest, and a smell of rot and mold escaped from the car. Uneasily he took a seat. The jagged edge of the ripped upholstery pressed upon his shoulder blade, and as he shifted to lessen the irritation springs within the seat creaked and popped. Just before he twisted the key, he noticed the crack in the windshield -- the one that used to remind him of a spider -- was now the size of his hand.

Beads of sweat formed on his forehead.

With the engine's roar, an impulse jerked his left hand from the steering wheel; but the part-time cook yelled "All right!" over the noise, and the remembrance of his ancient fear of the engine faded. Upon revving it twice he let it idle and tried the radio. Just as the first notes of an unfamiliar song crackled from the back speaker, his eyes gravitated toward the cigarette lighter, knowing it was infused with the same power that had reanimated the engine. He reached out to check the knob for warmth, but through the scar tissue of his fingers there was no heat, and no indication of its potential as a weapon. From his memory came the image of Michael wielding it -- the enflamed coil glowing brighter as it was brought closer. He extracted it from the console with a tentative hand. Just as it came free, the part-time cook slammed down the hood, and Jack fumbled it to the floor of the passenger seat. He leaned over to pick it up, touching only the black knob and not the metallic cylinder. An ember of pain pricked at his stomach.

"And just think, with my free labor, you only had to spend half of your one hundred dollars," called the part-time cook as Jack emerged from the car.

"Uh-huh," Jack agreed with a forced smile that ended when the exhaust cloud made him cough. After a simple exchange that concluded with a boisterous "See you at the game!" the part-time cook carried his toolbox back to his car and Jack was left behind with the Oldsmobile.

More dislodged rain peppered his shoulders and head.

He walked to the dumpster outside his bedroom window, and with an underhand toss cast the lighter into its depths where it clanged against the empty bottom with a metallic echo. In the window of his apartment hung the slowly spinning prism, and drawn to it, he stood on his toes to free its fishing line from the nail. It was dormant within the shaded aperture, but once in the sun, flecks of light shone against his skin in numbers equal to his own freckles.

And the pain in his stomach disappeared.

Aware of nothing but the prism, he made his way across the parking lot to the Oldsmobile, and delicately hung it from the rear view mirror just as Nick had years ago. Twisting it to the right as far as he could, he released it to unravel, twist anew, and unravel again until it finally bobbed in the space above the cracked dashboard.

He turned on the radio and pulled his door shut with two hands. Even with the car started and in gear the Oldsmobile didn't move; but once he'd remembered to release the emergency brake, it crept from its six-month parking spot, exposing a rectangular carpet of moss. Unaccustomed to driving, he pressed too hard on the brakes. An accumulation of leaves and twigs lurched from the roof of the car to the hood, and the prism pitched forward to collide with a *clack!* against the windshield. With relief he took it in his hand and observed it was not damaged in any way.

"I … promise, t … tl not h … happen again."

He gently lowered his hand until the fishing line caught the prism's weight, and lifted his foot from the brake. The Oldsmobile eased past the sidewalk and into traffic. With a caution that resulted in a pace well below the speed limit, he made his way to his soccer game via the exact route he was accustomed to taking on his bicycle.

Chapter 3

By the time the Rudy's Diner game was five minutes from concluding, Jennifer had put Charlie to bed, KC had notified everyone in the concession area that he wouldn't be available for a while, and Helena had arrived to handle the baby monitor responsibilities -- a presence that ensured KC wouldn't be dragged from his post outside the office at a critical moment. As the three gathered in a tight huddle near the video games, they spoke secretively, not wanting to be overheard by anyone passing by.

"This'll work out great," KC said, "because Helena and I can pretend we're just having a normal conversation right outside your office."

"I'll leave that up to you guys," Jennifer said, wasting no time directing her next comment to Helena. "It means a lot to me that you're here. I'm totally in your debt."

"Don't be. This is important. Do you have Logan's photo ready?"

"It's on my desk."

"Three minutes left," interrupted KC, who was monitoring the digital clock far across the field. He turned to Jennifer. "So you have it all down? What you're going to say to him, I mean?"

"Well, I don't have anything scripted. I'm just going to slow down, take it easy, and try not to frighten him." She let out a deep breath. "Actually it's me who's frightened. I can feel myself shaking."

"Well no wonder," said Helena. "You've spent the past ten years putting it all behind you, and now it's like … " An errant shot rattled the Plexiglas, causing both women to jump. " … it's like being thrust back in time. Just keep in mind your friends are quite literally just a few steps away."

"And believe me, that means everything," she replied. "But I'm still scared."

"Two minutes!" KC called out.

"Kase … really … that's not helping."

"Okay, I'll stop," he apologized.

"Hey. Listen to me for a sec," Helena said to her in a whisper as a group of people passed nearby. "Remember when we found all Logan's money, and I was a total basket case as we carried all his LPs to my car?"

"Like it was yesterday."

"Well I've never told you this before, but I thought you were so composed that day. There you were, just days after

Logan's murder, and in a situation we both thought was filled with danger. I was so scared … I don't even think I was able to back my car up to the house … and in the hallway I passed you with your flippin' gymbag! You were heading out to go put it on the hood of my car to make it look to anyone passing by like we were packing up some of your everyday things. I remember at that moment thinking you were stronger and cooler under pressure than I'd ever given you credit for."

"Yeah, and you'll recall I broke down in the car later when … "

Helena shook her head. "The point is, when you *had* to be, you were strong. Stronger than me. Stronger than almost anyone would have been. Compare that to now. What lies ahead is only about asking some questions. You're faced with *less* danger, *less* to fear, and *more* support from your friends. Besides, we don't even know if Jack was involved."

"Oh yes we do!" said an eavesdropping KC.

"You know, you're right. You're right about all of it. There's just one thing that's complicating things compared to back then."

"What's that?" asked Helena.

"I've got Charlie now."

"Okay boss, you're up," KC said just before the sound of the buzzer rang through the arena.

"Okay," she said. Taking a deep breath, she turned from Helena to see a scattering of yellow and aqua jerseys coming off the field. "Game on," she muttered with uncertainty to both of them.

"Game on," they responded in unison as she took her first step toward her encounter with Jack.

She spotted him on the field almost immediately, a mop of red hair standing out among players shaking hands at midfield. Arriving at the benches well before him, she waited while he accepted congratulations and slaps on the back from nearly every one of his teammates. Eventually he made it near her and she resisted the urge to pounce, opting instead to let the crowd thin while he gathered up a few of his things and toweled the sweat from his face, neck, and arms. When he was done and players from the next game were moving onto the field, she stepped in his path just as he attempted to move past her.

"Jack?"

He stopped and looked down at her.

"Hi. Remember me? Jennifer? The owner of this place? We kicked the ball around and talked for a little while the other week before your game?"

He nodded. "Y … You and th … th … boy."

At first she thought he was referring to KC, but then she recalled Charlie had come onto the field that day with his ripped homework. While Jack's remembrance of Charlie was unsettling, she maintained her friendly tone and revealed nothing more about Charlie or the unease his recollection caused. "Hey, if you have a minute, I'd like to talk to you for just a little while. In my office if that's okay with you."

"K … kay," he said after a considerable pause and a glance at his teammates.

"Great. Just follow me. My office is right over there," she said while directing him toward it. His resistance overcome, he followed her. In an attempt to calm him she asked a question whose answer she already knew. "So, did you guys win?"

"Uh … " he said while glancing back at the scoreboard and wiping sweat from his face with his shirt. "One to s … s … six."

"Oh. Too bad. It's still fun though, even when your team loses, isn't it?"

He didn't answer, and his silence continued as they walked past Helena who was listening to KC talk about how he'd had to unclog the men's bathroom toilet earlier in the week. They entered the office. She turned to him and tried to make her words sound casual and pleasant. "Well, Jack, you remember when we talked that time before, and how I said that I thought you looked familiar? That day we kicked the ball around?"

He nodded.

"Please Jack … have a seat."

A series of *zaps!* sounded, causing him to look about the office anxiously. He set his gym bag on the floor next to the chair and sat down. She was silent while closing the office door partway -- enough to give them privacy, but not enough to feel like an entrapment. Moving to the opposite side of the desk, she sat on the edge of her leather chair. "You see, I've been doing some thinking Jack, and I'm pretty sure I know where it is I remember you from."

His face told her nothing, and was covered by a sheen of fresh sweat.

"You still don't remember me at all?"

He shook his head and looked out the window where a mass of passing yellow T-shirts caught his eye.

"What I think I remember Jack, comes from a time here in Portland ten years ago. I lived in a house a few miles from here with my boyfriend Logan Salinas. Is that a name that's familiar to you?"

Again he shook his head.

She reached for the eight-by-ten photo that lay face down on her desk. "Well, I've got a photo of him right here on my desk. You see, he was involved in selling drugs, and someone … a couple of people probably … killed him for the money he made selling those drugs."

She turned the photo over and held it up for him to see.

Outside the office, Helena was talking to KC with her eyes fixed just over the edge of his shoulder to monitor the silent exchange taking place within the office.

"What are they doing now?" KC asked.

"I don't know. Just talking I guess. It all looks very calm."

"What about now?" he persisted.

"I don't know. He's shaking his head 'no' to something and she's pretty much doing all the talking."

He waited a few seconds. "How about now?"

"Kase … "

"Let's switch positions. I want to see what's going on for myself."

"Shhh. Just hold still."

"Okay, but at least tell me how he looks when he … "

"Wait a sec! I think she's about to show him the photo of Logan. Wait. Yep. There she goes."

Left with no better indicator of the events taking place behind his back, KC studied Helena's eyes. As they grew wider, her hand rose to cover her mouth, and she gasped with an exclamation of "Oh my God!" through her fingers. He spun, expecting to witness the worst, but instead was greeted by the sound of the office door colliding with the wall. It should have shattered the door's glass window, but didn't, and instead ricocheted off the wall to strike Jack's foot, nearly causing him to trip.

And their eyes met.

The look of wild panic froze KC, and in the next instant Jack bolted down the walkway with the urgency of an animal's escape from a predator. Plunging into an accumulation of players near the benches, shouts of "Watch it!", "Hey!" and laughter rang out. Ten seconds later he was gone, a departure punctuated by a final *zap!* which resonated from within the office.

Helena rushed past KC and into the office. "Are you all right?!"

Jennifer realized she was standing, and feeling faint, hastened to take a seat just as KC arrived in the doorway and parroted Helena's query. She held her hand flat against her sternum. "Yeah. Yeah, I'm okay. Just … just give me a minute. My heart's racing."

"Well no shit … so's mine," said KC. "What'd you say to make him freak like that?"

"I … nothing. I swear. All I did was this." She leaned forward in her chair and turned over Logan's photo so KC and Helena could see it.

"And that's all it took?" asked Helena.

"That and saying I remembered him from the time of Logan's murder."

From the concession area a chant began. "K … C … K …
C … K … C … "

"Hey boss, come talk about this at the tables. I don't want
to miss out on anything, but the natives are getting restless for
beer."

"Say no more. I could use a drink myself."

Or ten.

She rose to come around her desk, but stopped while
gazing at something that blocked her path. "His gym bag," she
said softly.

"He left it?" KC exclaimed from the doorway.

"Yeah, he took off so fast … "

It felt unnaturally light as she lifted it from the floor and set
it down upon her desk where both KC and Helena stared at it as if
it contained a human head. "Kase, really, go on ahead. Helena
and I will be right there." He dutifully departed to what sounded
like an ovation from the patrons, and she said to Helena, "I'm sure
as hell not feeling so strong right now. In fact, the more I think
about it, the more I think this whole thing is a big mistake and … "

But Helena interrupted her sputtering flow of doubt. With
a voice as soft as the touch of her hand, she came to her saying,

"C'mon. Let's go talk about it over that drink," and led her away once the gym bag had been stashed beneath the desk and the office door locked.

They walked hand-in-hand to the only vacant picnic table, and KC promptly brought over a pitcher of beer and three cups. Eventually he caught up with all food and drink orders, the shock of the encounter diminished, and Jennifer began to feel the calming influence of alcohol. As a precaution against being overheard, once they'd reconvened they huddled together as Jennifer quietly detailed the encounter, a recitation that concluded with, " … and basically you guys saw the result."

"That's it. He did it," said KC definitively. His hand slapped the table.

Helena whispered her rebuttal. "Shhh! Oh come on! He's as meek as they come. You never knew Logan, but I'm telling you he could have more than held his own against Jack in a fight."

"Well maybe it was him and someone else. Beside, why did he run? I'll tell you why … because he was scared he was about to get caught."

"I think you're jumping the gun big time Kase," said Helena.

"I agree," whispered Jennifer. "When you think about it, we really don't know any more than we did yesterday."

"C'mon. We know he knows *something*," said KC over the sound of Ian's whistle.

"Really, I don't think we even know that," said Helena. "Maybe he's just scared and thought he was being accused of something. It *was* a bit of an ambush."

"Ambush or not boss," inquired KC, "you have to admit he freaked out *after* he saw the photo … not before, right?"

The Plexiglas rattled as bodies collided against it.

"Yes."

"Well," KC continued, "that tells me at the very least he knew Logan. And you know what else? I bet there's something in that gym bag that'll help prove it!"

"Shhh! Oh come on! There's probably only a change of clothes in there," countered Helena in an argumentative whisper.

KC fired back not to Helena but to Jennifer. "But what if there *was* something in there, boss? Some piece of information … or maybe a clue. Don't you think you owe it to yourself … and to Logan to check it out?"

A maddening swirl of thoughts battled for priority in her mind as she refilled her cup with beer. Fear. Uncertainty. Loyalty to Logan. Protection for Charlie. Her own curiosity. The opposing advocacies of KC and Helena. With both of them staring at her for a decision, she stalled. "Let's put it to a vote. Kase, what do you say?"

"Open it."

Cheers erupted from the field as a goal was scored.

"Helena?"

"Abstain. This is your call Jen. Not ours. This isn't the time to flip a coin, call for a vote, or leave it up to fate. It's time for you to follow your heart and do what it says, like you always say. So what's it gonna be?"

She felt slapped across the face by her own words. Helena was right, and marshalling her strength with the help of a deep breath, she said, "All right then, let's see what's inside," and rose from the table.

They headed to the office with KC in the lead until he was thwarted by the locked office door. Like an impatient dog he pushed his way through once Jennifer keyed it open. "It's been stolen!" he exclaimed.

It's under the desk," Helena said calmly. To Jennifer she asked, "Are you sure about this?"

As series of *zaps!* sounded, KC retrieved the bag and brought it to the surface of the desk, and Jennifer gulped down the last of her beer. "I'm not sure of anything right now. That's why we're opening it."

With a constraint neither Jennifer nor Helena expected, KC put his hand on the bag's lone zipper and said, "Last chance to change your mind … "

Suddenly she felt sure it was the right path, and upon tossing her crumpled cup across the office where it banked neatly off the paper shredder and into the corner receptacle, she confidently said, "Go for it," and the bag was unzipped.

It contained only three things: a balled-up tan sweatshirt, a metal ring that held four keys, and a dilapidated leather wallet. While KC searched every cranny of the bag, Helena and Jennifer's gaze fell upon the wallet. It was Helena who picked it up first.

Clearing a spot on the cluttered desk, she cast a furtive glance out the office window to make sure they weren't being observed, and began pulling its contents from various compartments. A combination of money, scraps of paper, and wallet-sized cards were set in a pile, and KC immediately began to rummage through the money.

"Fifty-five. Fifty-six. A total of fifty-seven dollars," he announced as more *zaps!* sounded. Jennifer extracted a driver's license just as Charlie's voice resonated from the baby monitor stuffed in Helena's pocket. They all stiffened, but once they heard the giggles of Charlie's dream, they resumed their scrutiny of the wallet's contents.

"Well, his name is truly Jack Edens," Jennifer announced while holding up the driver's license. "He's six foot two, has red hair, brown eyes, and he's … let's see … twenty-nine years old."

Helena chimed in, "That's all there is," and put the empty wallet down.

"And he lives on Southeast twenty-eighth street. Not too far from here. And apparently he's an organ donor."

The faraway screech of Ian's whistle made its way from the arena into the office.

"Looks like he shops at Thriftway," Helena mentioned examining a supermarket discount card from atop the stack.

Jennifer picked up the next two items in the stack, one of which was a business card from someone at a Mormon church, the other an embossed punch card from Rudy's Diner which showed he was due a free lunch because he had paid for five of his own. Helena grabbed the driver's license while Jennifer, left with nothing new to look at, noticed KC was engrossed in a newspaper clipping he had unfolded and was reading. From his eyes and furrowed brow, she could tell he had found something of importance.

"What is it Kase?"

"You might want to see this," he said while handing it to her and unfolding a second one. Aged yellow with edges that had been ripped instead of cut, it had the feel and look of an ancient parchment. Helena came to her side to read it over her shoulder.

Pair Sentenced in

Drug Case

Portland -- Michael Bradford Edens and Nicolas LaTourelle were sentenced Friday for their roles in the distribution of cocaine. Judge Ryan Lind sentenced Edens, who has two prior felony convictions, to fifteen years. LaTourelle, who has no criminal record, was sentenced to an eighteen-month term. Both will serve their sentences in the Oregon State Penitentiary in Salem, Oregon.

No sooner had she and Helena finished reading, KC said,

"And then there's this one," and handed over a second article.

Inmate killed in Prison Fight

Salem -- An inmate at the Oregon State Penitentiary was pronounced dead after an altercation with another prisoner. Prison guards found Nicolas LaTourelle unconscious in his cell Saturday morning, and transported him to the prison infirmary where he was

> pronounced dead by the physician on duty. "Prison officials are questioning the deceased's cellmates," said prison spokesperson Mitchell Hayden. Hayden added that LaTourelle's death was likely the result of asphyxiation, but said preliminary autopsy reports were not yet available. Latourelle was serving an eighteen-month sentence for drug-related offenses.

"Any others?" Helena inquired.

"No, the rest is just receipts and junk," he said while setting some scraps of paper on the desk. "Those sound like some bad dudes." Then to Jennifer he asked, "Are the names familiar to you?"

"No. Other than ... of course ... this Michael fellow shares Jack's last name. I'd have to see their faces ... but even still, it was nothing short of a miracle I remembered Jack from so long ago."

"What about the journal?" KC asked hopefully.

"Well remember, the names in the journal are all codenames. Without knowing what these guys … well this Nick's apparently dead … without knowing what this Michael Edens looks like, I don't think there's any way to tie him to anything. I don't recall any entries for FRECKLE'S BROTHER. And even if there was, I don't exactly think it would prove anything."

The three of them silently stared at the accumulation of money, paper, keys, and the tan sweatshirt that covered her desk.

"So what does your heart tell you to do now?" asked Helena.

"To tell you the truth, it's telling me to call the cops."

Chapter 4

The next morning the sound of footsteps roused Jennifer from her nap. It was close to noon, and as she lay on her living room couch her initial thought was that it was only KC. When a second set of footsteps echoed the first, her lethargy shifted to alarm. Encumbered by a thick shroud of blankets, she spotted the cordless phone an arm's length away on the coffee table, and as the footsteps drew nearer she raised herself to her elbows to reach for it. At that exact moment KC's voice called out timidly, "Um, boss?"

She fell back onto the couch and exhaled with relief, "Yeah?"

He peeked his head around the corner. "The door was unlocked and … um … sorry to disturb you, but I have Ethan here for you."

She rose to her elbows again, certain she must have misunderstood him. But then Ethan stepped from behind KC, and she saw it was true. The contrast between the two men could not have been greater. Ethan's height dwarfed KC and his clothes -- a broad-shouldered and impeccably coordinated suit and tie --

matched with a panache found nowhere in the garishness of KC's zebra-striped T-shirt.

"Thanks Kase," she said, and as he departed, he threw her a wry smile before turning to walk back down the hall. The adrenaline spike left her wide-awake, while Ethan's presence filled her with an elation she strove to conceal. She sat up. "How come you aren't at work?"

"Oh, I had a meeting offsite and thought I'd stop by on my way back to the office. Really, I probably only have a few minutes."

He was the perfect tonic for the plague of her thoughts -- thoughts that darted between the newspaper articles, Jack's frantic flight from her office, KC's insistence on a confrontation with Jack at the address listed on the driver's license, Helena's call for restraint and a return of the gym bag to Jack's teammates, the multiple messages she'd left with the homicide division that hadn't been returned, and her own uncertainty of what to do next. Apart from the maelstrom stood Ethan, and like an elixir his mere presence gave her peace. Suddenly, and like never before, she knew what it was like to crave somebody, to want to grab hold of them and never let go. If he said anything to her now -- even the most preposterous lie or sentiment -- she'd believe it.

Instead he said nothing. As he fidgeted with his hands in his pant pockets, a crooked smirk appeared on his lips.

"What?" she asked.

"Nothing," he answered as his smile widened.

She longed for him to sit on the couch with her, and as if a miracle of telepathy occurred, he wordlessly took off his jacket, draped it over the back of a chair, and crossed the void between them. Taking a seat with his hip touching hers through the layers of blankets, he spoke of his prior meeting, his brief interaction with KC, and questioned her about the barrel of water in the entryway. She lay back down and detailed KC's improvisational fix, her relief that repairmen were due in the afternoon to look at the roof, and of her feelings of fear upon hearing two sets of footsteps upon waking. It felt unnatural to withhold from him the story of her recent encounter with Jack Edens, but she resisted. He likely hadn't the time for the breadth of the story, which would undoubtedly lead him down the path of an infinite series of questions. Instead the conversation remained light and easy, and for a span of time that encompassed fifteen minutes, yet felt like five, she imagined them a couple at the dawn of their relationship.

His hand rested on the back of the couch as he hovered over her --

an entrapment from which she desired no escape. Sinking back

into the depths of her pillow, she half-listened to him give a

lengthy account of the tribulations that occurred when he agreed to

let his sister cut his hair, all the while gazing up at his lips, smile,

and steady eyes, as would Sleeping Beauty awoken to find her

prince seated at her bedside.

Only there had been no kiss.

She couldn't imagine a time more opportune, and yet --

nothing. Even when she reached out to place a hand on his leg just

above his knee it failed to motivate him, and with each passing

minute of conversation and laughter her anticipation of intimacy

dissipated. And yet there was no disappointment. Instead, she

marveled that sitting with her was a person -- maybe the only

person in the world -- with the power to supplant thoughts of Jack

and Michael Edens. She could be in a trash-strewn alley in the

driving rain, in a hovel under a freeway overpass, or in a wasteland

devoid of any redeeming feature -- as long as he was with her, she

would be content. His 'few minutes' turned into twenty, then

thirty, then more, before she interjected, "I'll be right back," at a pause in their conversation. He stood, giving her the room to

extract herself from the cocoon of blankets, and she walked around

the corner while he seated himself back on the couch. Pushing

open the bathroom door, she suddenly remembered she'd meant to

ask if he'd like something to drink. Not wanting to yell, she

walked back down the hall. Upon reaching the corner with the

offer set to tumble from her mouth, an unexpected sight was

reflected back to her from the hallway mirror.

Sitting in generally the same position as when she left him,

in his hands he held the pillow upon which she had been resting

her head. While it was her favorite for sleeping, there was nothing

unique about it. In fact, it was typical in every way: its size, its

softness, and its adornment in a plain white pillowcase. For an

instant, she feared he was noticing her drool upon it, until he

brought it to his face and inhaled its scent -- her scent -- in a long

and luxurious breath. She watched as he did it over and over

again, closing his eyes to savor it each time, before her bladder

compelled her to head back down the hall.

At first she perceived it an oddity, an act not meant to be

seen. By the time the bathroom door closed behind her though, her

perception of it changed. It was a gift -- the first unadulterated instance in which she saw her effect on him through an action not meant to be seen, and within it was a verification of his heartfelt words uttered weeks ago at the Eastbank Tavern. While washing her hands and giving her teeth a cursory brushing, she wondered if he was still breathing in whatever scent he found so intoxicating. Exiting the bathroom, she walked heavily to make the wooden floorboards creak, and upon rounding the corner saw him seated with the pillow back in its prior position. She headed not to the couch but to the kitchen where she called out, "Care for anything to drink?"

He declined. With her back turned she sensed his approach from behind. "Let me see if I can find it," he said, and a moment later his hands were upon the back of her head -- a touch that compelled her to put down her iced tea and close her eyes. He was generally in the right area of the fishhook scar, but her hair was tangled from sleeping, and he was unable to locate it. Even her helpful comments, "Up" and "More to the left" and "It should be right in there" didn't help, and he eventually gave up and wrapped his arms around her in an embrace that felt like love. Covering his arms with her own and tilting her head back upon him, the position felt so natural she exhaled and let herself sink into his body further.

"So … Saturday?" He broke the embrace and took a step backward.

"Yeah, um … " she said while returning to her iced tea. "Up for stopping by?"

"I am. One problem though. I've got a farewell party for a friend of mine from college. He's moving back to Seattle and we're giving him a big sendoff. I probably won't be able to make it 'til later. Does that work for you?"

"Sure. Whenever. I'll be here."

She turned. He was still in hugging distance, and as she faced him his height was so pronounced, it occurred to her that they were ill-suited to kiss while standing. Staring down at her, he inquired simply, "So how are you doing?"

"Fine. Why?"

He reached for her hands. "It just occurred to me that I haven't asked you that question in a while."

While his question shut out the possibility of immediate intimacy, it meant much more. She yearned to tell him about Logan, the Edens brothers, Nick LaTourelle, the journal with the fleur-de-lis, and the anxieties that would course through her as soon as he left. But she feared it would all be too much -- too intense -- and instead of sharing with him a topic that could take hours to fully explore, responded, "I'm doing just fine," and allowed him to commence his departure with a tight squeeze and release of her hands.

"Oh, I almost forgot! I have something for you." He headed for his jacket and reached into an interior pocket, pulling from it a pen, followed by a tight cordon of white wire. "It's for you," he said and handed over the wire.

It took her a moment to discern what it was, but upon rotating it in her hand she saw it was a knight for her collection.

"I've got an uncle whose niche is hanger-art. He can make anything out of them! Seriously. His basement is devoted to it. 'Even built a full-sized statue out of a bunch of hangars as his lifetime accomplishment. 'Scared the hell out of me as a kid. Anyway, I was at his house the other week to help fix his computer, and I asked him if he could make me a chess piece in exchange for my services. He said, 'Which one?' and I said, 'The knight' and he said, 'Give me ten minutes.' He goes down to his basement with all his pliers and vices and stuff, and this is what he came up with."

It was the length of her index finger, the bottom half of which was comprised of a wide circular base and the horse's neck -- a rendering that was fairly unremarkable. The head, however, was nothing short of a miracle. Shaped by an instrument she could not fathom, the horse's jaw bulged outward with perfect symmetry on each side, concavities represented the eyes and nostrils, and upward kinks atop the head made for an alert set of ears. The white paint had been scraped from the revealed metal representing the line of the bridle and the hair of the eyelashes and mane, and scratched in a single strand of the wire near the base was the man's name and the year. She felt she held in her hand nothing less than a piece of art belonging in a museum, made even more special since it was spawned from Ethan's thoughtfulness.

"Are you telling me your uncle made this in just ten minutes?"

"Well, it actually took him more like thirty. I told him it was for someone special, so he put more time into it than normal," he said with a wink while putting his coat on. "He's got some sort of industrial spool he can wind the hanger around in nothing flat. The rest of it, all the bending and shaping, is what takes some time.

He's got some secrets he won't show anybody, and really that's about all I know. It truly is art though, isn't it?"

She set it atop the television where it stood upright and didn't tip or rock. "Amazing. Yes it is. Tell him thank you next time you see him, and that I'm proud to add it to my collection."

Smiling, and still holding the pen he removed from his pocket, he reached out for her hand. "Don't look."

With her eyes shut she felt him scrawl something on the back of her hand. Once finished, he said she could open her eyes, but held her hand as they walked out. Despite a craving to read what he had written, she resisted.

KC was nowhere to be found in the arena, and they walked the entryway and down the stairs hand-in-hand. They emerged out onto the sidewalk where a mid-day sunburst stunned their eyes with its brightness. He let loose his grip to shield his eyes, and she hastened to read what was written on the back of her hand.

SNIPES RULE!

While it wasn't I LOVE YOU, or I'M BREAKING UP WITH HER, the accolade for her soccer team was still endearing, and she laughed lightly to show her appreciation. They both

started speaking at the same time, a tangle of words from which he

sputtered a simple, "You first."

"I'd like to invite you to a Fourth of July party here at the

arena. We're gonna do what we tried to do last year, which was to

climb up to the roof with a lot of blankets and lawnchairs and stuff

… bring a lot of stuff to eat and drink … and watch the show they

light off from barges on the Willamette. So far I've got about a

dozen people coming. Me, Charlie, Helena's family, KC, a few of

the Snipes … "

"That sounds totally fun. Count me in."

"Really? Are you serious? You don't have to be w … I

mean … You don't have anything else going on?"

"Not that I can think of."

Her heart leapt. "Oh, and you're not afraid of heights, are

you?"

"No. Why?"

"Because you'll have to climb up the fire escape."

"Piece of cake," he said with a shrug. A delivery truck

rumbled behind him.

"Okay. Your turn. What was it you were going to say?" she asked while placing her hands on his leather belt and pinning him to his car.

"Tell me something about you I don't know," he said while his own hands landed upon her hips.

She gave her usual lament, and he gave his usual reply that he wouldn't accept her inability to remember anything. She scanned her memory for trivialities of even the most banal quality to satisfy him, but found her mind devoid of even these. Then, in a wave pushed forth by a force she normally would deny, but one that felt natural given his visit, his acceptance of the invitation, the wire knight, and their hands upon each other, she said, "Okay. I've got something. You ready?"

"Let's hear it."

She exhaled deeply. "I've fallen for you."

There was a pause and a smile spread upon his face as he gazed down. "Jennifer, you know I just can't accept … ", his eyes raised and met hers, " … things about you I already know."

Chapter 5

Though darkness had not yet fallen, and though he felt the pang of a hundred uncertainties, Jack Edens settled into bed immediately after arriving home from work and peeled off his rain-soaked shirt. Despite the smell of garbage coming from the open window, it was a relief to reach his apartment, where his room and bed held for him a comfort he coveted -- a comfort present nowhere else in life.

The past week had completely unraveled, starting with Jennifer, the owner of the soccer arena, producing a photo of the man Michael and Nick had killed many years before. It had all come rushing back to him in that cramped office. Violence. Control. The capacity for murder. It would all be unleashed upon the world, his world, on July first.

According to his wall calendar, in just ten days.

So urgent was his flight from the arena, it wasn't until he was out on the street that he realized his gym bag had been left behind, along with his wallet and keys. Lacking the will to retrieve them, he left the Oldsmobile behind, walked home in the rain, and entered his apartment via the open window by the dumpster. It wasn't until the next day that the landlord grudgingly provided him with a replacement key to his unit -- a fragment of all that had been lost. No one could replace his car keys or wallet, and left with no alternative, he'd reverted to biking to work, knowing his inability to pick Michael up on July first could never be adequately explained. Michael would be the one coming for *him*, and there would be a price to pay for his failure.

A dull ache stirred to life within his stomach.

He pulled up the sheets, rolled onto his back, and noticed for the first time a wasp poised at the junction of the ceiling and wall. Normally such a sight would have caused alarm, but on this day it was only worth a few seconds of his attention as he pondered the predicament from which there seemed to be no escape. While thoughts of Michael's return usually had the power to thwart sleep, on this night his exhaustion was of a greater potency, leaving his dreams as the only reservoir into which his worry could inhabit.

He found himself parked behind the wheel of the Oldsmobile, listening to the quiet radio in the dark and twisting the prism that dangled from the rear view mirror. The wind skipped leaves along the street and billowed tree branches high above the sidewalks.

Then two figures rounded the corner.

They walked slightly apart, a gap that widened as they neared. The larger of the two reached the car first and extended an arm for the opposite door of the Oldsmobile. The dome light came to life, and a hand smeared with blood thrust the passenger seat forward. Michael's body fell into the backseat with an exhausted thud, followed by Nick who eased in front seat and pulled the door shut behind him. The interior of the car plunged into darkness once more.

"Let's get the fuck out of here," Michael commanded from behind.

Jack turned the key in the ignition, momentarily silencing the radio. A light rain began to fall, and he flipped on the windshield wipers while stealing a look into the rear view mirror.

Darkness.

As he eased the car from the curb, the prism began to glow. Soon tiny rainbows danced within the interior of the car. Fascinated and hopeful, Jack followed their whirl with his eyes until he realized Nick no longer sat in the seat beside him. As the sounds of the radio, engine, rain and wind were silenced, warm light radiated from the backseat of the car.

A gentle voice spoke to him from behind. "You know they committed a murder that night, don't you?"

Jack turned in his seat, but was forced to shield his eyes.

"That's why you never had to go to that house again. The man from the photo was no longer alive."

He faced forward again and placed his hands on the steering wheel. Using the rear view mirror he tried to look into the back seat, but the light was overpowering. "Who … who are you?" he asked.

There was no answer.

"Uhhh … "

"You believe in angels, don't you Jack?"

He wanted to say "yes" but didn't. Closing his eyes, he imagined himself alone and the voice imagined, but the question came at him again. "You know they committed a murder that night, don't you?"

He nodded. There was only the sound of the wiper blades dutifully scything along the glass. Jack finally spoke. "I … "

"Did you know there's a way out? Confront your fears, and you'll find the way out."

A long pause was broken by, "Are you afraid?"

Jack nodded.

"Confront your fears, and you'll find the way out. You *do* believe in us, don't you Jack?"

"I d-do."

The voice was reassuring. "Then we'll be there. As long as you believe Jack, we'll always be there."

"I don ... "

"The rain striking the windshield. Do you see it?"

He gazed at the droplets that appeared on the glass in time between the wiper's cleansing swipes. Jack nodded

"Every single drop ... its size, its location, the soft sound it makes when it hits the glass, the entire constellation of drops right before it's wiped away ... it's all planned. We've the power to create things, shape things, and erase things, in a way and for reasons you could never understand. Like those raindrops, the pattern of freckles on your skin was planned long before you were ever born." Jack stared ahead, listened, and contemplated the array of the drops on the windshield before they were whisked away.

"Confront your fears, and you'll find the way out."

There followed only the sound of the wiper blades. He looked into the rear view mirror, and spun. The angel was gone, and in its place was only darkness. Rain strummed louder upon the car -- a hollow repetition that grew louder and louder until ...

His eyes opened. He sat on the edge of his bed for the next hour, watching the curtain billow with the incoming wind. As it had each rainy night for the past few years, water dripped from the gutter onto the dumpster's lid directly outside his bedroom window. His bicycle lay sprawled on the floor, his television perched atop cinderblocks and wood, and the calendar on the wall fluttered as it moved one day closer to July. Out of habit he turned to the window to see the prism, but it was miles away in front of the soccer arena, dangling from the rear view mirror of the Oldsmobile.

He would to do it. He would put his trust in the angel and go back for his keys and wallet the very next day. And if she asked about the murder, or Michael's role in it -- he would tell what he knew. The power of the angels was with him, and by confronting his fears he'd find a way out. For the first time in recent memory, his stomach no longer hurt.

"I b ... b ... believe," he whispered in the darkness before lying back down upon the bed. He rolled onto his stomach and soon fell asleep in his favorite position -- with one arm folded beneath him and the other dangling off the side of the bed where just his scarred fingertip made contact with the cool floor.

Chapter 6

"Mom, what's that on your hand?" Charlie asked as she drove him to Jonah's for the overnight.

She pulled her right hand from the steering wheel to show him Ethan's faded script. "Well hun … a friend of mine wrote 'SNIPES RULE!' on it. I'm not sure quite why. I guess he thought my current team is pretty good."

"Was it KC that wrote it?"

"Someone else."

And if you ask me who … I'll tell you it was just a friend.

"Snipes Rule," he muttered. "Mom? Can you write something on my hand?"

"No Charlie."

"How come?"

"Because I'm driving right this second."

"How about when we stop?"

"Tell you what Charlie. If you can find a pen to write with by the time we get to Jonah's, I'll write something on your hand. Deal?"

"Deal!" He tore into the glove compartment.

Good luck finding anything in there.

He rifled through old receipts, maps, and ancient cassettes, and triumphantly retrieved from its depths a silver instrument. "Found one!"

"Sorry hun. That's the tire gauge."

His search resumed. As the car wound its way down the Powell's tree-lined street, he discovered a forgotten pen in the space between their seats.

"Congratulations. So what do you want me to write?"

He slammed the glove compartment shut. "I don't know. Something cool!"

"Something cool, eh? That's a pretty tall order for a mom."

"I know."

"Well you didn't have to agree with me" she said with a smile. He laughed and avoided her attempt to tickle him above the knee. The car came to a squeaky stop in front of Helena's house, and upon killing the engine she said, "Don't look," and snatched the pen from his hand once he'd closed his eyes. Failing to recall a band he liked and unable to incorporate his graduation from third grade into a concise message, she wrote the 'I' in 'I Love You' until his *Something cool!* remark stopped her. Completely stumped, she resorted to drawing the four intersecting lines of a tic-tac-toe grid, and scrawled an X in the upper left corner.

"All done."

He looked at it with disapproval. "Aww mom!"

"Now hold on. Here's the deal. If you and Jonah figure out how to beat me, you each get five dollars. Deal?"

"Deal!"

Grabbing his overnight bag for him, she urged him out of the car and accompanied him up the sloping walkway where Roy awaited them at the front door.

"Hey guys, come on in."

She alone thanked him while Charlie preoccupied himself with the back of his hand, and by the time Roy informed her Helena was in the kitchen, Charlie had disappeared in search of Jonah. The aroma of coffee permeated the house, and it grew stronger as they made their way to Helena. Unbeknownst to her, Helena had told Roy the entire story of Jack's panicked flight and the newspaper articles found in his wallet, and though he rarely joined their conversations, as they walked through the house he advocated calling the police.

"I talked to them just this morning actually," was Jennifer's response as they entered the kitchen where Helena was doing a crossword puzzle at the kitchen table.

She put her pencil down and looked up. "And what did they say?"

"I was only able to leave a message with some clerk, but I faxed over copies of the articles and Jack's driver's license. They haven't called back yet." She sat down at the table next to Helena, impressed that the puzzle was nearly completed. "One thing I'm not sure is good or bad ... the detective that handled the case years ago has since retired, and they said someone else would be getting back to me. Some guy named Kovacs."

"Why would that be a *good* thing?" Roy asked.

She turned in her seat to face him. "Well, the detective originally assigned to Logan's murder didn't seem very attentive last time around. In fact he was nothing short of a disaster. Totally disinterested. Maybe not even competent. A new face could only be an improvement, even if he's less familiar with the details of the case."

"Well I think it's the smart thing to do. Calling the cops that is. Maybe they've got some records of those two guys from way back … ones they can look at again."

"I have to say, I'm not too optimistic. The whole investigation didn't impress me the first time around. It just seemed like they wanted to bury it and move on. Besides, it's not as if I have anything concrete to offer them other than a few names and a suspicion." She snorted and turned toward Helena. "KC on the other hand, thinks I should make a citizen's arrest on Jack."

Helena laughed and shook her head, but Roy stayed on the subject. "Well I just think it's the right thing to do … to report it to the police that is. At least now they have record of it."

The boys came running into the room with Charlie's left hand still clutching the pen from the car. "You're up mom!"

"Are you really gonna give us five dollars if we win!?" asked Jonah.

"Five dollars *each*," she said while studying Charlie's hand. Predictably, they'd drawn an O in the center square, and she placed an X in another corner, a move she knew would result in a tie game. They departed in pursuit of a departing Roy to ask for his help, and she and Helena were left alone.

"Sorry, I told Roy all about the Jack stuff. I hope that wasn't … "

"It's fine. Don't worry … really. I figure it's spousal privilege."

"I know, but I just figure you're probably sick of talking about it. Coffee? I just made a pot."

She shook her head. "I probably don't have the time."

Helena rose to get some for herself. "So are you excited about tonight with Ethan?"

She gladly switched topics, even though Ethan offered only uncertainty. "Well, once again, I'm not sure exactly what I feel or what to expect. He said he'd probably come by late, but I don't know exactly when. I know I'm prone to getting frustrated if I think he's gonna show up at a certain time and then he doesn't. And if I let myself think about it too much, I get all nervous. I guess I'll just try to stay busy and not expect too much. All in all though, it's gotten easier than before."

"What has?"

"My ability to understand him. I'm feeling a lot more confident."

"How come?"

She told her about Ethan's visit and what she witnessed in the hallway mirror, a tale she concluded with, "So what do you think?"

"What do I think!? I think he's so ga-ga for you, even smelling your scent on a pillow drives him crazy."

"Yeah but, do you think it's kind of weird or freaky in any way?"

"Oh no, not at all. When I was first dating Roy, I used to totally get off wearing his clothes. It wasn't like the clothes themselves were really great or anything, it's just that I loved being close to them, and the way they felt against my skin. The way they smelled. Not like body odor or anything gross like that. I just wanted to be so close to him all the time." She looked wistful for just an instant. "That was so … well, that was right about when I knew I was in love. I totally get what he was doing with that pillow."

"You think?"

"Oh yeah. Definitely."

"Well, all I know is after seeing him do that … "

The boys ran into the room again, the game of tic-tac-toe on the way to its inexorable tie. She made her third X, and the boys walked to the other side of the room to weigh their options, but not far enough to be out of earshot.

"All I know is that I feel stronger in his presence than ever before," she whispered. "Like seeing him do that made him vulnerable all of a sudden. Like I was the one in control for once. Of course then I had to blow it and tell him I'd fallen for him."

"You didn't!"

She nodded with regret. "I did."

Helena thought for a moment. "Well it's good. It's all good. Your confidence is good, what you saw was good. Do you feel like things are headed in a positive direction?"

She nodded again.

"I assume he didn't say anything about his girlfriend."

"Not one word."

The boys approached again, acknowledged they could not win, and headed for Jonah's room, there attention already switched to something else. "My advice Jen? Just do what ever it is that makes you happy tonight."

Jennifer rose from her seat and grinned. "That's *always* your advice."

"I know. It never changes. I guess that means it's worth following."

 After she said her good-byes to the boys, Helena accompanied her down the brick walkway to her car and exclaimed when they reached the curb, "Oh yeah! I totally forgot! What about the meeting with SoccerCity tomorrow?"

"What about it?"

"Well, what's your game plan? And what the hell's up with a Sunday morning meeting?"

"You know, this whole thing is setting up to be a sort of high pressure summit meeting. They're bringing an attorney and one of their investors. I'm just bringing little ol' me. It seems like they're taking it all very seriously. And honestly, I think they set it up for a Sunday just to throw me off. Or possibly they're holding a big tournament there and they want to show off."

"So are you nervous?"

"No. Ethan's tapping all my nervousness these days. It's hard to get nervous over SoccerCity when in the back of my mind I know I'd never sell to them."

"What if they offered, like, three million dollars?"

"I wouldn't do it."

"Come on … "

"Really. I wouldn't do it."

"Why not?"

"It's my home."

"So why even meet with them? I mean, why even go to the trouble?"

She took a seat upon the hood of her car. "Because information is power."

"Well, just don't let KC think you're gonna sell. He'd probably kill you before he let that happen."

"To be perfectly honest, the only interaction on my mind right now is the one that'll take place sometime later tonight."

"So, your belief in fate … and how it was fate that brought you to decide to build the arena?"

"Yeah?"

"Do you think it's fate that you and Ethan will be together?"

"You mean tonight?"

"No. I mean *together* together."

It brought to mind how she'd imagined them a couple while they talked on the couch. But she had no answer. "I wish I knew."

A glance down to her hand revealed the SNIPES RULE! was barely visible. "The only thing I *do* know is that I'm following my heart wherever it takes me. That … and that it's almost seven o'clock and I gotta go."

"Me too," Helena said as she moved forward for an embrace. "I hope your heart takes you somewhere good tonight."

Resting her chin on her friend's shoulder, she replied, "You and me both."

Midway up the stairs her thoughts of Ethan were interrupted when a pack of players stampeded past her in a race for the exit. Despite the activity of the arena -- the game taking place on the field, the loitering horde waiting to play the next game, and the mix of others drinking and watching -- she felt profoundly alone. In the off chance Ethan was early she scanned the tallest heads for his face, but to no avail. Passing through a mass of people near her locked office door, she was startled when a hand reached out to clasp her forearm.

It was KC. "Get your stuff on. You're needed to play."

"Huh?"

"The team in white?" he said while motioning toward some

players huddled nearby, "Their game's next and they don't have enough to field a team."

"Why don't you play Kase?"

"There's a problem with my genitalia."

"Excuse me?"

"They need a girl. Besides, I don't think I'm ready yet."

"All right. Tell 'em I'll do it." The digital clock across the field told her there were five minutes left until the next game started. As usual, Ian had things clicking away on schedule. "But Kase, trust me, you *are* ready. Promise me the next time you get an opportunity to play, you'll take it."

He held up three fingers. "I promise. Scout's honor."

They ran off, he to tell the team he'd found a female substitute, and she to the back for a change into soccer apparel. It ended up being a friendly game, and one in which she ran furiously throughout the first half, hoping to purge with her effort all her thoughts about Ethan and the Edens brothers.

And it worked.

She thought of little but soccer for the entire hour, even though her stamina, and that of her surrogate team, lasted only forty minutes. Worn down due to a lack of players, they gave up seven goals in the second half, and afterward she said thank-you and retreated to a picnic table to rest and gulp down some water. A hectic, standing-room-only crowd of around thirty people filled the concession area, and animated conversation and laughter drowned out all but the loudest noise from the field. Though still sweating she assisted KC, and upon drinking a beer and being drawn into various conversations, became infected by the exuberance that surrounded her. Someone spawned a round of toasts, and KC twice had to replace kegs of beers. She was happy, sociable, and so busy she didn't even think to take a shower or clean up in any way. Instead, she basked in the activity of the arena -- her arena -- and was almost able to trick herself into thinking no one special was due to arrive that night. As much as she tried to imagine it was just another Saturday night however, every time a *zap!* sounded, she found herself conditioned like one of Pavlov's dogs to glance up and see if it was Ethan who emerged from the entryway steps.

"Looking for someone in particular?" teased KC in the midst of one of her expectant stares.

"Maybe."

"Mmm-hmm," he hummed suspiciously and went back to his work without saying another word.

An hour later games were still going on but the concession area was less busy, and she began to think Ethan wasn't going to show. Hiding any disappointment in her voice, she told KC to keep an eye out for him while she took a shower.

"Why don't you wait thirty seconds and he can take one with you."

She turned and saw Ethan's approach, suddenly glad to have taken the opportunity to play instead of whiling away the hours awaiting his arrival. As he neared a smile grew upon his face. "And why are *you* so happy?" she called out to him.

"I'm here with you, aren't I?"

"Oh brother," muttered KC under his breath so that only she was able to hear it.

KC and Ethan exchanged the succinct greeting of "Hey" before KC's attention was drawn to someone's complaint about their corndog, and she and Ethan gravitated to a table that had just been cleaned. Amid the details of his farewell party and her account of the game she'd played earlier in the evening, KC served them beers without their asking, joined them, and gave a fictional account of her vicious on-field tactics earlier in the evening. Their three-way repartee flowed effortlessly between whatever topics KC or Ethan put forth, and soon after the last game of the night had concluded, and players drifted away from the arena in twos and threes. By the time KC announced his imminent departure, she felt the nervous anticipation of being left all alone with Ethan. He had the capacity to cast a spell on her with his mere presence. While she headed behind the counter to pour them two more beers, KC clicked off the MTV, plunging the arena into a deathly quiet.

"All right. I'm outta of here," he said as he shouldered his backpack. "Should I kill the field lights?"

She blew her excess foam into the sink and said, "Please Kase. Thanks."

He hit the switch that bathed the field in darkness, but left the lights on in the concession area, and moments later departed with a *zap!* which resonated from her office and punctuated their solitude at a picnic table. Immediately they ran out of things to say to each other, and as their lull progressed to silence -- a strange thing happened.

Neither of them felt compelled to speak.

They merely looked at one another, grinning and shifting the position of their intertwined fingers, but without uttering a single word. In the cavernous structure so full of energy just an hour before, it felt impossible that there could be no one else around, and at any moment she expected someone to burst from the bathroom, the phone to ring, or the sound of a ball hitting the Plexiglas.

Nothing.

It had all the ingredients of a prelude to a kiss, and she nearly initiated one, until he broke the silence with a whisper, "What are you thinking about?"

"Where's the penny?" she whispered back.

"What?"

"You know? The one for my thoughts?"

He felt around in his pockets, and merely shrugged.

"Your loss."

He finished his beer and disappeared to use the restroom, and by the time of his return she sat atop a picnic table with her feet dangling an inch from the floor. Beckoning him to come near, she ensnared him with her legs, an act that was meant to be playful, but felt overtly sexual. If he took it the same way she had no idea. Repetitively he ran a fingertip from her knee to the edge

of her shorts -- a touch that would have melted her had he not

chosen that moment to comment, "You know, I just can't get over

how, on the Snipes, the girls are better than the boys."

"And why is that so incredible?"

"Just that on ours it's the opposite. The men dominate, and

the girls really just fill the space. I think that's the way it is on

most co-ed teams … the speed and strength and all. You combine

that with an average skill level, and you've got superiority that I

don't think many females can match."

She freed him from her leg-vice. "All right Mr. Caveman

… why don't we find out?"

"Is that your way of saying I'm sexist?"

She nudged him aside and hopped to the floor. "No.

That's my way of saying you're wrong. Seeing as we represent the

genders of the superior portion of our teams, maybe we should see

who is better between you and I, and let that decide whether or not

girls have comparable skills as boys. Game on?"

He paused, uncertain what exactly she had in mind. "Game

on."

"Good. Follow me."

She led him to the place between the benches where three soccer balls lay amid Ian's beer cups and some other detritus. Upon finding two of them adequately inflated, she tossed one to him and mocked him when he said his tennis shoes were ill-suited for soccer.

"Oh *really* … ", he shot back. "Care to make a wager who'll win?"

"You want to bet money?" she asked.

"No. Let's make it interesting. How many articles of clothing are you wearing?"

Mentally she counted. Two shoes, four socks, underwear, shorts, her sportsbra, and her white shirt. It totaled ten. Stalling for a few seconds, she intuited why he had asked and took the time to estimate the number of items he wore before answering.

"Not counting jewelry?"

"Not counting jewelry."

Likely he's got eight.

"Eight," she lied.

"Perfect. Me too. Here's what we'll do. You perform some soccer skill, and if I can't beat it, I take off one of my eight items. If I can, then you take off one of yours. Ties mean no one takes off anything. We alternate turns. Loser is the first to give up, or run out of clothes."

"No calling the same shot twice?" she asked.

"Agreed."

"Then you've got yourself a bet."

While half the field was impossibly dark, the quadrant nearest the concession area shared its light, and he headed for it while walking backwards and bouncing his ball on his knee. "Ladies first," he offered.

"Very un-caveman of you" she replied before turning and heading toward the darkness. "Follow me."

They arrived at midfield where she stated simply "Kick it in the Snoopy goal." It was not an easy task given the distance the ball would have to travel across a darkened field, and sure enough, her shot missed the mark. Fortunately his missed as well, and for the moment, no clothes were shed.

"Okay," he said, "since you like shooting at a goal ... follow me." He led her to a white line on the field where, tapping her leg with his foot he told her to widen the gap between her feet, and when satisfied walked to a parallel line twenty yards away.

"You have to kick the ball through the other person's legs without it touching." He took his time lining up his kick, but ended up missing with the ball grazing the outside of her foot.

Her elated "Hah!" coincided with his "Dammit," and it was her turn. He formed a similarly-sized triangle with his legs, and it was with great satisfaction that she watched her shot sail cleanly through for a goal, prompting the removal of his left shoe.

She won five out of the next seven, and had him shirtless and barefoot with just Levis and (presumably) underwear left on his body. Her only loss was her left shoe and sock, until, as if growing accustomed to playing barefooted, he won four in a row. She found herself down to her shirt, shorts, and the undergarments beneath -- and desperate to reverse his momentum.

"Okay," he said, "you have to kick the ball through the playing field gate in as few kicks as possible. Kinda like golf. Oh, and you can't intentionally knock the other person's away." His hand pointing across the darkness of the field to the benches. "And you have to let it roll to a complete stop." Ten seconds later he had rolled his first kick perfectly, and even in the dim light they could both see the white ball just in front of the open gate.

Son of a bitch.

"One wonders, will you be removing your shorts, or your shirt?"

"Shut up. You haven't won anything yet," was her retort, but her shot couldn't match her bravado, and it bounced away from the gate leaving an impossible angle.

He punched his through easily, and lifted himself up to take a seat on the low wall to observe. *"This looks like a tough one ladies and gentlemen,"* he said with the hushed voice of a golf announcer. Her second effort deflected back onto the field, and with her hands clasped upon opposite hips, she pulled her shirt over her head, not at all feeling exposed in her sportsbra.

"Three left for you, two for me." He jumped down to the field. "Wait a sec … " he said while counting the items strewn across the soccer field with a finger stabbing the air. "You said … you … said … five, six, seven … you had eight items."

"Yeah?"

"So I see seven of yours already on the field. And you have three left … "

"I lied."

"No fair."

"All's fair in lo … ", she said before stopping herself.

He smiled. "Well it matters not you cheater. I'm gonna beat you anyway."

"We'll see about that. The ball that ends up closest to the wall … wins," she said, pointing to the border of the field just ten feet away. You can't intentionally knock the other person's away, and it's okay if it touches the wall." She sent hers to within three inches, a distance that easily won after his effort caromed from the wall many times that distance. He stepped out of his pants, revealing black athletic briefs that extended to mid-thigh.

"Sexy."

"Well I think so. I gave up the tighty-whities years ago."

It was his turn, and with only one article of clothing left, he was desperate. "The winner of this one bounces the ball on their knee the longest."

She groaned. Having seen him perform this particular feat for minutes at a time, she knew it meant an automatic loss. Mentally she began an assessment of whether to remove her sportsbra or her shorts.

Shorts it is.

"Go!"

They began bouncing soccer balls with their knees in a marchstep fashion. She lasted only five repetitions before losing control, whereas he continued for another twenty seconds to flaunt his win. He finally caught the ball with his hands. "Do you give up?"

Dropping her shorts to the field, she said, "Not even," and added, "My turn," after she'd kicked them aside.

He walked close to her and placed his hands upon her arms just below her shoulders. "Are you cold? I think I see goose pimples."

"Not half as cold as you're about to be."

As his hands slowly moved down her arms, the grip of her competitiveness grudgingly eased. In the shadows, the features of his cheekbones rose with his smile, and light from the concession area sparkled in his eyes. Reaching out, she placed her hand along the side of his face and felt his smile recede. With her thumb she slowly traced his lips, a gesture to which he responded by closing his eyes. She did it for at least a minute -- touching them as lightly as possible -- before moving her hand back to the side of his face. He took her hand in his own, and pressed it over his heart.

"It's your shot, Jennifer" he whispered.

"What do you say we call it a draw?".

"Agreed."

They moved closer. Her hand dropped to the groove beneath his ribs, and he placed his on either side of her jaw just as he had before their first kiss at the Eastbank Tavern. Their height was of such a disparity he had to hunch to kiss her, but she remedied it, first by standing on her toes, then by guiding him down to the artificial turf.

The electricity of the soft caress of his fingertips surged with the movement of his hands beneath her remaining clothes. Almost accidentally her right had drifted up and clasped upon his bony hip. It wasn't a part of his body she found sexy, or had ever even thought of before. But in this moment it became an instrument of control. She may not be able to tell him how to feel, to force him to not deceive her, or loosen the tethers that still bound him to his girlfriend. But with tight clasp of her hand she could control his hips, his torso, and his whole body. As if he read her mind his tongue moved up and down her neck, his hands moved to the exact places she wanted, and as she guided him into her the only thing that mattered was that she was in control of him … something she wanted more than anything else in the world.

Chapter 7

It was bigger than she ever remembered.

Five years had passed since the last time she'd set foot in SoccerCity, and while the atrium through which she walked remained familiar, there was a sparkle and spaciousness to the place that was new. It had undergone some sort of renovation, and as Preston Richardson led her past the glittering trophy case, a digital schedule of the day's games, and a wall decorated with poster-sized team photos, she had to concede it was money well spent.

Then they made their way into the actual arena.

Within a space big enough to house a blimp was the field -- free from rafters, dripping rain, and chicken wire. Every impeccable surface, coordinated color, and championship banner left her with the feeling SoccerCity was everything that her arena wasn't.

Exactly the impression they'd want me to have.

The image of a shirtless Ethan barged into her mind, but was forced out by Preston's inquiry about business license requirements in Portland. She answered without elaboration, which was just as well since they approached an office where two other men were waiting. Preston wasted little time with formalities, introducing her to their attorney and their principal investor. Once the handshakes were concluded and they thanked her for meeting on a Sunday, everyone took a seat.

"I believe directness is a virtue," Preston began, "so I'll come right out with it. The reason I … we, actually … wanted to talk to you is to make an inquiry about your willingness to sell to the ownership group of SoccerCity."

She felt a stab of nervousness, but it was overcome by an instinct to restate his statement to her advantage. "Well that *is* direct Preston. Tell me … what's behind the desire to buy at this particular time?" She sat back, listened, and nodded politely, all the while stockpiling further questions. On two occasions when there was a natural break in his presentation, she let the silence grow, and each time Preston couldn't help but fill the void with more words.

He's nervous.

When she finally did speak, it was a question intended only to feed their collective egos. "You guys don't waste any time, do you?"

The principle investor chimed in for the first time, "No. Time is money." He glanced at Preston, and as if a signal had been passed, Preston began a monologue history of SoccerCity that she found of little interest. She fought to keep Ethan out of her mind, and was relieved when Preston appeared to be finishing up.

"So you see we've had a good long run as a solo facility. SoccerCity is the preeminent indoor soccer facility in the city, and we're situated in an affluent location where people have no qualms about paying for soccer leagues. School-aged kids, especially girls, are getting into the sport more and more, and we can sell merchandise in excess of the price of many local sporting good stores … and we sell the stuff out. Honestly, were it not for a lack of available property, we'd build a second facility right next door."

Without warning, the recollection of Ethan's touch sent goosebumps across her skin. She repelled it with the query, "Why don't you just build where the parking lot is?"

"Oh we would," Preston replied, "but the city has some strict rules about commercial parking in residential areas, and the high school across the street has its own parking issues that contribute … "

She recalled the pinch of Ethan's teeth along her collarbone.

"And that's not counting all the zoning ordinances. We've tried to work with the City of Beaverton for some time, but have found … "

She felt Ethan pull her hair aside and move his tongue along her nape.

The principle investor interjected again, "But despite all that, we hold a fantastic advantage. We've got a lot of momentum, and the time is ripe for expansion."

She pushed aside the memory of Ethan gently working his fingers beneath her panties. "Well with all that momentum, why would you need to purchase my place ? Why not build a new facility on your own in some other location?"

"We've explored that possibility. As it turns out … "

She suspected she knew why. East Portland Indoor Soccer had hurt SoccerCity. At the time the grand opening there was rampant player dissatisfaction at SoccerCity over crowded schedules, a lack of "open" play times, and the latest round of price increases. Then the monopoly was broken. She immediately drew away many corporate teams that were closer to her anyway, and as its popularity spread it even began the unthinkable -- attracting

players from the suburbs. It offered an alternative at half the price,

cutting into the almost-constant play at SoccerCity, and forcing a

reduction in their fees.

"I think there's a real synergy that can be gained by sole

ownership of SoccerCity and your facility as eastside and westside

sister facilities," the principal investor said definitively. And we're

willing to put our money where our mouth is."

Have you guys actually thought this through to the point

where you're ready to make me an offer?" she asked and sat back,

recalling the sense of Ethan's heartbeat while running her hand

along his chest.

" … premature to comment specifically … "

She recalled the chill when his fingers move down her

back.

" … a revised marketing approach put in place the previous

fiscal year … "

The saltiness of his necklace when it tumbled into her

mouth.

" … economies of scale … "

How they'd gasped at the exact same time.

" … value in the transition period of ownership … "

How, as they lay entwined in the dark, a *zap!* echoed in the arena.

" … possibility of an advisory capacity … "

How, unaware of their stifled giggles, KC walked into the concession area and made his way into her office completely unaware Ethan and she were scrambling for their clothes in the dark.

"I'm sorry. Did I say something amusing, Jennifer?"

She realized she was smiling, and gradually let it ebb. "Oh. I, uh … I was just thinking … that's the first time anyone's suggested that I act in an advisory capacity for anything."

Cursed by the same swirl of thoughts that tormented her during the meeting at SoccerCity, she drove to pick up Charlie from his overnight. The one piece of information she wanted had been revealed to her. If she were to sell SoccerCity, they would shut it down. She'd have a small fortune to be sure, probably a lot more than she started with. But imagining it felt tantamount to being poor, and a return to the directionless time in her life pre-arena. Nevertheless, at the conclusion of the meeting the principle investor indicated they were almost ready to make her an offer, and she encouraged them to do so.

She pulled up to the Powell's house and stepped from behind the wheel. Helena was apt to pounce on her for details of her evening at the first opportunity, but once inside Roy indicated she was in the shower, and informed her that Charlie had had a "bad night" without further elaboration. After corralling Charlie, they left hand-in-hand as they walked down the driveway. She noticed an armful of tic-tac-toe games adorned his arms from wrist to sleeve, and asked, "By any chance do Jonah's arms look like yours, hun?"

"Worse."

"Oh good."

Minutes of silence in the car were broken by her next question. "So, Uncle Roy said you had a rough night. Did you have another bad dream?"

"Yeah."

"Anything you want to talk about?"

"Mom, what did my dad do?"

"You mean like what was his job?"

"Yeah."

"Well when I first met him he worked with me at a place called Eastmoreland Country Club. He helped people with their golf while I worked in the dining room. Being a waitress. After that though, he did some buying and selling of music. You know like the old records I have in the storage room back home."

"Did he ever sell drugs to people?"

"Uhmm."

"Jonah said he heard his parents talking late one night. Is it true?"

She weighed the merits of telling the truth against the protection of a lie, and chose the truth. "He did sell some, hun."

"Was it drug dealers that killed him?"

"Charlie, really I don't know. Maybe"

He asked no further questions, and she pulled to the side of the road.

"Charlie, I'm being honest with you about your father because I think you're old enough to handle the truth, and I think it's important you know what happened. Your father had so many great qualities, but he also had some faults, and one of them was not realizing the danger he was getting himself into when he sold drugs. He shouldn't have ever started selling that stuff. It was wrong, illegal, and dangerous, and not a day goes by that I don't feel bad because that I wasn't strong enough to make him stop sooner. It probably cost him his life Charlie, and it also cost him his life with you. That's what drugs do … rob people of their loved ones." She studied his expression but could read nothing in it. "I hope all this doesn't cause you any more bad dreams, hun."

He didn't answer, and she reached out to hold his hand.

"What was the bad dream you had?"

"I dreamed I was following him up the fire escape, and right when he got to the top, he fell, and I was so scared … I couldn't go up or down. I got stuck up there all alone, but I could see his body down on the street below." His lip began to quiver. Just before he broke into tears she reached out for him, and he accepted her embrace.

He cried into her shoulder for a few minutes before she said, "Shhh … don't cry hun. You'll never be alone so long as I'm around."

He sobbed for a while longer before managing, "I know mom. It's … It's just that I get …" he trailed off and blew his nose into a tissue she offered. "Mom? Do you always tell me the truth?"

"Usually, Charlie. Sometimes I leave out some stuff though. Because I'm afraid you might have a bad dream like you did last night, or because you're not quite old enough yet."

"What age will I be when you finally tell me everything?"

"You know hun … I think that time is coming sooner than I think."

The rest of the way home they lost themselves in their own thoughts, and upon returning to the arena Charlie ran back with his overnight bag while she walked past the benches where she was surprised to find Coach Morris carefully stretching.

"Game, Coach?"

"Not for thirty, but these ol' muscles of mine need some serious stretchin' beforehand if you know what I mean."

She nodded and said, "I know what you mean. Don't let me stop you," before hastening on. Relieved not to be trapped in conversation with him, but unable to spy KC anywhere, she headed for the back to find Charlie engrossed in a comic book Jonah had let him borrow. His overnight bag lay on the floor between his feet.

"Now I don't want to see that bag on the floor all day today."

"Okay," he replied without looking up.

She felt a growing headache whose epicenter lay behind one eye, and headed for the bathroom where ibuprofen awaited. Upon swallowing three pills she returned to the arena, again finding KC was nowhere in sight. "Hey Kase?!" she yelled out.

"Behind the counter!" came his voice. She approached, leaned over the countertop, and saw him seated on the floor amid a supply of plastic cups, forks, and paper plates.

"Games start in what? Thirty?"

"About that."

"Why is *he* here so early?" she said, referring to Coach Morris.

"Stretching, I guess."

There was lifelessness in his voice, and like Charlie engrossed by his comic book, he didn't give her the courtesy of eye contact. "Sorry if we scared you last night. You looked surprised to find you weren't alone."

"Don't worry about it."

"Did you realize we were in the arena when you first came back?"

"No."

Something's wrong.

"Are you okay, Kase?"

"Actually no. I'm not feeling so good. I think coming in today was a mistake. If it's okay with you, I think I'm gonna head home."

"Well okay … I can handle things here. Is there anything I can do for you?" She heard a door slam, and saw Charlie approach from the back.

He hesitated as if an answer was on his mind, but then simply shook his head and it remained unspoken. Shoving everything into the storage cabinet and rising from the floor, he thrust his hands in his pants pockets and gathered up the Sunday newspaper he had brought in that morning. While his behavior was puzzling, it was far from alarming, and she dismissed insisting he tell her what was wrong. Instead she headed to her office. Once she settled in her leather chair, the *zap!* signified KC's departure, followed shortly by a few more, but glancing up there was only the lonely sight of Coach Morris balanced in a painful-looking position with one foot planted on the ground and the other atop the three-foot wall. Hoping for a message from Ethan, she checked both her e-mail and voicemail.

Nothing.

Yet another *zap!* sounded. Shifting her attention to the menagerie of paper that covered her desk, prominently displayed atop it all was a fax that had been received only thirty minutes earlier.

From: Preston Richardson, SoccerCity, LLC
To: Jennifer Scott, East Portland Indoor Soccer
Re: Our conversation this morning.

Jennifer,

Thank you for your time this morning, and your interest in exploring sole ownership between our facilities. I thought our conversation was a fruitful one, and have taken the liberty of moving forward with the next step. Please find the following draft Letter of Understanding ("LOU") pertaining to our discussion.

The LOU represents that both SoccerCity, LLC and East Portland Indoor Soccer will negotiate exclusively and in good faith with regard to ownership by SoccerCity, will agree to an evaluation standard set forth by an independent third party, and that both parties will keep such negotiations confidential and solely between the parties.

Please have your legal representatives review the LOU, and if acceptable, please let me know so that I can have copies sent to your office for signature.

If you have any questions, pl …

"Mom, there's someone here to see you," Charlie said from the doorway of her office.

She didn't bother to look up. "Hold on hun, I'm right in the middle of … "

"But mom, I think he said it's important."

She looked up to a sight that chilled her. Standing beside Charlie was Jack Edens, and she choked on both breath and word. Only her eyes conveyed the horror she felt inside.

"Mom … "

"Uch … Charlie," she stammered while dropping the fax and hurrying from behind her desk.

"Mom, I was wondering … "

"CHARLIE, GO TO THE BACK RIGHT NOW!" she thundered.

Without another word he did as instructed.

Wide-eyed and afraid, she felt trapped within the confines of the office, but the fear that surged within her ebbed with one look into Jack's eyes.

He's scared too.

He'd visibly jumped when she barked at Charlie to leave, and they stood staring at each other without saying a word until she managed a breathy, "What is it that you want Jack?" before stealing a look past him and into the arena. Even Coach Morris seemed to have disappeared.

His fingers twitched as he struggled to speak. "I … to … g … g … get my th … things."

Her fear eased a little more. He meant her no harm, and she noticed his stare behind her desk where his gym bag was visible. "Yeah, you um … left your bag. You're … " she motioned toward it, " … you're welcome to it."

She stepped aside and he grazed her while moving past to get it. As he unzipped it she said, "You wait here Jack. I'll be right back," and left without waiting for an answer. Once outside the office she remembered KC had left for the day with his dubious illness.

Dammit.

The only soul around other than her son was Coach Morris, who she could see was seated on the field while he stretched his hamstrings.

He'll have to do.

Rushing up to him, she cut short another of his robust greetings with a forceful, "Do you have five minutes?"

"Well I uh ... "

"Good. Come with me."

Leading him by the hand to a picnic table, she asked him to have a seat. "Coach, I have to warn you. You're going to hear some personal things said, but I'll explain what I can to you later. Right now I really need someone by my side while I talk to the guy that's waiting in my office right now. Can you do that for me?"

"Well I ... "

"Good. I'm gonna bring him over here. Just hang tight." He stammered something else, but she just patted him on the shoulder, gave him a nod, and left him there. Rushing back to her office, she found Jack zipping up his gym bag. She conjured up a smile. "Jack, come with me. I'd like to talk with you for a bit." He gave her a nod, and she led him to the picnic table in silence.

He took a seat across from both her and Coach and clutched his gym bag in his lap. At first no one said anything, an awkward silence finally broken when she said, "I saw the newspaper articles in your wallet, Jack."

It was not what he expected to hear, and his attempt to respond disintegrated into a stammer, then a mere nod.

"Jack, is there anything about Logan's death you want to tell me? You remember … the man from the picture I showed you?"

He struggled with his words again. Just when it looked like their conversation would be futile, he pulled out his wallet and extracted the two newspaper articles. With shaking fingers he set them in the middle of the table.

"This Michael Edens," she said while unfolding one and adding a helpful nod. "He's your brother?"

Jack nodded.

"And this Nick whatsisname …" she said while unfolding the other. "Latourelle. Nick Latourelle. Is he also a relation of yours."

Jack shook his head.

"No huh? So then Jack, what is it about these guys? Did they know Logan?

Jack nodded and muttered, "Yeah."

"Did they have something to do with his death?"

He nodded again.

Stunned, she asked carefully, "Are … are you *sure* Jack?"

His nodding continued.

She stole a glance at a bewildered Coach Morris, and turned her attention back. "How is it that you know this? Were you … there when it happened?"

"Uhn … n … n … "

"Did they talk about it or something? Michael and Nick?"

"Uh … not … n … no."

Another *zap!* sounded from her office. "So how is it that you know this?"

"I was at … in the c … c … car."

She tried to be encouraging. "You were waiting in a car when they … killed Logan?"

He nodded.

"Was it day or night when it happened?"

Two of Coach's teammates had entered the arena and were stretching on the field.

"It w … was th … th …night."

"And what time of year was it? Hot like summertime, or cool and rainy like closer to winter?"

"Cool. It w … was … I 'member th … was l … l … leaves."

She tried to memorize his every answer, and wished she had with her a pen and paper. Tears began to build in her eyes. "Are you *sure* about this Jack. I mean, you don't have any doubt in your mind about it?"

"I … n … no … d … d … "

There were more *zaps!* "It says here," she said while wiping an eye and lifting a newspaper article from the table, "that Michael was sentenced to eighteen years. When was that? There's no date for me to tell."

"S … sixteen," he said, but then immediately began shaking his head. "S … s … six … "

"Six years ago. Are you sure?"

Another *zap!* sounded.

"So that means he'll be in jail for another twelve years, right?"

Jack shook his head, and she thought she'd have to explain the math to him. Instead, he pulled from his pocket the folded letter his mother had sent to him -- the letter that detailed Michael's early release from the Oregon State Penitentiary on July first.

She read it and set it down upon the picnic table.

"Are you telling me," she asked gravely, "that your brother's going to get out of prison in … in less than two weeks?"

He nodded, a look of angst causing a band of freckles to disappear within a wrinkle on his forehead.

She fought for control. "Can I … um … make a copy of this Jack?"

He nodded again, and she headed to her office copy machine, leaving Jack with Coach Morris. She couldn't imagine what they'd find to say to one another, but by the time she returned she caught the tail end of an exchange between them having to do with Coach's t-shirt. Her walk to and from the office quelled her tears, and in its place came a deep numbness. She handed the letter back to him, and he refolded it and tucked in his wallet.

Upon taking a seat again, she reached beneath the surface of the table and took Coach Morris' hand in hers.

"Okay, what else Jack?"

Out of sight, his grip tightened comfortingly over hers. Jack said nothing and gave her a vapid look as he played with his fingertip.

"Is there anything else you want to tell me Jack?"

He shook his head.

"Did you ever know Logan, Jack?"

He looked confused.

"You know … interact with him. Ever talk with him?"

He nodded that he did.

"What is it that you remember about him most?"

"M … the … m … music."

It was more than she could take, and she turned from the table as tears streamed down her face. She couldn't remember the last time she'd cried over Logan's death, but Jack's sputtered words transported her back in time to the days when she and Logan were so young. She wiped her tears away. "Jack, why is it you're telling me this now? Is it because you don't want your brother to get out of jail? Or are you just trying to clear your conscience in some way?"

He said nothing.

"Jack?"

"I … the … a … " he managed before trailing off with an incomprehensible mumble. Then he got up while clutching his gym bag to his stomach and walkedtpward the exit, never once turning around to look back at them.

"I guess he said what he had to say," remarked Coach Morris while letting go of her hand.

Shocked to find she'd been clutching it so tightly, she said, "Yeah, I guess," and let it go.

More of Coach's teammates arrived in the concession area. Ian was nowhere to be found and it was a few minutes past game time, so she was forced to referee. Heading to her office for a whistle, a player asked where KC was, and another informed her there was no more toilet paper in the women's restroom. She replied, "He's not here," and "Thank you," in quick succession, and ran to catch up to Coach Morris as she slung the whistle around her neck.

"Uh, Coach. I want to thank you."

"I'm not even sure's I know what I did. But if it was helpful to ya, I'm tickled to do it."

"So you probably figured out that this Logan, the one that got murdered, was involved in some … "

"You know little lady … much as I'm curious 'bout whatever that was all about, I've got a game to play. You ah … you okay?"

She sniffed and said "Yeah." It occurred to her she'd grossly misjudged him all this time. Denying the impulse to hug him, she extended herself to him in a different way. "Oh, one more thing Coach … "

"What's that?"

"Do you have any plans on the fourth of July?"

As hard as she tried to keep her mind on officiating, she failed, and thought only of Jack Edens as she ran up and down the field. Ian arrived close to halftime, apologetic and sober, and after transferring the whistle to him she sought out Charlie. He was alone in his bedroom, his eyes red and puffy, putting away the contents of his overnight bag.

"What's up, hun?"

"Mom, why did you yell at me like that?"

She walked closer. "Well you see hun, I was afraid right then. It didn't have anything to do with you or something you did. I'm sorry if I scared you."

"Afraid of what?"

"That man with the freckles that came to see me."

"Why were you afraid of him?"

"Well hun, I thought he might … I thought he might not be a good person. And if he was a bad person, then I wouldn't want him anywhere near you. As it turned out, I don't think he's bad like I thought."

"Oh."

"Come on out with me and tell me about the overnight?" she suggested while extending her hand to him. He grasped it and followed her out to the living room where they sat together on the couch. He was in the midst of telling her about the breakfast he and Jonah had cooked for Aunt Helena and Uncle Roy when the phone rang, and Charlie picked it up.

"Hello? Yeah I did. Uh-huh. Sort of. Yeah."

Her instincts told her it was Helena, and when he handed it over she knew a barrage of questions was coming her way.

"So tell me all about last night!"

"Hold on a sec, Helena."

She left Charlie in the living room where he was inspecting the hanger knight from Ethan, and turned the corner down the hall.

"You'll never guess who was just here!"

"Ethan?"

"Jack Edens."

"What!?"

She spoke in a hushed but excited tone lest Charlie be listening from the other room. "Yes! And you know what? They did it. Those characters from the articles ... Michael Edens and the one that died in prison ... they're the ones that murdered Logan."

"He *told* you that?"

"Yes. He didn't actually see it happen, but he was .. .he said they'd done it."

"What did KC say?"

"I haven't had a chance to tell him yet. He went home sick." She checked for Charlie, and finding him nowhere in sight, turned and whispered. "Oh, and I almost forgot. I slept with Ethan last night."

"What!?" was the disbelieving response.

"Yeah. It just kind of happened after everyone cleared out."

"Wow. I mean … hold on a sec." She heard Helena talk to Jonah in the background, and came back to the line. "Okay, I'm back. Boy, it's been a wild twelve hours … "

"You could say that."

"So how do you feel?"

"About what?"

"Everything."

"Well as far as Jack goes … Oh! I forgot to tell you! Hold on a sec." She walked all the way into the arena where she was sure Charlie couldn't hear her. In a serious tone she said, "Okay, I'm back. Jack's brother? Michael? He gets out of prison on parole in like two weeks. The article said he'd be in for another twelve years, but he's not."

"Oh shit. You've gotta call the cops again."

"As soon as I hang up."

"Do you need me to come down there to be with you?"

"No. I'll be okay. Thanks for asking though."

"So how are you holding up? How do you feel?"

"Scared."

"And how do you feel about the whole Ethan thing?"

She paused before answering. "Scared … " There was silence on the other end of the line, which she broke by adding, " … and *in love* at the same time."

"Did you tell *him* that?

"Oh, I get the feeling he's known for quite a while."

Chapter 8

Please. Someone pick up.

On the third ring her wish was granted. "Hello?"

"Yes. I'd like to speak to Detective Kovacs."

"He doesn't work today."

"It's urgent that I speak to him. It's about a murder investigation he's assigned to. Please … I've already left him multiple messages, and it can't wait any longer."

There was no immediate response, but then the voice said, "I can give you his pager number … "

"Please."

She got the number, dialed it, punched in her own, and was relieved when the phone rang just five minutes later.

"This is Detective Kovacs. Someone there paged me?"

"Yes, detective, this is Jennifer Scott. I've been trying to get in touch with you about the case of Logan Salinas … it's an unsolved murder from nine years ago that's been assigned to you. Previously it was one of Detective Quinn's cases."

"Yes … Jennifer. I've been meaning to get back to you. I got your other messages, but I haven't had a chance yet to look at the file to bring me up to sp … "

"I know who Logan's killers are."

There was only silence.

"Jack Edens, the one I called you about earlier? He was just here and told me his brother, Michael Edens, did it."

"Okay … let's take this one step at a time. You're telling me you've got an eyewitness who will testify that this Michael Edens … was the one that killed Logan Salinas?"

"Well he never said anything about testifying, and he didn't actually see it take place … but here's the other thing. This Michael Edens? He's in jail right now, but he gets out in just two weeks. On July first. I have a copy of a letter here, and it says he'll be released from the Oregon State Penitentiary on parole. That's twelve years earlier than the eighteen he was sentenced for his drug crimes."

"His drug crimes?"

"It's all in the faxes I've sent to your office."

"Look, I'm sorry … I haven't been able to see any of the … Could you hold on a moment?"

"Sure."

After a brief pause, he was back on the line. "Jennifer?"

"Yes?"

"Tell you what? It sounds like you've got some pertinent information there, as well as a verbal attestation that puts someone at the scene of the crime. Let me run by the office, get the Salinas file, come over to where you are, and compare what I've got with what you've discovered. I can be there by … mmm … how does this afternoon sound?"

It sounded great.

By mid afternoon, amid the backdrop of a game between a Hispanic boys team and some junior high girls considerably older, she sat across a picnic table from Detective Kovacs with the space between them stacked with blue file folders that represented the official investigation into Logan's murder.

Kovacs hair was almost all gone, with the contours of his skull visible beneath a few black wisps. Dark circles filled the sunken chambers of his eyes, and crimson grooves appeared on the sides of his nose every time he stopped reading, and removed his glasses to ask her questions. He wore a beeper, but not a gun, and was dressed in clothes that hadn't seen an iron in their lifetime. He moved through the files with agility, picking out information to substantiate or contradict the information she provided. He took care to hide from her the gruesome photos in a tan envelope labeled 'CRIME SCENE', and upon reviewing the background information, all the evidence collected, and Logan's autopsy report, he dove into the file containing interviews with people that were considered suspects.

She tired of sitting across from him while he read and sipped at coffee and on one occasion left him alone in order to climb the fire escape to observe the efforts of the company she'd hired to work on the roof, and also to check on Charlie who was watching TV in the back. Finally, after hours of scrutiny and multiple pages of notes jotted down on a legal pad, he closed the last file, perched his glasses upon his head, and gave the upper part of his nose a vigorous pinch.

"Is there anything else you have for me that might be useful? Any other evidence or any aspect of what you've heard from this Jack Edens that could be helpful. Anything at all."

She strained to come up with something in addition to what she was told by Jack, the copies of the newspaper articles and parole form, and Logan's fleur-de-lis journal.

"No. You basically know everything."

"All right. Here's what we've got … "

He laid it all out. How there was no evidence at the scene of the crime that pointed them toward any single suspect. How fingerprints taken in the bedroom and elsewhere in the house were either Logan's, hers, or were marred beyond use. How the motive was determined as robbery based on the drug paraphernalia in and under the house and in the trunk of his car. How the encrypted journals pointed to a method by which drugs sales were tracked. How Logan's cell phone had within it dozens of phone numbers which led to suspects, interviews, alibis, and a dearth of evidence necessary to press charges against anybody.

"Did they interview Michael, Jack, or Nick?"

"They did. Their number was in his cell phone." Upon thumbing through his notes he elaborated, "The report in the file indicates their alibi, just like many of the others, was either accepted or couldn't be disproved. It doesn't give any detail beyond that because unfortunately, I don't seem to be able to find the transcripts. They interviewed all three of them. The report considers any information provided by Jack to be unreliable, attributed to what they regard as 'greatly diminished mental capacity.' The other two … " he turned the pages of his yellow notepad, " … the other two apparently disavowed all knowledge, and I can only presume there was no evidence upon which to warrant further investigation of them."

There was a cheer from some parents as a boy scored a goal and was mobbed by his teammates.

"So what does that mean? Doesn't any of the information provided by Jack make a case against Michael Edens more compelling?"

"Compelling … yes. Conclusive … no." He put his legal pad down, edged forward, and looked her in the eye. "What you've uncovered tells us Michael and Logan probably knew each other, and likely were both involved in trafficking narcotics. But I've got to be honest … even if Jack was willing to testify to his brother's involvement in Logan's death, I don't think it would hold up. He's just not a credible witness given his handicap. Even the most inept public defender could make a case for the disqualification of such testimony."

"But Michael's behind bars right now on drug charges."

"I'd bet most of the characters on the initial suspect list have done time by now. The articles and the parole letter really have no bearing on Logan's murder." He looked at the parole letter and shook his head in disgust. "Sentenced to eighteen. Out in six. That's our penal system. Hard at work." He put the letter down. "The most compelling thing of all, is what Jack said to you … his knowledge about the murder, what he saw, and what he remembers. As testimony it's useless, but it *has* pointed us toward Michael Edens. I can review everything we've got on him, talk to his parole officer, and even bring him in for questioning once he gets out. It's possible we could find out more."

"Detective Kovacs, I think you need to know where I'm coming from on this. Part of me is concerned with the whole investigation and finding out who did this and bringing them to justice. But what's foremost on my mind … is what happens when he gets out. In my mind I've got Logan's killer set free in a week and a half, and frankly I'm scared. I'm scared to death. I've got a young son you know, and now Jack's just one conversation from telling his brother where I can be found. That scares the shit out of me."

He sipped his coffee and ran his fingers along his barren scalp. "Personally, I don't blame you. It's got to be hard … real hard … for you to find out about someone who could be Logan's killer, and at the same time find out that same person is about to be released from prison. But let me tell you, most ex-cons who've spent significant time in the Pen like this guy has, don't look to commit a crime as soon as they're freed. They're on a pretty tight leash with their parole officer from moment one, and the last thing they want is anything that's gonna send them back to the hell they just left behind."

"Am I supposed to take comfort from that?"

He sighed. "No. But look … I can do a couple of things. Inquire with Jack Edens at the address on the driver's license you photocopied. Get in touch with the parole officer of Michael Edens. Find out where he'll be living once he's released. Get a mug shot of him so you know what he looks like. I can even run a patrol car by here more often. I'll put all this information into the file, but I have to be honest with you, there's not enough here for me to do anything more than that. We might find out more, and if we do, we'll take what action we can and keep you informed. In the meantime if you're feeling scared about what could become known about you and your kid, you might consider what you can do to minimize that. You know, move, spend some nights elsewhere with family, hire a security guard. Buy a dog or a … well … you have options."

"Logan had a gun, and look what good it did *him*."

He looked back at her but said nothing.

"Detective Kovacs, you don't know how long it's taken me to find this place, turn it into something I'm proud of, and call it my home. I can't just cut and run."

"I admire that. Personally, I wouldn't either. No way I'd let some punk run me out of my home and business. Especially not some washed out druggie that's emerging from that shithole down in Salem. Let me tell you, that place ain't pretty. Let's say, hypothetically, *you* were this Michael Edens, and *you* got away with Logan's murder. You get nabbed for drugs after-the-fact and get put away. Then, after six years, you get released. Would your first thought be to commit a crime that's gonna put you right back behind bars again? I don't think so. I think you get out of there, head back to whatever family you've got that'll take you in, and try to get it behind you as soon as possible. 'Parole officer's checking in on you so often, you get so much as a speeding ticket you're right back where you came from ... I bet you're unwilling to spit on the sidewalk once you get out. Besides ... why would he *want* to come back after you?"

I can think of over eight hundred thousand reasons.

"Especially after doing serious time like that. Six years'll take something out of a person. Look, I know you're worried, and really I can't blame you. But here's what I'd do: I'd arm myself with information, lean the police as much as you need, and take the time to think about what you've built here … and how safe you'll feel. I wouldn't make any rash judgments based on what we've found out here today. I really don't think there's cause for it … and I've been doing this for over twenty-four years now."

Over the next few days Jennifer's mind floated from the dueling obsessions of Ethan and the Edens brothers. To thwart her mind's obsession with one, she steered her thoughts toward the other, only to have the distraction consume her with equal torment. For nearly a week she didn't heard a single word from Ethan, and his silence plunged her into renewed uncertainty. When she finally did speak to him on the evening of his next game, she found his ease bewildering, as if his axioms about "life being short" and her "casting a spell over him" were either forgotten or false. She thought it might help to tell him about the Edens brothers, but as she feared it led to an interminable series of questions about the past, and only drew him further from the future. She couldn't decide which frustration was worse, her inability to coax Ethan along a course toward their togetherness, or her inability to cull reassurance from Detective Kovac's predictions about Michael Edens behavior after his release on July first. As Ethan and the Edens brothers spun within her mind, their centrifugal force became unbearable -- a vortex from which there seemed to be no relief.

She engaged Charlie and Helena whenever possible, but when neither were available she only had KC to turn to, and his disposition remained icy -- an estrangement that felt silly one moment, but devastating the next. Even his sociability in the concession area disappeared, something she hadn't thought possible. It was on a Saturday, a day that marked a week since her night with Ethan and three days from Michael Edens' release from prison, that she overheard some players puzzle over KC's brusqueness.

This has to stop.

Making her way to him in the concession area, she was intercepted by Charlie, who was in the process of helping KC, and was struggling to carry an armload of empty soda containers toward the recycling barrel. After helping Charlie with his task she neared KC again, but a trio of players interrupted her with an inquiry whether anyone was available to fill-in and play on their team.

"How many you need?" she asked.

"One. Guy or girl. It doesn't matter."

All three of the players were looking in her direction, anticipating her acceptance of the offer. Instead she turned to KC. "Kase, why don't you play?"

"I uh … I mean, I'm kinda busy here."

"You said you'd play the next time someone needed a fill-in."

"I … "

"In fact, you promised. Remember? Scout's honor?"

Charlie added, "Yeah KC, you promised. I never get to see you play."

"That's because I haven't before," said KC in a high voice that parroted Charlie's.

"Well what are you waiting for?" Charlie said, having taken no offense. "Now's your big chance!"

Staring back at the expectant faces, KC agreed to play, an answer that brought a cheer from Charlie, a smile from Jennifer, and a look of mild disappointment from the trio -- who knew they were getting an inferior player. After changing into his ratty soccer shoes, some shorts, and his unblemished silver-striped Adidas shin guards, he donned a shirt tossed to him by a teammate and made his way out onto the field.

"Well bloody hell! Look who's decided to make a go of it!" exclaimed Ian after a quick test of his whistle. "Never thought the day'd come they got the likes of you to drop the girlie dishrag and get out from behind that counter."

"Yeah well it's the first time ever, Tubby, so take it easy on me, eh?"

Ian let loose a hiccup. "You'll get the same as all the rest. Just pace yourself young fella. Fifty minutes'll take the wind right outta ya, and I don't see as your team's got any subs."

They put KC on defense where he stood the best chance of contributing. Their team played well, resulting in a respectable one-goal halftime deficit, and just as everyone was resting and gulping water, two more teammates arrived to give them some added depth. Etiquette dictated KC continue playing if he so chose, and he did, remaining on the field to start the second half.

"He's playing pretty good, isn't he hun?" she asked Charlie as they sat behind the Plexiglas to watch.

"He's doing okay, but I want to see him score."

A *zap!* sounded as she put her arm around him and made a mental note to look to see who had entered. "That might be a bit much to ask."

"Why?"

"Because defenders don't score too often, and besides, it's his first game. His role is to stop the other team, not be a scoring machine." She looked to her right, and saw an unfamiliar man enter the arena. His wavy hair went down to his collar, and his goatee was short, black, and an irresistible attraction to the fingers of his left hand. By his uncertain gaze it was clear it was his first time in the arena, and by his clothes and leather jacket it was clear he was not there to play soccer.

"Did *you* score in your first game, mom? Mom?"

An associate of Michael Edens?

"Mom?!"

"What?"

"I said … did *you* score a goal in your first game?"

"Oh Charlie. It was so long ago. I really can't remember."

The leather jacketed man walked slowly past them and took a seat near the goal KC was defending. She continued talking to Charlie, glancing over his head at the stranger as she did. He sat with his hands in his jacket pockets as if cold, and his focus was drawn toward the action of the game. As numerous players battled on the field just opposite his seat, she heard him yell something, to which KC immediately stopped playing and replied, "Oscar?!"

KC stood frozen while play continued nearby. An uncertain look appeared on his face, one that was just turning into a grin when the ball not squirted free, leading to a shot, a deflection, and the ball's path toward his face.

He went down in a heap.

Charlie was one of the first on the field, offering his shirt to help staunch the blood which poured from KC's nose. Repeatedly KC said he was okay, but blood was still flowing as he was led off the field with his face pointed upward, and she, Charlie, and Oscar all escorted him to the back to lay down.

"Boss?" he croaked. "I'd like to introduce you to Oscar."

"I figured as much. Nice to meet you."

"And you," was the reply.

Oscar apologized as they walked to the back, believing himself at fault for the distraction and therefore, the injury. KC evidently agreed, for not only did he fail to accept the apology, but he didn't acknowledge him further. They got him on the couch with some Kleenex in place of Charlie's blood-soaked shirt, and minutes later she left him in Charlie and Oscar's care, found Charlie a replacement shirt, and went back out to run the concessions. After a few minutes of Charlie and Oscar's combined ministrations, KC told Charlie he would be all right, and asked if he could speak to Oscar alone.

"Has the bleeding stopped yet?" Charlie asked.

"Almost." In truth it hadn't, but Charlie was placated, and he returned to the arena without further fuss.

"So, I uh … saw you on TV," Oscar said.

KC didn't respond.

"You know … on the news? The piece on old news stories"

"Oh yeah? And what did you think?"

"That you did a nice job." He paused. "It's just that … "

"What?"

"Well … it's just that I never had you figured for soccer is all."

KC sensed condescension in the word *soccer*. "What's that supposed to mean?"

"Just … that I had you pegged for outdoor sports is all. This is … "

"What?"

"Just … odd. I never knew you had an interest in soccer."

"I never had an interest in trees either."

Neither of them spoke as they assessed the familiar lurking of an argument.

"The truth is," KC began, "my working here has little to do with soccer. You just witnessed the first time I've ever played. And maybe the last." He handed a bloody tissue to Oscar and pressed a fresh one against his nose. "It has to do with being part of something."

"Well congratulations. Although, I don't recall you getting bloody noses from dealing with forestry issues." With a serious tone he added, "This is beneath you Kase."

KC pulled himself up to an elbow, ready to engage, but suddenly lacked the energy. He wanted to speak of his feelings of loyalty to Jennifer. He wanted to say how his job was the best he'd ever had. How he was so taken by the place, a compulsion to try the inane sport had stirred within him. How, at East Portland Indoor Soccer, he felt part of a family for the first time in his life. Instead he merely grabbed a fresh tissue from the coffee table, laid back on the couch, and closed his eyes. "It doesn't matter if it's beneath me or not. The owner, Jennifer … she's gonna sell out soon, and I'm gonna get the shaft like I always do." He felt the mashing of cushions as Oscar sat near him on the edge of the couch.

"I'm sorry Kase."

Oscar stood, headed for the kitchen, and tossed Kleenex atop the bloodstained ones previously thrown in the kitchen wastebasket. As he did, KC raised himself up to an elbow again. "Oscar, why are you here?"

He turned in the doorway and leaned against the frame. "Well like I said, I saw you on TV and thought I'd look you up and say thanks and all."

Sensing it was not the truth, KC sat up and noticed far less blood on his tissue than before. Again, but with more insistence, he asked, "Oscar … why are you here?"

Oscar walked back to the couch but did not sit down. Instead he stood with his arms crossed defensively. "Well your mom said this is where you spend most of your time, and she gave me the address so … "

Interrupting, this time he said it softly, making it clear he would not stand for further evasions. "Oscar … why are you here?"

There came a sigh. A defeated grin fell over Oscar's face, and his arms released. He sat down on the couch, clasped his hands together, and took a deep breath. "The truth is Kase … the truth is I came because I've missed you."

PART V

Chapter 1

Accompanied by the owner of the roofing company and his adult son, Jennifer ascended the fire escape to inspect the recently-completed work on the roof. Despite the early hour and the chilling wind that increased with each gritty rung, she reveled in the climb -- imagining her torments swept away by the force that streamed across her face, up the back of her sweatshirt, and sent her hair cascading about her face.

Before she knew it, she was on the roof.

All alone for the moment, she felt at peace while staring out at the smaller buildings between the arena and the river. In the distant sky was a dark gray gloom, and beneath it, the cluster that comprised the buildings of downtown Portland. Regrettably, the moment came to a sudden end, spoiled by the grunting arrival of the two men.

While the fireworks party had been in a state of limbo all week, no significant rain had fallen in the past several days, the repairs proceeded as scheduled, and the team of immigrant workers had completed their labor the prior day. As the owner and his son detailed the technical aspects of their work -- something about layers, tar, and the binding time of polymers -- her interest lapsed and her thoughts spun toward the fact that just hours from now, Michael Edens would be released into the world.

"And it's a good thing we finished when we did," said the son with a satisfied grin. He thrust his chin toward the river and added, "It looks like rain."

She turned again to the West where the darkest clouds loomed, and pulled a strand of hair from her mouth. "But everything dried overnight, right?"

The owner spoke up. "Oh yeah. She's good as new. You shouldn't have any troubles for the next several years. In this section anyway."

"And it's fine if we have a party with a bunch of people up here, right?"

Both men stared at her as if her priorities were warped, but eventually confirmed that, yes, a party would cause no problems with the roof. She gave her final approval of the work, grabbed a pile of blue tarps, and took a few steps to the edge where she let them drop to the sidewalk far below. As a group they headed for the fire escape where father and son simultaneously motioned for her to descend first.

While the day's forecast had been for clear skies, the only evidence of the sun was a few diagonal beams that fought through an aperture in the clouds on the opposite side of the river. Contrasted against the dark backdrop of the coming storm, the scene was so striking she stopped her descent -- a delay that ended with the son's foot pinning her hand to a rung.

"Ahhh!"

"Oh! Sorry 'bout that ma'am!"

After accepting his apology she hastened to the ground and checked the abrasion of her knuckles. She gathered up the tarps, and though both men offered to help she declined and led them inside through the back door cracked open with the help of a brick. Dumping the tarps near the concession counter and leading the men to her office, she pondered placing another call to Detective Kovacs. He'd been true to his word ever since their initial meeting, sharing various pieces of information about Michael Edens whenever he came upon them. The knowledge of where he would be living upon his release (Prineville) and the frequency with which he had to meet with his parole officer (every two weeks) were of some consolation, but she would have felt better if Kovacs had been able to procure a photo, something he'd promised but hadn't yet delivered. Pushing open her office door, it dawned on her she hadn't seen KC all morning, but the ringing office telephone tore her from the thought.

"East Portland Indoor Soccer," she answered.

"Hey. It's Ethan."

"Hey yourself, stranger."

Dammit! Why'd I have to say that?

"Stranger? What do you mean?"

"Um … nothing. Hey, can I call you right back? I'm just finishing up with the repairmen. Where are you?"

"At work."

"I'll call you back in a couple of minutes."

She wrote out a check for over four thousand dollars to Barr and Sons Construction, shook their oil-stained hands, and walked them out. Ethan's call lifted her mood, and once father and son were dispatched she felt like rushing back to her office to call him back.

"So what was the damage for the repair?"

"In total? Just over eleven thousand."

He whistled and muttered, "Jeez, you could have bought a new car with that."

"Yeah tell me about it. I guess I'll just have to settle for the pride of owning my own business."

She laughed as he recounted an absurd argument between two of his coworkers, but her mood was shattered upon her innocuous inquiry of what he did last night.

"Oh not much. My friend Lonnie called. He and his wife are coming into town next month, and Beth and I are trying to figure out some way to hang out with them at the coast for a few days."

The casualness with which he mentioned his girlfriend in the inclusion of his future plans jarred her with a feeling of insignificance, and reversed the impression that their evening together had tipped the scales in her favor. Though she tried to keep her feelings hidden, the surge of grief that rose within her built to tears, and she was unable to speak to him with the same amicability as earlier in the conversation.

"Is … uh … there anything wrong?" he asked.

"No. Sorry. It's just … I'm just a little distracted."
Substantiating her lie, a *zap!* sounded in the office.

"Are you sure?"

She wiped away a tear she hoped would be her last, and watched as KC entered the arena. Seeing the receipt from Barr and Sons Construction on her desk, she was able to mask what she felt. "Yeah. So … with the roof repair all done, you're still up for the party, right?

"I wouldn't miss it for the world."

The bipolarity of his words almost prompted her ultimatum that he pick between herself and his girlfriend, but as quickly as the notion flared, it burnt out, and she was left without the will to challenge him. Something was holding him back. Something she couldn't see, or understand. Or overcome.

Is it because I have Charlie? What is it about me that's not good enough?

"Are you still there?" he asked.

"Yeah … sorry."

"So what time should I show up?"

She felt numb. "What … time … "

"For the fireworks party."

"Oh. Sorry. Why don't you, um … why don't you just plan on coming over sometime around sundown. That's when everyone else will get here."

After an exchange of good-byes, she got up from her desk desperate to sweep the conversation from her mind. The blue pile of tarps commanded her attention, and while KC was engrossed in the newspaper five feet from them, it was she who gathered them in her arms and headed for the cabinet behind the snack bar. She knew she should fold them up neatly, but her mood left her only with the patience to cram them into the unused bottom shelf -- an effort that ended in failure.

Why the fuck won't these fit?

She pulled them back out, lowered her head to the ground, and peered inside. Deep within the shelf were multiple stacks of paper, and pulling some out, she found them to be fliers advertising East Portland Indoor Soccer. There were thousands of them, but her inquisitiveness was drawn not to their number, but to the fact she couldn't remember them as leftover ones from KC's marketing blitz a year ago. They were more recent. Leaving the tarps behind, she stood and approached KC at the picnic tables where he was ferreting out the classified ads from the rest of the paper. "Hey Kase?"

"Yeah?" he replied without lifting his head.

She held the flier out for him to see. "What do you know about these?"

He looked up. Though momentarily silenced by what she held, he answered unremarkably, "Oh … that's just the latest flier."

"How come there's thousands of them behind the snack bar cabinet?"

He paused. "Because I didn't have anywhere else to store them."

"Let me rephrase. Why would there be thousands of them *anywhere*?" She set the flier on the table, and he swooped it up and brought it closer to his face.

"Because I haven't been using them up as quickly as I used to."

"Used to?"

He lifted his eyes from the flier and began an evasive response, but abandoned it and instead said with a sigh, "Boss, where do you think I go when I leave here at night after all the games are over?"

She shrugged.

"Part of me thought you'd figured it out and were okay with it, but I guess not." He straightened in his seat and pushed the newspaper away. "For the past year, I've been canvassing neighborhoods with my backpack full of these things. I've been doing it ever since I started." He gave a long pause, but she matched his silence. "Why do you think people started flocking here soon after we opened? The website?" He answered his own question with a shake of his head, and there was a slight quiver to his voice when he next spoke. "And why do you think people still mention the fliers from time to time? Because they held onto it for ten months and just got around to calling? I'll tell you why they still mention them ... because I haven't' stopped. I've hit every neighborhood on both sides of the river, every sports venue in town, and just about every athletic club around. Sometimes I just cruise random streets ... putting them in mailboxes and on windshields. Night after night I've done it until I've used all I'd stuffed in my backpack. Sometimes I'll even do it during the day ... parking lots downtown, the mall at lunch hour ... just to get the word out. Why is it you think we had that big surge last fall? I'll tell you why … because of the fucking fliers."

She was speechless, and he was spent. A hundred questions came to mind as she slid into the seat opposite him. Discarding the subject of fliers for the moment, she asked, "Kase? You've been in a snit all week. Would you please tell me what's wrong?"

He took a deep breath, but said nothing.

"Please."

With reluctance he said, "I saw the fax."

"The fax?"

"Yeah. You know. That legal document about selling the place to SoccerCity. I can't imagine there's much future for me here once that sale goes through. As soon as you sell, I'm gone."

She looked down and saw the classified ads in front of him. "Oh Kase. I think you've got it all wrong."

"Do I? I've gotten the shaft before, remember? Do you really think those assholes from SoccerCity'll want to keep the me around? I don't want to be the last one to find out I'm expendable. I'd rather be on the front end of this one."

"No Kase ... I mean you've got the wrong impression about me selling. I've got no plans to do so. Quite to the contrary. I couldn't even imagine it."

"Please. I saw the Letter of ... the Letter of ... "

"Understanding."

"Whatever."

"Yeah well, you see I ... ", she began, but instead of explaining the entirety of her strategy of dealing with SoccerCity, she opted for the easier way out. She rose, said, "Come with me," and led him to her office. Halfway there Charlie emerged from the back and asked them what they were doing.

"Nothing hun. Hey ... maybe you can help me. Come on." Her arm fell around his shoulder while KC trailed behind. Upon entering the office she went directly to her file cabinet, unlocked it, and extracted both copies of the original Letter of Understanding from within. Holding it in front of her for both KC and Charlie to see, she said, "I only pretended I was interested in selling the place to see what they would say, and to see what I could learn about us and them. I've never had any intention of selling out."

Charlie looked confused, and KC was unmoved. A *zap!* sounded.

"And I'll prove it to you. These documents I hold are the official signature copies they sent me." She reached back into the file cabinet, "And this is the fax." She handed it all to Charlie. "Hun, would you please shred these for me?"

Happy for any opportunity to use the paper shredder, Charlie said "Okay!" and snatched them from her hand. Over the grinding of the machine that reduced both the document and KC's final doubts to tatters, she saw a softening within his expression. He motioned for her to follow him from the office. Once they were alone near the field he said with his head bowed, "I've been an ass."

"I know," she replied, "and you've thrown a mother of a wet blanket on this fireworks party we're having in a few days."

"I know," he replied with dejection. In a more upbeat tone he asked, "Jen?"

"Yeah."

"I'm sorry."

"I'm sorry too Kase." She felt like hugging him, but resisted in the remembrance of her past misjudgments. They stood facing each other in awkward silence until he took a step forward, reached out, and hugged her for the first time ever. It was such a shock she let out an audible gasp, but as her arms overlapped behind him and their chins rested on each others' shoulders, they held each other with the familiarity of their thousandth embrace instead of their first. It was he who initiated a break.

"You okay?" she asked upon pulling away enough to see his swollen eyes.

"Yeah. I'm just … "

"Relieved?"

He exhaled heavily. "*Happy* is more like it."

She placed a hand on his shoulder to say something more, but her attention was drawn to a flicker of movement within the rafters behind him. "What the hell was that?" she asked while pointing over his shoulder. He turned around, and on cue there was whirl of something flying between the beams. "Look! Right there!"

Casually he wiped away the moisture from one eye. "Oh, that's just the bat. He's been sharing your home for about a week now."

With an open mouth she stared as it darted crazily, and suddenly stopped. Losing interest, she stepped forward until she was just behind him, and whispered in his ear, "And it's *our* home

Kase, and don't you ever *fucking* forget it." He turned around with a smile on his face and was about to respond with reciprocal profanity, but Charlie had just emerged and was within earshot. Instead he asked, "So are you and I friends Jen?"

"It feels like it to me."

"It feels like it to me too."

Charlie walked to her side, announced that the papers were shredded, and asked if they were going to the store to buy things for the fireworks party. "Thanks hun. Yeah, we'll head out in a few minutes, so you'd better go get your shoes on. Oh, and hey … did you know that we have a bat living here in the arena?"

"Yeah. KC told me last week."

She turned toward KC with a smirk of being the last to know.

KC shrugged, and just as she opened her mouth to bring up his unsanctioned flier campaign, Charlie interrupted her by holding up a piece of paper. "Mom, who is this Michael Edens? There was this picture of him on the fax machine."

As she drove from the supermarket with food and drinks for the fireworks party, Charlie filled the car with chopped lyrics in search for the best song. It was of vague amusement to think that the issue she'd resolved today was one of which she was completely unaware. No sooner had the SoccerCity documents been shredded, KC dropped his sullen demeanor, discarded the classified ads into the recycling bin, and returned to his old self. His enthusiasm for the party returned as well, and he'd added to her shopping list a dozen things he claimed were essential for the party to be a success.

Charlie finally settled on rap music, but it played for only a few seconds before a commercial came on, and he switched over to heavy metal. With the change in music her thoughts of KC vanished, and in its place emerged the mug shot of Michael Edens faxed to her by Detective Kovacs. She'd imagined he would look like an ogre, or someone with the sinister leer of a comic book villain; but his photo had been neither terrifying nor threatening. Instead there was a vacancy -- eyes that saw Logan in life and death one autumn night ten years ago -- eyes that said 'So what?' as they peered back into hers.

"There's nothing good playing," Charlie whined.

"I know. It's a conspiracy," she replied. Seizing the opportunity to talk to him, she flipped the radio off. "Hun, I want to talk to you. How are you doing on the whole fear thing?"

"Fine."

"Are you still feeling anxious and insecure about things?"

"Sometimes."

He was reluctant, so she switched tactics. "Well now that we've got all the stuff from the store, and the weather's supposed to clear up starting tomorrow … there's no going back on the party now. I can't believe it's just three days away. Are you excited to have Jonah come over and see the show?"

She got a more lively answer. "Yeah. What time is he coming over?"

"Probably when the sun goes down hun. Now, you realize you're going to have to show me you can do the fire escape prior to the party. You'll need to show Jonah how to do it."

"Mom … I'm not a baby. I can do it."

"I know you're not a baby, Charlie, but I've never *seen* you do it, and I don't want to find out you can't after all the guests have already arrived like last time. I don't think you want that either, do you?"

He gave a sheepish, "No."

"Do you want to practice when we get home?"

He shook his head.

"Charlie … I really think we should … "

"I don't want to right now."

"Okay, tell you what? I don't want to pressure you, but I have to insist on you trying to do it prior to the party. How 'bout this? I'll give you until the morning of July fourth, but by then you have to show me you can do it. Deal?"

"Deal." They shook on it, their official recognition that the accord was final. "Mom, you don't have to worry. I know I can do it. I had a dream where my dad told me I could."

She wanted to ask him to elaborate, but with the inquiry on the tip of her tongue, she reconsidered. "I'm glad, hun."

"Mom, could you tell me something else about my dad."

"Well … okay … " The neighborhood through which they drove brought an immediate thought to mind. "Actually very near here is where your dad and I first met. At a place called the Eastmoreland Country Club where we both worked. Want to see it?"

"Yeah."

She pulled her car into the ECC parking lot as Logan used to -- stopping in the middle of the wide lot and backing her car into a space far from the clubhouse. After turning off the engine and staring out the windshield, she said, "I haven't been here in years. It's changed." Where she remembered landscaping there was none; and yet where she remembered little or no greenery, significant trees and bushes grew. The parking lot now had lights, and the bag shack had been torn down and replaced with a spot for valet parking.

Elegant.

"We used to pass notes to each other behind those bushes," she said while pointing to a distant honeysuckle she remembered as a waist-high shrub, but now was the height of the roof.

"What kind of notes?"

"*I love you* notes and all that kind of mushy stuff."

"Oh."

She recalled her secret meetings with Logan and the sense of anticipation that came from removing the sliver of cement and finding a note. It was a marvel how just a few scrawled words could make her feel so happy. After Logan was fired, they never again exchanged written sentiments -- a way of communicating

their love for one another they both undervalued, and lost.

"Wait here Charlie. I'll be right back."

"Where are you going?"

"Just to check on something. I'll just be a minute, I

promise."

"Can you leave the radio on?"

"Sure."

She left him with his music and crossed the parking lot

toward the honeysuckle. An Alfa Romeo sped in front of her, but

its driver didn't take any notice of her as it roared over the speed

bumps and headed for the exit. Passing beneath the enclosure, she

came to the spot where she and Logan used to meet. Flowers

bloomed where she distinctly remembered gravel -- and bees,

drunk with nectar, swerved between the white echinacea, the violet

petals of the pansies, and the honeysuckle's yellow buds.

She ran her hand along the brick wall.

It was just as she remembered, and her eyes darted to the

cracked cement behind which lay the crevasse. As a book would

be slid from a crowded shelf, she worked the gray sliver free with a single finger, and once its weight fell to her hand, she was stilled to see a folded piece of paper within the thin space.

It couldn't be.

There could have been no sight more unexpected, and upon dropping the shard of cement to the ground, she extracted it, and found herself reading twin sentiments crawled beneath the outline of a unicorn.

I Love You, Logan Salinas

-- Jennifer

Since you've moved in you've made my house a home.

Promise me it will stay that way forever.

-- Logan

Her tears flowed at once. If he'd only known selling drugs would condense 'forever' into four years, he'd have stopped, Charlie would have a father, and she'd be facing none of the fears that lay before her. Instead she was alone, and a yellow scrap of paper was all she had to show for the love they shared so many years ago.

She walked across the parking lot to the car while gingerly folding the note back upon its deep creases -- fourteen years having worn the paper to the point of disintegration. Before she even opened the car door, Charlie's music could be heard pulsing from within, and she gave her eyes a final wipe to keep from him the fact she'd been crying.

He turned the radio off as soon as she shut the door behind her. "Mom, why are you crying?"

With a snort she handed him the note. "Well hun, I found something your dad left for me long before you were born. It was in the secret meeting place I was telling you about." As he took it from her hand she cautioned, "Be careful. It's on the verge of falling apart."

He unfolded it with reverence and read it.

"If you take the unicorn from the collection … you know, the crystal one … it'll match the exact shape you see there."

"You guys really loved each other, didn't you?"

"Very much hun."

"Do you ever think you'll be able to find another person to be in love with again? I mean in addition to me?"

She was grateful he'd blended maternal and romantic love, because it allowed her to laugh rather than cry. With an amused smile she said, "I'm looking hun. I'm always looking."

They drove home speaking nothing more about love, the fire escape, Logan, or the note which Charlie kept folded and in his lap. Instead they spoke only of music they either did or didn't like as Charlie flipped from station to station. Stopped at a red light near home, Charlie rejoiced in a song she despised, and after a loud "Ugh … no way!" she reached out to change the station. He thwarted her, and their duel denigrated into a chaotic mixture of laughter and staccato bursts of music as the stations were changed back and forth. Aware only of their struggle to force their musical preferences on one another, neither of them noticed the white Oldsmobile stopped at the light next to them, where Jack Edens languished behind the wheel.

Chapter 2

Acid ate at Jack's stomach as he drove the Oldsmobile onto Crescent Street, Gardiner Lane, SE 22nd Avenue, and then Hawthorne Boulevard. On the backseat lay his gym bag, filled not with the accoutrements of soccer but an assortment of clothes and a few things from the bathroom. He stopped at a traffic light, gazed out at the clouds that threatened rain, and tried to find a comfortable position within the grip of his seat. Though it pressed upon him uncomfortably, the bulge in his back pocket reminded him of the presence of his wallet, and he wrung some comfort from the knowledge it was recovered -- just like the angel said. While the prism hung in its usual place from the rear view mirror, it was lifeless and still, and even as the car's motion caused its sway there was no indication of rainbows or angels.

Or hope.

The light turned green and as the car began to climb the freeway onramp. As it passed the building adorned with the giant painted soccer ball and the words EAST PORTLAND INDOOR SOCCER, recollections of playing drifted to mind, though they failed to break through. Soccer was a part of his past -- not his future.

He flipped on the radio and headed south from Portland toward Salem. Cars zoomed by as he stayed in the right lane, and the city dropped behind him -- first the big buildings of downtown, then the homes of the suburbs, and lastly the car lots and outlet malls that lined the freeway. For many miles there were only crops, dirt, and the license plates of enormous trucks to gaze at -- a monotony abruptly broken when he noticed a green freeway sign:

Salem Exits   8 miles

And a while later, a dark brown one that read:

Oregon State Penitentiary
Use Exit 239A

His stomach stung, and he looked to the prism for relief. Though lifeless, its touch gave him some comfort. Lifting its fishing line free from the rear view mirror, he brought it to his lap, squeezed it in his fist, and whispered, "I believe" again and again. Peering down at his opening fingers, he longed for light or rainbows, but skin tone was all that could be seen through the distortion of the facets.

The blast of a horn cut short his scrutiny.

He gingerly hung the prism back upon the rear view mirror.

As before it dangled a few inches above the dash, and just as he

took his eyes from it, a brown freeway sign came into view:

Oregon State Penitentiary
Next Exit

He followed the brown signs, making his way past trailer

parks, churches, and blackberry brambles, and into a mix of

farmland and forest. Tiring of the radio, he flipped it off and

looked up just as a distant structure of concrete came into view

through a break in the trees. Set against the verdant hills it looked

grand and dead at the same time, and as he drove closer more and

more cars materialized on the road. Soon the structure loomed

before him, and following the signs that led to a long driveway

lined with razor wire, the Oldsmobile soon became a middle link in

a taut line of cars. A man in a uniform stood near a booth and

waved people forward. He spent a few moments talking to each

driver, and by the time Jack pulled up next to him, the letter was

unfolded and ready in his lap.

"Where ya headed young man?" asked the before the car

had even come to a stop. Leaning forward and resting a forearm on the roof of the car, he watched as Jack shifted to P, stamped the emergency brake to the floor with his foot, and wordlessly produced the letter.

The man studied it. "Says here you need Parking Lot F. You know where that is son?"

Jack didn't, and shook his head.

"You go straight about five hundred yards, then turn left where you see the giant F. It'll be in big red letters. 'Can't miss it. Park as close to the building as you can." He looked at his watch, handed back the letter, and swept the interior of the car with his eyes. "They'll release 'em anytime between now and noon. You got all that?"

"Uh-huh," said Jack. He struggled to refold the letter and shifted the car to D. The car shuddered as the forces of the emergency brake and the engine fought against each other -- a conflict that continued until Jack released the brake with his left hand. Only then did he manage to drive off.

"You're welcome," said the man in the uniform and motioning the next car forward.

Jack found Parking Lot F and, as instructed, edged the Oldsmobile as close to the building as possible. There was barbed-wire between the building and the mass of parked cars, and despite a sign instructing visitors to keep clear, a dozen people stood near it gawking at whatever activity was taking place on the other side. Other vehicles shared the dilapidation of the Oldsmobile, and Jack parked behind a car whose bumper careened toward the ground on one side. A cigarette-wielding hand dangled from the car's window, while in the backseat two children alternated between fighting and casting looks out the rear window -- looks that turned into a contest to make the most insidious face.

He heaved the reluctant door open. Shifts in the wind brought the alternating smell of damp air and cigarette smoke his way, and misty rain began drifting to the ground. A break in the clouds allowed sunshine to grace the parking lot, but facing forward Jack failed to notice the rainbows that danced in the interior of the Oldsmobile behind him. Moments later the sunshine was gone, its portal snuffed out by the clouds shifting across the sky. Jack pulled up his collar to keep the moisture from his neck, and the hand that dangled from the car before him flicked the still-lit cigarette and retracted within the car.

"Hell of a day to be set free in the world," came a voice from his left.

Jack looked over to see an old man in a plaid shirt stuffing chewing tobacco into his cheek.

"Now that I think of it though, it was raining the day my boy was born ... but still, something ain't right about it. They should only release people on sunny days, don't ya think?"

Jack stared at the man with the bulging cheek who leaned back upon his truck, splashed the last of his coffee to the ground, and used the Styrofoam cup as a receptacle for his spit. Although the man had apparently spoken to him, there had been no eye contact, and Jack began to believe the man was merely talking to himself.

"Or at least a day with rainbows."

"Rain ... b ... bows?" inquired Jack.

The man looked up. "Yeah. Rainbows. You know ... like a sign the storm has cleared?" He approached with his cup in one hand and the other extended.   The name's Russell."

Jack tentatively shook the hand and sputtered his own name.

"Got my son bein' released today, Jack. 'Always tried to teach that boy right from wrong, but there's only so much you can do once they become an adult themselves. 'Know what I mean?"

Jack knew exactly what he meant.

"I brought him up Christian too … after his mother died. Church every Sunday. 'Didn't do no good though." He spat into the cup and wiped his mouth with the back of his hand. "You ah … you believe in God, Jack?"

"I … I, uh … I … b … a … ang … angels."

"Same thing I reckon. 'Makes you feel pretty small, don't it?"

Jack didn't answer, his attention drawn to a surge of activity by the congregation at the fence.

"Nothin's ever made me feel smaller than the day I realized God's already got a plan for me in my life. He's got a plan for everyone's life actually. Every aspect. From which day it is we'll leave our mortal selves behind, to the lessons we learn each 'n every day. Even down to the little things, like which parking spot you and I happened to choose this morning … "

A released prisoner was coming toward the gate.

" … to you and I standing here … "

The gate began to open.

" … to the entire constellation of raindrops on your car's windshield there."

He's heard that before from the angel in his dreams, and Jack turned, but the old man was busy spitting into his cup again. Once he'd wiped his lower lip he looked up -- not toward Jack but toward the gate.

"Ahh … there's Henry now. 'Looks different. Older. A little defeated maybe. You know, I can still see the little boy in 'im. Even now." He paused. "Well Jack, it was sure nice talkin' to you." The old man took a few steps forward, but then stopped, turned, and looked back. "I gotta say … 'sure is good to hear you believe in them angels of yours. Nothing's more important than believing." He winked, turned toward the gate, and moments later hugged his son in an embrace immune to time and circumstance -- an embrace Jack couldn't imagine would be duplicated between himself and Michael.

He stared at the two so intently he didn't notice Michael's passage through the gate -- an oversight only partially due to the distraction of the father and son reunion. As if a metamorphosis had taken place within the prison walls, Michael emerged as a different species -- a creature whose head was shaved and whose physique that showed muscles. Making his way between two parked cars, he slung a bag over his shoulder in a manner that accentuated the biceps of his left arm, and broke into an unforeseen smile as he approached. For just an instant Jack imagined prison had altered his personality as well as his outward appearance, and there would be a moment between brothers that would make everything all right.

But he was wrong.

Just as a smile began to spread on Jack's face, Michael said, "I can't believe that ol' jalopy still works!" and Jack realized the smile was meant not for him, but for the car. As he came within a few paces Michael held out his hand, but as Jack lifted his own to shake it Michael only smirked and said, "No, dumbass … the keys," prompting Jack to dig into his pocket and meekly hand them over.

"I haven't driven in so long, I'm not sure I remember how." He tossed the key ring into the air, snared it, and headed for the trunk. Jack turned, not toward Michael but to look for the old man and his son, but all that remained was a Styrofoam cup perched in the middle of a wet parking spot.

Michael threw his bag in the trunk and slammed it shut. "Momma said you had some trouble with 'er, and she had to send you money to get 'er fixed. 'She running okay?"

"Uh-huh."

"Well don't just stand there. Let's get the fuck outta here and over to Momma's 'fore they change their mind."

Jack headed for the unfamiliar passenger side of the car, and opened the door with the ease of only one hand. Michael overpowered the hinge of the driver's side door, and once inside tossed a pack of cigarettes onto the dash. He turned the key, gunned the engine, and threw it into reverse -- but the car made a horrible screeching noise and crept backward with a shudder.

"The br ... brake ... e ... mer ... gen ... "

"Yeah, yeah. I got it," Michael said while pulling the release on the emergency brake and easing the car backward. "I don't know why you gotta use it though. It's not like we was parked on a fucking hill or nothing."

Jack silently stared at the children making faces in the rear window again, before shifting his gaze to the dangling prism. In its sway there was only a vast emptiness.

"God, I could use a beer. I swear I forgot what it tastes like," Michael muttered. "So, momma been sendin' you money all these years?"

"No. I ha … have … a … a job."

"Yeah? Doing what?"

"W … wash … ing … d … di … dishes."

"Washing dishes, eh?" he snorted. "That sounds about right."

An uneasy silence set in. For minutes only the sound of the windshield wipers filled the void, a repetition to which Michael eventually added music from the first radio station he could find. From behind they approached the booth where the man in the uniform was giving instructions to the incoming cars. Michael honked the horn, raised his middle finger, and muttered "Here's a little farewell gift," before turning onto the road that led toward the mountains.

It rained for an hour but when it stopped, steep hillsides and churning rivers opened up before them. As the Oldsmobile climbed, the songs on the radio became riddled with static, and Michael muttered as he tried to improve the reception. Eventually he gave up, settled for a garbled tune, and grabbed the pack of cigarettes from the dash. "You think there'd be a fucking store

along here somewhere," he blurted before turning to look at Jack.

"You still don't say very much, do ya?"

Jack shook his head.

"I suppose it's just as well. So … how often you talk to

momma? Once a week?"

"N … not … no … "

"Not much at all?"

"Uh, y … yeah."

"Well she was coming to visit me all the time when I was

locked up. Drove me fuckin' crazy. She's pretty unclear on

things." They passed beneath a set of power lines that rendered the

radio unlistenable, and Michael flipped it off. "Always talking on

and on about how her baby's comin' home, and how she's gonna

throw some sorta party and cook some special meal or some shit

like that. I always preferred it when she wrote cuz then I could just

throw the damn letter away 'stead of having to sit there and take

it." He did a wheezy impersonation of her -- a dose of mockery in

which Jack could find no humor -- and concluded in his own voice

with, "And get this … she wants me to stay in Prineville and live

with her."

A spike of hope rose within Jack.

"As if I'd *ever* live in that shithole again." He placed a cigarette in his mouth and reached for the lighter, only to find it missing. "What happened to the goddamn lighter?"

"L … los … I uh … l … lost it."

"You lost it?"

"By a … a … acc … i … dent."

Michael muttered a repetition of Jack's words, but said nothing more. With the cigarette still dangling from his lips, he reacquired his prior topic. "Like I was sayin' … 'last thing I wanna do it sit around and take care of her. It'd be like being a nurse in one of them homes … waitin' on her hand and foot and all. First chance I get, I'm coming back to Portland with you. I'll give her some line about my parole officer or something. She'll buy it. She always does. She don't think so clear now anyway."

As the broad face of a dam came into view, the road thinned to a single lane in either direction, and they soon found themselves beside a lake whose surface sparkled with the midday sunshine.

"You got space for me at your place, right?"

"N … no … it's … t … small."

"I'm used to *small*. I just spent six fucking years in a cell the size of a closet. Remember?"

"No … n … no … it's … "

"I ain't askin' Jack. I'm tellin'. I'm coming to stay with you." He pulled the cigarette from his mouth and tucked it behind his ear. "You think things is changed between you and me?"

"I … n … no."

"Mmm?"

"N … no … I … uh … "

"You think you can say 'no' to me like things is changed? Maybe you think somehow you're better than me cuz I went to jail and you didn't. 'That it Jack?"

With the pain in his stomach worsening, Jack shook his head and stared at the lake as it came into view around each turn. Hundreds of exposed stumps dotted the no-man's-land of mud left behind by the receding water.

"See Jack, I have a plan … and you gotta part in it."

As a series of logging trucks passed in the opposite direction, Michael detailed a return to buying and selling something called 'meth' -- and without being told, Jack knew exactly where he fit in his brother's business plan. "See the thing about prison is … you got time. Nothing *but* time actually. Time

to sit back, listen, and learn from those guys who got busted just

like you. What mistakes they made. What they coulda done better

to avoid gettin' caught." Michael flipped off the windshield

wipers, ending the repetitive squawk of rubber on dry glass. "If I

coulda had the chance to listen to them years back, I wouldn'ta had

to piss away six years of my life lifting weights and sittin' around

doing nothing."

Through a band of trees Jack could see a dock whose last

plank hung in the air far from the water's edge.

"And most of those guys I learned from in the Pen?

They're out now. Some of 'em headed back to Portland once they

got out. Those guys are smart sons-of-bitches. Not like Nick, or

you." After a time he added, "They said for me to look them up

when I got out, and you know what? That's exactly what I'm

gonna do. No reason we can't be as big as we was before."

"B … but, I … "

"I ain't askin' Jack. I'm telling."

"But … I al … r … r … ready w … work … a … at … "

"Like fuck you do. You're just a goddamn dishwasher!

You think they couldn't replace a dishwasher in a second with some other retard? When we get back to Portland, your job is to help me, do what I fuckin' tell you, and get back to makin' deliveries jus' like you always did."

Jack looked to the prism in a plea for help, there was no sign of the angels. His stomach groaned at the confirmation of his worst fears -- his future would be controlled by his brother.

"Your six year vacation is over."

Imprisoned within the car, Jack could only stare out his window. The Oldsmobile rounded a turn and approached a bridge, on the opposite side of which was a marina and a general store.

"Hot damn. A market. I need to get me some matches and beer. Gimme your wallet."

Jack straightened in his seat, wrest his wallet from his back pocket, and handed it over.

As if talking to a dog Michael said, "You stay," as he parked in front of a white propane tank flanking the store. He exited, thrust the wallet in his own back pocket, and slammed the door shut. Left alone, Jack considered his options. He could get behind the wheel and drive back to Portland -- but no sooner had he thought it, he realized Michael had taken the keys with him. He could run away, hide for a few hours, and hitchhike his way back to Portland on his own -- but Michael would eventually show up, and the punishment for his flight was certain to be severe. Desperate and bereft of options, he reached for the prism.

"I be … believe," he whispered again and again, a repetition that ended when Michael burst from the store carrying a paper sack. Jack tore his hand from the prism, but it continued its pendulous swinging long after Michael had returned to the his seat.

"So I got some questions for you," Michael said, He popped open a can of beer, took a long drink, and slammed the door shut. "Look at me Jack."

Suddenly fearful, Jack turned to face his brother.

"So I'm in there, picked out my beer and gettin' my matches, and the lady behind the counter tells me how much it costs. So I go to open the wallet, and I pull out some cash to pay 'er, and then I notice … GODDAMMIT, LOOK AT ME JACK!"

Jack raised his head from its fallen position.

" … and then I notice these … these old newspaper articles inside." He held them up for Jack to see, but Jack was looking down again.

"Why you had these in here? Something for your scrapbook maybe?"

Jack said nothing.

After an exhale of frustration, Michael took another gulp of beer. "We ain't moving until you answer me."

Jack glanced up at the prism and began to sob.

Michael dropped the articles to the seat between them, belched, and set the can of beer upon the dash. "I suppose you thought getting' rid of the cigarette lighter was a good idea. One less thing to worry about." He fished around in the front pocket of his pants. "Well I got news for you." He produced a book of matches, folded it back upon itself, and pinched a match between the covers. "Bad news."

He pulled.

A flame burst to life with a *pop!* that made Jack jump. "In every store on the road between here and momma's … they give these books of matches away. Just give 'em away." He shrugged. "You don't need to pay for 'em or nothin'. Hell … they'd probably even give 'em to *you* if you asked." Michael paused, watched the flame for a second, and turned his full attention toward his brother. "Look at me, Jack."

Jack raised his head just enough to see his brother out of the corner of his eye. In his hand was a match alit with a teardrop of fire that Michael blew out just as it reached his fingers. "You think they burn any less than a car cigarette lighter? Mmm? Well let me set you straight … they hurt just as bad." He lit a second match. "Fire's fire Jack. It don't matter where it comes from. You wanna see what I mean?"

Jack shook his head.

"Yeah. I think we should try one out."

Jack recoiled, but instead of the horror he imagined, Michael picked up one of the newspaper clippings from the seat, lit its edge, and blew out the match. The brittle paper was engulfed so fast it surprised even Michael, and he hastened to throw it to the floor where his foot quickly extinguished it. The smell of smoke permeated the car.

"So why you got these articles in your wallet?"

Jack shook his head and began sobbing again.

Michael lit another match and reached for the second newspaper clipping. "Maybe you don't care about these articles. Maybe you don't even care how much it'd hurt if I held this here match against your skin." The second article went up in flames and was thrown to the floor to suffer the same fate as the first. "But maybe there's something here you *do* care about." He held the still-burning match to the fishing line of the prism, and the filament immediately ruptured, dropping the orb into his waiting hand. Jack looked up with alarm, a reaction that told Michael all he needed to know about the importance of the prism. He blew the match out.

"You tell me why these articles was in your wallet, or this thing goes out the window and you never see it again."

"N … no … I … "

"Okay, you asked for it … " Michael said, and feigned a throw toward his open window.

"NO! Mn ..Don't … O … k … kay. O … kay."

"I'm listening."

Through a succession of sobs, Jack spoke. "I sh … showed th … them t … to … to … s … s … someone ah ... ah … "

"Who'd you show 'em to?"

"Th … the girl … l … at … soccer … pl … pl … place."

"Why would you be showing 'em to some girl at some soccer place?"

"She … she thought … k … I … k … k … killed that … m … m … man from w … way b … ba … back … "

Michael took a quick sip, and interrupted. "What man? You talking about that miserable fuck Logan?"

Jack nodded. "Sh … she … thought … t … t … I … d … did it. But it … t was you an'… N … Nick d … did."

"Yeah? And what about it? That guy was cheating us out of money for years before we … " There was an ominous pause before Michael next spoke. With slow severity he asked, "Jack, why'd this girl think you had anything to do with Logan?"

The pain in Jack's stomach built. "Sh … she was w … w … with Lo … Lo … "

"She was Logan's girl?"

Jack nodded as Michael thought.

"Are you telling me you bumped into Logan's girl at some soccer place and she remembered you from way back then?"

Jack nodded again.

"And you went 'n showed her these articles!?"

"N … n … no. She … f … found th … em in m … m … wallet. I … I … I … lost m … m … "

Michael's voice fell into a matter-of-fact intonation. "So she remembered you from back then …you lost your wallet and she found it … and when she found the articles that just *happened* to be inside, you … you told her it was me an' Nick that killed Logan, and not you?" Throughout his recitation of events, he nodded and raised his eyebrows -- an agreeableness that masked whatever was to come next.

Jack nodded and feared the worst, but instead of the rage he expected, Michael's bellowing laugh exploded with a power that made him jump. Michael tried to speak, but his words competed with the laughter until he finally formed a coherent sentence. "Oh … you know … you really … you know you really … you really are a stupid fuckin' retard. You know … you're really … you're really even dumber than I thought."

Eventually his laughter died away. "You think there's any way in the world someone's gonna take your word over mine? I could just as easy say it was you that did it. Ever think about that? Maybe I say you was prone to violence and lost control. Maybe I say you an' Nick went there and the two of you killed him. Maybe I say Nick told me that was what happened, and I kept it quiet all this time because you was my little brother. Maybe I say you don't think so clearly, and was seeing things like them fuckin' angels all the time. Hallucinatin' that things was there when they really wasn't." He shook his head as if there was a library of fiction to choose from. "You're a funny guy Jack … a real funny guy. Just remember one thing though … if it ever comes down to my word against yours, there's no way they believe yours. Ever. People don't like retards. They feel sorry for 'em and all, but they don't like 'em and more 'n anything they don't trust 'em. And they're never gonna trust you." He took a lengthy drink of beer, tossed the can over his shoulder and into the back, and popped open another.

Jack said nothing, past experience telling him to be quiet.

Confident his point was driven home, Michael's mind shifted gears. "You think she's got his money? Mmm? We was never able to find it … Nick panickin' and all after I ... " he trailed off. "We left the house 'fore we could look for it good, but word was it was there. More than you could spend in a year. I bet she's got some of it somewhere."

An impulse to dissuade his brother rose within Jack. "I don't … d … don't think th … they … h … h … have ... "

"They? Whose *they*? She gotta a new man running things?"

Jack faced forward in silence, and this time, Michael had no patience for the leverage of matches or the prism. Giving in to his innate tendency to use force, he grabbed Jack by the back of the neck and bellowed, "WHO'S *THEY!?*"

With his shoulders hunched up, Jack sputtered, "a b … b … boy," through gritted teeth.

Michael lessened the pressure only slightly. "You sayin' a boy … like a kid? You sayin' Logan's girl from back then's got a kid?"

Jack tried to nod, but couldn't, and croaked, "uh … huh."

Michael released his grip and looked wistfully out the window. "Back before … I remember trying to get payment from that Carlton scumbag. You remember? That guy with them twins?"

Jack didn't remember, but nodded anyway.

"I remember one time he didn't want to pay. Nick and I threatened him with all sorts of stuff and no matter what, it didn't do no good. But when we threatened his boys … talked about what we was gonna do to them, and made 'im believe we was willing to go through with it. We had the money quick."

As a bead of sweat crept down his side, Jack watched Michael repetitively toss the prism a few inches into the air and catch it each time.

"Maybe she's still got some of his money … and then again maybe she don't. But we're gonna need a bankroll to get us started again. If we could get our hands on just some of it, we could pick up where we left off." He weighed the risk and the promise of pursuing it, and slowly nodded his head -- the allure of quick money combining with the alcohol to override his sense of caution. "Yeah. We gotta pay her a visit. And Jack … you're gonna help me."

Jack was beyond protesting, and merely stared at the prism Michael tossed so casually.

Upon starting up the engine and after another sizable drink, Michael backed the car from its spot near the propane tank and looked over at his brother's rapt attention at what he held. "What the fuck is this thing anyway?" he said, giving it a final toss and holding it up between his thick fingers.

"It … t … was … N … Nick's."

"That right? Nick's? And you kept it all this time?"

"Uh-huh."

Michael pulled the Oldsmobile onto the road, took another pull of beer. "It must mean a lot to you for some reason. I saw the way you was looking at it."

Jack relaxed just a little. The worst seemed to be over.

"Want it back?"

Jack nodded.

Instead of handing it over, Michael flung it in the opposite direction where it flew out the driver's side window and into the forest.

"NOOOO!" Jack cried.

Michael laughed. "Sorry. My darn hand musta slipped or something. Acc ... i ... dent, I guess. You know. Just like the cigarette lighter."

They were the last words spoken for the next hour, words that echoed in Jack's head as he looked out the back window desperate for a sign, any sign that the angels were still with him and following. But there was only a wet stretch of curving pavement surrounded on either side by lush forest, and as they drove farther up the mountain grade. He longed to be in any of the cars kicking up a plume of spray as they headed in the opposite direction.

After a long silence Michael began to talk intermittently, and to each soliloquy Jack responded with a rote, "Uh-huh" -- the safest response he knew. In the dream the angel had said to be

strong and stand up to his fears; but his confidence, like the details

of the dream itself, had faded. Michael's power was undiminished,

as was his will to wield it to get whatever he wanted.

While rain clouds obscured the tops of the mountains ahead

of them, mid-day sunshine broke through from above, causing

ghostly wisps of steam to rise from the wet asphalt and swirl atop

the road. A few miles before they reached the closed ski resort at

the mountain pass, Michael announced, "I gotta take a piss," and

pulled off the road to a flat clearing big enough to accommodate

hundreds of vehicles. Apart from the occasional passing car and a

group of leather-clad bikers who congregated at the extreme end of

the turnout, there was no one else around. Aluminum cans,

antifreeze containers, and plastic boxes that once contained tire

chains all littered the landscape of gravel and mud, and as Michael

pulled the car up to the edge of the overlook far from the

motorcyclists, he obliterated a puddle that had accumulated in a

deep tire rut. Butterflies rose from the edge of the water, and to

Jack's astonishment, one of them landed on the windshield.

Jack studied it for a while before pressing his scarred index

finger to the cool glass beneath it. Transfixed by its slowly-pulsing wings, he began to contemplate it was a sign of the angels, or even that the creature was an angel itself. Focussed on nothing else, he didn't see Michael's hand move forward or hear the Oldsmobile's windshield wipers activate, and with a mix of surprise and horror saw a single swipe of the blades mangle the creature against the outside of the glass.

"Gotcha!" Michael exclaimed with a triumph.

Jack recoiled in his seat but said nothing as he stared at the pitiful remains flattened by the repetition of scything rubber.

"You best take a piss now cuz I ain't stoppin' later," Michael said as he turned the wipers off and muscled open his door.

"I ... don't ... d ... not ... h ... have ... to ..."

"Suit yourself," Michael said before slamming the door shut and walking to the edge. With his back turned and a hand on one hip, he leisurely peed and drank at the same time.

The crushed butterfly remained foremost on Jack's mind, and he exited the car to pluck it from the glass. It was no longer alive, but one of its fragile wings was unmarred and beautiful -- a mix of fiery colors he studied before the wind whisked the corpse from his hand. Several strides away, Michael arched his head back to finish off his beer, and Jack approached from behind with steps that crunched on the wet rocks. The sound of a truck's air brakes drifted across the valley -- a noise engulfed by the starting and revving of multiple motorcycles. There was no guardrail between Michael and the chasm into which he peed, and as Jack closed the distance he thought of what it would take to push his brother off. He would only need to force him to take a single step -- a single step that would change everything; but no sooner had he contemplated it, he realized it was impossible. The muscles of his brother's arm and neck bulged as if squeezed by his T-shirt, and Jack knew he had neither the might nor the courage to act on such an impulse. Besides, the motorcyclists were passing, and there had been no sign from the angels indicating this was the way to proceed. Of course without the prism, the angels couldn't communicate like they normally did. All these considerations flashed within Jack's mind in the time it took him to take the final steps and stand beside his brother.

"Change your mind?" Michael asked as he zipped up his fly.

"Huh?"

"About peeing, dumbass. Change your mind about peeing?"

"Uh … n … no."

Michael snorted and wiped his mouth with the back of his hand. "Hell of a view, ain't it?"

Stretched out before them was a valley miles wide. Trees, interspersed with clear-cuts, covered the opposite hillside, and far below on the valley floor was a lake, another dam, and a triumvirate of powerlines that disappeared over a ridge. While both brothers mused about where the electricity was destined -- Michael imagined the light bulb and electric razor back in his cell, while Jack imagined the appliances back at Rudy's Diner.

"On second thought," Michael said upon dropping his beer can to tumble down the path of his urine, "I'm feeling beat. You drive the rest of the way. I'm gonna catch some shut-eye in the back." Jack watched the aluminum can bounce down the escarpment, taking some loose rocks and dirt with it until it spun from sight. Michael pulled the keys from his pocket, barked "Here!" and tossed them into the air. Jack fumbled them, but managed to pin the keys against his aching stomach.

"It's a damn good thing you caught 'em," said Michael. "If you'da dropped 'em over the side, maybe you'da had one of them *acc ... i ... dents* goin' down after 'em."

Michael headed for the Oldsmobile. He transferred the case of beer from the backseat to the trunk, rifled his bag, and pulled forth a single blanket. "Piss or get off the pot," he called out after slamming the trunk shut.

Backing away from the edge, Jack picked the correct key from the key chain, and after a slow walk to the Oldsmobile, struggled to open and pull shut the driver's-side door. The familiar torment of the ripped upholstery grated against his shoulder blade, and he watched in the rear view mirror as Michael stretched out in the backseat as best he could, though he momentarily sat up to kick Jack's gym bag to the floor and cast empty beer cans out the open window. He grunted, pulled the blanket over him, and rolled onto his side. "And don't wake me up until we get to momma's place. You got that dumbass?"

"Uh-huh," Jack responded before turning the key and starting the engine. Out of habit he reached down to release the emergency brake, only to find it had not been depressed. He shifted to R and backed up, gunning the engine to make sure the front tires crossed the rut. Once accomplished, he shifted to D and steered the Oldsmobile toward the road. Apart from a passing pick-up truck there were no other vehicles around, and once he checked both right and left, he lifted his foot from the brake to pull out onto the mountain road.

Until he looked up.

There, set against the dark clouds hovering above the mountains, was a rainbow. It spanned the entire sky before him, a panorama within which each band of color was distinct from the next. Leaning forward in his seat, he hit the brake and stared the sight with his chin upon the steering wheel. He would have remained that way indefinitely had a voice not called out from the back.

"Are we fucking gonna get going or what?"

"Uh … jus … m … minute," Jack replied without moving. The rainbow's radiance increased, and as Jack stared at it with awe, a strange feeling coursed through him. It tingled his skin, instilling in him a disregard for his brother's impatience -- a disregard from which strength was born.

It had to be the angels.

"H … have to … p … p … pee," he said in an attempt to buy time, and from the back Michael groaned with contempt, but said nothing more.

Turning the Oldsmobile around, Jack drove back to the car's prior position, set the car to P, opened the door, and walked to the edge. The scene stretched out much as it had before, the only exception being the brilliant arc dominating the sky to his left. He looked down only long enough to pee, deepening the channel Michael had previously carved with his urine. When finished, he zipped his fly and turned to his left. It was still there -- a river of colors in the sky high above him.

"I … b … believe," he whispered.

Insensate to fear, he headed back and plunged into the car's open doorway. Pulling the gearshift down from P to D, a feeling of exhilaration swept through him, and he ran a few steps away before looking back over his shoulder in anticipation of the Oldsmobile moving forward toward the ledge.

But instead it remained still.

Immediately he realized why. Out of habit he had hit the emergency brake, and as he weighed the action necessary to release it, his strength evaporated. It would require getting near

Michael again, a proximity no more than an arm's length away.

He took a tentative step forward, and between the front seats could see Michael was still lying in the back, facing the rear of the car just like before. There was still time to forego the impulsive plot and drive to Prineville as planned -- still time to retreat to safety; but there could be no real safety as long as Michael was in his life. The angel's words replayed in his head -- words that encouraged him to be strong and believe, and everything would be all right.

And a resurgent courage coursed through him.

He walked to the open doorway, bent down, and released the emergency brake. It snapped back against the underside of the dash with a jarring rattle, and after scurrying away from the car, he turned around.

But as before, the Oldsmobile failed to move forward.

He couldn't imagine what force would keep it anchored in its position, until he took a step back and saw the rear tires were stuck in the rut.

"Hey! Are you done fucking around yet!?" Michael called out.

Jack froze.

All his will flushed from him, and beads of perspiration ran down his arms, back, and forehead. Michael still had no idea what had taken place, but if it took much longer, there could be no doubt his wrath would compel an investigation. He considered that even now he could retreat to the car as if no contrary plan had been conceived and partially carried out, and drive onward to Prineville as planned.

Or he could proceed.

It was now or never, and Jack turned to the rainbow. The multiple colors still shone against the dark clouds, but his attention was drawn to something else instead.

Something much closer.

A butterfly, like the one crushed against the windshield, fluttered before him. He extended his open hand toward it, and was transfixed as it landed on the fleshy area beneath his thumb and walked to his scarred fingertip. But for its quivering wings it didn't move, and the more he stared at the fragile creature, the more he saw the precariousness of his own existence.

As if siphoned into the insect's tiny body, all fear passed from him. He could never go back to the way things were years ago. He'd rather fail and be cast into the ravine himself than endure a repetition of life as Michael's drug courier; and most of all, he knew he could never live with himself if he played any role in any harm that came to the girl who owned the soccer place, or her young son.

"Okay," he whispered, and blew the butterfly from his hand.

While heading back to the Oldsmobile he thought of calling out to announce there was nothing to worry about, but Michael had an ability to read things in his voice, and instead he chose silence. Calmly he planted his feet in the gravel as best he could, and began to push the car forward. After a few heaves he'd made little headway, but within his failure lay a kernel of discovery. In the car's rocking motion was a progression, and as he began to time his pushes, the back tires made greater and greater headway toward the crest of the rut. It seemed impossible his plan hadn't been discovered by now, and as Jack looked in the rear window he was both relieved and amazed to be able to see through the car all the way to the hood ornament.

Michael still didn't realize what was happening.

Sweat ran down his ribs as he rested the side of his head on the trunk and concentrated on timing his pushes with the car's momentum, but when he lifted his head again he was riveted by the sight he least wanted to see in all the world.

Michael had risen to a seated position.

The tires settled to the bottom of the rut. While his arms were strong and willing to try again, his legs were not, and his shoes slipped in the gravel as he hastened to rock the car anew.

"What the fuck is going on?!" Michael bellowed from within the car. His head pivoted as he peered out the side and front windows, but it wasn't until he glanced out the back that he saw Jack engaged in some sort of strange hunched effort.

"Hey! What the fuck you doin' out there!?" he called, but Jack paid him no attention. "HEY! ASSHOLE! I SAID … WHAT THE FUCK YOU DOIN' OUT THERE!?

Again, Jack didn't answer. The car was alternating between lurching forward and settling back, and while unclear about what his brother was attempting, he recognized they were in approximately the same position as before -- pointed toward the edge. Tempered by lethargy, the flirtation with sleep, and the sedative effect of alcohol, his anger subsided and he was left without the energy for further yelling. Rubbing at his eyes and gazing forward with a sleepy calm, his attention shifted from the notable crack in the windshield, to the fissure in the dash, and to the gearshift. Oddly, it appeared the car was in Drive.

Jack's incomprehensible rocking continued.

Squinting and leaning closer he found it was true, the car was in gear and the engine was running, even though the car did not move. He turned to look at his brother again, and as Jack lifted his head and their eyes met, Michael saw in Jack's gaze a steely determination unlike any he'd ever before seen. An unfathomable concept rose in his mind, severing the last of his lingering sleepiness.

Jack meant to kill him.

The tire neared the forward crest of the rut, but Michael's sudden movement within the backseat shifted the car's weight, hindering his progress. Within the rear window he could see Michael, with his blanket still wrapped around him, urgently pull himself between the front seats where he became momentarily wedged. Thrusting the car forward using all the force in his legs, arms, and back, Jack's feet slipped -- but then held -- and the car balanced on the crest for just a moment before falling back into the groove. It would only take one more push.

Michael shed his blanket with an urgent flail of his right arm, while at the same time a mighty tug at the steering wheel freed his torso from the vice of the front seats. Sweat dotted his scalp and brow, but inside he felt a burst of relief. The open doorway was just a lunge away.

Jack brought the tire against the forward crest of the rut again. He could see Michael's legs and rear through the window, and his frantic effort toward the open door. Setting his chin upon the hood, he found better footing to his right, and shifted his hands and body as well. His new grip positioned his right palm over the hole of the exhaust pipe, but despite the searing heat that melted through the layers of skin on his hand, his effort was undiminished, and was rewarded when the tire topped the crest and fell to the other side. The Oldsmobile began moving forward.

Michael felt the car lurch forward, compounding his urgency. Pulling one leg free from between the seats, he braced it beneath him and prepared to lunge for the opening. Just as he planted it however, he felt his other foot held back by a force he could neither fathom nor overcome. Looking back, he saw his foot had become wrapped in the strap of Jack's gym bag.

Jack stumbled forward and stood with his hands on his knees, watching the Oldsmobile head for the edge. He could see Michael struggling inside, and heard a blurted yelp of exertion. For once, the tenor of his voice was not one of authority or anger. Instead it was tinged with a quality he knew all too well. It was the sound of fear.

In the span of a precious second, Michael realized that pulling against the strap was futile. With a grunt he relaxed his leg, reached back, and freed his foot from the nylon manacle. The Oldsmobile was approaching the edge, and with his weight leaning back he was no longer positioned to lunge for the open doorway. Unable to reposition himself in time, he jumped before he was set, and just as he did the car pitched forward.

With wide eyes Jack watched the drama unfold within the car. The desperation of Michael's movements increased as the car reached the edge, and just before it dipped, he saw the dark figure of his brother vault toward the open door.

Michael's head careened against the interior roof of the car, opening a cut along his scalp and propelling him to the threshold of unconsciousness. While his head and left arm technically made the opening, the rest of his body did not, and remained anchored within the car. As the Oldsmobile barreled down the slope, its open door struck a tree stump, slamming it shut against Michael's neck with such force, no amount of muscle could prevent it from snapping the vertebrae of his neck and the spinal cord within.

The last Jack saw of his brother was his muscular forearm. Disembodied, reaching from within the car, and with a hand clenched in a fist, it appeared for just a second at the driver's side door before it, and the car, were gone from sight. After the initial rumble of a collision everything went silent, an eerie pause that lasted a few seconds before the destruction of metal and glass erupted from the valley -- a sound that was strangely familiar.

Then he placed it. It was the sound the garbage truck made when the dumpster was emptied outside his apartment window back home.

In the time it took for the Oldsmobile to bounce off a tree stump, vault through the air, and disintegrate as it rolled to the valley floor, Michael felt neither pain nor fear. As a riot of destruction flooded his ears, a single awareness consumed his mind. In that moment he realized his invincibility had been an illusion, shattered not by the police, rival drug dealers, or notorious fellow inmates, but by the most unlikely and person of all.

Jack walked to the edge and looked down. Nothing could be seen of Michael or the Oldsmobile, and the only evidence of what had happened was the dust that began to drift up in a faint cloud. He felt neither exaltation nor relief -- emotions that would come later and over time. Instead he was numb with the comprehension of what he had done. Turning to the rainbow, he found it had disappeared, and in its place all that could be seen was the stagnant darkness of clouds. Pain radiated from his hand, and when he brought it before him he found a white, puffy circle in the center of his palm. It hurt to close it or open it wide, so he kept it

in the position that caused the least pain -- half-open with his

fingers curled and apart, as if stricken with arthritis.

Then he realized he was not alone.

A butterfly fluttered erratically nearby. He reached out for

it, but instead of landing on his hand and healing the burn as he'd

hoped, it headed to the rut where it joined two others at the edge of

the murky water. In slow independent rhythms, each of the three

fanned their wings while they drank.

The oncoming rush of a distant car carried to Jack's ears,

and he staggered toward the road. Just as he reached the asphalt a

minivan came into view, and with his good hand he waved it

down. He could see it was occupied by at least two people, and as

it approached and slowed, a window rolled down. It pulled up next

to him and a woman in the passenger seat inquired, "What's

wrong?"

Hundreds of words formed in Jack's mind. Explanations.

The truth. Lies. Evasions. After a significant hesitation in which

she repeated her inquiry, Jack found one word rise from the tangle

of shock and disbelief at what had just occurred. Motioning with his good hand toward the edge, he uttered a simple explanation for

what had taken place.

"Acc … i … dent".

Chapter 3

Just before six o'clock on the morning of July fourth, the rumble of a truck on MLK shook Jennifer from her slumber. She could tell she'd recently had one of her recurring dreams involving Michael Edens, but on this morning the details lingered only as an ill feeling without images or dialogue. Morning light seeped through the windows high above her bed, and before long her mind ticked off the things she'd have to get done prior to the party. Ethan hadn't contacted her since their telephone conversation a few days ago -- a hiatus she'd anticipated, but one that plagued her nonetheless. The notion to demand he choose between herself and his girlfriend came to mind, but a confrontation was so contrary to the path she thought their relationship would travel, she dismissed the thought outright.

Somewhere on the other side of the brick wall a second truck rumbled by, then a third, and she forced Ethan from her mind by rising to check on Charlie. With ankles creaking she walked to his room, and from his doorway observed him asleep within the tangle of his covers. The crystalline unicorn was at the front of over one hundred knights that watched over him from atop his headboard, and drawn to it, she walked over and saw it alone sat atop Logan's ancient note. Picking up both items, she held them together so the faded outline matched the unicorn's profile with the perfection of puzzle pieces.

That's what we were once. A perfect fit.

Charlie stirred.

At first she froze, but then arranged both items as they were before and exited his room. Her second destination of the morning was the arena and the concession area coffeemaker -- until she heard the familiar squeak of her office chair, followed by a faint flip of paper. Likely it was KC, but not wanting to take any chances she edged to the office window so she could peek inside without being seen.

At her desk, hunched over a sketch, labored her sole employee -- and friend.

She ended her covert observation and joined him. "What in the world are you doing here so early, Kase?"

He was unsurprised to see her, even as she stood in her pajamas. "Well … when you stumbled upon all my fliers, and dug that one copy out, I got to thinking it sucked and could be so much better. Here's what I've come up with so far."

He handed her a traced action shot from a soccer magazine, set against a backdrop of the city skyline and Mount Hood. Above it was written DOWNTOWN'S PREMIER SOCCER COMPLEX, and beneath it was a blank space she presumed would be filled by the phone number, the web address, and other information.

"I don't know. Doesn't 'Downtown's Premier Soccer Complex' make it sound more grandiose than we actually are?"

"Oh come on, boss! That's called *marketing*. We need a fresh flow of people in here! You know … kinda like how the tobacco companies need new smokers when they kill all their customers off. We've got character. I shouldn't have to tell you that. We may not have the fancy digital schedules of those SoccerCity bastards, but if we can get people in here, let 'em get a feel for the ambiance … or even better if I can get a drink or two in 'em … I bet you get a lot of them to look past the surface inadequacies that don't really matter."

Surface inadequacies?

"Besides, you said this was my place too. Remember? That thing you told me not to *fucking* forget? Well I haven't forgotten, and as part-owner I say we officially re-re-start the flier campaign."

She knew he was right. They couldn't just rest on their heels now that they were turning a profit. People were bound to leave the arena, or the sport altogether, and they needed to bring in new people if their success was to continue. If newcomers could be persuaded to try the place out, at least some of them would stay and become regulars. They might be P.E. coaches, attorneys, investment bankers, or just people who appreciated a hidden bastion of warmth and camaraderie within a desolate industrial stretch of East Portland. "You know Kase, we both know it's gotta be about the soccer, but let's not forget the social aspect of the place." She directed his attention to the partially-completed flier. "Is there somewhere on here where we can promote special events, or better yet, send the message that this is the kind of place to spend the evening rather than just … "

Without even realizing it, she'd capitulated to the first of a wave of a niche marketing campaigns -- some targeting families, some targeting minorities, and some targeting downtown businesses -- that would keep a continual flow of people trying out East Portland Indoor Soccer for years to come.

Despite the assault of Ethan and Michael Edens upon her every idle thought, the morning it wasn't bad. With the arena closed for the holiday, Charlie rolled out of bed at half past eight, they ate a breakfast of doughnuts and pound cake KC bought at a bakery up the street, and near mid-day they ventured out to buy some sparklers from a fireworks stand near Charlie's school. Without the churning rotation of constant games, the arena -- and life itself -- played out with one carefree hour following the next. The tranquility came to an end however, when she and Charlie ventured out to the fire escape in the afternoon to practice his ascent.

Even before they set out she scolded herself for waiting this long, but there was little time left to do anything but have Charlie give it a try and hope for the best. The first sign of trouble appeared when Charlie's foot began quivering on the neck-level fourth rung. She tried to nudge him upward, but when he did he shrieked, and she backed off. Trying encouragement instead it proved no more successful. For ten minutes he remained in place on the fourth rung while she grasped at anything that would help him take the next step. Desperate, she found herself reminding him of the dream in which Logan assured him of a successful ascent; but after several words she reconsidered, fearing the mention of Logan's guarantee would somehow tarnish the dreamstate relationship he'd created.

She tried more coaxing, but in a reaction borne from fear he yelled at her, and she gently asked him to calm down. He fell into apocalyptic crying as he descended to the sidewalk, and slumped in defeat as he trudged to the arena back door. Even after they were back inside his tears didn't slow, and she sent him to their living room couch to lie down. He offered no protest, and after an hour of sobbing headed to his bedroom where at last he fell fast asleep -- a slumber that consumed much of the rest of the afternoon.

"How's Charlie?" KC called to her from the concession area as she emerged from the back with a packet of sparklers. A giant commercial loomed above him on the big screen TV before he shut it off.

"Still asleep last time I checked on him. I think he's exhausted from crying. There hasn't been a single peep." She realized she'd forgotten to move the monitor's with him from the living room couch to his bedroom, but she pulled the receiver from her pocket nonetheless to make sure it was on. Sure enough, a green light shone in an upper corner.

KC walked over to her as she took a seat at a picnic table covered with blankets, collapsible chairs, grocery bags filled with food, an ice chest, and two watermelons. "People should start arriving soon, I imagine," he commented.

"Yeah. Probably in the next half hour." She glanced at the clock and tucked the packet of sparklers within the food.

"Sorry about Charlie boss. Maybe he's just afraid of heights."

"I think he's just afraid, *period*. I wish I could change that in him," she said through a sigh, "but I can't." She rose just as a *zap!* made them both pause with the mental inquiry of who it might be.

"That's probably Oscar," he said with a trace of excitement. "I told him to come early."

With a nod she left him and walked down the hall toward Charlie's room, noting the phalanx of knights he'd lined-up along either side of the hallway floor. Except for Ethan's gift, the long parallel lines made up the complete collection. The hanger-knight had been so cherished -- a gift she deigned representative of his love and kept it apart from the others on her office desk. Seeing

Logan's unicorn between Helena's bamboo knight and KC's

seahorse however, made the exalted status of Ethan's gift seem

suddenly ludicrous. Detouring back to her office, she plucked it

from her desk and returned to place it with the others, equalizing

its status within the herd.

A quick check on Charlie revealed him still asleep, and she

returned to the arena to find KC and Oscar together. Their

postures were rigid, as if uncomfortable with each other, or in the

aftermath of a fight.

Then again, maybe that's just the way they are.

"Still asleep?" KC inquired as she drew near.

She exchanged hellos with Oscar before answering, "Yeah.

I figure it's a good thing. He'll stand the best chance of attempting

it again if he's rested."

"Are you sure you don't want me to assist? You know …

be there when you try to get him up to the roof again?"

"Maybe," she said while noticing Oscar fidget. "I'm

willing to try anything at this point. I'll let you know."

"Well Oscar and I will set everything up on the roof, although those watermelons don't look like they're going to be easy."

That's nothing. Wait 'til you see how much the ice chest weighs.

A *zap!* sounded again, followed by a stereo, "Mom!" that sounded from both the receiver in her pocket and the open door to the back.

"Thanks Kase. I'll be back in a minute to help."

She walked back, but Charlie met her in the hallway with a sleepy stumble and disheveled hair. "Feeling better, hun?" she asked in as upbeat tone as she could conjure.

He didn't respond, and instead rubbed his eyes with one hand and clasped hers with the other as they headed to the arena.

"You still sleepy?"

"Yeah."

She observed what seemed to be a budding argument between KC and Oscar near her office, and when KC saw Charlie and her, he ushered Oscar into the office itself.

She sat down at a picnic table to get down to his height. "So hun, what is it that you … "

"Mom you wouldn't believe the dream I had."

Uh-oh.

He began a tale of Logan and waking in the middle of the night to find him at his bedside, but before continuing he looked beyond her and said, "There's that man again," immediately widening her eyes.

She pivoted and Jack Edens approached.

With KC and Oscar nearby she was technically not alone, but the two were deep in conversation and noticed nothing else. With the protective instincts of a mother she told Charlie to "wait here," rose, and walked forward to engage him as far from her son as possible. Her breathing shortened as the space between them vanished, and she blurted out a coarse, "What is it you want Jack?" before either of them had taken their final steps.

"I … uh … I … y … you … s … see … "

Without taking her eyes off him she called out, "Charlie! … Why don't you go see what's on TV?"

"Okay," he answered.

She meant for him to retreat to the back, but moments later she heard the big screen TV surge to life in the concession area. Before she could redirect him, Jack was sputtering syllables and single words again, a struggle that ended when he suddenly gave up, and with a hand wrapped with gauze, pulled a piece of paper from his back pocket. It was a newspaper article similar in size to those they found in his wallet weeks ago, however this one was relatively new, with scissorred instead of ripped edges, and in the font of an unfamiliar newspaper.

She took it from his outstretched hand.

Accident kills
local man

Santiam Pass – A Prineville man was killed Tuesday when his vehicle went over the side of Highway 53 at Milepost 90 and crashed into the North Santiam River Canyon.

Michael Bradford Edens, 32, of Prineville, who had been released from the Oregon State Penitentiary earlier in the

```
day,        was
pronounced
dead    at   the
scene.       The
victim's
brother
witnessed    the
accident,    but
was  not  in  the
car    at    the
time,   and  was
not     injured.
Marion   County
investigators
have  ruled  the
crash        an
accident,    but
further
commented   that
alcohol   likely
played  a   role
as   well.    The
results        of
toxicology
tests        are
still   pending
and   will   not
be     available
for     another
week.
```

She was stunned. "So … Jack … your … your … Michael

died?!"

He nodded.

"And his car … it crashed down the side of a mountain at

some milepost?!"

Again he nodded. Shifting in place, he raised his hand to wipe the sweat from his temple, but then not wanting his bandage shown, pulled it behind his back.

"And you were there when it happened?"

He gave another nod, and she vowed her next question would elicit a spoken response. "How'd it happen?"

He shrugged, but she remained silent, and he began a stuttering reply in which only every third word was intelligible. Finally, he stopped and gave a succinct explanation for it all. "Acci ... d ... dent."

It was unfathomable that the menace of both thought and dream had been eradicated, and in fact had been gone for three days. Even as she read the article a second time it seemed too fantastic to be true. By the third time through, she scrutinized Michael's name for signs there might be some mistake, misidentification, or typo. But on all accounts it was incontrovertible -- a miraculous incident on a faraway road had changed everything, and in a single instant swept her worst fears from the present to the past.

He started backing away, but she implored him to wait. "Jack, this was your brother so I'm sorry. If any part of this has been hard on you, then I'm so sorry. It's just … this is just … it's just so … ". She stared down at the article again, knowing little of what she felt could be communicated with words. Instead, an impromptu idea rose in her mind. "Jack, I don't … mmm … I'm not really sure how to say this, but we're having a fireworks party here tonight, and I want to know if you're at all interested in joining us. We'll have a bunch of people from my soccer team coming, and KC and … "

But before she could finish extending the invitation, he declined with a shake of his head and resumed his retreat toward the exit. This time she didn't stop him and watched him leave -- a departure finalized by the *zap!* that sounded shortly after he disappeared. Filled with relief, she walked back to Charlie and gave him a wordless embrace from behind, but before either of them could speak KC ran up to her from the office. She detached from Charlie and looked up with surprise to see not just KC, but in the distance behind him, Ethan, whose arrival must have coincided with Jack's departure.

"Did I just see Jack Edens leaving!?" KC called out.

Her eyes were locked on Ethan as she responded, "Yes," and handed KC the article.

KC accepted it with a "What's this?" which she ignored and instead greeted Ethan with a "Hi!" which he echoed back. Before she could say anything more he added, "Hey … um … can I talk to you alone for a second?" It sounded ominous, and he looked serious as he led her away from KC.

"Listen, as it turns out I can't stay. My dad came into town … sort of unexpected and all … and the two of us are just gonna sort of hang out tonight."

"He could join us if you'd like?"

"Mmm … you know, he's a little frail, and I don't really think the fire escape is for him."

She nodded. The impediment of the fire escape made complete sense, and her disappointment was tempered by a vision of Ethan and his father witnessing Charlie's difficulties on the very same apparatus. KC's presence nearby left her conscious of what she spoke of next, but before she could say anything else Ethan spoke again.

"Actually, I need to call him, and I left my cell at home. Do you think I could use your phone?"

"Sure." She turned to KC and asked, "Hey, is Oscar still in the office?"

"HE DIED?!"

Oh great.

"Kase!" she implored with a glare to signal him to shut up about the article. Then she repeated her question. Just as he answered "Yeah," Oscar emerged from the office doorway with a sour look on his face.

KC saw it too. "I uh … I better get back there. We'll talk about this … uh … article about the grocer down the street who died, later."

Oh brother.

"Are you guys okay Kase?" she asked, referring to what she surmised was an ongoing fight.

"Oh yeah. This is just the way we are … I mean *were* … I mean … um … we'll talk later."

She told Ethan he could use the phone in the back, and watched as he disappeared down the hallway. Turning to observe KC and Oscar, the two schizophrenically seemed to be enjoying each other's company, and she laughed at her inability to gauge their relationship with any accuracy. Left alone within the triangle of the three men that mattered most in her life, she gravitated toward Charlie -- finding him not watching TV, but writing on some paper.

"What are you doin' hun?" she asked while picking up the remote.

"Writing a thank you letter to my dad."

Before she could even ask the baby monitor in her pocket crackled with Ethan's garbled voice.

"Who's that mom?"

She clicked off the TV. "Oh, that's just my friend Ethan. He's using the phone in the back." Ethan's words came through more clearly, and reaching into her pocket with the intent to turn it off, her finger was poised on the switch when his words made her stop.

" … worry about a thing, sweets. No. I'm just now on my way."

"Don't worry. We'll just stay home, you and me."

"I don't know, love. Fifteen minutes or so? I'm sure there'll be no traffic."

"Uh-huh. I love you too. Bye."

Each word he spoke punctured what she'd thought was built between them, and unable to respond to Charlie's inquiry of whether *rooftop* was one word or two, her senses returned only

when Ethan's footfalls could be heard from the hallway. Hastily

she implored Charlie not to say anything about the overheard

conversation.

"Why?"

"Please Charlie," she implored. "Just do what I say."

"Okay," he agreed.

Ethan emerged with nothing in his expression to indicate

deception. It would have been easier if there was a self-satisfied

smirk or an aversion to her eyes, but he gave her neither and

instead looked incapable of the words she'd heard with her own

ears. It was the inverse of her witnessing him breathing in the

scent of her pillow. The phone call, like his being drawn to her

scent, represented the truth; only this time a painful truth that his

heart was not aligned with hers. Not only had their night together

failed to tip the scales in her favor, he was never weighing a choice

between her and whatever it was that bound him to his girlfriend.

At worst he'd deceived her all along, and at best he was the coward

Helena had long hypothesized. Either way, whatever the thing was

he felt for her -- an impulse -- lust -- a strong connection -- it wasn't love, and its whatever it was its cost was more than he was ever willing to pay.

He reached her, and she cleared her throat to drive the coldness from her voice, "So you gotta get going to your dad?"

"Yeah."

"I'll walk you out."

He apologized for not being able to stay, compounding her ill-will by the time they pushed upon the front doors and emerged out onto the street where his car was parked. Free of traffic on the holiday, it was eerily quiet, and the shadows of late afternoon began to merge with the dusk. Somewhere a street or two away someone lit off a string of firecrackers -- and when the ten-second crackling came to an end, so too did her ability to hold back what she'd overheard. As she laid out her awareness of his lie he looked at her calmly, not interrupting with a single word of contradiction.

"So all I ask of you Ethan, the one thing that matters to me more than anything else, is that you don't lie to me. You told me once you'd never deceive me again, and I'm asking that whatever you do, you don't do it now. Okay?"

"Okay," was his simple reply.

"Your dad's not here tonight, is he?

He dropped his eyes with his answer. "No."

"And what you've said about your feelings for me ... have those been lies too?"

His eyes shot directly to her. "No they weren't. I ... " He took her hands in his, but she held them limply, not releasing him from the responsibility of his words. "I love you Jennifer. I really do. When I'm with you I feel like I'm with the one person who's the perfect fit for me."

"But if that was true, and you felt like I was absolutely *the one* ... the one person meant for your heart and soul ... you wouldn't have picked her over me tonight."

"You don't understand. It's not easy for me. You could never understand what it's like for me ... for me to ... " He failed to translate his feelings to words, and as his explanation trickled off into silence, his gaze again fell to the sidewalk.

She pulled her hands free. "It's not strong enough. What you feel for me, that is. It's not quite strong enough ... is it?"

He had no answer, and could only finger the antennae of his car.

"What you said to me at the Eastbank Tavern, and what you said to me in your e-mails ... were they exaggerations Ethan?"

"No. It's just … they were all the truth. Every single word. I swear it."

Tears built and began to fall down her cheek when Ian McMannus and some woman she'd never seen before, walked up arm in arm. Pulling up in his truck at the same moment was the unmistakable figure of Coach Morris, and Ian, recognizing they were encroaching on a private discussion, snared him and steered the three of them inside the arena's front doors.

She resumed before the front door had even slammed shut. "I'm not quite worthy of the sacrifice, am I? Not quite worth the cost of an unpleasant break-up."

"No. That's not it."

"Well then what is it, Ethan? Talk to me." She wiped away the tears that drowned both eyes. "Is it what your girlfriend would think?" she managed, "Or what others … your family and friends would think of you if you broke up with her?"

"It's not what *anyone* would think. I truly do love you!" he uttered in a raspy whisper.

"Ethan, I've had love … for a few years anyway. And you know what? You'd do anything for it. And once you've got it, you'd do anything to keep it. It's the only thing that matters. And everything else … friends? … family? … what others think about you? … it's all secondary. You may love me in your own way, and I may make you feel different than anybody else has, but it's not love. Love isn't a secret you have to hide, and I deserve more than being someone's secret."

He had no response.

"What's it like Ethan?

He looked at her quizzically.

"What's it like to have your heart tell you something, and you choose to ignore it? If your heart's breaking right now like mine is … how are you okay with that? For months I've been standing here with my arms open, beckoning you, and you've stood still, even though you say you feel the same thing. How can that be?"

He withered under her words, but was given a reprieve when the Powell's car pulled up. Though her tears momentarily stopped, the puffy redness in her eyes told both Helena and Roy there was something wrong. She motioned them inside along with Jonah, informed them KC was in charge of showing everyone how to get to the roof, and exchanged a nod with Helena that said she'd be okay. No sooner had they disappeared inside than a van filled with her teammates on the Snipes pulled up. Unlike the Powells' they were oblivious to the fact anything was wrong, and it took a minute's worth of conversation before she was able to prod the last of them up the entryway stairs.

They stood looking at each other -- a silence in which she felt the impulse to wrap him in her arms and hold him. Instead, in her spoken word she found the strength to resist. "You go on Ethan. You go be with her, because I can't compete with whatever's holding you back. There's no cost to you when you choose her over me. It's only me that has to pay, and you know what? I'm broke." After withholding her feelings for so long, to speak from her heart to the very person embedded in her thoughts and dreams, felt empowering. "Ethan, tell me something about you that I don't know."

"Something about me ... "

"Yeah. Something I don't know. I'm not going to settle for no response, or something about you that's already known." She looked him in the eye and held his gaze in the singular pursuit of an answer. "Something ... anything that's in here," she added while putting a hand to his chest. The touch reminded her of being on the field with him late at night, when her competitiveness melted away and her resistance to him was overcome. Only this time nothing melted away, and her resolve remained as strong as the ferocity in her gaze. Finally, it was she who broke the silence. "I don't know what's in there either Ethan, but I know what's *not* in there … me … and while that hurts, I know I can't force my way in. Someone else got there before me and shut the door, and you know what? Good for her. She wins, and for now, I lose. But someday I'll be the one that wins … and when that day comes, *this* day will feel good instead of how it feels right now."

With that, she dropped her hand from his chest and walked to the entrance, reeling from an exhaustion that deepened with each stride. By the time she stood on the threshold she managed to turn around. He gave her the same look she'd seen so many times before -- a look that summoned her to come back to him. To give him another chance. To wait. But something in her own heart had hardened. She turned away, and with an unwavering hand reached for the handle and passed through the arena front door.

The door slammed shut behind her, and using the stairway railing for support, she succumbed to the full weight of her heartache and lowered herself to a seat on the third step. Helena, waiting behind while everyone else climbed to the roof, investigated the *zap!* and wordlessly sat down and held her in an embrace that didn't ease until long after the sound of Ethan's car had faded away. After a while the tears gave way to silence, and she pulled away to dry her eyes with her shirt.

"You're a mess," Helena said. "I hope everyone's arrived for the party already, because if anyone comes in right now they're gonna see you and head in the opposite direction."

Though it was said with a laugh, Jennifer did not return one, and the comment did little to improve her mood. However it did make her aware of the spectacle she'd become, and within self-consciousness was a measure of relief. She let out a groan, tucked her hair behind her ears, and grabbed the iron railing to lift herself up.

Helena rose at the same time. "Hey. You know how soccer takes your mind off things when you need a distraction?" she asked.

"Yeah?"

"Well imagine what a fireworks show will do. What do you say we go join the others."

"Okay."

They climbed the first few steps arm-in-arm until she said, "Oh shit, I've still got Charlie to deal with," and summarized the difficulty they'd had earlier in the afternoon.

"Poor guy. Where is he anyway?" Helena asked.

"Well he's in the arena. At one of the picnic tables last I left him. Didn't you see him?"

"Actually no … I never did."

They pushed their way past the interior doors near the field and sure enough, Charlie was nowhere to be seen. "Where's everybody else?" she asked while breaking from Helena and scanning every corner of the arena.

"KC took them all up … just like you said."

"And you never saw Charlie?"

"Not once. I just assumed you knew where he was."

She hastened through the concession area. "Well, he was right here at the picnic tables when I left him." She called out his name to no avail, and she and Helena plunged into the back.

After a minute of futile searching Helena said, "Okay. Let's not panic. He's probably around here somewhere," and they both headed for the arena yelling Charlie's name. They met up again once the office and bathrooms had been searched. "Okay."

Helena repeated, "Let's not panic. I'll go up and get KC." They walked to the back doors and found them wide open, something even KC would not have been irresponsible enough to overlook as they led directly out onto MLK. Horrible scenarios filled Jennifer's head -- that Jack's article was a phony and Michael was alive and had kidnapped Charlie, that Charlie had run away, that Charlie had been purloined by a stranger who wandered in, that Charlie was stuck on a high rung and about to fall. They hurried through the back door only to find stillness -- a sidewalk and street devoid of people and cars. Laughter and music could be heard from the rooftop.

"I'll be right down with KC," Helena said before climbing the rungs as quickly as possible. Left alone to scour the streets for Charlie's diminutive form, she jogged along MLK calling his name, only to have a homeless man look at her with unwelcome curiosity. She retraced her steps and ran beneath the fire escape toward Hawthorne Boulevard, but before she got there Helena called down to her from the rooftop.

"JEN!"

She skidded to a stop and looked up to find Helena's beaming face peering down.

"He's up here!"

"What?!"

"Charlie! He's up here!"

She'd have thought it a joke had Helena not seen how worried she was moments earlier, and she climbed to the roof to find it was true -- within a cluster of people seated on an array of blankets, was Charlie.

"I DID IT MOM!" The pride in his voice burst forth for all to hear.

She felt a mix of emotions -- anger at having been made to worry, the throat-tightening exhaustion of recent tears, relief, happiness, amazement, and bewilderment. Overwhelmed by the turbulence of all she felt, she could only stare, walk closer to him, and give him a hug as he explained, "I never got to tell you mom … the dream I had about my dad. He told me just to put one hand above the other, and not to look down, and that he'd make sure my hands didn't slip. And it worked! I didn't slip or get scared or anything."

The last ember of her panic was drowned by his beaming smile, and she took a seat behind him with her arms and legs enwrapping him in a tight hug identical to Roy's embrace of Jonah.

Charlie sipped at his soda and said, "Mom, do you think my dad is looking down on me and saying, 'Now there's one brave kid?'"

"Oh, I'm certain of it, hun. And you know what? You're more than just one kid, Charlie. You're more like one and five eighths."

She smiled with the remembrance of their moment together with his fractions homework as wisps of pink clouds shone and then faded to gray. Darkness fell, and the sound of intermittent fireworks popped and shrieked from the street below. A few faraway bursts from a show far to the north whetted their appetites, but the show they awaited was fired from a barge on the river, and wasn't scheduled to commence for another hour. After the consumption of chips, beer, soda, watermelon, an abortive game of charades, and numerous accounts of the disastrous prior year's party, the first firework erupted in the sky before them.

From their front row seat they watched as the space above the river was filled with a mosaic of colored sparks, while skyscrapers on the opposite side of the river reflected the spectacle back to them as would giant mirrors. Huddled on blankets amid the oohs and ahhs, everyone plunged into a languid trance within which their independent thoughts stirred.

For KC, there was joy that came from knowing he had found a place in the world that truly felt like home.

For Oscar, there was the realization that any future with KC meant he'd have to integrate with KC's world, instead of KC having to integrate with his.

For Jonah, there was jealousy of the place Charlie got to call home.

For Roy, there was the realization that the arena neighborhood had real estate potential for more than just warehouse storage.

For Helena, there was little interest in the show. Instead her attention drifted through the sea of heads to where Jennifer's face shone in the flashing lights. Her embrace of Charlie was the very definition of maternal love, and the contentment on her face didn't waver once in the few minutes she watched. Satisfied that her friend would be okay, she ran her hand along Roy's back and reclined to give her full attention to the show.

For Ian, there was the contemplation of how inferior his can of PBR was to a pint of Guinness stout.

For Charlie, there was the hope his dad was looking down at that moment, and could see the show.

For Jennifer, there was momentary happiness. Surrounded by friends, entangled with Charlie, and atop the structure she was destined to create, she achieved contentment -- one that would evaporate as soon as the show was over, and would only gradually rebuild as Ethan seeped from her heart. Leaning forward to kiss the back of Charlie's head, she felt his soft hair give way and bounce back just as Logan's used to. Beneath the thunderous noise in the sky she whispered, "I love you," -- words that meant everything, yet were audible to no one. Not even to herself.

For the moment she was happy, and that was enough.

Twisting backward on his bicycle seat, Jack Edens viewed the eruptions in the sky with one foot balanced upon a pedal and the other resting on the curb. The angels had startled him at first -- announcing their presence with the power to cause buildings to tremble; but the noise only strengthened his feeling of security. Glancing forward, the red hand in the crosswalk continued to forbid his passage, and he looked back again at the window of sky framed between the warehouses and the power lines. Angels celebrated in the sky, and in their screams and pops Jack felt the warmth of a celebration, applause, and the assurance his future was his own. With the angels on his side, there was no longer any

reason to be afraid.

The roar of an automobile suggested the light had changed,

and facing forward again he saw the red hand at the other side of

the crosswalk had turned into the strolling profile of a pedestrian.

With a smile on his face, he leaned forward on the handlebars,

pushed away from the curb, and began his journey home.

EPILOGUE

KC popped his head into the office and said, "Hey boss, we've got a no show."

"Who?" she asked while staring at the clock in the bottom corner of her computer screen. It was 6:16 PM.

"Those losers from Harvest Bakery … you know, that team that flaked out last week? They're supposed to play Rudy's Diner. I hope they paid for the season up-front."

Her thoughts wouldn't be drawn to finances. "So what do you wanna do?" she asked while standing to look out to the field. Amid a mix of yellow shirts kicking balls back and forth in an aimless fashion, the distinctive red hair of Jack Edens was once again nowhere to be found.

"Well, between you, me, Ian, Charlie, Jonah, Helena … hey where'd Helena go?"

"The bathroom in the back."

"Between all of us, plus a player or two from their team, I don't see why we couldn't get a friendly game going."

She needed no further prodding. "Okay. You go back and round up the boys and Helena, and I'll go talk to Ian and the folks from Rudy's." She rose from behind her desk, and before he was out of earshot yelled to him, "Oh, and bring out a couple of white T-shirts as well."

He nodded and disappeared, and she remembered to grab the shoebox from beneath her desk. Depending on what the boys were doing they could refuse, but she put her faith in KC's persuasive enthusiasm, and headed off to the field. Even KC might not have been enough to sway Charlie to play months ago, but since the Fourth of July a transformation had taken place. Even though his soccer skills were no greater than before, he didn't shirk from playing in games anymore, and weeks had passed since his last bout of crying.

She did a double-take with her first stride upon the field. Facing away from her, Jack Edens lay on the ground mimicking a teammate's stretching technique. It was the first time she'd seen him in months, and while every ounce of her felt like stopping and talking, or at the very least watching him, she felt obligated to head for an accumulation of five conversing players from Rudy's Diner. It took little effort or time to persuade them to make use of the hour playing a friendly game, and she turned her attention to Ian who was idly drinking beer as he sat atop the midfield wall, "You up for a game?"

He gave a simple nod between sips and she turned back to the others. "We'll need two from Rudy's Diner to round out our team."

A girl said agreeably, "Okay. You pick 'em."

She didn't hesitate. "Okay. We'll take Jack and yourself."

KC ran up to her, indicated the boys and Helena were on their way, and tossed her a couple of T-shirts. He inquired, "What's in the box?"

She forgot she was carrying it. "Oh! Well, it's sort of your birthday present. I was going to wait, but I figure you probably could use them right now." She removed the lid to reveal a new pair of black indoor soccer shoes, laced and ready to go. While handing them over she explained, "It'd just kill me Kase, if you twisted an ankle wearing those tattered things you discovered months ago in the lost and found."

At first he was speechless, but eventually he lifted his eyes from the open box. "Size nine and a half?"

"Size nine and a half," she confirmed with a broad grin.

He smiled, gave her an awkward hug which compressed the box between them, and headed for the benches to put them on. Charlie, Jonah, and Helena came onto the field, but her attention was galvanized by Jack Edens who approached, having been told he'd be switching teams.

He put a finger on his own chest. "I ... I'm on y ... y ... y ... your ... t ... team?"

"Just for today. Here. Put this on." She handed him a white T-shirt, but he didn't put it on until he saw a teammate strip off her own yellow shirt and don a white one. He did the same, and once he'd pulled it down over his freckled torso she saw on his was an ancient shirt from a soccer camp she attended in high school -- one that featured a giant upright mosquito and beneath it, the singular word, DEFENCE. She made a note to see what KC thought of it for its wall-art potential.

Helena herded the boys together, KC finished tying his new shoes, Ian finished off his beer, and their makeshift team gathered in a huddle of which she seized the role of unofficial captain. "Okay, I'll start out in goal. Jonah, you and your mom are back on defense with me. Jack you and ... I'm sorry what's your name again?"

"Michelle."

"Jack, you and Michelle play midfield. KC and Charlie go on offense. Switch around if you want to, and we don't have any subs … so if anyone gets tired, you can always come back and take over the goalie spot for me. Anyone got any questions?" She looked at Charlie's face, a latent fear telling her he would be distressed to play in a game with adults. Instead he looked eager, and she smiled to see in his face the same excitement and anticipation that flowed through her at the start of a game. Instead it was Jack who looked nervous, and after the huddle broke apart she took him by the arm and said understandingly, "Don't worry Jack. It's just a friendly game."

As ease came over his face. "I … know," he said, and trotted off to his position.

Walking back to play goalie she overheard Ian and KC's playful banter.

" … and try not to break your nose this time, eh bloke?"

"One more crack like that and I spit in your next beer, uber-toad."

"You wouldn't."

"Please boys … be nice," she called out to them jointly, and the latest round of their verbal sparring concluded with no clear victor.

Her own skill level, combined with that of Ian and Helena, made up for the fact they had two children on their team, and the score was tied 2-2 late in the second half. Ian had by then taken over for her in goal, a fortuitous substitution that allowed her to witness a magical moment. With the aggressiveness she'd never seen before, Charlie plunged into a crowd of players, somehow came away with the ball, and whether it was intentional or not -- passed it to Jack when a defender came toward him. Jack dribbled once and kicked it -- a short shot that went directly between the legs of the goalie for a score. Unbridled joy shone on both Jack and Charlie's faces, and she stood and watched in amazement as they exchanged an awkward high five. She felt like joining their celebration, but something told her not to insert herself into their moment, and instead she yelled her congratulations from afar while feeling blessed at whatever force had propelled Charlie's self-confidence from its cocoon. Making her way back to the other end of the field, she became embroiled in a conversation about KC's new shoes, all the while unaware that far away near the opposite goal, Charlie had noticed something on Jack's hand.

"What *is* that?" Charlie asked.

Jack looked puzzled.

Charlie pointed. "That. That thing on your hand."

At first Jack pulled his hand behind his back, but unable to thwart Charlie's persistence, he slowly produced it and uncurled his fist revealing the circular brand in the middle of his palm. Jack's hand trembled slightly, but when Jonah came over to see what they were looking at, he spread his hand fully to allow their inspection. While the unnoticed scar on his fingertip was a reminder of evil, the purple circle represented its departure, and Jack felt a strange satisfaction at showing his hand to the very boy whose protection was paid for by what he, and the angels, did months earlier. For the first time he felt proud of what he'd done.

"What happened?" asked Jonah.

Jack didn't hesitate. His answer, unencumbered by a single stutter or hesitation, came out clear and succinct. "Accident," was all he said, followed by the slow closure of his freckled hand.

They played for ten minutes more, and Jack's goal against his own team held up for a 3-2 win. The next game started and ended, players came and went, and on a rainy Saturday night, fingers of water probed for new ways to circumvent the roof. While the makeshift team -- minus Ian who had resumed officiating -- mingled at the picnic tables with players from Rudy's Diner, Charlie ran to his bedroom and brought out the crystalline unicorn to show everyone.

"Charlie. Just be careful with that." Jennifer cautioned.

"I will."

Jack, his attention drawn to the glass object Charlie was showing everyone, immediately remembered the prism, and how much he still missed it. "C … could … I … s … s … see?" he asked.

Charlie handed it to him. He caressed it with both hands for a full minute before saying, "It … it's n … n … nice," and offering it back.

"Yeah. It's from my dad," Charlie said as he took it from Jack's hand. He walked back to the table where Jennifer, Helena, and KC were seated. "Mom, could I take this one from the collection and have it for myself."

"Why, hun?"

"I dunno. I guess I want to pretend like it's a present from my dad."

"Well okay ... but only if you put it back in your room where it's safe."

Charlie ran to his room, set it upon his bedside dresser, and flipped off the light on his way out. Far from the sight of those in the arena, the crystalline unicorn began to glow with a light from which hundreds of tiny rainbows burst forth. For a few seconds they twirled around the room, spinning upon Charlie's bed, the clutter on the floor, and the posters on the walls -- before the colors stopped, faded, and disappeared back within its icy depths.

51487152R00320

Made in the USA
San Bernardino, CA
23 July 2017